CITY OF ELDRICH
BOOK 3

GODS & SWINDLERS

CITY OF ELDRICH
BOOK 3

GODS & SWINDLERS

LAURA KIRWAN

Cover design by James T. Egan of Bookfly Design
Book design by Maureen Cutajar of Go Published

ISBN-10: 0-9913023-4-6
ISBN-13: 978-0-9913023-4-5

CHAPTER ONE

London, Anno Domini 1098

THE CLOAKED MAN strode through the dark town. At this time of night thieves and cutthroats roamed freely, but the man had no fear. Although not a wizard, he was a gifted conjurer, skillful with certain smaller magics. If he couldn't conjure away a hazardous encounter, odds were good he could talk his way out of it. Failing that, he had his dagger. Even with only average physical gifts, centuries of practice had made him lethal when the occasion demanded it.

He pulled his cloak closer. Down by the river, the mist grew thick, the dampness sinking into his bones, and he suspected he'd have a long wait. His cousin's behavior had grown even more erratic of late. He knew, despite wanting to believe otherwise, that their long association was at an end. One last caper, one last magic sword, and then he planned to gather his earnings, retire from swindling, and head south.

Somewhere warm. The south of France perhaps, or Spain. Maybe Constantinople . . .

Lost in dreams of sunshine and leisure, the cloaked man was oblivious to the small figure stepping from the shadows.

"You know—" the figure said.

The cloaked man, startled from his reverie, groped for his dagger.

"You should never let a leprechaun sneak up on you." The small figure threw back his hood. "We're nefarious little bastards."

The cloaked man relaxed. "No, my friend, you're a nefarious little bastard. Most of your brethren lack the imagination for anything but average wrongdoing. And you're the only one in the worlds who can sneak up on me."

"Good thing I'm on your side." The leprechaun chuckled, then grew serious. "Where is he?"

The cloaked man sighed. "Where do you think?"

Now the leprechaun sighed. "In his cups, telling tales of past glory. If he keeps this up, they'll burn him for a heretic."

"He and my father both," the cloaked man said. "The age of the northern gods is over. It's time to move on."

"What are you saying?"

"It's time to get out of the magic sword and magic ring business and into something more modern. Sacred relics, perhaps."

The leprechaun nodded, pondering the cloaked man's words. "With a convincing story and a little magical dazzle, some people will believe anything. Particularly when a god is involved."

"Indeed. Plus, relics are easier to manufacture and transport. Add gullible and greedy buyers . . ."

"I like it. But what about him? How does he fit into this?"

The cloaked man sighed. "He doesn't. His work hasn't suffered yet, but it will. Provided he doesn't end up on a pyre."

"You don't mean that," the leprechaun said. "We can't abandon him. His leg—"

"Is an old wound and a convenient excuse. The drink is destroying him and I won't let it destroy us, too."

"Us? Is she—"

"She's at her breaking point."

"If you both leave, it will kill him." The leprechaun shook his head. "Are you sure about this?"

"Not in the least. I hate myself for even considering it. But if he's intent on drowning himself in mead, should we let him drag us under with him? Should our loyalty to him make our lives forfeit, too?"

The leprechaun stared at his small feet for a long moment. "No. I suppose not."

Neither spoke for several breaths.

A decision made, the leprechaun broke the silence. "About the relics—did you know it's not only lone fools? I've heard that whole towns are banding together to get them." The leprechaun chuckled. "They crow about stealing well-known relics from other towns to entice pilgrims and their gold."

The cloaked man smiled. "Because a relic somebody would willingly sell is not worth having?"

The leprechaun nodded, a wide grin on his handsome face. "And not being thieves themselves—"

"They're willing to pay well to procure such services." The cloaked man nodded.

"So, if we create a convincing relic, goosed with a little magic—"

"We can—guided only by our piety—reluctantly sell it to one town and get paid to steal it for another." The cloaked man laughed. "You nefarious little bastard."

"And we know a certain woman with lovely golden hair who might have reason to disguise herself—"

In his excitement, the cloaked man had forgotten his dreams of retirement. "As a saintly woman who has shorn her hair to prove her modesty and humility—"

The leprechaun nodded. "Giving us several feet of lovely golden hair—"

"To cut into locks from the Virgin Mother's head. Pilgrims love holy hair."

"Giving us an easy way to earn enough coin to eat well whilst we set up something grander for ourselves."

"Much grander," said the cloaked man. "We could get paid at least three times on one relic if we steal it back from the town we stole it for. Or even more, depending on how many times we can steal it before they grow wise . . ."

They basked for a moment in the glow of their scheme. Then the cloaked man thought of his cousin, the kinsman he had decided to leave behind, and felt a stab of guilt. But there was no alternative. For his own sake, for her sake, and for his cousin's sake. It was only a matter of time before the drunken lout turned his frustrations upon his wife, only a matter of time before he lost what meager control he had over his magical gift and it destroyed them both.

"Do we wait for him any longer?" the leprechaun asked.

The cloaked man shook his head. "No. She's waiting with the cart. At the church near the bridge. The one place she knows he won't be."

The leprechaun's eyes widened. "You're already packed? You're really serious about this."

The cloaked man nodded. "I am."

"But what about tonight? We have a sword to deliver."

The cloaked man gestured around them. "Do you see a sword? The drunken fool still has it. I don't relish walking in there empty-handed. This buyer won't hesitate to cut us down with one of his many less-than-magical swords if he thinks we're trying to cheat him."

"I guess we can't sell a sword we don't have. Not to this buyer." The leprechaun shuddered. "Better we disappear. But I have a few things to do before I can leave."

"We were thinking about heading south." The cloaked man

sighed. "To be truthful, I was thinking about heading south. She wants to go north."

The leprechaun nodded. "Which means you're going north. Norwich?

The cloaked man nodded.

"I'll find you," the leprechaun said.

"You always do." With a final smile, the cloaked man turned and disappeared into the fog.

Chapter Two

"HOW CAN YOU ask me that?" Meaghan held out the thick blue-rimmed glass as Elena poured. "Of course, I want another margarita. What a ridiculous question."

Elena flipped her dark hair over her shoulder. "Silly me. But you still haven't answered my other question. Why are you here?"

Meaghan watched the setting sun paint the western sky red. It wouldn't last long—sunsets in Arizona never did—but for the moment, the view from Elena's deck was spectacular.

"I wanted to see you," Meaghan said. "It's been a while."

Elena nodded. "Yes. It has. I'm thrilled you're here, but I come back from Portland—"

"I'm sorry about you and Dennis," Meaghan said.

"Thank you. We have a very successful divorce, much more successful than our marriage, and you're trying to change the subject." Elena scrutinized Meaghan over the edge of her margarita glass. "I come back and hear you've lost your job, sold your house, and blown town without telling anybody."

"I told people," Meaghan said.

"You mean besides your real estate agent?"

"I told plenty of people."

"You didn't tell me. Or my mom."

Meaghan fidgeted in her chair, fighting back the tears that had grown even more frequent since Labor Day. It had gotten so bad, she could barely get out of bed some mornings. February in Arizona and February in northern Pennsylvania were not remotely similar. The moment her plane had touched down at Sky Harbor, she'd felt better. Actually, she'd felt better the moment the puddle jumper from Williamsport to Philly had broken through the ever-present cloud cover to reveal sunshine and blue sky.

Elena waited patiently for Meaghan to respond. Elena had been Meaghan's best friend since Meaghan had arrived in Phoenix as a child. Meaghan knew that Elena would slowly, but inexorably, push, like lava flowing across the land, until Meaghan told her what was going on.

But how much could she tell her? Really tell her? About Eldrich, about her new life . . .

"It all happened so fast," Meaghan said. "I barely had time to register what was going on before I was there starting the new job."

"And they have no phones in this town? Is that why you show up on my doorstep without a word in advance?"

"I . . . yes." And now the tears did flow, because Meaghan desperately wanted to talk to Elena about everything, especially the paranormal and magical crap, but knew she couldn't.

Elena nodded and patted her hand. "I'll get the tissues. Drink your tequila like a good girl until I get back."

Meaghan snorted a giggle through her tears. Elena knew her so well. She dug a rumpled tissue out of her pocket and blew her nose, then a fresh wave of tears swept over her.

She's my best friend and I can't tell her what's going on.

But Meaghan knew that was bullshit the moment she thought it. *The magic is only part of it,* her calm, rational voice told her. *The magic isn't what made you run away from John. The magic isn't what's causing the nightmares.*

Elena returned with a box of tissues and a full dinner plate.

"What's that?" Meaghan asked, sniffling.

"Cheese enchiladas."

Meaghan's stomach rumbled, her tears forgotten for the moment. "Tía Nancy's?"

"Yup. Frozen into single-serve packets for emergencies."

Meaghan raised an eyebrow.

"I got divorced," Elena said. "It's a good divorce, but that doesn't mean it's been easy." She dropped the tissue box into Meaghan's lap and held out the plate. "Here."

Meaghan blew her nose, then took the plate. Nobody made enchiladas like Elena's aunt Nancy, not even Meaghan's brother, the chef, because Tía Nancy used the cheapest flour tortillas she could find, canned enchilada sauce, and Velveeta cheese.

Tía Nancy's enchiladas were the Mexican food equivalent of SpaghettiOs and the supreme comfort food of Meaghan's youth. She loved them with all her heart. Russ, on the other hand, considered them a culinary travesty.

Between bites, Meaghan said, "My brother would have a stroke if he saw me eating these. He thinks Velveeta should be banned by treaty, like nerve gas. His enchiladas take at least three days to make."

Elena smiled. "Russ is the gayest straight man I've ever known."

Meaghan laughed, inhaled a bite of food, and started coughing. When she got her breath back, she said, "You don't know the half of it."

"Yeah, it didn't surprise me to hear that love spell made him gay for a day."

Meaghan sprayed her sip of tequila as she began choking again. Elena knew? Elena, her best friend from Phoenix, sensible down-to-earth Elena was clued in?

"Before you start wigging out, I know, I've always known, and I'm so relieved that now you do, too." Elena drained her margarita.

"How?" Meaghan managed to gasp. "How do you know?"

"My mom's a witch," Elena said. "She and Tía Nancy both."

"What about you?"

Elena shook her head. "Nope. I'm a little psychic, but that's it. And it's not like Mom and Nancy are Eldrich-type witches. They have to go up to Sedona to get that kind of power and you know how much Mom loves Sedona." She rolled her eyes. "If it weren't for the vortices, she'd never go near the place. That New Age stuff annoys the crap out of her."

"So, you know about me?"

"Yeah, sweetie. Always have." Elena reached forward and grabbed Meaghan's hand before she could pull away. "And if you start in with the 'everybody lied to me' whine, I'm gonna brain you with that dinner plate."

Meaghan bristled. "I wasn't going to—"

"Yeah, Meg," Elena said. "You were. Psychic, remember? You think your father left you guys unprotected? It wasn't a coincidence that we moved in next door right after you got here."

"You—"

"No, I was your friend because I wanted to be your friend, not because Mom asked me to get to know you. I didn't befriend you because it was a job or because I knew you had some big-time destiny."

"Stop doing that," Meaghan said.

"Doing what?"

"Reading my mind."

"Oh, please. I don't need to be psychic to know how your

mind works. Russ gave me a heads-up. He figured you'd show up here when he got your note. And before you start with the 'everybody's conspiring behind my back' crap, we only do it because we love you and know how much shit has been thrown at you in the last year."

"You know about Eldrich?" Meaghan asked in a small voice.

"Yeah, all of it," Elena said. "Russ—what do you guys call it?—clued me in. So, what's going on? What's really going on? Why did you run?"

There hadn't been one defining moment, no epiphany or precipitating event. Meaghan had simply woken up that morning, looked at the heavy gray sky, smelled more snow in the air, and decided she was done with it. Done with Eldrich, done with magic, done with her destiny. She was going home.

"Bullshit," Elena said. "It was that guy, John, after you rejected him again." She paused a beat. "Okay, I did read your mind that time. He's crazy about you. What's the problem?"

"You're the one reading my mind," Meaghan said, her voice sullen. "You tell me."

"I'm only a little psychic, remember? Talk already."

"He's an alcoholic."

"In AA, right?"

"That's no guarantee he won't drink again."

"This again?" Elena rolled her eyes. "Meg, life doesn't come with a guarantee. Just because you won't let yourself make mistakes, doesn't mean the rest of us aren't human." She shrugged. "Mostly human . . . humanoid . . . you know what I mean."

"I make plenty of mistakes," Meaghan said.

"Yeah, and then never forgive yourself for them. Did it ever occur to you that hiding from life so you don't screw it up is the biggest mistake anyone can make? So, tell me, if you let him in, and he starts drinking, what will happen? What's the worst that will happen?'

"I . . . he'll . . ." She glared at Elena. "He'll leave. Or I'll have to leave."

Elena shook her head and sighed. "Well, sweetie, then the worst has happened already. You've left. And he hasn't touched a drop." She leaned back in her chair. "Don't shake your head at me. He wasn't drinking when I talked to him before you got here. He's worried and he's hurt, but he's sober."

"You talked to him?"

"Mmhm, I did. He has quite an interesting accent to go along with that sexy voice. He knows something's wrong. This isn't only about his past. There's something else you're not telling anybody."

Meaghan shook her head as the tears fell again.

Elena stood up. "Hold that thought. I have something that might help."

Meaghan blew her nose and tried to regain her composure. There was something she wasn't telling anybody, something she could barely articulate to herself.

Back in September, she'd promised Russ and Natalie, their much younger half-sister, that she'd see a therapist about the bad dreams and sleepless nights. But in the aftermath of Labor Day—rebuilding city hall, finding homes for the Fahrayan diaspora, trying to learn more about the dangerous magical creatures that had tried to enter the human world—she'd never gotten around to it. They all had bigger problems, and it seemed, to Meaghan at least, like everyone had wanted her and John to live happily ever after like some fairy tale.

So, she played along. She tried to stuff her fear and uncertainty as deep inside herself as she could and be strong. She was surrounded by people who had suffered real trauma—Jamie, despite pretending otherwise, still had a long way to go to recover from his ordeal in Fahraya, and Marnie . . . six months had passed and she was still hiding in Brian Cressley's guest room.

Meaghan and John had begun to date, but despite what everyone believed, had not had sex yet. He remained patient, but Meaghan wondered for how much longer. She wanted him—at least she thought she did—but whenever they came close to physical intimacy, she panicked.

Her nightmares had coalesced into one awful dream. The giant scorpions, the waving tentacles of the mystery monsters, dead Jamie excoriating her for failing to save him, Natalie burning and screaming atop the bonfire in the city square—they'd all been upstaged by a wizard. A paunchy, balding, middle-aged wizard, who pinned her to the ground and fumbled for the zipper to her jeans, while she heard a male voice growl, *"The bitch needs to learn her place."*

Before the wizard could go further, she always woke up, with the covers snarled around her and a scream in her throat. But the worst part was the way the fear bled into her waking life whenever things got too far with John.

Meaghan had faced so much in the nine months she'd lived in Eldrich—starting with the discovery that magic was real and she was impervious to it. Her father had died. She had been attacked by wizards and had fought monsters. She'd saved the world—twice.

She'd even managed to fall in love. She knew she loved John and that he loved her. That wasn't the problem. And, to be brutally honest with herself, neither was the risk of him drinking. That was merely a convenient excuse.

The real problem was that every time John touched her below the waist, her mind was filled with the balding wizard crushing her to the ground, leaving her weak and powerless.

The bitch needs to learn her place.

But Meaghan hadn't been raped. The wizard's companion had shoved him away from her, not to save Meaghan from the wizard, but to save her for something worse.

But that hadn't happened either. Meaghan had to keep reminding herself that the monsters hadn't gotten past her. Jamie had survived and was getting better. Natalie hadn't been burned alive.

Meaghan hadn't been raped.

But when John touched her and the panic rose in her throat, when the nightmare came alive in her waking mind, all she could think of was escape. Not from John, but from that wizard and from the realization that there had been nothing she could have done to stop him.

And the worst part was, she couldn't tell John. She couldn't bring herself to tell the man she loved that his touch reminded her of a man who had tried to hurt her.

She couldn't tell anybody.

CHAPTER THREE

B EFORE MEAGHAN COULD spiral any deeper, Elena reappeared holding what looked like a tablet computer.

She held it out to Meaghan. "Here. You need this more than I do."

Meaghan examined it. "I thought these things were supposed to weigh less."

Elena shook her head. "It's not an iPad. It's a light box."

"A what?"

"A light box," Elena repeated. "For seasonal affective disorder. Seasonal depression. Winter blues. I got it when we moved to Portland. That first winter, I thought I was gonna die. It rained all the time, and the sun went down at like four thirty. Then somebody turned me onto this."

"I don't have seasonal depression."

"Bullshit, you don't," Elena said. "You can't deal with the PTSD until you deal with this. You sit in front of it every morning. The owner's manual is in the house and there's a lot of stuff on their website."

Meaghan looked at it skeptically. "I don't have PTSD."

"You sure about that?" Elena sighed. "You moved really far north after spending most of your life in one of the sunniest places on earth. Seasonal depression is biochemical. It's not a sign of weakness, and you need it."

"I guess. I do feel a little better since I got here."

"Moving back fixed my problem. That and divorcing Dennis. That helped, too." She laughed a moment, then grew serious. "But moving back here isn't an option for you and we both know it. Tell me what's going on."

Meaghan was silent a moment. Where to start? "What do you know?"

"I know about that Fahraya place and what they did to John and his son. Jamie, right?"

Meaghan nodded.

"And I know Jamie went all wacky and blew up city hall—"

"Not all of it."

Elena waved her hand dismissively. "Whatever. And I know you kept some really awful scary monsters out of our world, but I don't know how."

"I chucked a stapler at them," Meaghan said.

"A stapler? For real?"

"It was big stapler, made out of steel. They don't like that. I also beat up a wizard with one of Russ's chef-grade saucepans."

Elena nodded, smiling. "I heard about that. You beating the snot out of a wizard really didn't surprise me. Remember when you beat up Eddie, down the street? When he said you liked his older brother?"

Meaghan smiled. "Yeah. I do. I got a black eye."

"He got a broken nose. I still can't believe you didn't get in more trouble for that."

"I talked my way out of it. Besides, he started it."

"Um, no, I was there. You threw the first punch."

"Which I wouldn't have done if he hadn't been ribbing me about his brother."

"Dominic. You totally liked him."

Meaghan laughed. "You have no idea. I was so in love with him. He didn't know I was alive."

"I saw him not that long ago. I was downtown for something and ran into him. Still thinks he's God's gift."

"How'd he look?"

"He still has his hair, I'll give him that, but now it's on top of a much rounder guy. And I remember him being taller." Elena smiled. "And you, Ms. Sneaky, changed the subject again. Russ and Natalie—I also know she's your sister, by the way—tell me you've been kicking ass and taking names. The magical bad guys are terrified of you. So what's the deal?"

Meaghan sighed. "Can I have another margarita?"

"Oh, for God's sake. Yes, but you have to come inside while I make it and start talking. No more stalling." Elena shivered. "It's getting cold out here."

"Seriously? This isn't cold."

Elena rolled her eyes. "One winter up north and she thinks she's a polar explorer. I have thin Latin blood. Humor me."

With glasses, dinner plate, and light box in hand, they moved into the kitchen. Elena made another pitcher of margaritas, heated up more of Tía Nancy's enchiladas, and sat down at the tiny dining table with Meaghan. "Now you have your drink and more cheese. Start talking."

Bolstered by the tequila and the enchiladas, Meaghan told her everything—from the call last May from her brother begging for help with their father to her deciding to flee to Phoenix, leaving out only one thing. With the rest of the story told, both of them sleepy with tequila, Meaghan knew she couldn't hide it any longer.

"I haven't told you everything," she said.

Elena nodded. "I know. I can feel you holding something back."

"Right. You're psychic now. I gotta get used to that."

Elena smiled. "I always have been. Just never talked about it. And you're better than most at blocking me."

"I am?"

"You are. What haven't you told me?"

"I . . . there was . . ." Meaghan's stomach lurched, making her acutely aware that she'd filled it with almost nothing in the last twelve hours but Velveeta and tequila. She sat up straighter and burped up the acid in the back of her throat. The time had come. She looked away from Elena, sudden shame making her face grow hot. "I almost got raped."

There was a moment of stunned silence. In a hushed voice, Elena said, "Shit, girl. Nobody told me about that."

"That's because nobody knows it happened. It was crazy. The mob had grabbed us and they were dragging Jamie and Natalie away, and Sid and Annie had disappeared. A wizard—"

"One of those Order guys?"

"Yeah. He grabbed me and punched me in the face"—Meaghan heard Elena suck in a sharp breath—"then he knocked me to the ground. My arms were under me and I couldn't move. And he . . . he tried to unzip my pants." Her eyes filled with tears. "And he said 'the bitch needs to learn her place.'"

Elena moved to her side and hugged her. "No wonder you're so upset."

Meaghan shook her head. "That's not it. He didn't rape me. The other wizard knocked him off me."

"Thank God."

"But, you don't get it." Meaghan's voice sounded loud and harsh in her own ears. "It wasn't anything I did. I couldn't stop him. In my whole life, I've never been so powerless. He was just a normal looking guy. He wasn't big, he wasn't strong, but there was nothing I could do."

The tears—the real tears—arrived. Meaghan stopped resisting and sobbed on Elena's shoulder.

Elena held her and rocked her until the storm passed. "I'm so sorry you had to go through that. I'm so sorry."

Meaghan groped for the tissue box. "But that's the problem. I didn't go through it. I'm supposed to be leading everybody, and I'm falling apart over something that didn't even happen."

Elena shook her head. "Something did happen."

"Not like what happened to Marnie. How can I fall apart over almost getting raped after what happened to her? How weak does that make me?"

"Meg, honey, it's not a competition. People deal with bad shit in their own ways. Minimizing your pain doesn't help her at all."

Meaghan blew her nose again. "No. I guess it doesn't. I promised Natalie I'd see somebody about it. A therapist."

"Excellent idea. Only find a clued-in one, otherwise you'll get committed." Elena smiled. "Most people don't accept this stuff as easily as you have."

"Most people don't see their coworker disappear in a flash of light and reappear eight inches tall with wings."

Elena giggled. "I hear you got an eyeful."

Meaghan smiled. "Did I ever. You've been talking to Kady?"

"Yeah, I caught her once when I called to see how you were doing. When's her baby due?"

"Um, March fifteenth, last I heard, although she looks big enough to pop at any moment. She's naming him after my father."

"Nice," Elena said. "How long do you plan to stay out here?"

"The original plan was forever, but now I think I have to go home before then."

"You called Eldrich home. Did you notice that?"

"Shit. Now I have to go back."

Elena stood and grabbed their glasses off the table. "I'm not trying to rush you. Work's been slow. I have a few things to take care of, but nothing major. Stay the week. We can book a spa day, eat out, go on some hikes. You need to decompress a little. You want me to call Russ and tell him?"

Meaghan pushed herself to her feet. "No, I will. First thing in the morning. It's after midnight back there."

When Meaghan woke the next morning, she found a plate of Mexican pastries, a carafe of hot coffee, and a note from Elena saying she'd run into the office and would be back by lunchtime.

Russ picked up on the second ring. "Hi," was all he said, his normal ebullience muted.

Because the jerk lied to me once again, and I caught him at it. "You said you told me all your secrets. You missed one."

"That wasn't my secret to spill," Russ said. "She told you?"

"Yeah."

"She made me swear—some crazy Mexican *bruja* thing. She said you had to hear it from her."

Meaghan sighed. "You do know she's not a witch, right?"

"She's not? She said I'd get boils if I told you."

Meaghan snorted. "And you believed her?" She laughed. "That's the same shit she did to you when we were kids."

"Yeah, ha ha, very funny. So, what gives? When are you coming back? *Are* you coming back?"

"I'll be back next week. I need a little break."

Russ sighed with relief. "Thank God. We've all been really worried."

"Well, don't worry anymore. Except for a little tequila hangover, I'm safe and sound."

"Good. But that's not what we're worried about."

Meaghan was silent for a long moment. "Something happened to me on Labor Day and nobody knew and I've had a hard time dealing with it. I don't suppose you know any good clued-in therapists?"

"Therapists? No, not personally, but I can get you some names."

She could hear the relief in Russ's voice. "I don't want to go into details right now, but we can talk when I get home." She shut her eyes, dreading the answer to her next question. "Is John okay?"

"Yeah," Russ said. "He's fine. Why wouldn't he be?"

"He's sober?"

Russ sighed again, this time exasperated. "We've had this discussion. You need to ask him. Or Terry, if he'll talk to you about it."

Terry was John's AA sponsor. He had moved in across the street right after Labor Day. Meaghan liked him and his wife, Steph, but they were hiding something from her. From everybody but John, it seemed, who had hinted about Terry once having been a big deal to "his people" whoever they were.

Terry was a blacksmith and had built himself a forge, surrounded by a steel cage, in a garage he rented in Eldrich. Iron and steel were as impervious to magic as Meaghan was. Terry's forge was basically a magic-proof safe room. He had built a similar forge in a shed in the backyard of his and Steph's ramshackle Victorian house on Holly Lane.

In addition to odd jobs around town, Terry made decorative swords he sold online and at renaissance fairs, along with iron gewgaws and whimsical kitchen cabinet knobs and handles. When they moved in, Terry presented the other five homeowners on Holly Lane with wrought iron weather vanes, which he installed on each roof himself. The dead-end street consisted of a half dozen Victorian houses in various stages of renovation and the weather vanes complemented their ornate gingerbread trim.

Terry and Steph seemed like a normal middle-aged couple, despite Terry's biker appearance. He had graying red hair halfway down his back and a full red beard that Steph was always nagging him to keep trimmed. At Christmas, he'd asked Natalie to whip up a little charm amulet that turned his hair and beard white, so he could transform himself into Santa Claus for the Christmas village the city sponsored on the square. Steph, a cheerful, solidly built woman with lovely golden blonde hair, worked the renaissance fair circuit with her husband and managed his online business. In her spare time, she volunteered at a hospice down in Williamsport.

They exuded the well-worn comfort of a couple who had weathered more than a few storms—not surprising considering Terry's alcoholism—and had come out stronger for it. They were good neighbors, despite their mysterious and likely magical backstories.

When Meaghan had pushed Terry a little about John, he'd given her a warm grin and said, "Not a chance. You want to know stuff, you talk to him."

"Terry won't tell me anything," Meaghan told her brother.

"Then I guess you'll have to talk to John," Russ said. "As far as I can tell, he's sober and patiently waiting for you to come home. But Meg—don't get mad—I've done this dance with women before, so I know what I'm talking about. He's been lonely a long time. If you don't want him anymore, let him find someone who does."

Meaghan couldn't respond or she'd start crying again, because she knew Russ was right. "I'll call you in a few days," she said, "when I have my flight info."

Chapter Four

A WEEK OF sunshine and laughter improved Meaghan's outlook. The nightmares eased. She hadn't realized how tired she'd been until she got a decent night's sleep.

Elena saw Meaghan off at the airport, parking the car and staying with her until it was time to go through security. Hugging her fiercely one last time, Elena said in her ear, "You better stay in touch this time."

"Or you'll put a curse on me? Give me boils?"

Elena giggled. "Your brother's such a sucker. I can't believe he fell for that." She stepped back. "You sure you're ready to go back?"

"No," Meaghan said, "but I have the whole destiny thing I gotta deal with. Hiding in Arizona won't make it go away. Too bad there aren't a cluster of magical gateways in Scottsdale or Paradise Valley."

"You can't afford either one," Elena said. "Go home and get your head straight. And get laid. Don't let Mr. Tall, Blond, and Sober get away."

Meaghan nodded. She'd missed John intensely during her week in Arizona—missed everything about him—to a degree that surprised her. "I promise. Assuming he still wants me."

"Only one way to find out. You're going to use that light box, right? And find a therapist?"

Meaghan rolled her eyes. "Yes, Mommy."

"I'll give you boils if you don't."

"Yeah, yeah. You and whose coven?"

Elena laughed. "And I'm coming out for a visit sometime this summer. I need to see this freaky little town of yours."

"It's really nice in the summer. It's the winter that sucks."

A loud mob of travelers—it looked like an extended family—was slowly making its chaotic way toward security. Elena gave Meaghan one last hug and shoved her gently toward the TSA guy waiting for her boarding pass and ID. "You need to get ahead of that bunch."

With a final wave, Elena turned and melted into the crowd.

The flight was uneventful. Meaghan stared out her window most of the time, watching America unroll eastward. It was a clear day until they passed over the Great Lakes, where the clouds thickened into a floor of cotton balls beneath the bright blue sky. Up here, it was sunny, but underneath she knew, it was gray and cold. Everyone had assured her spring was on its way, and that Eldrich was glorious in the springtime, but right now it felt like it would always be February.

Hell's not hot, Meaghan thought. *Hell is cold, damp, and cloudy. Just like Eldrich.*

When Meaghan got to Williamsport, she discovered cold, damp, and cloudy had given way to frozen, snowy, and clear. The evening stars gleamed in the sky like the points of sharpened icicles. She shivered on her way from the tiny terminal to her car and wrestled into her down coat—it was like a sleeping bag with sleeves—and her heavy winter boots as quickly as she could. She started the motor and turned the defrosters and heat on full blast.

Thankfully, she had all-wheel drive—her sleek Audi sedan had been destroyed by the Order during the Labor Day madness and she'd replaced it with a more practical Audi wagon. She pulled carefully out of the lot and onto the road. It was clear and dry, but wouldn't stay that way once she got out of the city.

When she stopped to gas up the car and grab some coffee for the road, she texted Russ she was on her way. He texted back immediately. He worried less now about her driving through the forest surrounding Eldrich, but he still wasn't comfortable with her being out there alone after dark.

Meaghan might be immune to magic, but she wasn't immune to swords, spears, or claws. She was feared and mistrusted throughout the magical worlds for her perceived role in the destruction of Fahraya. A wrong turn through a gateway and Meaghan could find herself very far from home, surrounded by enemies.

She knew enough to stay to the paved roads and she was immune to magical efforts to entice her into the thick trees or trick her onto a twisty logging road to nowhere. And she knew that if she got lost, she should call for help—if she had a cell signal—or wait for someone to come find her. Meaghan never entered the forest without letting somebody know her route and expected arrival time. Even those residents who were in denial about the area's supernatural aspects made sure to check in with somebody before entering the forest.

The forest was not a place to wander.

Witch Hollow Road, the main road into Eldrich, remained clear and dry. She began to relax and drive faster.

When she hit the black ice, her first thought was *idiot, you're going too fast.* The car spun in a full circle, slid gently sideways down a small incline into a snowbank, and stopped. The landing was so soft the air bags didn't deploy.

Meaghan pushed at her door, but the snowbank blocked the driver's side. Cursing her stupidity, she scrambled over the console and crawled out the passenger door to examine the car.

There didn't appear to be any damage. Using the flashlight app on her phone, she peered into the several-inches-wide gap between the left side of the car and the snowbank. Everything looked fine there. The tires, the top half at least, looked okay. The bottom half were buried in the thick wet snow.

Meaghan had learned enough about winter driving to know that, even with all-wheel drive, she wasn't going anywhere without help. She felt a bloom of anxiety in her gut, which blossomed into fear when she discovered she had no cell service.

Taking a deep breath to steady her nerves, Meaghan struggled through the snow to the road to see if she could get a signal there, but no luck. She took a few more deep breaths. *Okay, time for Plan B.* Her only option was to wait in the car until help showed up. If she didn't make it home soon, Russ would come find her.

"If I don't freeze to death first," she said out loud. She was immediately sorry she'd spoken. The words sounded flat, as if the air were absorbing the sound waves like a dry sponge.

Something's out there. An ancient part of her brain told her a predator was watching. Hair standing up on the back of her neck, Meaghan whirled around trying to see into the blackness on either side of the road.

Get in the car. It's safe in the car. Trying to hide her panic, trying not to run, Meaghan picked her way carefully down the small, icy bank.

A shadowy figure crouched near the passenger door. Dread rose in Meaghan's throat, then she remembered the phone in her hand, useless for communication, but still a functioning flashlight.

She clicked on the light and pointed it ahead of her.

Nothing was there.

Meaghan snorted in disgust. *Dopey me, afraid of the dark.*

Then she looked down and saw the small footprints. Something *had* been there. Unable to smother the whimper in her throat, Meaghan charged for the passenger door, tore it open with shaking hands, and dove inside. She locked the doors and shone the tiny beam of white light behind her. She scrambled into the backseat and checked the cargo area.

The car was empty.

She pulled out the survival kit Russ had insisted she carry and crawled back to the front seat. Meaghan weighed which seat to slide into—control or escape?—and chose the driver's seat. The car wasn't going anywhere, but she could use the horn and lights and manage the heater, and, besides, there was no way in hell she was going outside.

Save the phone and car batteries, she thought. Fighting her fear, Meaghan shut everything off. The dark silence settled around her. *Get a grip. You're surrounded by steel.*

Iron and steel were impervious to magic, but cars weren't invulnerable, Meaghan knew. Natalie had once blasted the doors off an SUV by exploiting a slightly opened window. Glass wasn't impervious and neither was plastic or rubber or aluminum. But a car was enough of a barrier to scare off casual predators. Most scary monsters would wander off in search of easier prey.

Except for the ones who'd love to kick my ass. She shivered, pulled the space blanket thingy out of the survival kit, and hunkered under it to wait for Russ.

Something else got there first.

She saw the shadows slink from the trees and surround the car. They weren't from the Order. Too short. The Order contained children, but they weren't sent out as decoys and magic fodder until they were tall enough to masquerade as full-grown wizards. Meaghan had grown adept at telling the difference. The dangerous wizards were well fed, while the decoys were bony and half starved.

Leprechauns? She dismissed that idea immediately. The figures outside were a bit too tall and the leprechauns liked her, as far as she could tell. And even if they didn't, she didn't owe them money, their magic didn't work on her, and leprechauns generally didn't slink. Leprechauns were thugs, but direct and plain dealing thugs.

There was an element of theater to this . . .

The fair folk—was she finally meeting the notorious fair folk?

CHAPTER FIVE

THE FAIR FOLK were a magical race with the ability to shift their appearance and manipulate magic. Unlike true shifters, who could physically rearrange their bodies, the fair folk used magic to project a desired appearance into the mind of the viewer.

Their actual name was about thirty syllables long and unpronounceable with human vocal cords, but translated into something like "glorious wonders who are better than you."

The fair folk fed off emotional energy and were the source of much elven mythology—most particularly the tall, graceful, supermodel/movie star variety. They had a particular taste for fanaticism, judgment, and dogmatic belief, with the occasional meal of awe and wonder when they could find it. They liked to co-opt belief systems and, in addition to the glamorous elf routine, tried to pass themselves off as gods.

But they were neither. In reality, they were short and skinny with pointy ears and bad skin. Their vanity had made them hate Meaghan's father and now Meaghan, because impervious humans could see their true faces, could see how physically unimpressive they really were. But that didn't make them any less dangerous.

They despised the modern world, hated humanity's ongoing advancement, hated how they were steadily losing sway over the human mind. They wanted to see the world plunged back into the pre-Iron Age. The fair folk had been waging a simmering war on humanity for centuries, possibly millennia.

Meaghan still didn't have all the facts because, under the terms of the last truce, all references to the war in magical and non-magical lore had been expunged. The only reason she knew about the war at all was something her mother had told her in a dream when she'd first arrived in Eldrich. She still knew only the barest outlines of the story.

She reached under the seat for the tire iron her brother had placed there for her when she'd bought the car. "If I get a flat, I'll call for help," she'd told him.

"This isn't for changing tires. It's for bashing monsters," Russ had replied. "Humor me, all right?"

"Whatever," Meaghan had said, rolling her eyes, but she'd kept the tire iron under her seat as directed. She now sent a wordless message of thanks to her brother.

The cloaked figures surrounded the car.

Meaghan gripped the tire iron and tried to think. Physically, without magic, they were no match for her, but they could still drop a tree on her. She could hear the windows rattling and smelled burning rubber. The car wouldn't protect her for long.

"I'll be damned if sit here and wait for them," she muttered. Meaghan started the car, flicking on the high beams and leaning on the horn as she revved the engine. As she suspected, the car barely moved, but the four spinning wheels showered several of the cloaked figures with muddy slush. Their disdain of the modern world caused them to sneer at technology and underestimate the power it gave humans. They jerked backwards in terror as the strange beast suddenly came to life.

Meaghan crawled over the console to the passenger seat, leaned on the horn one more time, and opened the door, the tire iron held in front of her like a club. She had no plan beyond getting out of the car. If she could get to the road, she could run. Maybe a car would pass or Russ would arrive. It was a slim chance, but better than sitting in the car like a trapped animal.

"I hate this town," she snarled at the nearest figure. "I can't even get home before you assholes start screwing with me." She swung the tire iron. The figures moved back a few steps, but did not retreat. "You're breaking the truce. And yeah," she added sarcastically, "I know all about the war."

The figure hissed something and the circle closed in.

If I gotta go, one of you is coming with me, Meaghan thought as she grasped the tire iron in both hands like a baseball bat. With a wordless cry, she swung and nearly fell when the tire iron failed to connect. The figure had evaporated.

"You fuckers can teleport? Goddammit, that's not fair!" Filled with the manic rage that she usually felt on the heels of terror, Meaghan stomped forward. "Come back here, you elven piece of shit, so I can kick your scrawny ass."

The circle tightened, its members vanishing like smoke before the tire iron could connect.

Meaghan feinted forward, then dove to her right. This time the tire iron hit something solid.

The figure screamed and fell to the ground.

Meaghan grunted with satisfaction and charged. She straddled the creature and held the tire iron firmly across its thin neck, pinning it to the snow. The creature's shrieks grew louder, more desperate. "Back off or I'll lean in. My body weight is more than enough to snap his neck."

The other figures hissed and spat, but no one moved forward.

Meaghan knew if she killed the elf, she'd lose her only bargaining chip. *Now what?* Her knees hurt and the rage-induced warmth in her limbs was already starting to abate. She had no idea how the cold affected her attackers, but she knew if help didn't come soon, she'd be in trouble.

"Looks like we got us a standoff."

Meaghan looked up at the sound of the deep, booming voice. In the din of the elf's screeching, she hadn't noticed the arrival of the pickup truck now sitting on the road above them.

The sudden beam of a spotlight blinded her. She blinked a moment and looked around. She could see the cloaked figures cowering in the bright light. She looked back toward the truck.

Silhouetted in the spotlight Meaghan saw a large man, holding a sledgehammer in one hand and a long straight stick in another. He stood silent for a moment and then said, "Hey, Meg. Nice move with the tire iron. Need a hand?"

"Terry?" she gasped.

"At your service." He held up the hammer. "Wanna play whack-an-elf?"

"You!" One of the figures hissed at him.

"Me," Terry said in a cheerful voice. He held up the long stick. "Steel rebar. Good for skewering. Pin and smash. You remember how good I am at that."

The fair folk hissed and spat at each other and then vanished, leaving their companion trapped under Meaghan's tire iron.

Terry stared down at the now crying creature on the ground. "Wow. Without the magical enhancements, these things are ugly. Almost too pathetic to kill." He turned so the light illuminated his face. With a wide grin, he lifted the hammer. "Almost."

The creature shrieked and squirmed, then looked up at Meaghan and said, "Spare me. Please."

"Did you hear that, Terry? He said 'please.' You can see what they really look like?"

"This one, yeah, because of the iron you're holding to his neck."

"What did the other ones look like?"

"Like extras from the *Lord of the Rings*. Supermodels playing epic fantasy dress up."

"That's not how they looked to me."

"Because you can see what they really look like," Terry said. "They hate that. So what do you want to do with this one?"

"How dangerous is he on his own?"

Terry shrugged. "With the two of us? Not very, so long as we keep some iron on him."

Meaghan nodded. "I want to have a chat with him. Somewhere warmer than this."

"Okay. He'll keep until we get home and then the witches can do some buffering spells."

"Will the fair folk come after him?"

Terry shook his head. "Probably not. Loyalty's not their thing. Hang on to him for a sec. I'll be right back."

He rummaged in the bed of the pickup and came back with a length of chain and a padlock. "Let's wrap him up nice and tight."

Meaghan stood up. Terry yanked the elf to his feet and wrapped his arms and torso with the chain.

"It burns," the elf whimpered.

"Don't be such a baby," Terry said. "I'd forgotten how whiny these things are. There we are, all trussed up. Come on, Legolas, let's go for a ride."

Terry tossed the elf over his shoulder and looked around him, eyes narrowed. "There may be other stuff roaming these woods. We can dig out your car tomorrow. Get what you need. Bring the tire iron."

Meaghan nodded and, under Terry's watchful eye, grabbed her things, turned off the headlights and engine, and locked the car.

Together they trudged up the hill to his truck. Terry tossed the elf in the truck bed, locked him to a tie-down ring, and reached a hand out for Meaghan's suitcase. "Okay if this rides in back?"

She nodded and climbed into the warm truck cab with Terry. "Is he gonna be okay? It's cold out there."

Terry smiled. "You're mommying an elf now?"

Meaghan scowled. "Hell, no. But if he freezes to death, I can't question him."

"Right. Don't worry. It won't be comfortable, but it won't freeze to death. It takes a lot of kill those things."

"Like pinning and smashing?"

"Uh . . ."

"Before I chat with the elf, I think you and I need to have a little talk. Who are you?"

Terry grinned. "Did you hit your head or something? I'm your neighbor. Terry Donner. Remember?"

"No, I didn't hit my head. You're Terry Donner now, but I don't think that's who you've always been."

He sighed. "It's a long story."

"We've got at least twenty minutes until we get home."

"It's a really long story."

"And you're not gonna tell me."

"Nope," Terry said. "I'm not. I like to leave the past in the past."

"One day at a time?"

He smiled. "Yeah. Something like that."

"I'll get it out of you eventually."

Terry grimaced. "Yeah, that's what I'm afraid of. The thing is I wasn't always a nice guy like I am now. I used to be a major dick."

"When you were drinking?"

"That was part of it."

"How old are you?"

"Old enough to know better."

Meaghan snorted in disgust. "I should be used to this shit by now. So, if you won't tell me who you are, then tell me what you are."

Terry sighed again. "Your brother is right. You're like a damn bloodhound that's caught a scent. What I am is your friend. I hope you believe that."

Meaghan relented. "I know you're my friend. You saved my ass back there. Thank you. How did you find me?"

"I was in Williamsport finishing up a job. Your brother called me and asked me to keep an eye out for you."

Meaghan nodded. "I am like a bloodhound sometimes. I'm sorry." She paused a moment. "But you haven't answered my question. Are you human?"

"Yeah. I think. I started out that way at least. And that's all I'm willing to say for now."

"But—"

"It's a long story and I'm not sure I'm ready . . . I used to be a *major* dick." He glanced at her for a moment, then turned his eyes back to the road. "And it's not only my story. It's Steph's, too. We have—had, before tonight—a nice little life here in Eldrich. Now that the fair folk have shown up, I don't know how long that can last. Let me talk to my wife first. Digest all this a little. Okay? Please?"

Meaghan nodded. They rode the rest of the way in silence.

The secrets never stop, she thought. *What else aren't they telling me?*

Chapter Six

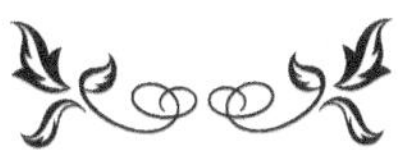

"Where are we taking him?" Terry asked as they drove through town.

"My house, I guess. Hang on." She pulled her phone out of her purse and called Russ.

"Are you okay?" Russ sounded frantic.

"I'm with Terry. I'm fine. I got stuck in a snowbank."

"Where are you?"

"On Main, heading north. We should be home in about five minutes. Is Natalie there?"

"Why didn't you call earlier? Of course, Natalie's here. With Lynette. We were about to leave to try to find you." His voice shook with anger.

"Relax. Geez. The cell service is super spotty tonight." Meaghan felt herself grow defensive and took a deep breath. "I'm sorry. You're right. I should have called. We had an incident out in the woods, and I got kind of sidetracked. Don't let Natalie and Lynette leave. We'll need them."

"What for? Are you sure you're okay?"

"We had a visit from the fair folk. You know—the ones I told you about?"

"Shit, Meg, what happened?"

"I'll tell you when we get home. Tell Natalie and Lynette we're going to need some heavy-duty protective magic. We've got one chained up in the back of Terry's truck. Once he thaws out a little, he's gonna be pretty pissed off. We'll be there in a minute."

Terry nudged her as she put her phone away. They were turning onto Sycamore, the street that accessed Holly Lane. "Should I go in through the alley?"

Meaghan shook her head. "There's no room," she said. "Russ's car and the food truck are parked back there. Use the driveway."

Russ, Natalie, and Lynette dashed out the front door as Terry pulled in.

The elf began hissing and shrieking when Terry approached the truck bed. Terry grabbed the sledgehammer, lifted it, and hissed something back. The elf's eyes widened and it grew still. Terry turned back to Meaghan. "Where am I taking this thing?"

"Your house?"

Terry smiled. "Steph hates these things even more than I do. She'll kill it on sight, like a cockroach."

"I thought you said they were hard to kill."

"Steph's a determined woman, and she doesn't mind getting her hands dirty."

"Yeah. I'll bet. Will he be okay in my basement? He can't blow up the house or anything, can he?"

Terry shook his head and threw the elf over his shoulder. "The iron weakens them and some good protective magic should take care of the rest."

Natalie nodded. "We're on it." She smiled at Meaghan. "Welcome home. I've got some names for you, some ..." Natalie lowered her voice to a whisper. "You know."

"Therapists," Meaghan said. "You can say it."

Russ nudged Natalie aside and hugged Meaghan. "Elena did set your head straight. Before you left, if we even hinted at therapy, you'd flip out."

"And she didn't even have to give me any boils," Meaghan said. She kissed Russ on the cheek. "I'm sorry I've been closing you out. Old habits are hard to break, I guess."

Terry shifted his weight. "I'll go take Happy the Elf downstairs. Then I need to get home and talk to my wife." He glanced at Meaghan. "And then maybe we can talk to you."

She nodded. "If it's relevant to fighting these things, I need to know."

He sighed. "It's relevant. Let me talk to Steph first. We knew they'd find us eventually, but it'll still be hard for her to hear. You can unlock its arms, but make sure you keep a chain on it somewhere. It'll tell you it burns, but ignore that. If you try to be kind, it'll think you're weak. It won't be grateful and the fair folk can't be trusted. Ever. For any reason."

"What do we need to do magically?" Natalie asked.

"Neutralize its power every way you can," Terry said. "Don't let it mess with your head."

"Come on," Lynette said to Natalie. "I've dealt with these things before. A long time ago. Let's get to work."

Russ grabbed Meaghan's suitcase out of the truck and they headed inside. Meaghan took a deep breath as she entered the house. As usual, it smelled wonderful.

"Did Elena make you those wretched Wonder Bread and chemical cheese enchiladas?"

Meaghan laughed. "Yeah, she did, and they were so yummy."

Russ shuddered. "Good God. Those things are an abomination."

"A tasty abomination." Meaghan kicked off her boots near the front door and wrestled out of her coat.

"I'll take your suitcase upstairs. There's chicken noodle soup on the stove if you're hungry." He grabbed her coat. "*Real* chicken, raised properly. And handmade noodles."

Meaghan rolled her eyes. "Hey, next time you go shopping, grab some Velveeta, okay?"

"Philistine," Russ said, as he headed upstairs.

Terry, on his way up from the basement, passed her on her way to the kitchen. "I'm not promising I'll tell you everything, but I'll tell you what you need to know."

"I guess I'll have to live with that."

He nodded and left.

Meaghan sank into a chair. She let out a deep breath and buried her face in her shaking hands. She'd been doing a good job keeping it together, but now that she was alone, the fear swept over her. Those things could have killed her. She could have died—again—simply driving home from the airport.

You weren't helpless, her calm rational voice told her. *You held your own.*

But Terry had to save me. Like Brian saved me when he shot that wizard, she countered.

And you think having people in your life willing to fight for you makes you helpless? Time to call the shrink, honey.

"Here I am arguing with myself."

"You are talking to yourself, too," John said behind her. She whirled in shock. She hadn't heard him come in.

"I . . . God, it's good to see you. I'm so sorry." She felt her eyes fill with tears. *Goddammit, again?* She willed them back down. She'd done enough crying to John. "I have something I have to tell you."

His smile disappeared.

She shook her head. "No, it's good . . . well, it's not a good thing, but it's good that I'm finally admitting it."

He let out the breath he'd been holding. "I thought you were saying you didn't want to see me anymore."

Meaghan patted the chair next to her. "I'm afraid you're going to say that to me."

"Never," he said. John moved the chair close to her, put his arms around her, and kissed her. After a moment, he pulled her onto his lap and held her even closer. "I thought you had gone away forever. I am sorry if it is too soon. I don't mean to push."

"Push?" She cradled his face in her hands. "Honey, you are the most patient man alive. I've been acting like a crazy woman and not telling you why. I think I can now."

Natalie and Lynette clattered up the basement stairs.

"Not yet though, right?" John asked.

"Not now. Stay, okay? Sleep here tonight? I missed you so much."

He smiled and nodded. "Of course. I was hoping you'd ask me that."

"See?" Natalie said. "I told you she didn't want to break up with you. She's just a little nuts right now."

Meaghan gave her a look. "A little?"

"A little more than usual." Natalie grinned. "I'm so glad you're back. You scared the shit out of us."

"How's our little guest?" Meaghan asked.

"Displeased with the accommodations," Lynette said. She sat down at the table with a groan. "I'm too old for this nonsense. I'm supposed to be making cookies and fussing over grandchildren, not hexing evil elves."

Natalie walked over and picked a cobweb out of Lynette's tidy gray bouffant. "Give me a break. You're a kick-ass old broad, and you know it."

"What's going on?" John said. "Who is in the basement?"

"Terry didn't tell you?"

John shook his head. "We didn't talk. He was moving his truck when I got here."

"I had a little accident on the way home. Nothing major. I slid off the road."

"Are you okay?"

Meaghan nodded. "Fine. Didn't even set off the air bags. Only—don't get upset—something was waiting for me."

John clutched her reflexively as his look darkened. "What was it? Is that what's downstairs?"

"Honey, relax. It's okay." She hugged him. "I hit one of them with a tire iron and sat on him, and then Terry arrived and chased the rest away."

"Terry?"

Meaghan nodded again. "Yeah. It turns out he has a history with them. The fair folk? Has he told you about them?"

John's face smoothed into the deliberate mask he wore whenever he tried to conceal something from Meaghan. "I . . . maybe."

"You are such a lousy liar," Meaghan said. "It's kinda cute. Don't worry. Terry and I had a talk—"

John's eyes widened.

Oh, this is gonna be good, whatever it is. Terry, who the hell are you?

"And he said he'll tell me some things about himself after he talks with Steph," Meaghan continued. "Not all of it, but some."

John visibly relaxed.

Meaghan shook her head. "Don't ever play poker. Or be a spy."

He looked confused. "What?"

She kissed him again. "You're the worst liar I've ever met." She turned her attention back to Natalie and Lynette. "Terry has a history with these things. So does Steph. He didn't tell me much, but enough that I know this isn't a good thing for them. He wants to break the news to her first and then he'll tell us what he knows about them."

Russ walked in. "Your bag's in your room, I put fresh sheets on your bed, and . . . well, we have news, too."

Before he could say more, the front door opened with a bang, and a female voice shouted, "Where is that little shit?"

Meaghan felt a brisk draft blow through the kitchen. *What the hell? When did the wind kick up?*

Steph Donner stormed into the kitchen, her blonde hair streaming behind her, Terry on her heels.

"Baby, calm down," Terry said. "It's safe. We've got it contained."

"The only safe elf is a dead elf, and I can't believe you didn't kill it on the spot." She took a deep breath, then noticed Meaghan. "Meg, sweetheart, how are you?"

"Fine, Steph, fine. How are you?"

"Enraged. Sorry to barge in, but—"

"Don't blame Terry," Meaghan said. "It was my idea to bring the elf home. So I can question him. It wasn't safe to stay in the woods."

Steph rubbed her temples like she was in pain. "I thought we could have a normal life for a while." She looked at Terry. "So, you want to tell her or should I?"

Terry looked nervous. "I'll do it. I'm the one who got us into trouble with them in the first place."

"So," Meaghan said. "Who are you? What are you?'

"Er, well, I'm . . ." He gestured at Steph. "We're kind of—"

"Immortal," Steph said.

CHAPTER SEVEN

"IMMORTAL HOW?" MEAGHAN asked. *My neighbors tell me they're immortal, and I go right to the details. I don't even have denial moments anymore.*

"What do you mean, how?" Terry asked. "We don't die, that's how."

"Yeah, but how did you get that way?"

John looked sick. "I swear I told her nothing."

Terry nodded. "It's okay, Johnny. We knew our cover would get blown eventually."

"We don't know for sure," Steph said. "We were born human and then one day something went boom, and most of the village and people were gone, and we stopped aging. Or at least stopped aging at the regular rate. We were in our twenties back then and now we're middle aged. So, I guess, technically, we aren't immortal."

"Something went boom?" Meaghan asked. "Magic?"

"Yeah," Terry said. "But we don't know who did it or why. But we think we know now what happened to everybody who vanished."

"They are my ancestors," John said. "We think this is how Fahraya was made."

"Seriously?" Meaghan looked around. "Does everybody else know this?"

Judging by the looks on everyone's face, Meaghan felt confident that this was news to them, too. "So, how did you figure this out?"

John shrugged. "Their story fits our story. I told you the Fahrayan legends about how wizards had a war and created our world, and how magic was taboo because we don't want them to come back?"

Meaghan nodded.

"Terry told me about his village, and how he and Steph came to be like they are now."

Steph nodded. "After it happened, we all had magical abilities we hadn't had before."

"You're a witch?" Natalie asked.

Terry shook his head. "Nah. Nothing like that. One-trick ponies, most of us. Like one person's power—"

"Shattered," Steph said. "I've got practically nothing. Some of us got more. Terry's cousin—"

Terry gave her a warning look. "Leave him out of it."

Steph rolled her eyes. "This again?"

"He has as much right to his privacy as we do." Terry turned to Russ. "You got any coffee? I could use some coffee."

Russ grinned. "You want a mocha? I've got some new organic chocolate I want to try out."

"You read my mind," Terry said.

Cousin? Meaghan was intrigued. But she knew that Terry would clam up if she pushed too hard. Time for a side step. "So the Fahrayan thing. Beyond the magic, what leads you to think the two events are related?"

Steph pulled out a chair and sat down. "Russ, could I trouble you for a cup of tea?"

"No trouble at all." Russ busied himself making beverages. "There's soup if anybody's hungry."

It turned out everybody was. After the soup was dished up, Meaghan renewed her line of questioning. "So how are you related to Fahraya?"

John piped up. "There are things similar in how we talk and how we write. We have stories about the time before the wizards made Fahraya that are like what Terry and Steph know."

"What we remember," said Steph. "It was a long time ago."

"How long?" Meaghan asked.

"We don't know for sure. It's hard to keep track after a while," Terry added, before sipping more coffee. He held the mug in front of him like a shield.

That's how he copes, Meaghan thought. *He's replaced alcohol with coffee.* "I guess this is a sign I've been in Eldrich too long, but I know a leprechaun, Owen Finnerty, who says the same thing."

Steph nearly spilled her tea. Terry began coughing. They exchanged a quick glance.

They know Owen. "Give me a rough estimate."

"Uh," Terry began, "I was still working with copper and bronze, and iron didn't catch on in a big way in Europe for at least another few hundred years, so three thousand years ago?"

"That sounds about right," Steph said.

"Wow," Meaghan said. "So, what's the deal with the fair folk?"

Terry and Steph glanced at each other again.

"Look," Meaghan said. "I get it. You've got some big dark history you don't want to disclose. Fine. But at least tell me what we're dealing with. If you don't want to tell me why you're hiding from them, that's your choice. But I need to know why they're here now and if it's about more than tracking down the two of you."

Terry sighed. "Best case scenario—for the rest of you at least—is them tracking us down. Worst case—"

"The war's starting again," Meaghan finished.

"You know about that?" Terry asked.

Meaghan nodded. "My mom told me about it in a dream. And Dad did a purposefully crappy scrub job on his files. The references to the war were expunged, but in a way that left obvious holes in the record. And Owen told me a little."

Terry and Steph exchanged a glance.

You'd think after three thousand years they would have learned how to lie better, Meaghan thought. *They're as transparent as John.*

"Did Owen tell you about the fair folk?" Steph asked. Terry opened his mouth as if to object and Steph held up her hand. "There's no point in pretending we don't know him. I told you both that we couldn't pull that one off for long."

Meaghan smiled.

Steph smiled back. "I could see you connecting the dots. Yeah. We know Owen. From way back in the day. Did the little stinker rat us out?"

Meaghan shook her head. "No. He didn't say a word about you guys."

"This is all very interesting," Lynette said, "but it's getting late and we need to figure out what we're doing about your house guest. Does he need a guard?"

"Yes," Steph said. "They're sneaky little shits. You should have a witch monitoring things all night to make sure the spells are holding."

"You want me to call the troops?" Lynette asked Natalie.

"Yeah, I guess," Natalie said. "Call Susan. And Gretchen. This might be a good learning experience for the apprentices."

Terry shook his head. "No. You don't want newbies down there. You want tough-as-nails experienced witches."

"They don't get tougher than Gretchen," Natalie said. "Susan's pretty good, too."

"Susan's in the Bahamas playing golf," Lynette said.

"Oh, hell." Natalie rubbed her eyes. "I forgot about that. Let me think about who else we could call."

Lynette sighed. "It's times like this I miss Marnie."

There was a frozen silence until Lynette broke it. "Oh, for goodness' sake. If you all want her to feel normal again, you have to start treating her that way. She'll never get her power back if you treat her like she's made out of glass. Or pretend she doesn't exist. She's a tough girl or she wouldn't still be here."

Meaghan felt her face flame and stared at the table. Marnie had been raped repeatedly by the Order wizards when they'd taken her back in August. When Meaghan thought of Marnie, she felt ashamed again that she was struggling to deal with an attempted rape, when Marnie had been through so much more.

John slipped his hand into Meaghan's and tugged her gently to her feet. "A lot has happened. Meaghan needs to rest. We'll go upstairs now, okay?"

Russ nodded. "Okay."

Natalie said to Lynette, "Call Gretchen for now, okay? We can figure out the rest of it tomorrow. Tell her she can stay in the guest room. So can you. We can take shifts."

Meaghan looked at her. "What about Jhoro? Where's he sleeping these days?"

Russ sighed. "Yeah, about that. Remember I said I had news? Jhoro took off a couple days ago."

"Where'd he go?"

"Somewhere in South America. With Sid."

"South America? What the hell?"

"Shaman training," Russ said.

"That druggy rainforest stuff?" Meaghan asked.

Russ rolled his eyes. "You can take the grandeur out of anything. Yes,"—he made air quotes—"that druggy rainforest stuff."

Jhoro, John's nephew, was a self-taught shaman, at least until now, using substances that had been available to him in

Fahraya. The high levels of background magic, in addition to forcing mutations in the human inhabitants, like reduced size and wings, also affected the plant life. In addition to a trippy high, the roots and fungi Jhoro had experimented with also gave the user temporary, but powerful, psychic abilities.

Meaghan had taken her own little trip back in June, when she had journeyed to Fahraya to rescue Jamie, and was still having occasional flashbacks. Jhoro had psychic abilities that transcended anything that anyone in Eldrich had ever encountered, but the language barrier, and Jhoro's overwhelming grief for the lover he'd lost when Fahraya had been destroyed, made his powers difficult to assess.

"He's with Sid?" Meaghan asked Russ. "How'd they get there?"

"Owen set it up. That guy he works for has a fleet of corporate jets and the pull to grease any entanglements along the way."

"Like the fact Jhoro has no official human identity," Meaghan said, "and therefore no form of identification, and Sid is blue and has tusks?"

Sid was Troon. A non-magical race with a fluid concept of gender, they were the universal translators of the magical worlds. The Troon language was so complex it made everything else seem easy, particularly primitive human languages that required only one set of vocal cords to pronounce.

"Yeah, basically. Owen says with enough money you can take anybody anywhere. And I guess his boss has enough money."

Meaghan glanced over at Terry and Steph who were not exchanging a glance in a very deliberate way.

So, Owen works for the mystery cousin, Meaghan thought. *The reclusive venture capitalist guy. If he's got that much money, there has to be a paper trail somewhere.*

Instead of pointing at Terry and Steph and saying "aha!" like she wanted to, Meaghan instead asked, "Is Jhoro coming back?"

Russ shrugged. "Eventually. I guess." He looked at Natalie. "You know anything?"

Natalie stared at her feet. She was still embarrassed about her role in the infamous Labor Day love-spell fiasco. She'd cast a spell to make Jhoro, who was gay, feel attracted to women and fall madly in love with her. She'd succeeded, partly, only instead of Natalie, Jhoro had hooked up with Marnie, which resulted in Marnie enduring her ordeal at the hands of the Order.

"Sid says he can't wait until Jhoro learns enough Spanish so that Sid can get out of there," Natalie said. "Jhoro says he's coming back, but Sid doesn't know when. Sid really hates the rainforest."

"Yeah," Meaghan said with a smile. "I bet he does. Too many bugs and not enough celebrity gossip." She turned to John. "Did you know about this?'

"Uh, maybe," John said. "Don't get mad."

"Have I really been that bitchy?" Meaghan asked.

"Yes," everyone said.

CHAPTER EIGHT

MEAGHAN WOKE UP with her bladder full and her nightgown damp with sweat. John was curled around her, snoring gently and radiating heat like a furnace. She slid slowly out from under his arm, trying not to wake him, and checked the bedside clock. A few minutes after five. It wouldn't be light for another hour and a half at least.

She used the bathroom in the dark and then fumbled through the clothing pile on top of the hamper to find something to pull on. Her sleep hadn't been interrupted by any nightmares, but from hard experience, she knew she wasn't going back to sleep.

Time to try out Elena's light box. On her way to the window seat, where she'd left her suitcase, she stubbed her toe. With a grimace but no sound, she hobbled the remaining couple of steps and felt around until she found what she was looking for.

With the lightbox under her arm, Meaghan cracked open the door and made her way as quietly as she could down to the kitchen.

She flicked on the lights. Russ had filled up the coffeemaker the night before and all Meaghan had to do was press the start button. He'd left her a note. "Staying with Annie. I thought you guys might like some privacy. There's bread in the pantry if you want toast."

Like everyone else, Russ assumed that she and John were having sex. *If only they knew. The gossip mill would explode.*

With a heavy sigh, Meaghan set the light box on the table and fetched a mug from the cabinet. She stared at the coffeemaker, willing it to brew faster. Toast was not outside her limited culinary skill set, but not until she'd had some coffee.

With the full mug in hand, she sat at the table, and plugged in the small tablet-shaped box. She pulled out the stand on the back and flipped it on.

The bright white light made her blink. She'd tried it a few times at Elena's house while reading the morning paper and it hadn't seemed this bright. *That's because everything else was so much brighter.* At Elena's the sun had been shining and the windows open, the warm air perfumed by the blooming orange tree next to the deck.

Meaghan could feel the grayness sinking back into her brain. She shivered. She was always cold, deep in her bones, and her brave words about dealing with her fear mocked her now as she sat in her brother's kitchen, clutching the warm coffee mug in her hands. Spring would never come and John wouldn't wait much longer and people were still keeping secrets and—

You done yet? Or are we doing the full pity-party checklist?

"Go make toast, little Miss Pathetic," she said to the empty kitchen. Relatively immune to self-pity, the rational part of her mind might annoy her from time to time, but it had kept her going through the difficult winter. That was the part she needed to nurture, she knew, but sometimes, the dark was so seductive.

Bread sliced and in the toaster, she went back to the light box. She sat for a whole ten seconds before realizing that she hadn't seen any signs of anybody in the house but her and John. Where were the witches?

The elf. Where is the elf?

Meaghan, now wide awake, her heart pounding, crept to the cabinet near the stove where Russ kept his smaller pans and skillets. She found her favorite saucepan, the one everyone called the wizard beater, and pulled it out as quietly as she could.

Taking a deep breath, Meaghan eased open the cellar door and stared down into the darkness. *The light should be on.* She listened. She heard a gasp and then silence. Too much silence. As she stood on the top stair, her finger on the switch, pondering what to do, she heard a loud bang and a whoosh.

Meaghan yelped and hit the light switch.

The furnace, idiot. That was the furnace.

Realizing that the element of surprise was long gone, she yelled down the stairs, "Who's down there? I got a saucepan and I'm not afraid to use it."

Wow. Some threat. I'm sure the elf is terrified now.

"Holy shit, Meg, what the hell?"

"*Owen?* What are you doing here?"

"Guard duty."

"Where's Natalie?"

"Um … I'm down here, too," Natalie said, sounding out of breath. "What's wrong?"

You mean besides you being in the dark in my basement with a leprechaun?

"Just wondering where everybody was," Meaghan said, her face growing pink, realizing she'd interrupted something. "You want me to turn the light off?"

"Yes," Owen said.

"Everything okay with the elf?" Meaghan called as she flipped off the light switch.

"Gretchen got tired of listening to it whine," Natalie said. "She zapped it with a sleep spell. She went home after Owen got here."

No one said anything for what seemed like a very long moment.

"Um, okay," Meaghan said. "I'm shutting the door now."

"Sounds like a plan," Owen called back as Natalie started giggling.

Meaghan shut the door and set the saucepan on the counter. She finished making the toast and warmed up her coffee, trying very hard not to listen. Or think.

"That was something I could have lived my entire life never knowing about," she mumbled.

Why? Because he's short?

Meaghan snorted and chomped on a slice of toast. She was arguing with herself again. *Hey, he's taller than John used to be. A lot taller.* The giggles took her then and segued into big belly laughs. She grabbed the dishcloth from the stove handle to try to muffle the sound.

It didn't work.

She was snorting back a laugh when John stepped into the kitchen, wearing only sweatpants, with Meaghan's eyebrow tweezers in his fist like a tiny dagger.

"What are gonna do with those?" Meaghan asked through her laughter. "Pluck somebody to death?"

He stared at her, confusion on his face. "It was the only steel I could find in your bathroom. What are you doing?"

"I'm laughing hysterically all alone in the kitchen. There's coffee. You want some?"

A puzzled smile on his face, John set the tweezers on the counter. "You sit. I'll get it. What's so funny?"

Meaghan started giggling again. "Don't go in the basement for a while."

John sat down with a mug of coffee. "Why? The witches?"

"Um . . . no, just one witch. And—"

"Is that safe? With the elf?"

"Gretchen zapped it with something and it's asleep. And Natalie's got company."

John raised an eyebrow. "Company who is not a witch?" He smiled. "Is it Brian?"

Meaghan grimaced. Brian still hadn't relented in his determination that he was done with Natalie. After several months of crying and moping, Natalie had apparently reached the same conclusion. "No, not Brian."

John squinted, thinking. "She isn't with a Fahrayan, is she?"

"No." Meaghan got up and refilled her mug. "You want toast?"

"Okay. Are you going to make me guess?"

Meaghan sighed. "Owen. She's with Owen."

He scowled. "The *leprechaun?*"

John's aversion to leprechauns was well known. One crew had tried shaking him down years before for protection money from his honey business, and a different crew had tried to start a loan sharking operation in the Fahrayan refugee camp right after they'd arrived in Eldrich.

"I thought you liked Owen," Meaghan said. Owen was thoroughly Americanized, and from what little information Meaghan had been able to dig up, appeared to be a legitimate businessman. At least at the moment.

"I do, I suppose. He's all right for one of them. But as a companion for Natalie?" He swallowed some coffee. "No. It's all wrong."

"Why?"

"He's too—"

"Short? As I recall, when we met, you were only eight inches tall without that magic amulet of yours."

John scowled. "Yes, but that was different. I was taller . . . looking."

Meaghan snorted with laughter. "That's the argument you're going with?"

John tried not to smile. "I give up. He's a leprechaun, but other than that, I guess he's all right."

Meaghan brought him a plate of toast. "Even the dirt Sid had on him wasn't that bad."

John gave her a blank look.

"You know," Meaghan said. "That supposedly horrible thing he did that got him booted out by the other leprechauns and that Sid acted all scandalized about?"

"What did he do?"

"Stole some magic sword. He gave it back. Everybody got their shorts in a bunch over it, but no harm done, as far as I can tell. Even Sid had to admit it really wasn't that big a deal and, if Owen hadn't been a leprechaun, everyone would be over it by now. I think the bigger problem is he's defying stereotypes. The other leprechauns hate him."

John's look brightened. "Why didn't you say that first? If they hate him, he must be okay."

Meaghan took his hand. "I missed you. I'm sorry."

"Sorry for what?" He brushed a strand of hair off her forehead. "I'm sorry if I am pushing."

"I think I'm ready to tell you what's going on. I should have a long time ago, but I thought I had to be strong. And I was scared. And you're not pushing. Not at all."

John's smiled at her, but his eyes looked worried. "Okay. I have wondered if I have been too eager."

Meaghan shook her head. "That's not the problem. It's not you. It's me."

John's eyes widened and he squeezed her hand tighter.

The look on his face couldn't have been any clearer. *He might as well have a comic strip thought bubble hanging over his head.* She laughed. "Will you relax? I'm not breaking up with you."

He sighed. "Good. I have heard that said and it's never good for the one hearing it."

"Yeah, except I'm not using it as an excuse. You've been wonderful. Patient." She felt the tears begin to prickle. *I must be getting better. I should have been full out weeping by now.* She took a deep breath. "Okay. Here goes."

Before she could continue, someone—or something—in the basement began to shriek.

CHAPTER NINE

MEAGHAN GRABBED THE saucepan off the counter and pulled open the cellar door, John right behind her. The shrieking grew louder. She flipped on the light switch and they ran down the stairs.

Natalie, naked except for the sheet wrapped around her, was standing in the middle of the basement, glaring at the elf. "Stop leering at me, you sick bastard pervert!" She whirled toward Meaghan and John. "That asshole elf was pretending to be asleep."

The elf wasn't shrieking, Meaghan realized. It was laughing, at a pitch and volume that made her ears feel like they were bleeding. She looked around. Owen hopped out of the shadows, zipping up his trousers.

"Can you shut this thing up?" Meaghan shouted to him.

"Sure." Owen grabbed the saucepan from Meaghan and backhanded the elf across the side of its face. With one final shriek, the elf crumpled to the ground. Owen gestured toward Natalie with the saucepan. "I told you hexing wouldn't work. When they start caterwauling like that, it's cold iron time."

John stepped toward the elf and stared down at it. "I thought they were supposed to be beautiful. This one is not."

"It's all the dampening spells," Owen said. "It can't mess with your head."

"No," Natalie said. "It just likes to watch." She kicked the unconscious elf several times. "Pervert."

"Calm down, Red," Owen said. "I think we got him."

Natalie, her anger waning, took in Meaghan and John gawking at her, then looked down at the sheet she wore. "Oh. Shit. Um ..." She looked back at them, her face flushing. "We were ... um ..."

Owen handed the saucepan back to Meaghan. "They know what we were doing." He grinned at Meaghan. "Don't kick my ass. I really like your sister. I have for a while." He nodded at John. "Sorry for the drama."

John grinned at Meaghan. "I like this one. He's not like the other leprechauns."

"So," Meaghan said, feeling her own embarrassment. "I guess we'll be heading upstairs now. Leave you ... to it. Um ..."

"I think we're done for now," Owen said. "Mr. Elf will be out cold for a while, if you want to head upstairs." He smacked Natalie lightly on the bottom. "Come on, firecracker, let's go clean up a little and let your sister process all this. When does Lynette get here?"

"Six, I think." Natalie adjusted the sheet more tightly around herself and bent to pick up an overnight bag. "What time is it?"

"Five forty-three," Owen said, looking at his watch.

"Oh, shit." Natalie scurried for the stairs. She caught Meaghan's eye on the way past. "Don't tell her anything, okay?"

"Not a word," Meaghan said.

"The gossip will start and I'm ..."

Meaghan looked at Owen. Natalie was obviously embarrassed, but Meaghan couldn't tell how much of it was being caught like this and how much was being caught like this with Owen.

Owen winked at Meaghan. He didn't seem to care.

Which made Meaghan feel a flash of sisterly protectiveness. She stared at him, eyes narrowed.

Natalie must have been paying better attention than Meaghan realized. "I really like him. This has been brewing for a while. Don't get all impervious and ass-kicky, okay?"

John snorted back a laugh.

Meaghan raised an eyebrow. "Have I really been that touchy?"

"Yes," Owen and Natalie said in unison.

Meaghan sighed. "We'll keep an eye on him until Lynette gets here. Go get dressed." She glared at Owen. "If you're just getting laid—"

"I know. You'll kick my ass, blah blah blah." He and Natalie climbed the stairs, giggling.

"Would you get me some more coffee?" Meaghan asked John.

He stared at the unconscious elf.

Meaghan hoisted the saucepan. "I'll be fine. If he wakes up, I'll give him another little tap."

John nodded and headed up the stairs.

Meaghan looked around the basement. Russ had done a lot of work down here since their father had died. He'd gotten rid of the boxes of random junk and set up the space as a rough but serviceable recreation room. There was a slouchy old couch with a new cover Annie had made for it, a card table, and a newer futon sofa, which was now open and covered with rumpled bedclothes.

Not sitting there. Meaghan moved over to the couch and sat down. While she was okay—theoretically—with the idea of Natalie and Owen being together, she didn't want to know any of the details.

The elf had been chained by an ankle and a wrist to one of the support columns in the center of the room. A pallet—it looked like an inflatable sleeping bag pad and a couple of quilts—had been placed on the floor, along with a galvanized bucket and a plastic jug full of water.

Meaghan had been so amped on adrenaline out in the woods she hadn't really looked at her attackers. The elf was small, not as short at Owen, but far more slender, almost child-like. It wore a plain gray tunic and leggings, not the rich fabrics and colors she'd expected. The clothing was like a blank screen, she supposed, and the elf projected on it whatever it wished.

As Owen had described, the elf had sallow pockmarked skin and pointy ears. There was nothing beautiful or glamorous in the least about its actual appearance. *No wonder they hate the impervious so much. We're like the kid who told everybody the emperor was naked.* Even the thing's laughter was unappealing, like tomcats having a fight.

The elf stirred, groaning. Meaghan had assumed it was a he, but up close, she wondered. These things seemed as genderless as the Troon.

When the elf saw Meaghan, it bared its pointy, yellowed teeth and began to hiss.

She merely stared back.

The elf began to hiss louder.

Meaghan, her face impassive, held up the saucepan.

It cringed back toward the column.

"You be nice," Meaghan said. "The leprechaun is strong, but I've got leverage on my side. I'll hit you even harder."

The elf stared back, its face twisted in revulsion.

"Do you understand what I'm saying to you?" Meaghan asked. "Do you speak English?"

"No one speaks this. You grunt it," the elf hissed. "Like pigs. This is barely language."

Meaghan raised an eyebrow. "You really don't get what's going on here, do you? You're the one chained to a post. Insulting me is probably not your best strategy at the moment."

"Impervious," the elf spat. "You are a disease. Worse even than the rest of the humans."

Meaghan smiled. "For you, yeah, I'm your worst nightmare. Because if everyone could see what I'm seeing, you'd be finished. What's your name?"

"You couldn't say it with your human excuse for a voice."

"Try me."

The elf sneered at her. More high-pitched shrieking erupted from its mouth.

Meaghan clamped her hands over her ears. "Enough, already. Shut up."

"You wanted my name," it said, smirking.

"That's your name?" Meaghan shook her head. "And you're insulting English? You got a shorter version of that?"

It shrieked again, sounding like a rusty hinge.

"Fine," Meaghan said. "We'll come up with something on our own. Why are you here?"

"You attacked me and then brought me here."

"I attacked you? You bastards jumped me in the woods."

"You broke the truce," the elf said.

"I broke the truce? How?"

"You brought him. The smith."

Terry? "I didn't bring him. He just showed up. After you attacked me."

"Your feeble gods can't protect you from what's coming."

Meaghan frowned. Was it still talking about Terry? "What feeble gods?"

The elf hissed and bared its teeth again. "Those who are no more."

"So what's your problem with the smith?"

The elf glared at her but said nothing.

Meaghan nodded. "It's the iron thing, isn't it? It was the iron smiths who put the hurt on you guys. Well, I got news. You got bigger problems than one blacksmith and his thoroughly pissed-off wife."

The thing's eyes widened.

"Huh. You're more scared of her than him." Meaghan smiled. "You should be. If it were up to her, you'd already be dead. She really doesn't like you guys."

"Who?" John, no longer bare chested, asked, as he headed down the stairs with two mugs. "I was cold. I had to get a shirt and then make more coffee."

"We were chatting about Terry and Steph. He's scared of Steph. Don't suppose you know why?"

"Uh . . ." John handed her a mug. "She is very scary?"

Meaghan sighed. "You're going to tell me eventually."

"I don't know the whole story."

Meaghan took a sip. He'd gotten the cream and sugar exactly how she liked. "Mmm. That's good. And you know more than you're telling me."

"Uh . . ."

She smiled up at him. "I get you're protecting him. It's sweet. Infuriating, but sweet."

The elf squinted at John. "You. You are a Fahrayan."

"Was a Fahrayan," John said. "We are human now."

The elf twisted its mouth in a humorless grin. "Not all of you."

John's coffee mug slipped from his hands with a crash. "What are you saying?"

"Would you like your wings back?"

John gasped. "Who are you?"

Too late, Meaghan noticed John was looking at a point about two feet above the elf's head. "John, no, it's—"

John gasped and fell to his knees.

Meaghan ran to him.

John, still kneeling, wrapped his arms around her, his body shaking. "I can feel them. My wings."

Meaghan glared at the elf. "What did you do?"

"I gave him a taste of what he lost." The elf smirked at her.

"Stop it," Meaghan shouted as John clung to her, sobbing. The red fury rose up in her mind and she could see herself smashing the elf with Terry's sledgehammer. "Stop!"

She dimly registered the sound of feet clattering down the basement stairs, shouting, and then the elf's shrieks again, before the sound was shut off like a radio. In the welcome silence, John's sobs seemed to grow louder.

Meaghan felt a hand on her shoulder and turned to see Lynette standing beside her.

"Where is everybody?" Lynette asked. "Who's been guarding it?"

"Natalie was here," Meaghan said in a rush, "but it started shrieking, and Owen hit it with the saucepan and knocked it out, and told us it would be out cold for a while, so I thought it would be safe. Then John came downstairs."

"Where's Natalie?"

"Upstairs," Meaghan said. "Taking a shower."

"Where's Owen?" Lynette asked, frowning.

"Um . . ." *You promised not to tell.* "Around."

"Damn it," Lynette said. "What happened to Gretchen?"

"She put a spell on it to make it sleep and then went home."

Lynette gestured toward John. "What did that thing do to him?"

"Made him feel his wings again," Meaghan said.

Lynette gasped. She'd been there the day John had escaped from Fahraya with bloody stumps where his wings had been. She'd help dress his wounds and had watched the aftermath. "We'd better call Terry."

Meaghan nodded. "As soon as I get John upstairs."

CHAPTER TEN

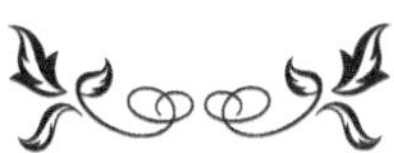

LYNETTE CALLED GRETCHEN, who zapped herself there in moments. Natalie, her hair still wet from the shower, joined them. The three witches put up multiple spell walls. With Lynette standing by with a stunning spell, Gretchen and Natalie trussed the elf as tightly as they could with the steel chain and strung from it every piece of iron and steel they could find, including several rusty cast-iron skillets Russ had picked up at swap meets but hadn't cleaned yet.

By the time Meaghan got John to her bedroom, he had calmed down quite a bit, enough to object to being removed from the basement.

"I am fine now. It was only the surprise. I want to talk to it again."

"Not a chance in hell," Meaghan said. "That thing got in your head somehow and until we figure it out, you need to keep your distance."

Meaghan led John to the bed, but he refused to lie down. "I am not sick. Stop. I don't need this. I am going downstairs again."

"Not until we know what went wrong with the buffering magic."

"Nothing went wrong with it," Lynette said as she walked into the room. "The magic was working. Did you call Terry?"

"On his way. What did you see when you came down the stairs?" Meaghan asked. "What did the elf look like?"

"Small, ugly, and dressed all in gray," Lynette said. "It looked the same as it did last night."

"No," John shook his head. "Something else was there. Tall. Beautiful." He glared at Meaghan. "You did not see it?"

Meaghan shook her head. "There was no one else there. You were looking above its head when you were talking to it. That's when I realized what it was doing."

"No, that's ... I saw it like you did when I came downstairs and then someone else was there. The one who ..." John's face twisted in revulsion. "They were the same? How could I not see that?"

"Because it was affecting your perception," Lynette said. "Somehow. Even with the buffering magic. It's what they do. When you're under their influence you can't tell truth from lies. You only see what they want you to see."

"You've dealt with them before," Meaghan said.

Lynette nodded. "Before the truce. Before we let the evidence of what they really are be erased." She shook her head, her lips in a tight white line. "I never agreed with Matthew on that decision. I know he was trying to keep things from dragging on any longer, but it was a mistake to let them hide from their crimes."

"The information wasn't erased." Owen strolled into the room. Instead of his typical impeccably tailored dark suit, he wore a black turtleneck and jeans. "It was removed and put in storage. And I know how to get it."

At their first meeting, Owen had made Meaghan a proposal. He would provide resources to help care for the misplaced

Fahrayans in exchange for Meaghan's assistance in negotiating the release of Matthew's redacted files from the people keeping them. But then all hell broke loose, and together they'd fought love-crazed witches and power-mad wizards, and barely stopped the invasion of mysterious hellish monsters who appeared even worse than the fair folk.

When the dust settled, Owen offered his help with the Fahrayans, no strings attached, and told Meaghan not to worry about it for now. The fair folk seemed like a lesser problem in light of the threat posed by the "extra-dimensional stinky space squid," as Natalie had dubbed them.

Not anymore.

"The elf got into John's head even with all the buffering magic in place," Meaghan said.

"Yeah, I heard." Owen looked at Lynette. "You couldn't see any tampering?"

"No. Unless . . ." She groaned. "Damn it. I know better and I still fell for it. Unless he hexed me to think that's what I saw."

Owen nodded. "That's what the fair folk do. It's like mirrors in a funhouse. They can bewitch you so badly you have no idea anymore what's real."

"Yeah," a deep voice said. "That's what they did to me for a while." Terry walked into the room and peered at John. "You okay, Johnny?" He looked around. "What happened?"

Owen sighed. "Uh, there's something I haven't told you all."

Terry shook his head. "They know we know each other. Steph and I are still going back and forth on what else we want to tell them."

"That's a relief," Owen said.

Terry nodded. "What happened?"

"The elf," John said. "It got in my head. It made me feel my wings again."

Terry grimaced. "You okay?"

John nodded. "I think." He gave Terry a small smile. "But this may be a one-moment-at-a-time day."

"Whatever it takes." Terry squeezed his shoulder. He looked around. "You had spells up?"

Lynette nodded. "Several. But it still got to John. Then it tricked me into believing the buffer spells were still working."

"Yeah, they'll do that," Terry said. "Little fuckers. That's why Steph wanted to kill it last night. She says there's no safe way to be around them. You shouldn't have taken the iron off."

Lynette shook her head. "We didn't."

Terry frowned. "You're telling me you had the chain on it and it still managed to mess with your head?'

"Around an ankle and a wrist."

"You said it wasn't a big threat on its own as long as we kept some iron on it and put up spell walls," Meaghan said.

"I was wrong," Terry said. "This one is stronger than it looks. Usually any iron is enough to short-circuit them. We need to get it better secured."

"Already done," Lynette said. "It's chained around the torso and we added every piece of steel and iron we could find. And we added several additional barriers. Is that enough?"

Terry nodded. "Probably. But you need at least two experienced witches down there at all times, and I think I'd better pay a visit and make some threats. Remind it who I am." He wore a worried scowl. "If it's resistant to iron, then it might have let itself get caught. So it could size us up."

"So then let's make it three witches," Lynette said as she walked toward the door. "I'll be in the basement with Natalie and Gretchen if you need me."

"I'll head down there with you," Owen said.

"Good," Lynette said. "You can tell me all about you and Natalie."

"Uh . . ."

"I'm sure Gretchen's already gotten it out of her. Come on."

Owen rolled his eyes as he followed Lynette out of the room.

"It said something," John said, his voice sounding choked. "About not all of the Fahrayans being turned human. Is that possible?"

Terry shook his head. "It's screwing with you. You told me yourself you're sure the missing Fahrayans are dead."

"But what if they are not? What if they're out there? I have heard the stories—"

"The gossip," Meaghan said. "It saw a soft spot and went for it, that's all."

Unless it knows something we don't. The gossip continued to circulate in magical circles that the missing Fahrayans had been grabbed for nefarious purposes when fleeing the destruction of their world. Even older gossip claimed that a band of Fahrayan raiders, gone missing in Europe during World War II, had been captured by the Nazis and taken to a secret lab in Berlin.

Conspiracy theories aside, many Fahrayans were not happy with their human transformation. They grieved their lost family and friends, and they wanted their wings back. Desperately. It was exactly the sort of longing the fair folk exploited to garner devotion.

Terry put his hands on John's shoulders. "Johnny, these things are liars. Everything about them is a lie. They're the most evil creatures I know of, and I've tangled with some scary things. Meaghan is right. It went after the one thing it knew would hurt you the most."

John nodded, his face etched with misery. "I still want to talk to it."

Meaghan shook her head. "Absolutely not. You heard what Terry said."

"I was sober on and off for fifteen hundred years before AA. I can't blame the fair folk for every time I fell off the wagon, but they definitely pushed me a few times. You need to keep your distance. Trust me. That thing downstairs would love to see you pick up a bottle."

"All right." John sighed. "I need to check on my bees today anyway."

"Would you stay up here for now?" Terry asked. "There's more of these things skulking around and they got your number. Let me talk to Meg and sort out a plan. After that, I've got nothing going today, so I can stick close. If you'd like the company."

John smiled. "Sure I'd like the company. Or is it babysitting?"

Terry laughed. "A little of both. And not only for you. These things have me rattled, too." He turned to Meaghan. "Meet me downstairs, okay? We need to talk about this some more."

Meaghan nodded, then turned to John. "We still need to talk too, but—"

"Now is not the time." He wrapped his arms around her. "I understand. Go. Do your job."

"My job … Oh, shit. I'm supposed to go into work today and walk through the new offices and finalize the furniture and—"

"Can somebody else do it? Jamie, maybe?"

"No, it has to be me. How is he, by the way?"

John shrugged. "He seems to be better, but—"

"You don't believe it."

"I don't know. I think maybe I am seeing too much of myself in him. And he still doesn't tell me much. More than he did, but some wounds are slow to heal. I can't make up for all those years away when he needed me."

"All you can do is be here now."

He nodded. "And then there is Patrice."

Patrice, Jamie's wife, had exhibited mysterious superpowers during the Order's siege of city hall. Cooper, the head wizard and all-around bad guy, had made cryptic sneering references to Patrice's "sisters," and Patrice—or more accurately, whatever had possessed her at the moment—had called herself a vessel. As soon as the danger was past, Patrice's powers receded and hadn't reappeared. At least not as far as anyone knew.

Meaghan sighed. "Yeah. We need to figure that one out, too. But first, there's the evil elf infestation to take care of. Let me go talk to Terry and get you sprung from house arrest."

"It never stops," John said.

"Look on the bright side," Meaghan said. "At least we haven't seen any evil wizards."

His look grew dark. "Yet. We haven't seen them yet."

Chapter Eleven

TERRY MET MEAGHAN at the bottom of the stairs.

"So now what?" she asked.

Terry pointed at the floor and shook his head. In a cheerful voice, he said, "Why don't you come over to my place for a cup of coffee?"

She gave Terry a quizzical look and pointed at her ear and then the floor.

He nodded.

"Let me get my boots and coat," Meaghan said, then added in a whisper, "Should I let them know I'm going?"

He nodded, then leaned over and murmured in her ear, "Keep it casual."

Meaghan made her way back to the kitchen and pulled open the basement door. She took a steadying breath. "Guys? I'm running across the street for a minute."

"Okay," Natalie called back.

"Who's down there with you?"

"Owen, Gretchen, and Lynette. We're fine. It won't be pulling anything else on us."

"Call me if you need me," Meaghan shouted. She pulled on her boots, found her coat in the hall closet, and followed Terry outside.

The gray clouds were back and the air was still and hushed. "It's going to snow again, isn't it?"

Terry nodded. "Feels like it."

"Is it safe to leave them?"

He nodded again. "I took a look and made some threats. They've got it locked down tight."

"So why the secrecy?"

"Not here," he said, his voice tight.

Meaghan raised an eyebrow. She pointed back toward her house.

Terry shook his head, pointed at his eyes, and then gestured around the neighborhood.

"Here?" she whispered, her heart pounding.

"Maybe," he said. "Let's get indoors."

In silence, they trudged across the street to Terry's house. He and Steph were in the middle of remodeling and the place was a maze of plastic sheeting and construction materials. They found Steph, still in her quilted bathrobe, sipping coffee in the outdated kitchen.

"Meg," she said, with a smile.

Terry shook his head, put a finger to his lips, and pointed toward the backyard.

Steph nodded and headed toward the tiny mudroom. She stepped out of her slippers and into her boots, grabbed a jacket from a hook near the door, and the three of them headed out the back door into the cold. The previous homeowner had let the holly run wild, but Terry had cleared a wide path back to his newly constructed forge.

His magical safe room.

Okay, this is bad, Meaghan thought.

He slipped a key into the deadbolt and unlocked it, then pulled an amulet from around his neck, squeezed it, and muttered something.

They stepped inside and Terry pushed the door closed. He exhaled a shaky breath and leaned his head against the door a moment as if to steady himself.

Steph put her arm around him. "You okay?"

He nodded. "For now." He gave her a worried look. "I'm sorry this keeps happening."

She shook her head. "Nothing to be sorry about. We knew it was only a matter of time."

Terry moved away from the door and gestured toward a battered folding chair. "Meg, have a seat. Sorry I can't really offer you that coffee."

Meaghan sat. "This guy isn't your typical elf, right?"

"No." Terry turned to Steph. "They sent one of the heavy hitters and it let itself be caught."

"How heavy?" Steph asked.

"It managed to mess with John and with one of the witches, even with a spell wall and an iron chain around its ankle."

Steph clutched the collar of her robe. "Where is it now?"

"Still in the basement, but with a lot more iron on it. There's three witches guarding it, plus Owen."

Steph relaxed a little. "Okay. I still think we should kill it."

"I agree," Terry said. "But not before we try to pry some information out of it."

Meaghan frowned. "How are you going to do that?"

"I have some ideas," Steph said, with a dark look.

"Now, honey—"

"I know. We can't stoop to their level. But after—"

"I know," Terry said.

"I wish you'd at least try to—"

He gave her a warning look. "You want to talk about this now?"

Steph glanced at Meaghan. "No. I guess not."

Meaghan sighed. They were obviously frightened and while she wanted to respect their privacy, she had to know what she was dealing with. "I get it. I know you have things you don't want me to know, but this cryptic shit is driving me crazy. Keep your secrets, fine, but tell me what we're dealing with."

Terry sighed and ran his fingers through his beard. "Like you said, that thing in your basement is not a typical elf."

"Yeah, I got that. Which is why we're hiding out here—"

"Freezing our asses off," Steph added.

"Oh, yeah. Right. Hang on a second." Terry fiddled with some knobs and within moments had a steady flame going in a small square box that sat on a pedestal in the middle of the concrete floor.

"What's that?" Meaghan asked.

"Gas forge."

"I thought this whole thing was a forge."

"No, not technically. The forge is really the heat source where you soften the metal so you can work it. But people also use the term to describe the entire workshop." He stopped puttering and looked up at Steph. "Better?"

She smiled. "Thank you." She looked at Meaghan. "I don't manage temperature well. Imagine going through menopause for several centuries."

"Ew. No thanks," Meaghan said. "If that's the price of immortality, you can keep it."

Steph rolled her eyes and pointed at Terry. "You sound like him."

"Immortality's like sobriety. You manage it one day at a time." Terry leaned back against the anvil and looked at Meaghan. "So, you want to know why we're having this conversation out here."

Meaghan nodded.

"It's been rumored for a while," Terry said, "that some of the fair folk were developing an immunity to iron. Like how humans are developing immunity to magic."

"And that's bad?" Meaghan asked.

"Very bad," Steph said.

"But if their magic doesn't work on humans, they're no threat at all, right?"

"Yeah," Terry said. "Eventually. But we're not there yet. There're still plenty of humans who have no immunity at all."

"Iron has always been the one thing that could short-circuit the elves' magic," Steph said. "At least enough for humans to begin fighting back. It was the sheer volume of iron and steel used in the modern world that gave humans enough of an edge to force them to a draw."

Meaghan mulled Steph's words a moment, then said, "This is what I don't get. If we forced them to retreat, why are they still screwing around in human affairs?"

Steph snorted. "Because it was a draw. Not a victory. They agreed to stop killing humans and we agreed to stop killing the fair folk."

"But it's okay to feed off us?"

Terry sighed. "Yeah. You aren't the only one who wasn't thrilled with that resolution."

"So then why did you agree to it?"

"Hey, don't blame me. I wasn't even there. I had nothing to do with it. You need to ask your father."

"Or Luka," Steph said. "Who has the advantage of still being alive."

The mystery cousin?

"Steph, we talked about this—"

"No," Steph said. "You talked about this. I didn't agree to anything. If the fair folk are breaking the truce, he's going to get involved, you know that."

"Yeah, but—"

Steph nodded. "I know you don't want to dig up the past. But, if the—"

"Everyone will be afraid of me."

Steph went to him and put her arms around him. "In Eldrich? Doubtful. There's much scarier things here than you."

"Like the stinky space squid," Meaghan chimed in. "Or Patrice. We still don't know what's up with her."

At the mention of Patrice, Terry glanced at Meaghan, a guilty look on his face, then looked quickly away as his cheeks grew pink. Steph, curled up under his arm, didn't notice Terry's reaction.

What the hell? But Meaghan knew better than to push him. She filed it away with the mystery cousin as something to look into later. *Time to change the subject.* "So, did you guys know my father?"

Terry shook his head, obviously relieved not to talk about Patrice. "Not personally, no. But we knew of him. My cousin knew Matthew a bit."

"Is that Luka?"

Terry gave Steph a warning look. She scowled back and said, "Yes. And don't you look at me like that. Meg already knows Owen works for him. Ninety seconds on the Internet and she'll know all about him anyway." She turned to Meaghan. "Luka Volkhov. Because I know you'll start Googling the moment you get a chance, and you won't let it go until you find him. This saves us both some time."

Meaghan smiled. "Thank you."

Terry threw his hands in the air and pulled away from Steph. "Geez, why don't you just tell her the whole thing? Spill all our secrets?"

"Don't be such a drama queen," Steph said. "I'm only telling her what she needs to know." She turned her attention back to Meaghan. "Nobody was happy to let the fair folk keep feeding, but like I said, it was a draw. I wasn't involved either, so I don't know the details about what happened. But I know somebody who was."

"Luka?"

"Somebody else." She looked back at Terry. "I called her while you were over there."

Terry nodded.

"Called who?" Meaghan asked.

There was small knock on the forge door. Steph smiled. "How's that for timing? Am I good or what? Honey, go let her in."

CHAPTER TWELVE

A SMALL BLUE face peered around the door. Melanie.

She was Sid's mother . . . parent . . . Meaghan still hadn't gotten a grip on Troon reproduction. They were hermaphrodites and the decision as to which set of organs were used by which parent in a particular pregnancy was made carefully, based on health, physical capabilities, and lifestyle.

But apparently not based on gender preference. Melanie could easily be Sid's father, despite her feminine behavior. Most Troon were androgynous, but others—particularly those with more extensive contact with humanity—exhibited a variety of gender characteristics. Sid claimed everyone was okay with this, but Meaghan wondered. Sid, whose mix of gender characteristics and sexual preference played in the human world mostly as male and gay, spent as much time with humans as he could, which—considering he had blue skin and tusks—was not in itself an easy choice.

Meaghan hadn't worked up the courage to ask Melanie about it. Maybe gender was a lifestyle choice for the Troon, but

Melanie seemed feminine to her core and reminded Meaghan—painfully sometimes—of Meaghan's mother.

Meaghan gave her a big grin and waved. She hadn't seen Melanie since the aftermath of the mess in Fahraya, and she felt a rush of relief to see her now. Melanie had translated for Matthew and knew most of his secrets, maybe even whatever was hidden in the redacted sections of his journals.

Melanie rushed to Meaghan's side. "Oh, Meggy, I was so worried." She pulled Meaghan to her feet and into a hug and gripped her tightly for a long moment, then stepped back. "Although I hear you gave them a fight."

"Tried to," Meaghan said. "But I'd have been in big trouble if Terry hadn't shown up."

Melanie eyed Terry with concern. "Are you all right? Still in control?"

Terry nodded. "I'm fine. Haven't thought about drinking once during all this."

"What about . . ." Melanie trailed off and gave him an appraising look, "the other thing?"

"That's under control, too. Don't worry. All the stuff we did is still working."

Melanie knows the secret, if I can pry it out of her . . .

"It's not my secret to disclose, dear," Melanie said. "And no, I'm not psychic. I merely know how your mind works."

"I didn't—"

"You're like your father," Melanie said. "You hate mysteries. You're watching and listening and gathering scraps of information, and the first free moment you have, you'll be digging away at it."

"Which is why we should tell her," Steph said. "Don't you give me that look."

"Fine," Terry grumbled. "Tell her whatever you want, but first, can we please get back to the current crisis? The evil, iron-immune elf in Meaghan's basement? Remember him?"

Melanie sucked in a breath. "Truly immune?"

"No," Terry said. "At least as far as I can tell. But resistant to a higher degree than I've seen before. He managed to screw with John's head while making everyone else think the spell wall was holding—even the witch who conjured it."

Melanie shook her head. "You have to keep the iron in contact with their bodies."

"We did," Meaghan said. "He was chained at the wrist and ankle."

Melanie's eyes grew wide with fear as she clutched Meaghan's arm. "Then it's true. I was hoping it was merely propaganda. This is bad. Very bad."

"Why is it bad?" Meaghan asked. "Here, sit down." She guided Melanie to the chair before she collapsed and dragged Meaghan to the floor with her. "Unless they're growing immune to iron faster than humans are growing immune to magic. Are they?"

Terry shook his head. "Nobody knows for sure, but my guess is humans are winning that race. We evolve faster."

Something stirred in Meaghan's memory. Something Melanie said. "When you were telling me about Fahraya, right before I went to get Jamie, you told me that magic is like radiation and it can cause genetic mutation. Wouldn't they be affected by that?"

"No. They've always lived in a magical environment," Melanie said. "They're used to it."

"Then what's forcing these changes? What's making them less sensitive to iron?"

Melanie sighed. "That's a very good question, but there's no one to research it. The magical worlds don't trust technology and science, and humans who understand science, who have the skill and knowledge to unravel it, generally don't believe in magic."

"What about the Troon?" Meaghan asked. "You guys are non-magical. You have technology, right? Science?"

"To a degree," Melanie said, "but we also have an economy based in large part on providing translation services to magical species. Nobody wants to rock that particular boat."

Meaghan sighed. "So science gets subordinated to politics. Gee, we don't have any of that going on in the human world."

"No shit," Terry said. "But I still think—based on nothing but my gut and three thousand years watching humans change—that we're changing faster than they are."

"Which is still bad because it means they need to be aggressive," Meaghan said. "They need to get to the finish line before we do."

"Yes and no," Terry answered. "Those who are completely immune to iron are even rarer than impervious humans. Like unicorn rare. Rumored but never encountered. Humans are definitely ahead of the curve on that front."

"Ultimately, they're fighting a losing battle," Steph said. "Unless—"

Meaghan pushed down her growing anxiety. "Unless they can root out the impervious *disease*, as that little jerk called it, before it spreads any further."

Steph nodded. "That's what happened to the guy who located your father."

"Lou," Melanie said. "Poor Lou."

Meaghan nodded. "He told me in a dream that he got killed right after he found Dad. That's what Mom was talking about."

Terry looked at her quizzically.

"In another dream. Before I got clued in. My mom told me my father had kept his distance from me and Russ when we were kids because the war had started and it wasn't safe. They were coming after me?"

"They wanted to, but we forced them to a draw first and they retreated," Melanie said. "Until now."

"Which means another bunch of magical nut jobs trying to kill me." Meaghan sighed. "But it's not like I'm gonna pass the impervious gene on. My window of opportunity closed a long time ago."

"You're a powerful symbol," Terry said. "If they could get into your head, they'd turn you against the rest of us. Instead, they'll have to kill you."

"Then why didn't they do it last night?"

Steph shivered and pulled her robe closer. "Because they like to draw it out and they need to make an example of you. Drive you mad with fear before they close in for the kill."

And right behind the fear, here comes the rage . . . "Seriously? I had my entire understanding of reality turned inside out—at age fifty, mind you—and a week later, I was in another world kicking ass. I stared down those mystery stinky tentacle things when everyone else was crapping their pants."

"Yes, Meg," Melanie said, "but—"

"But nothing. I've saved the world. Twice now. And a bunch of scrawny, screechy, mind-screwing elves think they're gonna bully *me*? Yeah, good luck with that."

Steph pulled Meaghan into a tight hug. When she pulled back, Meaghan could see tears in Steph's eyes, but she was smiling. "They don't stand a chance against you."

Meaghan took a deep breath. "You do know I'm only talking big because fear makes me angry, right? And that you can gauge the degree of my terror by how pissed off I am? Don't start the victory lap yet."

"No," Melanie said. "We know we have a battle on our hands. But you do have a reputation. Which is why they sent your prisoner in. To find out more about you."

"And you've acquitted yourself pretty well so far," Terry said. "If you're scared, you aren't showing it."

Meaghan sighed. "Yeah, I usually don't. Unless you know what to look for."

"Like towering rage?" Terry asked.

"Yeah," Meaghan said with a smile.

Terry smiled back. "I know a little about that."

"From back when you were a major dick?"

Steph rolled her eyes. "Not only then."

"Hey," Terry said. "I'm a teddy bear compared to how I used to be. I'm Santa. Remember?"

Steph stood on her tiptoes and gave him a kiss. "Yes, you are." She smacked his belly. "And Santa better lay off the mochas, or next year he'll be so fat he'll need more reindeer to get his sleigh off the ground."

"Ha, ha." Terry smiled down at her.

They stood in the now-warm shed, silent for a long moment, until Meaghan broke the silence. "So, now what do we do?"

"Get out the thumbscrews?" Steph asked.

Terry sighed. "Honey—"

"I was kidding," Steph said.

"Even if we used . . . intimidation"—Melanie wrinkled her small nose in disgust—"it wouldn't get us useable information. But if we let the elf go, it will scurry back to its masters with information to use against us."

"It's not moving into Jhoro's room," Meaghan said. "I know that. So our options are killing it or letting it go?"

Terry sighed. "I'll go get the sledgehammer."

Maybe there's a third way . . . "No," Meaghan said, with a smile. "No, we don't kill it. We're going to let it go."

"And it will use everything it's learned to hurt us," Melanie said, shaking her head.

"So then we make sure it learns what we want it to learn," Meaghan said.

"We scam it," Terry said.

"Exactly," Meaghan said.

"Time to call Luka," Steph said.

This time, Terry didn't argue with her. He merely nodded. "Time to call Luka."

Chapter Thirteen

THEY AGREED TO keep the elf under guard in the basement until they developed a plan. Meaghan knew she wanted to misdirect the fair folk, but she wasn't sure what idea she wanted to plant in their heads. She hoped the mysterious Luka would help her figure it out.

"Luka's in Seattle," Steph said.

Terry looked surprised. "How do you know that?"

"Owen."

Terry frowned. "This was always gonna happen, wasn't it? No matter how I feel about it."

Steph smiled back. "Yes. Yes, it was." Her face grew serious. "They're here and we have to deal with them. We can't do it without Luka and you know it."

Terry sighed. "You want to call him or should I?"

"Owen called him last night. He'll be here this afternoon."

Terry nodded. "What's he doing in Seattle?"

"Schmoozing a tech titan, I suppose. He's friends with all those guys."

Terry allowed himself a smile. "They're friends with him, you mean. Or his money, at least."

"Something like that." Steph turned her attention to Meaghan. "See? Mystery solved."

Not by half, Meaghan thought.

They agreed to wait until Luka's arrival to figure out what information to feed the elf. In the meantime, Terry would accompany John on his day's errands, the first of which was digging Meaghan's car out of the snow. Meaghan would borrow Russ's car and go into the office as she'd originally planned. Steph and Melanie would head over to Meaghan's to help the witches stand guard.

"I won't kill the damn thing," Steph said. "Unless it needs killing." She glared at Terry. "That's the best I can promise."

"It'll have to do," Terry said. "C'mon, Meg."

They trudged back across the street. Meaghan said goodbye to John and promised him they'd talk later.

She almost succeeded in ignoring the relief she felt at not having to tell him about the attempted rape. She knew she had to deal with it, but not yet. She felt a flash of gratitude to the elf for arriving and giving her something else to worry about.

Gee, that's not screwed up, her rational voice said. *Denial by crisis. Nifty.*

"Shut up," she mumbled. "I'll do it tonight."

"Do what tonight?" Russ stood in the doorway to her bedroom.

"Goddammit, don't sneak up on me."

"Who were you talking to?" Russ said, with a worried look on his face.

Meaghan gave him a haughty look. "Myself. I was talking to myself."

His face softened into a smile. "Oh, that's okay then. Dad used to do that all the time."

Meaghan's eyes widened.

"Before he got Alzheimer's," Russ added. "Said it helped him think to hear it out loud. So, what's going on? Where is everybody?"

Relieved that he didn't seem to want an answer to his original question, Meaghan quickly filled him in on the morning's events.

Russ merely nodded at the bad news, but lit up with joy when he heard Melanie and Steph would be hanging out in his kitchen all day. "I haven't seen Melanie in months. And Steph promised she was going to show me some old recipes."

"When did she promise that?"

"Last night. After you and John went to bed." He waggled his eyebrows. "You guys practically ran up here. I got everybody out before it got loud."

Meaghan stared at him for a long moment, and then, to her surprise and utter mortification, she burst into tears.

Russ, horror on his face, rushed over and put his arms around her. "What? What happened?"

"Nothing," Meaghan choked. "Nothing ever happens because I won't let it. Because of Labor Day. Didn't Elena tell you?"

He rubbed her back and said, "She told me you had a big secret, but it wasn't her secret to tell. What happened? What about Labor Day?"

The story spilled out and as it did, Meaghan realized it was marginally less painful to tell than it had been the first time with Elena.

"It's not a contest," Russ said. "You don't need to be stronger than everybody."

"But Marnie—"

"Don't use her trauma as an excuse."

"It's not an excuse," Meaghan said, trying to pull away from him.

"Yeah, it is, and you know it. If you minimize your pain by telling yourself you don't deserve to feel it, then you don't need to deal with it."

Meaghan cried a little more because she knew he was right.

"John says we're only as sick as our secrets," Russ said.

"What?" Meaghan pulled away, and this time, he let her go. "Gotta blow my nose. Hang on."

Russ followed her to the bathroom. "It's an AA thing. Something Terry told him."

"Huh," Meaghan said, wiping her nose with a wad of toilet paper. "He should know. There's a guy with some secrets. The immortal thing is only half of it. He's got a past. John knows some of it. Melanie knows more. And they won't tell me, as usual, but I'll get it out of them."

Russ sighed. "Or you could accept that sometimes people keep secrets for reasons important to them, and you need to let them tell you in their own time, no matter how hard it is to know someone you care about isn't being straight with you."

Meaghan glared at him. "You … damn it. You always do that, you sneaky bastard." She punched him in the shoulder.

He smiled. "Do what?"

"Say what I need to hear instead of what I want to hear." She hugged him again. "Bastard."

"How long you gonna be at the office? Want me to pack you a lunch?"

She shook her head. "No idea. If I get hungry, I'll grab something downtown."

Russ nodded. "So, when are you gonna call one of those therapists?" He pulled a folded sheet of paper from his back pocket. "I wrote down the numbers for you."

Meaghan stared at the paper like it was a snake about to strike. *Not now. I can't do this now.* "Give me a break. First we gotta deal with the elf and—"

"Another excuse." His smile vanished. "Make the freaking appointment already. You need to pull your head out of your ass. You're no good to us like this. Don't you see that?"

Meaghan stared at him, his words like a bucket of cold water in her face. *So maybe this way you can accept it?*

Her rational voice waited for a response. "Yeah," Meaghan finally said. "I do now."

Relief washed over Russ's face. "Oh, thank God. I thought I'd pushed my luck right off a cliff there for a moment."

She smiled at him, feeling the weight lessen. "Next time, start with the tough love first, okay?"

He smiled back. "And I went with kind and patient. Silly me. I should know better."

Meaghan said goodbye to everybody and headed into town. The city hall reconstruction project was nearly done, with only the solicitor's office still to be completed.

The rest of the city departments had been back in city hall since Halloween, while the solicitor's office had been doing business in the Keeles' dining room. It had taken so long to complete their space because the attic where the office had been located had suffered the most damage. Plus, the space had been dramatically redesigned, some of it in what had formally been unfinished attic space, to make sure that the work spaces stayed clear of any mystical hot spots.

The building had been constructed specifically to channel and focus the mystical energies that converged on the site, with two points of focus located in the attic where the solicitor's office now resided. The stronger of the two had been in Jamie's office, a fact the Order had attempted to exploit in their quest to release their stinky tentacled monsters.

The same monsters Meaghan had vanquished with a stapler. She smiled as she pulled into her assigned parking space near the front door. *I fought monsters with a stapler and I won.*

So calling a therapist shouldn't be too hard, she reasoned. Russ was right. She wasn't any good to anybody this way.

Meaghan made it all the way in the front door and halfway

to the elevator before being intercepted by Emily Proctor, the city council staff director and second most powerful witch in Eldrich after Natalie. Before Labor Day, Meaghan and Emily had hated each other. After Labor Day, against all expectations on either of their parts, they had become friends.

Emily was going through her own rocky transition trying to escape from her former self. Not everyone was inclined to believe Emily's Labor Day change of heart, particularly Natalie and Jamie, both of whom were convinced Emily was up to something.

"You're back. Thank God," Emily said, sweeping onto the elevator with her. "I'll ride up with you." As soon as the door closed, Emily looked at her shyly and said, "I'm glad you're here. I wasn't sure we'd see you again."

"Don't ask me how I am," Meaghan said.

"I wouldn't dream of it," Emily said. "Are you here about the carpet?"

"What about the carpet?" Meaghan asked. "I thought I was here to look at samples."

"Um, well, yes, then Tony got involved." Emily stared at her feet. "While you were away."

Tony Diebler was Eldrich's clueless mayor. He was the most gifted practitioner of denial Meaghan had ever met. Even with all the evidence staring him in the face, including a nearly destroyed city hall and a secretary who regularly talked to dead people, Tony still refused to believe in the supernatural.

Meaghan groaned. "How bad is it?"

"They finished it late last night. I haven't seen it yet, but I can't imagine it's good."

The elevator door slid open. The landing had been repaired as had the office entrance, which was one of the few things that hadn't been relocated.

"Tell me it's not the giant roses. Or the geometric mess. That pattern could give you seizures just looking at it."

Emily sighed. "It sort of pulsates, don't you think? I'm sorry."

"That's what Tony picked?"

Emily nodded. "Partly. He asked them to use both. I tried to stop him, but, well, he's not afraid of me anymore. He's only afraid of you and you weren't here."

"Not even Natalie? He's not afraid of Natalie?"

"She hasn't been here either," Emily said, her face growing pink. "I tried calling her, but . . . well, you know how she feels about me."

"Give her time," Meaghan said. "You guys were enemies for years."

"I didn't mean for us to be," Emily said, a worried frown on her face. "I really thought I was doing what was best for everyone."

Emily had spent years wielding the legislative branch of city government like a club, retaliating for every perceived threat or slight, but Meaghan now understood the fear behind it. Even Emily's betrayal of Jamie back in June, when she'd helped the Order kidnap him, had been motivated by her mistaken belief that Jamie was a threat.

Then came Labor Day, and Jhoro, and Emily's mystical mind-meld thingy, and Emily had been reborn. Except nobody in city hall, other than Meaghan, believed it. Emily didn't even always believe it, resulting in a few instances of her old self returning. But Meaghan—although still somewhat a neophyte about magic—was an old hand at politics and could tell the difference. Politics she could deal with. At least now she could talk Emily down when she started overreacting.

"Jhoro left, by the way," Meaghan said. "He's in Peru."

Emily's mouth dropped open. "What's he doing down there?"

Before Meaghan could answer, something in the solicitor's office exploded.

CHAPTER FOURTEEN

"AGAIN?" MEAGHAN WRENCHED open the office door and a cloud of smoke rolled out. Except it wasn't smoke. It was mist. And it smelled like . . . "Doritos?"

Emily shook her head, a dazed look on her face.

"Come on," Meaghan said, dragging Emily through the door into the new reception area, which was blocked from the rest of the office by a wall and a security window. Visitors had to be buzzed in. No more wandering into the solicitor's office unannounced.

Meaghan had pushed for the increased security. While the old office had been heavily warded with spells to keep magical bad actors out, not all of their enemies were affected. The Order relied on guns as much as they did magic. Kady now had a panic button to alert the Eldrich police, as well as a hex bag to call the coven.

But security doors only worked when they were shut, which this door wasn't. "This way," Meaghan said. "Get a hex ready. We might need it."

Emily nodded and began muttering an incantation.

"Who's supposed to be up here?" Meaghan asked.

Emily held up her finger and muttered something else. "There. I'm ready. The designer was supposed to be here waiting for somebody. That's where I was going when I ran into you. To see if we could do anything about the carpet."

Meaghan looked down at her feet. "Oh, God. It really does pulsate, doesn't it?"

Emily eyed it, a suspicious look on her face. "Yeah, it does. This isn't right. This is—" She stared at Meaghan, fear on her face. "This is magical. Some kind of key." She pulled Meaghan's arm. "We have to go. They're back. The Order is back."

"Dude," a male voice said, "that's harsh. We hate those guys."

A pimply faced young man, barely out of his teens, wearing a robe of rough brown linen that matched his shaggy hair, stepped out of the steam. He smiled and waved a pudgy hand. "Hi. Are you Meaghan?"

"Who the hell are you?" Meaghan stared. "Is this the designer?" she asked Emily.

The kid looked at her and then Emily, and his smile disappeared. "Designer? No, I'm one of the keepers."

Meaghan shook her head.

"You know," the kid said, "the Brothers of the Word? The keepers of the archive? Didn't the leprechaun guy tell you about us? He's been bugging us for months. You were supposed to come see us? To explain why you wanted the . . ." He looked around, then leaned closer. "You know. The stuff"—he glanced at Emily—"about the guys? Who do the thing?"

Meaghan shook her head.

"With the magic?" he asked. "You know," he glanced around, then whispered, "the *war?*"

The pieces fell into place. Meaghan nodded. "My father's lost journal entries. The fair folk."

The kid looked panicked and shook his head. "Don't say their names," he squeaked. "Never say their names."

"Oh, for God's sake," Meagan said. "I can't say their names, remember? Don't have enough vocal cords. What other euphemism would you like? They who must not be named?"

"Is she a witch?" the kid asked, staring at Emily.

"Yes," Meaghan said. "A very powerful witch and if you don't start making sense right now, she'll turn you into a frog."

The kid paled. "A frog?"

Emily nodded. "A frog."

"I don't want to be a frog."

"Then start talking," Meaghan growled. "How'd you get here?"

"How do you think?"

Meaghan scowled. "Not through the front door, I'm guessing."

"Through the gateway," the kid said. "The one back there." He pointed in the direction of the less powerful mystic hotspot in what used to be unfinished attic.

"There's a gateway?" Meaghan asked. She glanced at Emily, who gave her a confused look and shrugged.

"Well, yeah," the kid said. "You should know. You opened it." He pointed at the floors. "Why else install carpet covered in sigils? You called me. It's kind of loud, to be honest."

"Ah," Emily said. "That's why it pulsates."

Meaghan glared at her. "Who the hell was the designer?"

"Some Italian firm. Bottaio Design. Tony recommended them, remember?"

Meaghan groaned. "Right. The firm he hired outside of the procurement rules. With the money from Owen's boss."

"Yeah," the kid said. "That Luka guy. What's his deal? Do you know?"

"No," Meaghan snapped. "Do you? And why does it smell like Doritos?"

"I picked up a bag at the 7-Eleven. Had them for breakfast. This rug's been clanging at us since last night, but I figured nobody would be here until morning, so I did a snack run. That's the hardest part of the job. No pizza delivery. No Big Gulps. Too much, you know, medieval food."

Meaghan nodded. She could sympathize. "My brother throws a fit anytime I try to eat junk food. What's your name?"

"Dustin. Um, Brother Dustin. Sorry. We tech guys aren't that formal with each other."

"What world are you from?"

"Oh, uh, this one. Originally. The archive isn't really in a world. It's a bubble. It's more like Fahraya used to be." His ears grew red. "Before you, you know, blew it up."

Meaghan rolled her eyes. "I didn't blow it up."

"Mmm," Dustin said and seesawed his hand in the air.

Meaghan glared at him. "All right, fine, technically yes, I did blow it up, but only to keep everybody else from getting sucked into the void. You're welcome, by the way."

"You need that frog spell yet?" Emily asked.

"Maybe," Meaghan said. "If Brother Dustin doesn't behave himself."

His eyes widened. "I am behaving. I'm here because you called me, okay? I've been in the brotherhood for like a year, stuck in that archive, trying to set up servers that won't get fried by all the background magic, and they sent me because I'm human and because everybody else is . . ." Dustin trailed off and stared at his feet.

"Everybody else is what?" Meaghan prompted.

Dustin cleared his throat and said, in a small voice, "Everybody else is scared of you."

Meaghan grimaced. "Give me a break." She turned to Emily. "Am I scary?"

"Yes," Emily said, "you can be."

Meaghan shook her head. "So, now that you're here, can I have those files?"

"I can help you put in a formal request." Dustin stared at his feet again. "It's not really up to me. They only sent me because I ... well, I volunteered. If I don't get some decent food and download some movies and games and stuff, I'm gonna go nuts. It's not like I got Wi-Fi over there."

"You aren't working with the Italian design firm?" Meaghan pointed at the carpet. "The ones who gave us this?"

Dustin shook his head. "No. Usually people use chalk on floorboards, that kind of stuff. They don't actually weave it into the carpet. Not sure how to handle that. The signal is super strong, but we thought it was this building. If somebody came up with this carpet design by accident, we're gonna have problems."

"Let me see if I can track them down," Emily said. "Somebody from the design firm was supposed to be here."

"Are they clued in?" Meaghan asked.

"Not that I'm aware of, but I'll see what I can find out." Emily pulled her phone from her pocket and headed for the stairs. "Excuse me a moment."

The kid, Dustin, breathed a sigh of relief. "I thought she'd never leave. I have something I need to show you." He held up his index finger. "Gimme a sec. Wait here."

He disappeared down the hallway. Meaghan heard a whispered conversation—an intense debate, it sounded like—then Dustin reappeared. "We heard about what happened last night in the woods. I told Sam this wasn't the time, but he really wants to meet you. Says he wants to help."

"Who's Sam? And how did you hear about last night?"

Dustin looked at the pulsating floor. "Uh, Melanie. The Troon."

Meaghan nodded. "I know Melanie." She wasn't going to add that Melanie was at her house. Dustin seemed harmless, but until she had more information, she was going to let him do the talking. "So, who's Sam?"

"He's not like the others," Dustin said. "Don't hurt him."

"Why would I hurt him?"

"Dustin, it is all right," a voice behind Dustin said, in a stilted accent that sounded familiar. "I believe she will not harm me if I do not give her cause."

"Huh, not sure I believe that, bro." Dustin's face grew pink.

"What kind of a psycho do you think I am?" Meaghan asked. "I don't randomly attack people. I promise I won't hurt him. Who the hell is Sam?"

A small figure, clad in gray, stepped from behind Dustin. "I am Sam."

One of the fair folk stood before her. She took a step back and scanned the room for something made of steel, anything. The city seemed to have hired the tidiest contractors they could find.

It's a construction site. There has to be something.

"Dustin," she said, trying to keep her voice calm, "you need to get back through your gateway and close it as fast as you can. I don't know what Sam looks like to you, but he's—"

"An elf," Dustin finished. "Yeah, I know. But he's a good guy. He's not like the others."

"He tell you that?" Meaghan backed toward the front entrance. If she could get down the stairs, she could grab a stapler, or . . .

"Please," the elf said. "Dustin, tell her what you see."

"Uh, he's about four feet tall and kinda skinny, and—no offense, dude—kinda ugly. He's not doing the *Lord of the Rings* thing on me. I can see him for what he is. Sammy, I knew she was gonna have trouble with this."

The elf held out his hands and walked slowly toward her. "Please. I am not like them. I am . . . I do not feed on humans. I need your help."

Meaghan was almost to the front door of the suite when she saw the toolbox behind the open door. She grabbed a claw hammer in one hand and a large screwdriver in the other and waved them at the elf. "Not one step closer. Dustin, get the hell out of here."

Dustin shook his shaggy head, his face twisted in misery. "I told you she wasn't ready. Please don't hurt him. He's my friend. Listen to him."

The elf kneeled in front of Meaghan and pulled something out of his shirt.

Then Natalie walked in, Emily on her heels.

Chapter Fifteen

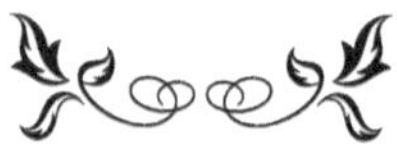

NATALIE TOOK ONE look at the scene in front her and turned on Emily. "That's your game? You bitch." She threw a hex at Emily, who countered.

Meaghan heard Dustin screech, "Oh, shit," as he dove to the floor.

She stared down at the elf and saw what he held in his hand. An iron nail twisted into a circle hung from a fine chain around his neck. The elf was wearing iron.

He was wearing iron. Voluntarily.

A spell crackled past her. Meaghan threw herself on top of the elf, protecting him from the spells Natalie was shooting at him. Meaghan looked up and saw Emily crouched over Dustin as Natalie threw spells at her. Colored sparks cascaded in the air near Emily but didn't touch her. Meaghan had seen enough witchcraft up close to know that Emily had conjured a barrier and Natalie's spells were breaking against it. It also meant that Emily couldn't shoot back.

"They aren't fighting back!" Meaghan shouted. "Goddammit, Natalie, stop!"

Natalie threw another spell at the elf.

Meaghan, still shielding him, felt a tiny static electric shock. *That one must have been a doozy.* "Knock it off! One more spell and I'm kicking your ass into the middle of next month. Dustin, Emily—you okay?"

"Fine," Emily said from her corner.

"No," Dustin wailed from the floor. "You scared the shit outta me. Is Sam okay?"

"Mmph," Sam said.

Meaghan realized she was crushing him into the magical carpet and rolled off him. "You okay?"

He took a shuddering breath. "Yes." He gazed up at Meaghan, awe in his eyes. "You protected me. My people are your enemy, but you protected me. You are as fearless as they say."

Meaghan shrugged. "Don't know about that. But I saw the iron. You wear it by choice?" She struggled to her feet.

He nodded. "As proof that I have forsaken the old ways. Magic is destroying my people. It is a drug for them and it grows scarce. This is the way forward."

Natalie stared at the elf. "You protected that?" She glared at Meaghan. "Are you nuts?"

Meaghan glared back. "No. Are you? Shoot first, ask questions later? If it hadn't been for me and Emily, you could have killed these two. The elf, okay, you got reasons there, but Dustin?"

"Who's Dustin?"

"I'm Dustin," he said as he pulled himself to his feet. He mustered as much dignity as he could in his wrinkled brown robe. "Brother Dustin, Keeper of the Word."

"Oh," Natalie said, a sheepish look on her face. "My bad." She pointed at the elf. "But where did that come from?"

"That is Sam," Meaghan said. "And he appears to be quite a bit different from the evil little shit in my basement."

Sam nodded. "That is why I am here. You have captured one of the—" he screeched something that sounded like a tomcat playing an out-of-tune violin. He glanced around at the confused looks. "I am sorry. Dustin keeps reminding me how discordant our language is to the human ear. The elf you have captured is a member of the secret . . . what is the word . . . police? The ones who are charged with keeping the old order."

Meaghan nodded. "He appears to be somewhat immune to iron. Even wearing a chain, he confused us—well not me, I'm impervious. But the iron didn't interfere with his magic."

Sam sucked in a breath, and looked at Meaghan with what appeared to be fear in his eyes. "I have heard tales of such ones. They do not fear iron but still have magic."

"Tales? Isn't that what you are?"

Sam shook his small head. "I am one of the . . . we have a word, but it will hurt your ears . . . it is an ugly word, even for our language. The *diseased* is the closest human word. We also do not fear the iron, but we have no magic."

Meaghan frowned. "What does that mean? You can't use magic?"

"We cannot use magic and magic does not affect us." His look grew dark. "They use other ways to control us."

Meaghan shook her head. "I have a better word than diseased. Impervious."

The elf's eyes shone. "That is an honorable name." He bowed. "Thank you."

Meaghan smiled at him for a moment. This Sam was either the most gifted bullshit artist she'd ever encountered, or he was truly something different. "But the one we captured. He does have magic—a lot of it apparently—and he's resistant to iron, but we're not sure how much."

Sam shook his small head. "This is very bad. We have heard they wanted to breed ones who could withstand the iron and have magic, too. But until now, they were rumors only." He shut his eyes for a long moment, still shaking his head. "The one you captured let himself be taken. You must not let him go or he will tell them all he has learned about you."

"Yeah, we already figured that out." Meaghan decided not to tell him any more until she'd spoken to Melanie, who, it seemed, had her own secrets. She'd mentioned a mysterious "we" a few times, but Meaghan hadn't attached any significance to it until now. And Melanie appeared to know all about whatever secret the Donners were keeping about Terry's past.

She felt the usual anger rise and took a deep breath. *Russ is right. People keep secrets for a lot of reasons. This isn't only about me.* She took another deep breath and felt the anger dissipate. One crisis at a time.

She glanced over at Emily. "You learn anything about the carpet?"

Emily gave her a grim smile. "Interestingly enough, our contact for Bottaio Design has disconnected his phone and their website has been taken down. I can't believe this"—she pointed at the floor—"was a coincidence. They knew exactly what they were doing when they installed it. They knew it contained magic."

"Uh," Dustin said. "These are the specific sigils to call us. Whoever did this wanted us to reach out to you."

"Knowing it would spur me to request my father's lost files and learn more about the fair folk." Meaghan glanced at the elf. "Sam, do you know anything about this? Did you set this up?"

Sam, looking bewildered, shook his head. "This is my first time in the human world. I have been hiding in the archive since I escaped from the ... there is not an exact word. The place where they force us to work until we die."

Meaghan felt sick, as her suspicion of Sam evaporated. Slave labor camps for non-magical elves seemed characteristic of what she knew about the fair folk. "Humans do have words for such places, too many, much to our shame." She touched Sam's skinny shoulder. "I'll help you. What do you need from me?"

"Meaghan, you can't trust—"

"Natalie, shut up. You sound like Steph. No one wanted me to trust Owen either and look how that worked out. If he's a traitor, we'll know soon enough." She squatted to bring herself eye level with Sam. "What do you need from me?"

"I need your help to find the smith," Sam said.

Meaghan smiled. *Terry, you and I need to have that talk.* "Big guy? Red hair? Bane of the fair folk?"

Sam's eyes widened. "You know of the smith? Do you know how to find him?"

Meaghan nodded. "Yeah, I know of him and I'm pretty sure I know where he is. But first, you're coming to my house. Dustin, you're welcome, too, as long as you don't tell my brother you had Doritos for breakfast."

"Dustin, it is a quest," Sam said, his small face beaming with gratitude. "You must accompany me."

"Quest?" Meaghan rose to her feet with a grimace. She was still having problems with the knee she'd busted up in Fahraya.

"Video game," Dustin said. "We've been playing a lot. There's not a lot to do over there." He nodded. "Yeah, Sam. I'll join your quest. I promised Melanie I'd look out for you."

"But—"

"Natalie, this is going to happen."

"I know, geez. What do you want me to do about the carpet?"

Meaghan glanced at her. Natalie wore the grimace Meaghan had learned to associate with annoyance rather than real anger. The storm had passed for the moment. "Good question. Dustin, will this stuff on the carpet open up any other gateways?"

He squinted at it. "Nah, it's specific to us, but this rug is like leaning on the doorbell. It's really annoying on our end."

Meaghan nodded. "Then we need to get rid of it. How soon can we get it pulled out?"

"I'll make some calls," Natalie said. "What are we replacing it with?"

"Something simple. No sigils. Or giant roses. God only knows what they summon."

"The city has a vendor contract with a carpet store in Williamsport," Emily said. "And I have the specs. I can order you something." She glanced at Natalie. "If that's okay. I can take care of it if you need to deal with other stuff."

Natalie glared at her.

Meaghan glared at Natalie. "Enough of this. I have zero patience with witchy shit right now. Emily, do what you have to do. We got money in the budget for more carpeting?"

"Plenty. What do you think of a warm gray? It's nice, has a white and sage fleck. It's what we used everywhere else."

"Perfect," Meaghan said. "As long as it's not mystical, I don't care."

Emily nodded.

"Are we sure the overall office design is okay?" Meaghan called after her.

"Natalie handled all that," Emily said. "I'm sure it's fine."

Natalie stuck out her tongue at the back of Emily's head as Emily headed out the door.

Meaghan rolled her eyes. "That was a compliment, in case you didn't notice."

Natalie shook her head. "I'd tell you she's up to something, but you'd only get mad."

"If you're right, you can have 'I told you so' tattooed on my forehead. Is there anything you can do to help Dustin's folks with the noisy gateway problem?"

"Yeah, yeah. I'm on it." Natalie trudged past her into the hallway and disappeared into the mist.

Sam watched her go, his eyes wide. "The Red Witch," he breathed. "I have been here not a day and I have already met Meaghan of Keele and the Red Witch."

Meaghan looked at Dustin. "Do they really call us that over there?"

"Officially, yeah. You know magic types. They're big on the fancy names."

Meaghan nodded. "Getting Sam into my house is going to take a little finesse. I have a whole house full of people who hate the fair folk, most particularly the smith's wife."

Dustin's eyes widened. "She's there? Oh, shit. She's scary."

"That's why we need the finesse. Do you have regular clothes? You can't walk to my car in that get-up. And we need a way to camouflage Sam."

Dustin nodded and pulled the robe over his head. Underneath he wore jeans and a Spiderman T-shirt. He ducked into an office and came back with a backpack and a down jacket.

"Sam handles the cold better than humans," Dustin said as he pulled a tattered red hoodie out of the backpack and handed it to Sam. "Put this on and pull the hood up, and I'll carry you. Pull the sleeves down over your hands. Let me do the talking."

Dustin turned back to Meaghan. "He's about the size of a seven-year-old. If anybody asks, he's my little brother who's home sick from school, and you're giving us a lift to the doctor."

Meaghan nodded. "You're good at this."

Dustin shrugged. "I'm the IT guy for an order of mystical record-keeping monks who live in an alternate dimension. I'm always making shit up."

Meaghan laughed, remembering a similar conversation with Sid in Fahraya. "You could be a lawyer."

Chapter Sixteen

THEY GOT TO the car without incident and headed home. Sam was so small Meaghan made him sit in the back seat. She didn't want to kill him with an airbag if she slipped on the ice again.

At the first light, she took a quick look at Dustin. He looked so normal. Like a college kid. "Dustin, how did you end up as a brother in the archive?"

The Brothers of the Word were a mostly human collection of archivists—all male with the exception of a handful of Troon translators—responsible for maintaining "the sum of all written knowledge." It hadn't started out as a mostly human institution, but humans were significantly noisier than all the other species combined, so maintaining what was predominantly humanity's prodigious output of writing had fallen to its own magical practitioners.

No had been able to explain to Meaghan why these duties had been relegated only to men. Tradition, everyone told her.

"I'm not a full-fledged brother." His cheeks flushed pink. "I haven't, you know, sworn the oaths."

"Oaths?"

"Constancy, loyalty . . . uh, celibacy." The crimson flush spread to his ears. "That last one is kind of a deal breaker."

A theoretical chance of getting laid being better than no chance at all.

Meaghan mentally slapped her wrist. *Don't be mean,* she told herself.

"So, you're their computer guy?"

"I manage the IT department," he said, in a lofty tone. "I have ten other guys working for me. The brothers were doing everything by hand and were having a hard enough time with the printing press, and then the whole digital thing happened and they couldn't keep up."

"I bet," Meaghan said. "I can't even keep up with my email."

Dustin nodded. "And most of it's garbage. They'd been saving anything in writing, but you know, one day of Twitter is like the whole Middle Ages so, yeah, big mess. We set up filters for the electronic stuff to save what's worth saving and now we're digitizing everything going forward, and beginning to digitize the backlog. They have no backup system. Can you imagine?"

"No," Meaghan said. Her knowledge of computers extended to how to turn them on and off, and how to swear at them. "Like I said, I can't even manage my email anymore."

"And no way to index anything. They literally have no idea what they have."

That caught Meaghan's attention. "So then how did they scrub all the references to the fair folk? They had to do that too, right?"

"Well," Dustin said, "you didn't hear this from me, but . . ." His voice dropped to nearly a whisper. "Yeah, they were supposed to, but they didn't. They did a magical search—at least they can do that much—and deleted what it pulled up."

"But the search didn't catch everything?"

"Not even close. And I can't prove it, but I think earlier brothers tagged stuff about the elves specifically so it would be overlooked if somebody wanted to pull everything up with magic."

"Is that what happened with my dad's files?" She took a quick glance at Dustin to see his reaction.

He grinned back at her. "Nope. Somebody made copies of those."

"With magic?"

"With a copy machine. They were still in the Kinko's bag when I found them. In a box under my desk when I took over the department. Hiding in plain sight."

"You have them?" Meaghan had to force herself to keep her eyes on the road.

"Not anymore," Dustin said. "But I know where they are, only the magic protecting them won't let me tell you. I have to show you and I can only do that if they give me permission."

"Not a rule breaker, huh?" Meaghan tried to hide the disappointment in her voice.

"I'm a hacker," Dustin said, annoyance in his voice. "Rule breaking's my thing. Which is why they made it all magical, so I can't cheat it. I can do basic charms and shields and stuff, but I never trained as a wizard and hacking magic is scary dangerous."

Meaghan sighed. "Fine. Official channels it is."

Dustin turned in his seat. "Sammy, how you doing back there?"

"I am well, my friend. I am well."

Meaghan looked in the rearview mirror. Sam smiled serenely in the back seat.

"Your turn, Sam," Meaghan said. "What's the deal with the smith? How do you know him?"

"He is a legend among those like me. We wear the twisted nail in his honor. He was the one who discovered the protection of the iron. You do not know his story?"

Meaghan shook her head. "No. He hasn't been exactly forthcoming with the details. He's been in hiding, I think. From your people."

"The fair folk are not my people," Sam said, staring out the window. "They have been telling me this my whole life. The impervious are my people."

"Welcome to the family," Meaghan said. "All one of me."

"There are more," Sam said. "We will find them."

Meaghan pulled the car over on Sycamore, at the entrance to the alley running behind her house. "We're almost there, but I need to make a call."

"Finesse time?" Dustin asked.

Meaghan nodded.

Russ picked up in one ring. "Yes, sister dear?"

"Where are you?"

"In the kitchen, where else? The witches are hungry."

"They've still got the elf locked down?"

"Oh, yeah. The little jerk's so loaded down with iron and steel he clanks when he breathes."

"Good. Where's Steph?"

"Right here. She's writing down Viking bread recipes."

"What about Melanie?"

"She's here, too."

"Let me talk to her." Meaghan knew Steph was her biggest hurdle. If she could get Sam past Steph, the rest would be easy. But she couldn't do it without Melanie's help.

"Yes, Meg?"

"I have a Brother Dustin here who claims he knows you."

"Ah." Melanie paused for a long moment. "I assume you've also met his compatriot?"

"Sam?"

"Yes."

Meaghan glanced at Sam in the rearview mirror. He gazed out the window, still smiling. She looked over at Dustin, who looked worried.

"Sam's looking for the smith," Meaghan said. "He and Dustin

were summoned by a swath of sigil-covered office carpet recommended by an Italian design firm . . . a firm that appears to have blown town in a hurry and not left any forwarding information."

She heard Melanie suck in a breath.

"I think the time for keeping secrets is over," Meaghan said. She tried to keep her voice level, but she could feel her temper pulling at the leash. "I need to know what this is all about. But first, you need to help me get Sam into the house without Steph killing him on sight."

"When will you get here? This will take some delicate—"

Her anger broke free. "Melanie, I'm done walking on eggshells with the Donners. I'm right around the corner on Sycamore sitting in the car, and I'm freezing my ass off, and I want to go home. I don't care what you have to do. I'm on my way. If Steph wants to hurt him, she's gotta come through me." She tossed the phone into her bag.

Dustin stared at her. "That's finesse?"

Meaghan shrugged. "As much finesse as I have at the moment. Nobody tells me anything, but I'm the one they're all looking at when Shit Creek starts to rise." She looked in the rearview at Sam. "Stay behind me, okay? I won't let her hurt you."

Sam smiled at her. "I know this. Thank you."

Big words, Meg. Big words.

Meaghan didn't want to pick a fight with Steph. She said she'd gotten practically no magic from the incident that created Fahraya, but there was something about Steph that frightened the hell out of the fair folk and Dustin.

She squeezed the car into the space next to Russ's food truck. He'd wanted to get it on the road for a fall season, but the stinky squid invasion had derailed his plan. He'd been working on outfitting it as time and weather permitted, and was getting ready for a grand opening tour in the spring. It was too big to fit in the garage, so it resided in the alley.

For now. The space technically belonged to Edna, their next-door neighbor, who was wintering in Florida. Edna would be back in April and the food truck would need to find a new home.

Steph was already out the back door and halfway across the yard, Melanie on her heels, when Meaghan ushered Sam out of the car.

Meaghan shoved Sam behind her and glared at Steph. "Stop. This is my house, and I'm bringing any one I want into it."

Dustin stepped next to Meaghan, visibly shaking with fear, but wearing a determined expression.

"No, you must let me do this." Sam shoved his small body between Meaghan and Dustin and took a few steps toward Steph, then knelt on one knee, his head bowed.

Steph stopped short, staring at him. "Meg," she said, through gritted teeth. "Get away from it."

Meaghan stepped next to Sam. "Not until you hear us out. He's not the same as the one downstairs. Not even close." She leaned and placed a hand on his small shoulder. "Show her what you showed me."

Sam pulled the twisted nail pendant from his gray shirt and held it up for Steph to see.

She stared at Sam, eyes narrowed, for a long moment. "That doesn't prove anything. The one downstairs was wearing iron, too, and it still screwed with us."

"Sam's wearing it voluntarily," Meaghan said. "It's in honor of the smith, he says, who his particular persecuted subset of the fair folk view as a legend to be honored. I'm assuming he means Terry."

"Lift your head," Steph said to Sam. "I want to see your face."

Sam lifted his head and stared back at her.

Steph circled him slowly, surveying him. She stared down at the top of his head and said, "Huh. You are different. Your skin's better and you don't have the bulge on the top of your head."

"They have always told me my head is smaller because I am stupid and not a—" He screeched something in the rusty hinge voice. "I am sorry. There is no exact word in your language. 'Person' is the only word and that . . . What they mean is that I am not one of them, that I am a . . ." He shook his head. "It does not translate. I am worse than not one of them. My existence disgusts and mocks them, and I am fit only to do their will."

Meaghan noticed Steph relax slightly. It wasn't much, but it was start. "He doesn't have magical ability," Meaghan said. "He escaped from a slave labor camp." She glanced at Melanie. "You knew these places existed? When the truce was made?"

Melanie nodded, but looked away, unable to meet Meaghan's eye.

"Which means Matthew knew, too." Meaghan shook her head, trying to control her anger. "Now I'm the one who's disgusted. Some truce." Meaghan squeezed between Steph and Sam. "I'd rather you were on my side, but if you can't do that, go home, because the only way you're getting to him is through me."

Steph glared at Meaghan, who glared right back, until Steph wilted. "I'm still on your side, Meg. That doesn't mean I trust that thing behind you, but I'll leave it alone for now."

"You'll leave *him* alone," Meaghan said. "And he's got a name. Sam."

"Dude," she heard Dustin say to Sam behind her. "Get up. Your pants are all wet. You're shivering."

"We're going inside," Meagan said. "Where's Terry?"

"Across the street with John," Steph said, still scowling.

"Get them back over here."

Steph nodded, and, without a backward glance, stomped around the side of the house toward the street.

Meaghan put her hand on Sam's small shoulder. Dustin had been right. She could feel Sam's small body shake, but whether it was from cold or fear, she didn't know. "Dustin, help him inside. Let's get you boys warmed up and get you something to eat."

And look at me. I've adopted another stray. Meaghan shook her head as she followed everyone into the warm kitchen. *Who am I, Mother Teresa?*

Chapter Seventeen

RUSS WASN'T FAZED in the least by Sam. If Meaghan and Melanie said Sam was okay, that was good enough for Russ.

"Thank you," Meaghan breathed into his ear, as he stood at the stove. She kissed him on the cheek. "If I'm wrong and he tries anything—"

"I'm surrounded by steel pans and steel knives. Not particularly worried. Go. Deal with shit. I'll take care of these two."

Sam approached Russ, bowed, and said, "Mister Russ, how may I assist you?"

Russ bowed back. "Call me Russ. No need for mister. Sam, you are a guest in my home, and it would be my honor if you would take a seat at the table and let me fix you some lunch."

Sam looked confused. "I am . . . I eat last, yes?"

Russ shook his head. "Nope. Not in my kitchen. If anybody's eating last, it's me." Seeing Sam's befuddlement, he added, "How about you help me clean up when we're done?"

Sam bowed again. "Thank you. I will do that."

Russ gave Meaghan a wide-eyed, open-mouthed, what-the-hell look. "That schmuck downstairs," he whispered, "I gave him a plate of food and he threw it at me. Told me it was fit only for human pigs."

"This one is different."

"No kidding." In a regular voice, Russ asked, "Guys, you want grilled cheese? Got some tomato soup, too. But first, Sam, you need some dry clothes. Let me grab you something to wear and a towel and you can change in the bathroom under the stairs."

Sam looked a question at Dustin, who nodded and said, "Sounds great. Thanks."

"Don't ask him for Doritos," Meaghan said. "Them's fighting words around here."

Russ made a face as he moved toward the hallway. "Don't you have any strategizing you need to be doing?"

"Yes. And don't put any fancy mustard on my grilled cheese," Meaghan called after him as he ran up the stairs. "That's just wrong." She glanced at Melanie. "We should probably go head off Terry and Steph before things escalate."

Melanie nodded. She still hadn't been able to meet Meaghan's eye. When they were on the front porch, Melanie said, "Meaghan, you have to understand. It wasn't a victory, it was a draw. We had to make sacrifices."

Meaghan turned on her, fury in her eyes. "No, you didn't. Sam did, and all those of his kind before him who were lost to their death camps. You should have kept fighting."

For the first time since Meaghan had met her, Melanie lost her temper. "Don't you tell me, girl, what I should have done," she hissed, her orange eyes glowing. "You weren't there. You were never there."

"How could I be there?" Meaghan said, her voice rising. "Nobody told me about any of this. I had to find out by accident, after you all blew up my life with magic. And you still don't tell me anything. Why am I only finding all this out now? If you needed my help, why didn't you ask?"

"Why didn't we ask?" Melanie's voice rose. "What would you have done if your father had tried to explain all this to you? You'd have thought him insane. Like your mother did. Like Matthew himself did for the first few years. You wouldn't even take his calls back then. He could have told you the sky was blue, and you'd have called him a liar."

She was right, Melanie was right, but Meaghan couldn't bring herself to admit it. "Too bad," Meaghan said, a snarl in her voice, "this impervious shit didn't pass to Russ, since you all seem to trust him so much more than me." *Stop now*, the rational voice said. *You like Melanie, she's your friend and ally. Shut up. Now.*

And for once Meaghan did.

Russ had stored the wicker furniture in the garage for the winter and there was no place else to sit, so Meaghan sat on the porch steps and patted the space next to her. "You're right. I'm sorry."

Melanie sat down, stiffly, and stared at her feet. They sat silent for a time, until Melanie said, "So am I." She sighed and finally met Meaghan's gaze. "Don't think the decision to abandon the non-magical fair folk was made lightly. It was one of the most shameful decisions of my life, and I tell myself it was unavoidable, but in my darker moments, I know better."

"I'm thinking the truce is over," Meaghan said. "We can't—I can't—let this go on. Besides, now they're bringing the fight to us."

"That's not how they see it."

Meaghan yelped and jumped off the step. Owen was standing right behind where she'd been sitting. "Shit, Owen. Don't do that."

"Do what?"

"Magically appear like that. The hiding-in-plain-sight shit." Meaghan tried to catch her breath, but the burst of adrenaline made her heart thump like a jackhammer.

"That doesn't work on you," he said. "This is me being sneaky in a totally normal way." He plopped down on the step and patted the space Meaghan had vacated. "I won't bite. Mel, I've told you, and I've been telling anyone who'll listen. We need to stop bullshitting around and accept that the truce is over. And we need to tell *her*"—he jerked his thumb toward Meaghan—"everything. Including about me and Luka and Terry and Steph. All of it."

Meaghan sat back down, Owen on one side, Melanie on the other. "Thank you," she said. "Finally somebody gets it."

"Provided," Owen added, "you tell us about the bug you've had up your ass since Labor Day. Don't complain about us keeping secrets when you're doing the same thing."

Meaghan's heart started pounding again.

The bitch needs to learn her place.

"I have to tell John first," she said, trying to keep her voice level. "I owe him that."

A red hatchback pulled into Holly Lane and slowed to a stop in front of the house.

Kady Cressley climbed out of the car. She still had three weeks until her due date, but the baby she was carrying overwhelmed her small frame. "Hey, boss," she called. "You back?"

Meaghan pushed herself to her feet and headed for the curb. "I'm back. I thought you'd be downstairs."

"Why? What's downstairs?"

"The elf?"

Kady's eyes widened. "The what? I was getting an ultrasound."

"Natalie didn't call you?"

Kady shook her head. "She texted me to say you were home, and I texted her back to remind her about the ultrasound. Did you go look at the carpet samples yet?"

"Hah," Meaghan said. "You've missed some stuff. Give me your arm and I'll help you up the driveway."

Kady snorted. "I'm pregnant, not disabled. I got it. Is that Melanie? And Owen? What are they doing here?"

They made their way slowly to the house "We'll be focusing on my other job today, I think," Meaghan said. "Where's Jamie?"

"Court, down in Williamsport, with Buzz. He's still helping out, until we get back into city hall."

Meaghan nodded. She still hadn't met Buzz Hallam, the city's outside counsel, in person, even after so many months in Eldrich. He had handled all the city's litigation while Jamie was out of commission, and Meaghan had still only talked to him on the phone. He was a friend of her father's, clued in, and competent, but beyond that, she didn't know anything about him. "Buzz is human, right?"

Kady shrugged. "I guess. As far as I know."

"But he knows all about Eldrich."

"Plenty of people know about Eldrich."

They got to the porch without incident until Kady slipped on a tiny patch of ice. Meaghan grabbed her arm and kept her on her feet.

Melanie's not the only one who regrets leaving them behind. The voice rang through Meaghan's mind, clear as a recording. It sounded like her father.

"Whoa. I guess I do need help," Kady said, with a laugh.

Meaghan shook her head to clear it.

"Meg?" Owen was watching her closely. "You okay?'

The voice was gone. "I thought . . ." *If I tell them I'm hearing voices, they'll start nagging me about therapy again.* "My ear was ringing. It's better now."

Kady looked at the three of them. "So, what did I miss?"

Melanie, Owen, and Meaghan exchanged looks. Owen gestured to Meaghan. "Why don't you take this?"

Meaghan sighed. "Okay. Let's see. I got attacked by the fair folk in the woods last night and got rescued by Terry Donner.

The Italian design firm the mayor stuck us with sold us sigil-covered office carpet that opened a gateway to that mystical archive place, and then they skedaddled. And there are two elves in the house. One's chained up in the basement being guarded by witches. The other is eating grilled cheese and tomato soup in the kitchen with Russ and the guy who does the IT work for the monks who run the mystical archive. Oh, and Terry and Steph are immortal. Sort of."

"Uh-huh," Kady said, gazing up at the sky as a few snowflakes floated in the air. "And here I was all excited because I saw the baby's little dingle in the ultrasound."

CHAPTER EIGHTEEN

OWEN AND MELANIE went across the street to find out what was keeping Terry and Steph, while everyone else went inside.

Meaghan ate lunch while Kady put Dustin and Sam to work. "The city's idiot IT guy is not clued in," Kady told Dustin. "He can't figure out why the system keeps crashing."

Dustin nodded. "Magic plays hell with electronics. I have some shielding charms that should help."

"You're hired." Kady smiled at Sam, who was wearing Meaghan's faded Arizona State T-shirt. It came to his knees. His legs were covered in a pair of Russ's gym socks. "So are you, cutie. You can be my intern."

Sam nodded, his face serious. "I will do my best to serve you."

"First task," Kady said. "Ask Russ to make me a sandwich. I'm starving."

Owen called a few minutes later. They had decided to avoid the Keeles' house until Luka arrived and they figured out their next steps. John would be staying with them for now.

Meaghan, relieved she wouldn't have to deal with John yet, and assured by Kady that there was nothing pressing on her work calendar, went upstairs to lie down for a little while.

Hearing Matthew's voice had rattled her. He hadn't reached out to her since Fahraya. Why was she hearing his voice now? She'd had the occasional psychic flashback since Jhoro had dosed her with Fahrayan peyote in June. Maybe this was another one?

Nah, she told herself. *That's too easy.* She groaned and kicked off her shoes, then plopped on the bed. *Early onset Alzheimer's? Or maybe I'm just nuts.*

Meaghan had a list of therapists to call, but she'd rather go for another moonlight drive in the woods. Therapy seemed so ... weak, wussy, pathetic—*necessary,* her sensible voice told her. "Shut up, you," she murmured. "I'm taking a nap."

She fell asleep right way and had a stupid dream about Russ throwing blocks of Velveeta cheese at her and then she woke up.

The light in the room had changed. She glanced at the clock. It looked like dusk, but it was only three. She'd been asleep for over two hours. She rolled off the bed and looked out the window.

Snow fell thick and fast and—if the last three months had been any guide—would likely continue through the night. Already several inches of new snow had accumulated. With a shiver, Meaghan grabbed another sweater off the laundry pile and headed downstairs.

She found Sam alone in the dining room office. He'd changed back into his gray leggings and tunic, but he'd kept Meaghan's T-shirt on over top. He sat at Kady's computer, on a pile of phonebooks, staring at the monitor.

Meaghan glanced out the front window. Kady's car was gone. "Did Kady go home?"

"Yes," Sam said. "The snow is hard to drive in, she said, and she wanted to return to her home while she could."

Meaghan nodded. "What are you doing?"

"I am looking at your Internet. It is very . . ." He stared at the screen. "Humans are very fond of cats."

Meagan couldn't hold back her laughter. "Among other things. There're some corners of the Internet you definitely want to avoid."

"And they are fond of arguing," he said. "And they do not like trolls." He shuddered. "This is wise. I met a troll once. In the wild lands before I found the gateway to the archive. I barely escaped."

Meaghan booted up her laptop. *Time to do some research on the mysterious Luka Volkhov.* "Not the same kind of troll. Internet trolls are merely extremely unpleasant humans. But you met an actual troll? My father wrote in his journal that they're almost extinct."

Sam shook his head. "Not extinct. They were banished by the fair folk. To a demiworld. Like the dragons and other dangerous creatures."

"Demiworld?" *Not the damn dragons again . . .* Melanie had mentioned the dragons before Meaghan went to Fahraya. The thought of dragons had been more terrifying than the reality of giant snakes. *No dragons. I draw the line at dragons.*

"A bubble. Like the archive. But these are sealed with strong magics. They are prisons, but sometimes things break free. Or are freed by accident."

"Or on purpose." Meaghan nodded, thinking of the Order's efforts to free the squid on Labor Day. Before she could follow the thought further, Russ leaned in, a worried look on his face. "Have you heard from Natalie?"

"I just woke up." She looked over at Sam. "Have you heard anything?"

"The Red Witch has not returned," he said, his face solemn. "Miss Kady worries and asks that we call when we hear from her."

Natalie lived within walking distance of city hall. "Maybe she headed home."

Russ shook his head. "I called Patrice and asked her to check. And she's not answering her cell."

"Where's Dustin?"

"Asleep in Jhoro's room," Russ said. "I guess the computer charms knocked him out."

"Let me check something." Meaghan dialed Emily's office line and got no answer, so she called her cell.

"Emily Proctor."

"It's Meaghan. Where are you?"

"In the car. Tony sent everyone home."

"What for?"

"Haven't you seen the weather report? This is only the start. We're supposed to get slammed. They're predicting record snowfalls."

Meaghan frowned. "Since when? They usually warn you about this crap days in advance."

"This one slipped under the radar, I guess. We get these freak snowstorms once in a while that blow up out of nowhere. Something to do with Lake Erie and the mountains, I think."

"Not magically induced?" Meaghan asked.

"Not any magic I'm familiar with," Emily said.

"Have you heard anything from Natalie?"

Emily gave a small polite laugh. "What have I done now?"

"You're fine. But nobody seems to know where she is."

"I'm the last person she'd call," Emily said. "You know that."

Meaghan smiled. "I thought maybe she'd drop by to glower or taunt or something."

"My office is still well warded against her. At least until she warms up to me a little. Listen, the roads are terrible. Even with all-wheel drive, I'm all over the place. I need to hang up and focus on driving. I'll call you if I hear anything."

Meaghan said good-bye and hung up. She looked at Russ and shook her head. "Who's downstairs? With you know who?"

"Gretchen and Lynette," Russ said.

"They've been here all day. I thought they were calling in reinforcements."

Russ shrugged. "Some new witches are coming later, I think. Lynette is being really picky about who's down there, I guess. At least that's what Gretchen says."

"Picky is good," Meaghan said, "until we have a better idea of our guest's abilities."

"I know who you speak of. I tried to talk with him." Sam smiled. "He was most displeased to see me."

"I bet," Meaghan said. "He's not all that fond of me either."

"He wanted to know how I got here." Sam's look darkened. "Anything we tell him, he will report back to the others."

Meaghan smiled. "We're counting on it."

"You mean to deceive them?"

"We do. Are they smart enough to see through it?"

Sam shook his small head. "They believe humans to be fools. Let him believe that he has tricked the information from you, and they will be certain of its truth."

Meaghan nodded. "Good idea." She turned her attention back to Russ. "Natalie was working on neutralizing the carpet signal in the archives. Maybe she's still there. You talked to Dustin?"

"No," Russ said. "He's been asleep. I think I'll go wake him up."

Which meant Russ was worried—he wouldn't disturb a sleeping houseguest otherwise—which in turn worried Meaghan. Besides being her baby sister, Natalie was still her biggest gun. She was, by far, the most powerful witch in Eldrich, and the last time any of them had seen her, she'd been heading into the archive.

And somebody had gone to a lot of trouble to make sure the archive gateway was jammed wide open.

If it had merely been an error, then why was Bottaio Design in the wind now that the job was done? Even if they were merely con men who'd spotted a fat mark in Tony Diebler, what were the odds that they'd inadvertently sell him sigil-covered carpeting?

Astronomical, she thought.

But why? It had been merely a fluke of timing that sent Natalie to the archive. It could as easily have been Kady or somebody else who ended up over there.

Meaghan's gut told her that this was about her, not about any of the witches. Who stood to gain from Meaghan getting a direct line to information about the fair folk?

Not the fair folk, that was certain.

So, it must be an enemy of the fair folk. But if it had been somebody sympathetic to Meaghan, then why the fly-by-night approach?

Meaghan thought of the adage about the enemy of your enemy being your friend. It had never made sense to her. In her experience, the enemy of your enemy could easily be a different enemy. If somebody wanted to destroy you, becoming allies for the sake of expediency gave them better access.

That left the Order, but Meaghan had no idea what their beef might be with the fair folk. Or could it be an enemy they hadn't encountered yet? "Sam, do the fair folk have any enemies besides humans?"

"Oh, yes," Sam said. "They are friends with no one. They have enslaved and imprisoned many species."

"Well, that narrows it right down," Meaghan said, with a sigh.

Sam gave her a confused look.

She patted his small back. "Don't mind me. I'm trying to figure out who was responsible for the sigil carpet. You keep looking at cats."

CHAPTER NINETEEN

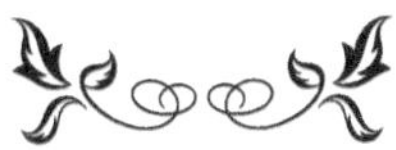

MEAGHAN HEARD THE snowplow before she saw it. She peered out the dining room window and expected to see one of the battered orange city plows. But this was a brand new pickup, extended cab, with the dealer sticker still in the side window, equipped with a snowplow blade and chains on the tires.

It stopped in front of Terry's house. Three figures bundled up in winter clothing stepped out. One of the men was huge, nearly as broad as he was tall. They all shook hands, and then the smallest of the three turned and trudged up Terry's driveway.

The other two headed toward Meaghan. After a moment, she realized the slender one was Jamie.

"Sam, we've got people coming. I'm going to pull this door shut for now. I'll come get you when I know it's safe."

He waved at her, totally engrossed in something online.

Meaghan closed the pocket door separating the dining room from the hall. When she heard them stomp onto the porch, she pulled open the front door.

The huge one saw her, grinned, and stuck out a giant hand. "At last we meet," he boomed. "Buzz Hallam."

She took his hand, tentatively. Buzz looked like he could crush her fingers into paste if he squeezed too hard. "It's freezing out here. Come on in."

He gave her hand a gentle shake, then followed her into the house. "The roads are already bad and this storm's only getting started. Caught a lift from Williamsport with your neighbor's cousin. His limo cancelled on him, so he bought a truck."

"With a credit card," Jamie added. He pulled his knit cap off, his dark blond hair crushed against his skull except for the hairs standing straight up from static electricity. "I thought the salesman was gonna have a stroke."

"Nice hat head," Meaghan said. "How'd you hook up with Luka?"

"Kady set it up somehow. She called Dad or Dad called her, they figured out I was already down there, and asked if I could give Luka a ride. But the roads were already so bad I knew my car wouldn't make it."

Meaghan nodded and turned back to Buzz. "While I'm thrilled to finally meet you in person, what are you doing all the way up here? I thought you lived in Williamsport."

He smiled down at her. He pulled off his own hat. Between his smiling, craggy face and shiny bald head, Buzz looked like an amiable boulder. "Got some family I need to check on up in Slepp's Holler. So I hitched a ride. Luka's gonna let me use his new truck to go out there. Nice fella for a gazillionaire."

She looked at Jamie. "What about you?"

He grinned at her. "I'm going to shamelessly mooch something to eat under the pretense of checking in at the office and then Buzz is going to drop me home."

Meaghan nodded. "You haven't heard from Natalie, by any chance?"

Jamie shook his head. "No. Why?"

"Just wondered," Meaghan said. Until she knew there was a reason to be worried, she wasn't going to tell him more. Despite his return to work and his outward cheerfulness, Meaghan could tell he was still struggling to recover from what had happened to him over the summer. The physical scars had faded, but there was a wariness about him that hadn't been there before, and dark circles remained around his eyes.

She stuffed their coats in the closet and followed them back to the kitchen.

"Buzz!" Russ shouted with joy. "If I'd known you were coming, I'd have bought more groceries."

Buzz pulled Russ into a hug and lifted him off his feet.

By Meaghan's calculation, Buzz had to be pushing seventy, but he moved like a much younger man.

"Russell, you snot-nosed brat, how the hell are you?" he bellowed, before setting Russ down. "I hear you got a new woman in your life. What's her name?"

Russ grinned. "Annie. I think this is the one, Buzz. This time I'm getting it right."

"Good for you, kid. I'm glad to hear it." Buzz had known Russ long enough to be familiar with his checkered marital past. "She live here in Eldrich?"

Russ nodded. "Yeah, she works in city hall, but she's down in Philly right now. Visiting family."

"Wait, is she the cute little blonde who works for the mayor? The medium?"

"That's her," Russ said with a beaming smile.

"Good job, kid. When she gets back, I want to meet her," Buzz said. "You got anything to feed a frozen old geezer?"

"Sit down." Russ punched Jamie lightly on the arm. "And don't you get any ideas. You're still the designated snot-nosed brat around here, no matter what Buzz says."

Meaghan pulled Russ aside as he headed to the fridge. "Don't tell him about Natalie until we know there's a problem," she whispered in his ear.

Russ glanced at Jamie. He was laughing at something Buzz was saying and not paying any attention to them. "Okay. I checked in with Dustin," Russ whispered. "He's trying to contact the archive and see if she's still there. The background magic is getting in the way. He'll keep trying."

Meaghan nodded. Time to break the news about the elves. She sat down at the table. "So, Buzz, what do you know about the fair folk?"

Buzz's amiable face turned dark. It was like watching time-elapsed video of a thunderhead forming. "They're nasty SOBs. I never bought that truce thing. I know Matthew had to make a hard call, but . . . well, he had to make a hard call. It's easy to second-guess somebody when you don't have to be in their shoes."

"You'd have made a different call," Meaghan said.

Buzz shrugged his huge shoulders. "Yeah, probably, but that doesn't mean it would have been the right one. I hated them so much back then, I couldn't have made any decision but to keep fighting."

"What if I told you the war seems to be heating back up?"

"I'm not surprised. Matthew knew it would only be a temporary lull. We needed a chance to catch our breath. And the world was different back then."

Russ brought Buzz a huge bowl of soup. "Working on the sandwiches."

"Where's my soup?" Jamie asked.

"On the stove. Get off your ass and dish it up. I'm not a waiter." Russ winked at Buzz. "Kids these days."

Jamie rolled his eyes and pushed away from the table. "Yeah, yeah, you lazy old fart."

Buzz tasted the steaming tomato soup. "Damn, Russ, this is

good. You must have learned this from your mom. Matthew could set the kitchen on fire making toast."

Russ snorted with laughter. "Maybe that's an impervious thing. Meg's not much better."

Meaghan ignored him. "How was the world different?"

"Well, it was the early eighties, during the Cold War. The fair folk were trying to work that to their advantage. It was only a matter of time until they manipulated things enough to make the nukes fly."

Meaghan felt her stomach clench. *Those were the stakes? I need to apologize to Melanie the first chance I get.*

"Shit," she murmured. "I had no idea it was that bad. But wouldn't destroying us have killed off their food supply?"

Buzz shook his head. "Nah. In some ways, it would have made it better. The radiation wouldn't have affected the elves, and in a couple generations, they'd have had what was left of humanity back to the Stone Age. Reduced supply, but a much more potent product from a better strain of livestock. What have the little shits been up to?"

"They attacked me in the forest last night," Meaghan said.

Buzz stopped eating, his spoon halfway to his mouth, a look of shock on his craggy face. "Attacked you?"

Meaghan nodded. "Terry—Luka's cousin, across the street—scared them off."

Jamie sat down next to her, his cheerful demeanor gone, a ferocious look in his eyes. "Are you okay?"

"Yeah, hon," she said, taking his hand. "I'm fine. Not a scratch. Don't worry."

He squeezed her hand tightly enough to hurt, and then gave a jerky nod of his head. He rose to his feet and stalked toward the hall bath. "Excuse me."

The door slammed behind him. A moment later, they heard a loud thump.

Russ nodded. "The wall punches seem to help."

Buzz sighed. "Poor kid. He's been through it this year, that's for sure. You ever figured out what those wizards were up to?"

Meaghan shook her head. "Gotta figure out the fair folk first. Here's the thing. There's two of them in the house right now."

Buzz rose to his feet, the chair crashing to the floor behind him. His huge hands clenched into fists. "Where?"

"One's in the basement, chained up, under guard. The other—"

"Is right here."

Sam stood in the kitchen doorway. He was trembling with fear, but wore a determined look on his face. He seemed even smaller and frailer standing in the same room with Buzz. "If you hurt her, troll," his voice shook, "you will have to answer to me."

Meaghan looked back at Buzz. "*Troll?*"

"Hey, Meg," Russ said, stepping in front of Sam. "I just remembered who I hadn't told you about yet." He looked around the room. "Oops. Who wants coffee?"

CHAPTER TWENTY

"HEY, KIDS," A gravelly female voice said. "What's going on up here?"

They all stared in the direction of the voice. Gretchen, small and plump and holding a fireplace poker, stared back. "I'd like some coffee. What are we doing?"

Nobody answered.

Gretchen, her white hair looking like the slovenly cousin of Lynette's tidy bouffant, stepped around Buzz and plopped down at the kitchen table. "You got a cookie or something to go with that coffee?"

Meaghan spoke first. "Who's down there?"

Gretchen yawned. "Relax. Lynette can handle it for a few minutes. Before I came upstairs, I had a nice graphic chat with our little friend about what I'll do with this fireplace poker if he misbehaves. Told him I was going to stick it in the fire, and get it nice and hot first. You got a fireplace, right?"

Nobody spoke. Nobody moved.

"Russ. Coffee," Gretchen said, waving the poker. "Chop, chop."

Russ nodded and moved toward the coffeemaker.

"Geez," Gretchen continued. "I feel like I'm in the middle of a bad western. Somebody draw or sit down already. Buzz, Sam's a sweetheart with an even bigger axe to grind with the fair fuckers than you. Sammy, Buzz and a wild troll have about as much in common as I have with a Playboy bunny. The basic parts are the same, but there's no way in hell you'd get us mixed up."

Russ handed her a steaming coffee mug and the vintage Godzilla cookie jar Natalie had bought him for Christmas. "You want cream?"

Gretchen shook her head. "Nah." She pulled a cookie out of the jar. "Homemade gingersnaps? Russ, you sexy beast." She took a bite of the cookie. "Oh, baby. That's so good. Everybody. Sit the fuck down. Now."

In a strangled voice, Buzz said, "Gretchen, you can't trust that thing." He pointed at Sam, his huge hand shaking, but whether from fear or rage, Meaghan couldn't tell.

Gretchen reached for another cookie. "Sam can't do magic any better than you can, Buzz, and if you pull off Sam's arms, Meaghan'll cancel your city contract. And you don't want that because then you'd have to get off your giant, lazy ass and look for clients. Play nice, boys, and everybody's happy. La la la, kumbaya, let me drink my coffee in peace."

"Would somebody mind explaining what the hell's going on?" Meaghan asked, her voice shriller than she would have liked. "I'm still trying to wrap my brain around the whole 'Buzz is a troll' thing."

The front door slammed. Russ looked into the hallway. "I think Jamie left."

Meaghan ran to the door and pulled it open. Jamie was headed down the driveway.

"Where are you going?"

Jamie turned fast and nearly slipped. Meaghan heard a muffled curse, then Jamie said, loudly, sounding out of breath, "Going to see my dad. I can't … I can't be around the fighting. It's too … it brings stuff up." He turned and stomped through the snow to the Donners' house.

Meaghan shivered and stepped back inside. The snow was falling so fast it hissed as it hit the ground. There were already a good five inches accumulated on the porch rail that had been bare and dry at lunchtime.

Her worry for Jamie was tempered by the knowledge he was reaching out to John for help. Nobody understood what Jamie was going through like John did, and John was desperate to make up for the years he'd stayed away, too ashamed to be part of his son's new life in Eldrich.

And besides, she had a war brewing in her kitchen. She didn't have time to worry about Jamie right now. She hurried back into the house.

Everyone was sitting at the table again, eating. Buzz was plowing through a couple of sandwiches, and Gretchen was happily crunching cookies. Sam had more soup.

Russ reached over Gretchen and stuck his hand in Godzilla's neck. "Don't bogart the cookies, you old witch."

"Hah!" Gretchen laughed through a mouthful of ginger-snaps. "You better back off, sonny boy, or I'll hex you."

Meaghan took a seat, then took a deep breath, and said, "So, Buzz. You're a troll?"

Buzz nodded.

"I thought trolls were made of stone," Meaghan said.

"There's a lot of different stories," he said, between bites of grilled cheese. "But we're flesh and blood, like you. Didn't you read any of your dad's journals?"

"He said you were almost extinct," Meaghan said. "That's it."

"Full-blooded, wild trolls, yeah. The rest of us are part human, but on the large side. Real trolls are a magical species that the fair folk used to use as enforcers. Huge, strong, not too bright—or at least the fair folk didn't think they were. They turn up in the folklore as giants and ogres, too. Got locked up in a demiworld a long time ago because they started defying their masters."

Meaghan reached for a cookie. "Defying them how?"

"The fair folk liked using trolls because we're so big," Buzz said. "But the real advantage is we've got thick skins where magic is concerned. It's hard to hex us. Takes some effort and planning."

"But they hate the impervious," Meaghan said. "Ask Sam."

Buzz looked across the table at Sam. "Sorry, kid. I shouldn't have jumped to conclusions. It's only—"

"My species deserves the mistrust all others feel for us," Sam said. "I have been treated as something separate, something that offends them, all my life. But, to you, I appear no different from them. I must earn your trust."

Buzz smiled at him. "And I guess I have to earn yours. If you don't hex me, I won't pull your arms off."

Sam grinned. "I will abide by this."

"It's a deal," Meaghan said. "But I still don't get why the fair folk would find a troll's immunity to magic to be a good thing."

"We're not immune, exactly. Trolls can definitely be hexed, but it takes slow deep magic that takes some time to brew up and needs to be maintained. The less human blood there is in the mix, the harder it is. You can throw quick defensive hexes at a troll—even a hybrid like me—all day long and you won't do more than piss us off. But if you set out ahead of time to control us, well . . . think about it."

"It would make trolls the perfect enforcers," Meaghan said. "You couldn't defend against a surprise attack because you wouldn't have time to do deep enough magic."

"Bingo." Buzz finished his second sandwich. "Even magic-wielding humans couldn't stand against full-bloods."

"Then the trolls started figuring out how to block the fair folk's magic," Gretchen said. "And suddenly the thick skin was a problem instead of an opportunity."

"Trolls aren't naturally stupid," Buzz said. "They were hexed. Drugged, is more accurate, because the fair folk spiked their food supply with potions to keep them under control. Their higher brain functions were dulled. The made-of-stone thing comes from a potion used to immobilize trolls in certain conditions, like daylight, as punishment for defiance or to prevent escape." He shook his head. "Bad shit. Finally, the fair folk locked them away. The full-bloods, at least."

"Would you want to see them freed?" Meaghan asked.

Buzz nodded. "Sure. If the war's starting up again, they'd be a big help."

"They can even pass as humans," Gretchen said. "Some of them at least. Huge humans. The NFL and NBA would go batshit with joy."

Buzz smiled. "The only problem is trolls, even the hybrids, live a lot longer than regular humans. I'm going to need to start pretending I'm old before too long and then fake my death. Pain in the ass. If we got the demiworld opened up, I could re-invent myself as a sports agent." He pushed back from the chair. "That hit the spot, Russ." He yawned. "I need to get out to Slepps's Holler tonight. Check on the Millers. You don't have a travel mug, do you? For coffee?"

Russ smiled. "For you, Buzz, I'll go the extra mile. I'll pour you a mug and fill you a thermos."

"The moonshiners?" Meaghan asked. "They're trolls?"

The Millers, Eldrich's notorious moonshiners, were also no-torious recluses. They had a handful of friends and neighbors who brought them supplies and distributed their product, but the general population never saw them. They were Eldrich's analogue to Bigfoot. Rumored to exist, but seldom seen and assumed by many to be nothing more than local myth.

Buzz nodded. "That's them. Even trolls can get hammered on that rocket fuel they brew."

"You sure you want to go out there in this shit?" Gretchen asked.

"No," Buzz said. "But I haven't been able to get in touch with them for a few days, and if we're in for the blow they say we are, I need to make sure they're okay. Even a troll can freeze to death if you drop enough snow on it. And they're only part troll."

"Where you sleeping, Buzzy?" Gretchen winked at him.

"Don't know, Gretch," Buzz said. "You offering?"

"Bring a few jars of 'shine back and you can sleep with me," Gretchen said. "I promise I won't get too rough with you."

Buzz grinned. "Gretch, you're the most wicked witch I know."

CHAPTER TWENTY-ONE

MEAGHAN TOOK BUZZ aside before he left, told him nobody had heard from Natalie since the morning, and asked him to run by her house to check if she was there.

"Jamie know?" Buzz asked.

Meaghan shook her head. "I don't want him to worry until we know there's something to worry about."

Meaghan waved through the living room window as they plowed their way out of Holly Lane.

Dustin walked into the living room wearing a worried look.

"I can't get through to the archive," he said. "My hex bag isn't working and neither are the sigils."

Meaghan's stomach clenched with worry, but she kept her voice steady. "Any idea why you can't get through?"

Dustin shrugged. "It's Eldrich. There's so much magic flying around this town. That could be a problem." He looked outside and shivered. "Or maybe it's this weather."

"But doesn't the magic help boost the signal? That's the way it's always been explained to me."

"Yeah. That's what I thought, too. Do you know any reason why anybody might cast a dampening spell? Something to deflect magic?"

"Well, yeah. That thing downstairs."

Dustin shook his head. "Already took it into account. It's not Gran and Lynette doing this. It's something else."

"Gran? Gretchen's your grandmother?"

"On my dad's side. I thought you knew that."

"I don't know anything it seems." *Although on the scale of magical secrets, that's a pretty minor one.* "You're from Eldrich?"

"No, I grew up in Ohio. Mom and Gran don't get along very well. Mom hates the whole magic thing. I spent some summers here, though, when I started showing signs I had ability."

"But the thought of hanging with all those crazy old ladies made you decide to be a hacker instead of a wizard?"

"Yeah." Dustin laughed. "Something like that. Gran and Melanie hooked me up with the archive job. Said I could use both my talents that way."

"Right now I need your magical expertise." Meaghan looked through the window at the house across the street. "Could you use a dampening spell to hide magical ability? To make yourself look like a normal human?"

Dustin plopped down in the armchair near the sofa. "Yeah, I guess you could. But usually magical types with any juice want to show off their power. You don't hide it. You flaunt it. Try to look bigger and badder than you are."

"But if you did want to hide, would you use a dampening spell?"

"Maybe, but there're easier ways to do it." Dustin chewed his lower lip, thinking. "Generally, dampening spells are to shut somebody down, like an enemy or somebody with more juice than they can handle. You know anybody like that?"

Meaghan nodded. "Yeah. I think I might." She pulled her phone out of her back pocket. She surveyed her caller list. Which one of the band of conspirators to call first?

Before she made up her mind, the phone rang in her hand.

"You know where Natalie is?" Owen barked before Meaghan had a chance to say hello.

"No," Meaghan said. "Last I saw her, she was heading into the archive through the gateway in my office. You know anything about somebody around here casting dampening spells? That might be interfering with efforts to contact the archive?"

"Uh . . ."

"Owen, I'm done bullshitting around on this."

Meaghan heard Owen say, "They won't let me," to somebody else, then in the background, a male voice said, "If she's as good as you say, she can handle it. Give me that." There were the muffled sounds of a phone being handed off.

"Hi, Meaghan," the mystery voice said.

"Who's this?"

"I'm Luka, Terry's cousin." His voice was a warm baritone, without a trace of an eastern European accent. "We need to talk."

"Yeah, no shit," Meaghan said.

"Under the circumstances, I think meeting over here would be best. Bring your monk with you and we'll see what we can do to restore communication with the archive."

"On my way." She nodded to Dustin. "Get your coat. We're going across the street."

Even the short trip across Holly Lane felt like an expedition. The air was bitterly cold, colder than it had been all winter, and the snow fell so fast it stung Meaghan's face. New snow already covered the plowed roadway, and the wind was beginning to kick up, drifting even more snow across the road.

She was halfway past the buried car in Terry's driveway before she realized it was her Audi, rescued from the forest. Not that it made any difference. Even with all-wheel drive, Meaghan didn't have the winter driving skills to tackle this kind of weather. This snowstorm felt lethal. It felt dangerous in a way the rest of winter hadn't. This weather would quickly kill anyone foolish enough to venture into it unprepared.

The front door opened, a rectangle of warm orange light shining in the swirling white snow.

Meaghan slipped and Dustin caught her arm before she fell. Together they trudged up the porch steps.

A middle-aged man with short reddish brown hair, wearing a muted blue turtleneck that looked like cashmere, stood in the doorway, smiling, then stepped aside to let them in.

The living room had been tidied up since the morning, with the drop cloths pulled off the furniture and the construction materials shoved into a corner. A fire glowed in the hearth. A big leather sofa and a couple of armchairs had been pulled up close, and Terry, Steph, Owen, and Melanie huddled near the fire.

"Where's John?" Meaghan asked.

"Upstairs taking a nap." Terry stood up and walked toward them. "Meaghan, my cousin Luka. Luka, Meaghan."

She surveyed Luka. He was a pleasant looking man, not handsome exactly, but he had a warm twinkle in his blue eyes. Nothing about him betrayed him as a man of wealth or power. He seemed normal, average even. Nothing about him set off her alarm bells.

Or at least nothing would have if she hadn't already known he was several thousand years old and possessed magical skills of some sort. With this man, first impressions were deceiving.

"You have questions," he said, smiling.

"I do," Meaghan said. "Are you going to answer them?"

He nodded. "I'll try."

"Do we have to freeze our asses off in Terry's little magic-proof shed in the backyard while you do it so the bad guys don't hear us?"

Luka laughed. "No, no. There's no point now. They know we're here."

"Can't they hear what we're saying?"

He shook his head. "Not if I don't want them to."

Meaghan raised an eyebrow. "One of your magical gifts?"

Luka nodded. "One of them."

"You a wizard?" Dustin asked.

Luka smiled. "Dustin, right?"

"Yeah," Meaghan said. "Sorry. I should have introduced you."

"No," Luka said. "I'm not a wizard. More a conjurer really. It's mostly parlor tricks with a few helpful additions. They know we're talking, but I can throw up enough magical noise to keep them from hearing what we're saying."

Meaghan saw her chance and went for it. "Dampening spells help with that?"

Melanie began coughing.

Luka smiled. "You're like your father. I told them we couldn't hide anything from you for long. Have a seat."

He offered Dustin and Meaghan the armchairs, while Terry pulled a couple of metal folding chairs out of the corner.

Luka frowned slightly at the dusty chair. Terry snorted and wiped the seat with the sleeve of his sweater. "There, your highness. All nice and shiny."

"All right," Luka said, ignoring Terry. "Ask your questions."

Meaghan nodded. "Who the hell are you?"

Luka laughed. "You don't waste any time, do you?"

"No," Meaghan said, "and questions don't count as answers."

"I've had a lot of names over the years. And I'm older than I look."

"Yeah, yeah. I got it. Immortal from a magical accident."

Luka nodded, but didn't add anything.

Meaghan sighed. Time for a different strategy. "I get you guys want to leave the past in the past. Let's narrow this down. What's your beef with the fair folk?"

Luka sighed and ran his hand through his short hair. "They don't like us much."

"They don't like any humans much. What makes you special? Besides your longevity?"

"With long life comes long memory and too many opportunities to cross paths," Luka said. "We—Terry, Steph, Owen, and I—haven't always been the model citizens we are now."

"Huh," Terry said. "I'll say."

Meaghan looked his way. "No. You used to be major dicks, right?"

Owen snorted back a laugh.

"Not all of us," Luka said, his blue eyes twinkling. "Owen and I were always charming. Dishonest, but charming as could be. Most swindlers are."

"Ah," Meaghan said and looked over at Owen. "I thought you were a legitimate businessman."

"I am," Owen said, indignation in his voice. "Now," he added after a moment.

"But once upon a time you were a more typical leprechaun?"

Owen glared at her. "Never. Those guys are idiots. Small-time thugs with no style and no brains. Even when I worked with them, I was always trying to find a way out."

"And one day," Luka said, "he was in a small village in what's now suburban Dublin trying to collect a debt from a certain smith—"

Terry grinned. "A bronze axe I'd lost in a wager. Had a problem with gambling for a while, too."

Meaghan nodded. "And then the world blew up."

Luka smiled. "And Owen found himself with new skills and new friends."

"After you pried Terry's hands off my throat," Owen said. "He thought I'd caused the explosion. Hell, everyone thought I'd caused the explosion, including the fair folk."

"And did you?" Meaghan asked.

Owen glared at her. "Of course not. It created a damn

demiworld, and look what it did to these guys. That's takes huge scary power."

"Um ..." Dustin held up his hand. "I'm sorry to interrupt, but we need to contact the archive.? I'm getting really worried. I've never had my hex bag not work before. It's like somebody changed the locks."

Luka nodded. "It's probably the dampening magic. Let me see it."

Dustin pulled a small leather bag out of his jeans pocket and handed it to Luka.

Luka held it between his hands, eyes shut, and muttered something. "There, that should—"

Meaghan felt the hair on the back of her neck rise. She looked around the room. It wasn't only her. Everyone's hair was floating with static electricity.

"Oh, *shit*." Terry jumped up, put one foot on the sofa and pushed hard. The sofa, still holding Steph, Melanie, and Owen, skidded back several feet.

Luka grabbed Dustin and Meaghan out their armchairs, wrapped his arms around them, and pushed them to the floor.

Over Luka's shoulder, Meaghan saw Terry grab his metal folding chair and hold it above his head. There was a blinding flash of light and a huge cracking sound and everything went dark.

Chapter Twenty-Two

MEAGHAN FELT SOMEONE lying on top of her. She had a moment of panic—*the bitch needs to learn her place*—and shoved hard. The weight rolled off her.

She smelled something burning, almost a chemical smell, and heard running footsteps. A moment later, she felt rough calloused hands patting her face.

Meaghan opened her eyes and saw John's face in the dim orange light from the fireplace. "Mmm." She shook her head trying to clear it. "I'm okay. Check the others."

He kissed her on the forehead and moved away.

With a groan, Meaghan sat up. Dustin was stirring at her side. Luka, on her other side, had pulled himself onto hands and knees and swayed unsteadily, his head hanging down.

"You okay?" Meaghan asked.

"I think," Luka said, his voice slurred. "Give me a minute."

Meaghan stood up and groped for the phone in her back pocket. She needed her flashlight app. But her phone was dead, the screen cracked.

She took a few tentative steps across the room in the dim firelight, and tripped over something that felt warm through her heavy wool sock. She reached down to touch it, and yelped and pulled her finger back. Whatever it was, it was sizzling hot.

Meaghan squinted at it, as her eyes adjusted to the darkness. With a shock, she realized it was a charred metal folding chair.

Like the one Terry had been holding.

She saw him now, hunched on the floor in front of the sofa. Steph had her arms wrapped around him and was stroking his hair, murmuring something to him. John crouched nearby, his hand on Terry's shoulder, speaking to him.

As she stepped closer, she could see Terry shaking.

Meaghan glanced at Owen. His face was set in grim lines. Melanie stood next to him, looking equally grim.

"Everybody okay?" Meaghan asked.

Owen nodded. "Mostly."

"What happened?"

Before he could answer, the front door opened and Russ ran in, his hair and jacket dusted with snow. "Did you guys see that?"

Meaghan got to him before he could move further into the house and pulled him down the hallway toward the kitchen. "What did you see?"

"I didn't see it," Russ said. "Well, I saw a flash, but I heard it. The thunder. It sounded like it was close."

"Yeah," Meaghan said, now understanding the significance of the charred folding chair. "Really close. Like in the living room."

"You guys got struck?" Russ's eyes widened.

"Not all of us," Meaghan said. "Only Terry." *And he knew it was coming.*

"Oh, shit, Meg, we need to call 911."

Meaghan shook her head. "Not sure they can help us with this. Let's find out how he is first."

It's like somebody changed the locks.

Dustin's words ran through her head. Like somebody had changed the locks after they'd used the sigils to pry open the door. The door Natalie now appeared to be locked behind.

And then Luka makes a little tweak in the dampening magic around Terry's house and down comes a lightning bolt. A lightning bolt Terry knew was coming for him.

Terry had his eyes closed, his head in Steph's lap. Luka sat with them, his arm around Steph's shoulders.

"Is he okay?" Meaghan asked.

"He will be," Luka said. "It's time for that talk." He glanced at Steph. "You got this?"

Steph nodded, her eyes blazing. "I wanted him to try again, but not like this. It's the elves. They did this."

Luka nodded, squeezed her shoulder, and stood up. He nodded to Meaghan. "Let's go in the kitchen." He glanced at Russ. "You're Meaghan's brother, right? Russ?"

Russ nodded.

"I'm Luka, Terry's cousin. Got a few minutes?"

Russ nodded again. "Let me send a quick text and let the witches know everybody's okay."

Luka headed for the kitchen, with Meaghan and Russ following.

"Your phone's working?" Meaghan asked.

"Yeah," Russ said. "Your phone isn't?"

"The lightning," Luka said. "Mine is out, too. Let's find some lights."

Luka flicked the wall switch, but nothing happened. He rummaged through the pantry for a moment. He came back with a battery-powered camping lantern, which he set in the middle of the table, and they all sat down.

"I'd offer you a drink, but there's nothing here," he said. "I could really use a drink at the moment to be honest." He stretched in his seat, rubbed his face, and—looking much older than he had when he'd greeted Meaghan at the front door—said, "I don't know where to start."

"Terry got some kind of lightning power that day," Meaghan said, "the day of the explosion and he really doesn't want to use it anymore. Is that what he's hiding from?"

"To describe it that way implies he can control it. Which he can't. Or at least couldn't when he was drinking." Luka sighed. "We—Steph and I—have wondered over the years if now that he's sober, maybe he could learn to really control it. Then he wouldn't need dampening spells and magic-proof rooms and lightning rods and all the rest of it."

"So the safe rooms, the forges, aren't to hide him from the fair folk?" Meaghan asked.

"Partly, yes, they are, but they're also to keep the lightning away. It's part of why we had to move around so much back then. When people—superstitious people, mind you, because this was long before anybody knew how electricity worked—when they saw a big guy with a hammer get struck by lightning and walk away unharmed, they made certain assumptions."

Russ's mouth dropped open. "Are you saying what I think you're saying?"

Meaghan looked at him. "What are you talking about?"

Luka smiled. "You read much mythology?"

"Not really," Meaghan said.

"How about comic books?"

Meaghan snorted. "Of course not."

"Holy shit," Russ said. He stared at Luka for a long moment. "And that means you're—"

"Yes," Luka said with a sigh.

The lights came back on, blindingly bright to Meaghan's dark-adjusted eyes.

"Holy shit," Russ said.

"Shit, yes. Holy, no." Terry stomped into the room, Dustin on his heels. "I need some coffee."

"Coffee?" Luka said, his eyebrow raised.

"What I want is a fucking drink," Terry said. "More than I have in a really long time. So, yeah, coffee."

Luka raised his hand in conciliation. "Sorry. Whatever you need."

"I'll make it," Russ said, jumping to his feet, staring at Terry in awe.

"Russ," Terry said. "I'm not him."

"Well . . ." Luka said.

"You shut up," Terry said, "or I'll sew your damn lips shut like the story says."

Meaghan looked at Russ. His hands were shaking as he tried to put the filter into the coffeemaker. On the other side of the room, Dustin stared at Terry, his eyes wide, like a small child meeting Santa Claus for the first time.

Terry sighed and moved over to the coffeemaker. "Russ, man, let me do it."

Meaghan threw her hands in the air. "Will somebody tell me what the hell is going on?"

"They're gods, Meg, geez," Russ said. "Figure it out."

"We are not," Terry said. "Not even close." He pointed at Luka. "He's a swindler and a thief. I'm a drunk. Luka's father— my uncle, by the way, not my father, thank you very much—was a first-class liar and grifter who got so crazy by the end he start- ed to believe his own bullshit. The only decent one in the bunch of us is Steph."

Meaghan ignored Russ's comment and Terry's response. Her mind was not ready to go down that path. It was easier to focus on the practicalities. "I have a question."

Terry groaned.

"Not that question," Meaghan said. *Definitely not that ques- tion.* "How is the house not on fire? How is the house still standing? I had a law school friend whose house got struck and he said it broke all his windows and collapsed the ceiling."

Terry turned the coffeemaker on and sat down next to Meaghan.

"The first thing I do in every house we live in is install lightning protection."

Meaghan could see his hands were still shaking. "The doodads you put on everybody's roofs when you moved in—those are lightning rods?"

He nodded. "But that's only part of it. Generally, lightning follows the path of least resistance to the ground. Which means plumbing, electrical lines, that kind of stuff."

"And you," Meaghan said, her own hands shaking a little.

"Yeah," Terry said. "Me."

"Why the chair?"

"It was already coming for me and I can walk away from it unharmed. You guys can't. I wanted to make sure I gave it a big target so you guys wouldn't get caught in a side flash."

"Why isn't the floor burnt up?"

Terry shrugged. "No idea. I seem to absorb a fair amount of it. There's a magical component to the lightning I attract that bends the usual rules a little."

Meaghan nodded. She felt oddly calm considering the circumstances. "This happens often?"

Terry shook his head, a look of misery on his face. "Not since I quit drinking. Since AA. The two always went hand in hand. Between sobriety and dampening magic, I've managed to control it. But if the lightning's back . . . oh, fuck." He buried his face in his hands. "I don't want to be that guy again."

"Then don't be," John said as he walked into the kitchen with Owen right behind him. "It is up to you what you do with this. I have been talking with Steph. Just because the drinking and the lightning happened at the same time doesn't mean they are the same thing."

"I've been dealing with this a long time."

John shook his head. "That's not what Steph says. She says you are not dealing with this for a long time."

"Johnny, I—"

"What is it you tell me when I first go to AA? You tell me if I fail at being a father when I'm drinking, it doesn't mean I will fail when I am sober. That the only way to know if I can be a father again is to try."

Terry didn't say anything for a long moment, then stood up. "Smart ass. I did tell you that. The coffee's done. Who else needs some?"

Everybody raised their hands.

CHAPTER TWENTY-THREE

MEAGHAN GOT HER coffee and headed out to the living room. Terry was too upset to answer questions—both from the lightning and from Russ and Dustin staring at him in awe—and Luka was too busy trying to calm Terry down to talk to Meaghan.

Steph patted the sofa next to her. "Sit down, sweetie. Ask your questions."

Meaghan sat down. "Where's Melanie?"

"She went back to your house to try to keep everybody calm."

"Okay." Meaghan nodded. *Time for the big question.* "So, are you guys really gods?"

Steph laughed. "Not even close. A case of mistaken identity that turned into a sometimes useful con."

"Mistaken identity?"

Steph nodded. "The belief was there. The gods were there. We gave a few of them faces."

"Did people worship you?"

"Of course not," Steph said. "At least not us personally. The thing you need to understand is that what the modern world knows as Norse mythology comes from stories written down after Christianity had supplanted the belief system. The actual beliefs . . . well, the eddas are more accurate than the comic books, but not by much. Celtic mythology is even worse. It was written down centuries after the fact."

"Then Terry's not . . ." Meaghan took a deep breath, "the guy they named Thursday after?"

Steph smiled. "No. Not really. Thunder gods were very common back then. Every culture, every tribe, had one. They were as good an explanation for what was going on up in the sky as anything else. We didn't understand how all that worked. So you had a name and a concept, and then along comes Terry and suddenly here's this thunder god with a big red beard showing up all over Europe and Scandinavia."

Meaghan nodded. "And Terry's a blacksmith so he probably always had a hammer nearby."

"Exactly. In Celtic mythology, the god was called Taranis. He got Terry's big red beard, but Terry hadn't started working iron yet, so Taranis was pictured with a wheel—the wheel of the sky—and a thunderbolt. When we moved east, the red beard stayed, but the wheel became a hammer."

"Because he was working iron by then." Meaghan sipped her coffee. "He's always had the beard?"

Steph nodded. "He's shaved it off from time to time, but he gets really bad razor burn and ingrown hairs—it's kind of a mess. It's easier to have the beard."

"Wow." Meaghan finished her coffee. "So, was Luka's father. . ." *Yup, I'm really about to ask this.* "Odin?"

Steph rolled her eyes. "No. He only liked to pretend he was. Odin was an existing deity, but Cian embellished him quite a bit, mostly to mooch free drinks."

"Key-un?" Meaghan asked.

"C-i-a-n. His Irish name. There's a series of stories about Odin visiting the human world as a one-eyed old man, Wegtam the Wanderer, who wore a tattered gray cloak and a broad-brimmed hat. Cian seeded those stories around and then bought himself the cloak and the hat. Got a lot of drinks out of it." She chuckled, but there was no humor in it. "Until the con went bad and he got burned at the stake for heresy."

Meaghan grimaced.

Steph nodded. "He started to believe his own stories. He really thought he was Odin. We're not sure if the fair folk did that or if it was simply dementia. He was pretty old by then. Either way, we couldn't save him. Owen smuggled a potion to him that killed him right before they lit the pyre. Didn't feel a thing. Cian could be an asshole, but nobody deserves to die that way." She shuddered. "Nobody."

"Who was missing the eye? Odin or Cian?"

Steph leaned back against the sofa cushions. "The written mythology says that Odin sacrificed his eye to gain wisdom. Cian got stabbed in the eye during a bar fight. I couldn't tell you which one happened first."

"From what you're telling me, my money's on Cian." Meaghan shook her head. "You know, maybe I'm cynical, but magic has turned out to be a lot less magical than I thought it would be. Like fairies—they turned out to be filthy little cavemen."

Steph laughed. "And then you blew up fairyland."

Meaghan laughed along with her. "Yeah, right, I did. And fairyland was a dump, let me tell you. Now it turns out elves are narcissistic parasites—"

"Who like to pretend they're gods. Except for the Norse pantheon, who are grifters and swindlers."

"Reformed grifters and swindlers," Meaghan said through her laughter. "Now Thor's a coffee-drinking handyman and part-time Santa Claus, and Loki's a venture capitalist."

She and Steph began laughing so hard they couldn't speak for a few moments.

"Oh, Meg," Steph said when she'd regained her composure. "I'm so glad you're taking it like this."

Meaghan wiped her eyes with the back of her hand. "Russ is in there staring at Terry like he's Superman. I guess I'm harder to impress. What about you? How do you fit into all this?"

"Hang on. You're sniffly." Steph got up and rummaged in a storage cabinet on the far wall. She came back with a box of tissues. "Here."

"Thank you." Meaghan blew her nose. "Don't try to dodge the question."

"Thor got himself a wife named Sif. She didn't do much except have long golden hair."

"Is that your original name?"

Steph shook her head. "No, Sif basically means wife. She doesn't even have a name in those stories. I also got mixed up with a couple of Teutonic goddesses. Long blonde hair again."

"You do have nice hair. What did these goddesses do?"

"Oh, they were your basic weather, farming, and homemaking goddesses. Generally benevolent, except when they were being scary."

Meaghan nodded. "Yeah, for somebody who supposedly doesn't have much magical power, there sure are a lot of folks afraid of you."

Steph sighed. "Yeah, well, I do have a temper. And if I'm really pissed off, I sometimes make the wind blow."

"And? You don't get a reputation for being scary because you stir up the occasional breeze."

"Says the woman who's hated and feared as a world destroyer."

"It was just the one," Meaghan said.

Steph nodded. "Well, there you go. Mostly I've always had a big mouth and strong opinions and no problem with fighting dirty. Add a few anger-induced windstorms, simmer for a few hundred years, and you've got Holda of the wild hunt."

"The what?"

"Old myth. Oh, there's the Valkyrie thing, too."

"You're a *Valkyrie?*"

"Again, one simple skill and hundreds of years with nothing to do on the long cold evenings but tell tales that keep getting taller, and next thing I know, I'm the gatherer of the slain. You know I volunteer at a hospice, right?"

"Yeah," Meaghan said. "You aren't a medium like Annie, are you?"

Steph shook her head. "That girl has a real gift. And I think she and Russ are great together, don't you?"

"Yes. Annie's awesome. Get back to the Valkyrie thing."

Steph made a face. "Fine. The hospice. It's not a big thing I do, but for people teetering on the brink, I can give them a little nudge, I suppose, to help them get to the other side."

"Nudge?" Meaghan asked, trying to keep the suspicion out of her voice. "What kind of nudge?"

Steph scowled. "Psychic, of course. What do you think? I walk around with a pillow, looking for people to smother?"

Meaghan rolled her eyes, trying to hide her relief. *That's exactly what you were thinking, dummy, weren't you?* "Of course not."

"Needless to say, I suppose, but back in the day we didn't have hospices." Steph paused for a long moment, staring at the floor, then said, "Mostly I used it on battlefields."

"To ease their suffering?" Even in the dim light, Meaghan could see Steph's face flush.

"Yeah, let's go with that." Steph wouldn't meet Meaghan's gaze. "It also made it easier to steal their stuff. We weren't good people, Meg."

Meaghan reached out and touched Steph's arm. "We all have shit in our past we're not proud of and you've had a lot more time to accumulate those bad moments. You're good people now, right?"

Steph sighed. "We're trying to be."

"Trying to be what?" Luka walked into the room.

"Good people." Steph patted the sofa next to her. "Lou. Sit down."

"Lou?" Meaghan asked.

"Original name," Luka said. "Spelled L-u-g-h."

"I don't know much mythology," Meaghan said. "But aren't you supposed to be kind of evil?"

Luka grimaced. "Bad press. I mean I was a crook, yes, but I only scammed jerks who deserved it."

"Are you a crook now?" Meaghan asked.

Luka smiled. "Not for a long time. I don't need to be anymore."

"Why not?" Meaghan heard Steph snort with suppressed laughter.

"Because I'm filthy rich for one thing. But the real reason is Owen and I got to America and realized we'd come home." Luka chuckled. "We turned into capitalists." His look turned serious. "I'll tell you all about it when we have time, but now we have to figure out what happened. I'm not even remotely strong enough to dismantle the dampening magic Terry had in place. All I did with Dustin's hex bag was harmonize it so the spells wouldn't conflict. That much I can do. It's standard maintenance and I've done it before—so has Owen—and we've never had a problem."

"Somebody set this up," Meaghan said. "Whoever had that damn carpeting installed. That fly-by-night design firm the mayor brought in."

"Dustin told me about that. Something Italian?" Luka asked.

Meaghan nodded. "The only reason Tony could hire them outside of the city bid process was because he was using your money instead of city funds. When I was on vacation in Arizona,"—*when you fled to Arizona, you mean*—"Tony gave them the go-ahead to install it."

"Sigil-covered carpeting," Luka said. "You know that wasn't an accident."

"Yeah, I do now." Meaghan felt the anxiety rush back into her gut. Natalie was still on the other side of a locked door. "So, the fair folk did this?"

Luka, chewing on his lower lip, stared at nothing for a long moment and then shook his head. "I don't think so."

"If they want to destabilize Terry, this is a good way," Steph said.

"Yeah," Luka said, "except when they had him in the past, they threw up their own dampening spells. They couldn't control the lightning any better than we could."

"But he was drinking then," Steph said. "Maybe now—"

"He could control it," Luka said, nodding. "Except he won't try."

"Now he's got to try," Steph said. "That strike was like the old days, the thunder god days. When he still had a handle on his drinking."

"Yeah, but even then, he didn't really have much control over it."

"He had enough to keep the fair folk at bay," Steph said. "Imagine what he could do now, when he's drinking coffee instead of mead."

Steph and Luka stared at each other for a long moment, then Luka began to nod.

"If it's not the fair folk, then who's responsible for that damn carpeting?" Meaghan asked. "And what do we need to do to get that gateway opened and get Natalie back?"

Chapter Twenty-Four

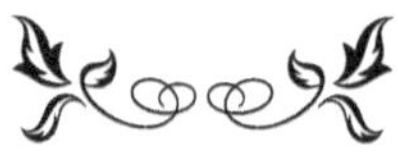

As soon as Meaghan asked the question about the carpeting, the answer came to her.

The Order. Cooper and his band of evil wizards.

The bitch needs to learn her place . . .

She shoved the fear down. No time for it now. "You guys ever deal with the Order?"

"Those guys from Labor Day?" Steph asked. "The wizards?"

"Yeah."

Steph shook her head. "No. They're new kids on the block, or so I've heard."

Luka jumped to his feet and moved to the fireplace. "We need another log on the fire."

"Luka," Steph said, "you ever deal with them?"

Luka poked at the embers until the new log began to smolder. His voice tight, he said, "Not with the Order."

Meaghan could see the poker trembling in his hand.

He's scared. "Interesting way to answer the question," Meaghan said. "If not them, then who? Cooper, maybe?"

Luka flinched.

"Who's Cooper?" Steph asked.

Why am I not surprised? "The leader of the Order," Meaghan said.

Steph looked at Luka, her eyes narrowing. "You know this guy?"

Luka poked some more at the fire. In a tight voice, he said, "We've crossed paths before."

"When?" Steph said. "Who is he?"

Luka stared at the fire for a long moment before answering. "Remember when we left London and headed to Norwich? When you left Terry again and we got into the relics business?"

Steph nodded. "Yeah, I remember. You cut off all my hair to sell to pilgrims." She looked at Meaghan. "It was down to my waist. I told him he could have a foot of it and instead he cut it all the way to my ears. While I was asleep."

Luka shrugged. "You needed a different look, we needed the money, and hair grows back. But the night we left, we were supposed to sell a sword. Tyr's sword—"

"Right," Steph said. "Terry made a pile of those," she explained to Meaghan. "We ran that one scam for over a thousand years." She turned back to Luka. "Didn't you sell one of those to Attila the Hun?"

"No. We only said we did, to build up the legend. Guys like Attila don't need magic swords." Luka sighed. "The mark that night was a young would-be wizard. Scary, but in a conventional psychopath sort of way. I couldn't feel any power from him, and if he'd any training at all, he wouldn't have fallen for the magic sword bit."

"Why?" Meaghan asked.

"Because there's no such thing as magic swords." Terry stepped into the room.

"There isn't?" Meaghan asked, as she surveyed Terry. He looked a lot calmer than he had in the kitchen. She tried to picture him as a mead-swilling, Viking thunder god, but even with as many times as she'd seen him with a hammer in his hand, she couldn't do it. Despite what she'd seen and heard in the last half hour, Meaghan was relieved to discover to her at least, he was still Terry.

"Of course not. Steel's impervious," Terry said as he walked over to the sofa and sat down beside Steph, who reached over and took his hand. "You can make a sword out of other metals, but—even with magic—it won't stand up against a well-made steel blade."

"But put a simple spell on the slag in a cheap blade," Luka said, "and make it throw sparks or shine like a rainbow and presto, magic sword."

"Slag?" Meaghan asked.

"Everything in the ore that isn't iron and didn't get processed out in the forging," Steph explained.

"Your so-called magic sword is a piece of crap that will shatter in your hands," Terry said. "It's inferior steel. It's only special effects."

Luka smiled. "But a certain type of man will fall for it every time."

"Like Vitellius." Terry nodded. "What a sucker that guy was."

"Vitellius?" Meaghan asked.

"He was a Roman prefect," Luka said. "Somehow he got himself named general of the army up near the Rhine and then got himself proclaimed emperor in the chaos after Nero died. But his position was shaky at best, so I convinced him I had a special sword, imbued with magic that would keep him in power. A sword I was willing to sell for a reasonable price so the great Vitellius could protect the empire." He shook his head. "Some marks are so easy. A little ego stroking and some mystic dazzle and you're in."

"What happened to him? How long was he emperor?" Meaghan wanted to get back to Cooper, but it was hard to resist the urge to question people who'd been on speaking terms with ancient Romans.

"For like five minutes," Terry said.

"Eight months actually," Luka said.

"Seven and half of which he spent drunk. He was an even bigger lush than me," Terry said. "Anyway Luka spun some bullshit about the sword originally belonging to Tyr—"

"The Norse god they named Tuesday after," Steph said.

"Really a god?" Meaghan asked. "Or a cousin I haven't met yet?"

Steph chuckled. "The god Tyr already existed in the belief system. Cian made up stories about him, but they were based on a bunch of different people."

"Who are we talking about?" Owen walked into the room.

"Tyr and Vitellius," Luka said. "I was telling her about the sword."

"Let me guess," Meaghan said, looking at Owen. "You stole it back."

Owen grinned. "Yup. And replaced it with a rusty piece of shit right after Luka sold it to him, so we could get Vitellius to pay us to steal it back or pay a ransom for it. But the old sot was so drunk he didn't notice the switch."

Terry nodded. "Meanwhile, Vespasian rolls into town at the head of the eastern army and takes charge. The story goes that Vitellius finally discovered his magic sword was gone and he was so freaked out from losing it, he hid in his palace until he was dragged out and executed."

"Did you try to sell it to Vespasian then?" Meaghan asked.

"Hell, no," Terry said. "We were long gone by then. Besides, Vespasian was a real soldier, a good one. He wasn't the type of guy who believes in magic swords."

Meaghan looked at Owen. "Was this the same magic sword that got you in trouble with everybody?"

Owen rolled his eyes. "No. Well, yeah, that was also Tyr's sword, but a later version. Honestly, those monks. They know how magic works. They should know better. They're such a bunch of fanboys. 'But the Norns decreed,'" he said in a whiny voice. "'That's what the Druid priestess said. There's a prophecy. Whoever wields it will rule the world.' Morons."

Meaghan looked at Steph, who grinned back, and said, "Yeah, that was me. Vitellius wasn't the first guy we suckered with that sword."

"So that's why Vitellius fell for it. There was a prophecy." Meaghan rolled her eyes. *And look how he dodged the original question.* She stared at Luka. "Tell me how you know Cooper."

"Cooper?" Terry asked.

"The wizard from Labor Day? With the tacky witch girlfriend?" Owen looked to Meaghan for confirmation.

She nodded.

"He's the one we were supposed to sell the sword to on the night we left London." Luka looked at Terry. "When we left you."

Terry nodded slowly. "Right. A sword I never delivered to you guys because I was too drunk to finish it."

Owen stared into space a moment, then went pale. "I thought he looked familiar."

"The wizard who caused all the trouble last summer?" Terry shook his head. "Can't be the same guy. The guy back then came at me in an alley with a sword the day after you left. Seemed pleased with himself to find me unarmed. Kind of the sneering gloater type."

"Yeah," Owen said. "That's him."

"I tried to warn him off, but he wouldn't listen. I had a really bad hangover, and I'd just read Steph's goodbye letter, so I had even less control than usual. I fried the bastard where he stood and for once I didn't feel that bad about it."

"You killed him?" Meaghan asked.

"I didn't stick around to check if he was breathing, but it blew him right out of his boots. He sure looked dead."

"Don't be so sure," Owen said.

"He was smoking," Terry said. "Actual smoke rising off him."

Owen shook his head. "Doesn't matter. It was him. Cooper. I mean, I only saw him a couple of times back then, but . . . I'm sorry, Meg. I should have put it together a whole lot sooner."

Terry frowned. "That was almost a thousand years ago. This guy's like us?"

Luka nodded. "It appears so, but not as old. I'm sure he was genuinely a young man back then. Vicious and lethal, but still kind of wet behind the ears."

Steph started nodding. "He was the barrel maker's son, wasn't he? I remember him. Sneered at the family business, but he was only too happy to spend daddy's money."

Luka stared at the fire. "Cooper is another name for a barrel maker. He eventually did the work to become a real wizard, I guess. He doesn't need a sword anymore."

Now Meaghan was confused. "Witches and wizards don't live longer than normal people." She glanced around the room. "Do they?"

Luka sighed. "Not usually, but there's some old magic, dark stuff to prolong life. You need to make a blood sacrifice. Family blood."

Meaghan had a quick mental flash of Jamie, bloody and battered, clinging to her in terror as the Power offered John a deal. *This has something to do with Fahraya.*

"Oh, hell." Owen shook his head. He looked sick, his face pale. "The cooper—the father—he and his whole family were killed, did you know that? A few years later. In a big fire. There was all that pitch and tar in the workshop. The bodies were burnt so bad they looked like lumps of charcoal."

Luka's eyes narrowed. "You sure it was the same family?"

"Yeah, their workshop was down near the docks. Where we were supposed to meet him that night. I always thought his father was a merchant, not a cooper, so I never put that together either."

Terry frowned. "The guy survives a direct lightning strike and the fire that burned up the rest of his family, and now he's a wizard?"

Steph sighed. "Sweetie, he *killed* his family. The blood sacrifice. The fire was probably to hide it and to make it look like he died, too."

"Yeah, giving him extended lifespan and now he's a wizard," Owen said. "A powerful one."

Meaghan looked at Luka. "You said he didn't have any power."

"Not then," Luka said.

"He sure had plenty in September," Owen said. "If it hadn't been for Natalie and whatever crazy shit Patrice was channeling, we'd all be dead now."

Meaghan glanced at Terry when Owen mentioned Patrice. This time his face was rigid. Too rigid, like he was making an effort not to react.

Luka sighed and sank down onto the metal chair not burned by the lightning strike. "Yeah. About that."

"What did you do?" Steph's voice had a growl in it Meaghan had never heard before.

"Honey," Terry said. "Calm down. We don't need any more weather disturbances in the house today.

Luka looked at them. "You may want to rethink that. I may deserve smiting for this one. This Cooper guy getting big power may be my fault. I threw him in the path of the fair folk to keep them away from us."

"But there's no way he got his power from the fair folk. They'd only promise it, bask in his worship, and then get him to do something awful ..." Terry's eyes widened. "Right. His family. Which is why he's still alive. But the power—the fair folk wouldn't give him that. Where did the power come from?"

Meaghan glanced over at Owen. "When you hear someone else say it, it's so obvious." She looked back at Terry. "The Power. His incorporeal sidekick."

Terry looked confused again.

This is about to turn into who's on first. "Power with a capital P," Meaghan said. "The thing that possessed John's brother."

Luka nodded. "And whatever that thing is, it's worse than the fair folk. We may have a two-front war on our hands."

CHAPTER TWENTY-FIVE

"THE STINKY SPACE squid," Meaghan said. "Cooper calls them his masters, but thinks they're working for him. Or at least he did until they showed up."

Luka laughed, but it was harsh and without humor. "Yeah, he would think that, but I'm sure it's the other way around."

"What do you know about them?"

He shook his head. "Not much more than you do. They're rumor mostly. Something ancient and evil from before time."

"More evil than the fair folk?" Meaghan grimaced. "That creepy Power thing seems to be on a similar diet, except for the awe-and-wonder part."

Luka nodded. "Those creatures' disappearance seemed to have opened an ecological niche for our nasty little elf friends. And it sounds like these things also use magic to manipulate the minds of their prey."

"Yeah, everyone was shitting bricks in city hall when they showed up," Meaghan said, "including Cooper."

"They were . . ." Owen shuddered. "I'm still having nightmares."

"What did they look like?" Steph asked.

"They ..." Owen trailed off and stared into space for a long moment. "It's funny. I don't remember exactly. I can't describe them, only how they made me feel."

"I can describe them," Meaghan said. "The smell was beyond disgusting, but honestly, they weren't that scary to look at. I've seen worse stuff on TV. All I saw were some gray, slightly scaly tentacles. Hence the name stinky space squid."

"Wait," Terry said. "They're from space? Like aliens?"

"No," Meaghan answered. "I don't know. Maybe. Or another dimension? But wherever they came from, they're stuck between worlds."

"In a demiworld," Luka said. "Like Fahraya." He paused a moment, then added, "I think."

"I was told it was a space between the worlds," Meaghan said. "I assumed it was similar to the void the Power stepped into when it destroyed Fahraya."

Luka shook his head. "That ... nobody knows what that is. And nobody else is able to do it as far as I can tell."

"Nobody still here, at least," Steph said. "You said they were ancient, right?"

"Maybe," Luka said. "But if they could go around tearing holes in reality, why are they trapped?" He looked at Owen. "Isn't that what Cooper said? That they were trapped?"

Owen nodded.

"But Finn—"

"Finn?" Luka asked.

"Jhoro's dead boyfriend," Owen said.

"Right," Luka said. "Sorry. What about Finn?"

"Finn described them as the Power's masters. So did Cooper and the Power." Meaghan sighed. "But then I've worked for plenty of morons who I called boss even though I was the one really in charge."

Owen smiled at Luka.

"Don't get any ideas," Luka said back.

"Whatever you say," Owen shot back. *"Boss."*

"Boys, behave," Steph said.

"So, how did they get into a demiworld?" Meaghan asked.

"Somebody put them there," Luka said. "Demiworlds don't happen without magical intervention."

"Like the explosion that created Fahraya?" Meaghan glanced around the room. "That created you guys? You said it was an accident."

Luka nodded. "Yeah, but an accident that wouldn't have happened unless somebody was playing with big scary spells."

"Like trying to lock up these squid things?" Steph asked.

"No," Luka said. "The timing's wrong. These things were gone long before us. I think somebody was trying to free them."

Meaghan felt a chill in her gut. Cooper had pried open that door in September and Meaghan had only managed to close it at the last moment. "Somebody else who thought he could control them?"

"This Cooper guy really thinks he can control them?" Steph asked.

Meaghan nodded. "Although he might be rethinking that after Labor Day. He was as terrified as everybody else when they arrived." She looked back at Luka. "What exactly do you know about them?"

"Like I said, it's mostly rumor and conjecture."

"Do they have a name?"

Luka shook his head. "Not really. It's all along the lines of the ancient ones, the old gods, the terror that sleeps, that sort of stuff."

Meaghan nodded. "Then stinky space squid it is."

Luka raised an eyebrow.

"I'm not dignifying these things with a fancy euphemism."

"These things are dangerous, Meg. Even to you." Luka said. "Especially to you, because I'm betting they won't like the idea of impervious humans any better than the fair folk do. Don't underestimate them."

"I'm not. I was there. The only thing that stopped them was that damn stapler I chucked into their prison." She took a deep breath. Meaghan had never articulated this before to anyone, not even to herself, but she'd known it that moment in city hall. "A lump of steel worked last time, but the day may come when the only impervious thing to throw at them is me. Trust me. I get how dangerous they are."

"Who's dangerous?" a female voice asked.

Natalie.

Meaghan had been so focused on Luka she hadn't seen her come in. She leapt to her feet and pulled Natalie into a crushing hug.

"What?" Natalie tried to wriggle out of Meaghan's embrace. "You're squishing me. Did you see all that snow out there?"

"Where have you been?" Meaghan released her grip and glared at Natalie. "Why didn't you call? We've been worried sick."

"As soon as I got over there, the door slammed shut and I couldn't open it back up. What did you do? Rip out the carpet yourself? And there was some kind of dampening magic on this end." Natalie glanced at Terry. "That was you, right? Do we still call you Terry?"

"Yeah. Please. I'm still me," Terry said. "I'm not him. I never really was."

"Tell Russ." Natalie rolled her eyes. "He's in full geek-out mode. He's getting the boys all wound up, too."

"The boys?" Meaghan asked.

"The monks." Natalie rolled her eyes again. "They're even geekier. Dustin is actually the cool one, if you can believe it."

"Aw, hell," Terry grumbled. "I'd better get in there. Before it gets any worse." He rose to his feet, and stomped out of the room.

Meaghan glanced at Owen. She could see the relief on his face, despite his obvious efforts to be nonchalant.

Ah. Haven't told the family about Natalie yet, have we?

Meaghan looked over at Steph.

Steph winked at her.

Meaghan chuckled.

"What?" Owen said.

Meaghan gave him her best innocent look. "I'm happy to have Natalie back in one piece. Aren't you happy to see her?"

"Of course I am." Owen's face flushed. "Why wouldn't I be?"

"No reason," Meaghan said.

Steph snorted back a laugh. "Owen, you dope, we know all about you and Natalie."

Owen's mouth opened. He and Natalie exchanged a quick look.

"Everybody knows about you and Natalie," Steph said. "Worst kept secret in town. Give the girl a kiss already." She stood up. "Take my seat. I have to go check on my husband."

Natalie and Owen sat on the sofa next to Meaghan.

"You must be Luka," Natalie said. "The boys are even more geeked out about you."

Luka rolled his eyes. "Of course they are. Thanks to dear old Dad and his stupid stories. Time for damage control. Nice to finally meet you by the way."

"You know, too?" Owen stared at Luka, a shocked look on his face.

Luka smiled as he walked past them. "Of course. I've known you for three thousand years. I knew how you felt about her before you did."

"How did you get here?" Meaghan asked.

Natalie shrugged. "Dustin chalked the symbols on the pantry floor and the gateway popped right open. Where the hell did all this snow come from? I've only been gone since this morning, right?"

Meaghan nodded. "Did you know Buzz Hallam is a troll?"

"Yeah," Natalie said. "You didn't know that?"

"No," Meagan said stiffly. "Nobody bothered to mention it to me."

Natalie sighed. "Not this again. I thought you knew. If you don't know something now it's because we all assume someone else told you."

"Then why did Kady lie about it? You're telling me she doesn't know?"

Natalie shrugged. "How should I know what she knows? Buzz doesn't walk around telling people he's a troll, but he doesn't hide it either. You're making this into a big deal and it's not. It's not some plot against you. We're not that organized. You saw what a crappy job we did hiding the truth about Eldrich. We wanted to give you a few days to settle in, but all we managed was a few hours before the spells were flying. Along with Jamie."

She's right, you know. If you want to know stuff, ask more questions. Meaghan took a deep breath, then nodded. "Sorry. I'm . . . it's a sore spot."

"No kidding," Natalie said. She took her own deep breath. "It's not like you don't have a reason to be suspicious, but my secrets are spilled, I promise." She glanced at Owen with a smile. "Even this one."

Owen rolled his eyes. "Most of my secrets are forgotten, to be perfectly honest. I can't remember half the shit I've done after all these years." He glanced at Meaghan. "Now you know about me and Luka and the Donners. How you doing with that?"

Meaghan rubbed her face. "I'll tell you when it hits me. The swindler part doesn't really surprise me, but I'm still trying to wrap my brain around Terry being a thunder god."

Natalie giggled. "He sure doesn't act like a god."

Owen snorted. "Well, not like a modern one, but smiting under the influence was all the rage back in the day. Fortunately,

Terry—even when falling down drunk—usually remembered he was a stand-in, not the star. Unlike Cian. I always hated that guy. The way he treated Luka was shitty."

He looked up at Meaghan, a defensive gleam in his eye. "Luka never scammed anyone who didn't deserve it. And he's done a lot of good since we went straight. He's not the bad guy Cian's stories made him out to be."

So you say. I'm reserving judgment. Meaghan nodded. "Good to know. I have too many bad guys to deal with already. Including the elf in my basement. Time for you guys to scam someone who deserves it."

CHAPTER TWENTY-SIX

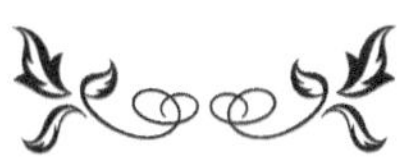

MEAGHAN FOUND JOHN and Steph back in the kitchen, watching Terry and Luka try to explain themselves to Russ, Dustin, and three awed monks.

Steph grinned at Meaghan. "Come to see the show?"

"Yeah, I guess."

John held his arms open and Meaghan moved to his side. "Now I understand why they didn't want me to tell you," he said in a low voice. "But you're more sensible than these." He frowned at the monks. "They're struggling. So is your brother."

Meaghan nodded. "I've never seen this side of him. Maybe because he isn't in his own kitchen. If we were home, he'd be too busy making dinner to care."

"Food is important to him," John said in a solemn tone. "His form of magic."

Meaghan surveyed the three robed monks standing with Dustin. They were all staring intently at Terry.

Two were human. The third one . . . Meaghan wasn't sure. He had his hood up and he was much smaller than the other two.

Elf? She quickly dismissed the idea. The mystery monk was too stocky to be an elf. He was on the small side, but he could be a Troon. The archive had several Troon. Or he could be one of the many species she hadn't encountered yet.

Or he could be a small human.

Terry groaned. "I'm not a god. I'm a big dumb guy who could hold his mead and got struck by lightning a lot. Nothing divine about it."

One of the humans, about the same age as Dustin, with a shaved head and glasses, scowled. "You mean you don't have a hammer?"

"Well, yeah, of course, I do. I'm a blacksmith. And a handyman. I got shitloads of hammers."

"Mjolnir?" another human asked. This one looked even younger than Dustin, with sloppy blond hair and multiple freckles. "Is one of them Mjolnir?"

Terry rolled his eyes. "You want a magic hammer?" He yanked open a drawer and pulled something out. "Here."

"What's its name?" said the first monk, eyeing with suspicion the claw hammer in Terry's hand.

"Craftsman." Terry held the hammer out for inspection. "See?"

"That's not a magic hammer." The second monk couldn't hide his disappointment.

"Do you know how good the warranty is on this thing?" Terry dropped the hammer back into the drawer and slammed it shut. "As long as I hang onto the receipt, it's guaranteed for life. If I bust it, I take it back to Sears, and they give me a new one. How much more magic do you want?"

Steph laughed out loud.

"Neither of us are gods," said Luka. "We have that settled. Who are you guys?"

Dustin stepped forward. "Uh, this is Todd." He pointed at the bald one, who turned pink and stared at his toes. "And Clint."

The freckled one raised his hand. "Yo."

Luka turned to the final figure. "How about you?"

"That's Brother Enoch," Dustin said. "He's taken a vow of silence."

The small figure nodded. Meaghan looked for a telltale flash of blue that would identify Enoch as a Troon, but the hood was deep enough that Meaghan couldn't see his face. She glanced at his hands. He was wearing gloves. Whatever he was, he was doing his best to hide it. Her fear returned. If Enoch was a disguised elf and she outed him here, he'd either teleport or she'd end up with another prisoner and still no idea what the fair folk were up to.

She glanced at John. His brows were knitted as he stared at Enoch. *He's suspicious, too.* She squeezed his hand and, when he glanced at her, she gave a tiny shake of her head and mouthed "not here."

John nodded.

Todd pinned Luka with a skeptical stare. "So, you aren't trying to kill him?"

Luka shook his head. "Nope. That's only in the movies. I have nothing but affection for him."

Terry snorted. "You're so full of shit."

Luka smiled at him. "I love you, too." He turned his attention back to the monks. "So, Eamon O'Malley, when did you change your name to Enoch? And a brother of the Word? I can't wait to hear the story behind this one."

The other monks took a step away from Brother Enoch, who took his own step away from Luka and Terry.

"Eamon O'Malley?" Terry asked Luka. "You sure?"

Luka nodded.

Terry started laughing. "Owen's gonna love this."

Brother Enoch held up his hands and furiously shook his head. He backed away from Luka toward the still-open gateway in the pantry.

As the small monk neared the table, John reached out, grabbed Brother Enoch, and pulled the deep hood from his head.

A small sweaty face topped with dirt-colored hair appeared. "Shite. You giant bastard, whaddya do that for?"

"You," John said, his eyes narrowing.

The unmasked leprechaun took a closer look at John. He moaned with fear. He wrenched free and scrambled in the other direction. "Not the bees. Not the bloody bees again."

Bees? He had to be talking about John's honeybees, who had a tendency to swarm in his defense.

Terry scooped up the little monk, holding him in the air by the back of his robe. "Eamon." He grinned wolfishly. "How you doing?"

"This keeps getting worse," the leprechaun squeaked.

Steph got to her feet and sauntered over to Terry. "And worse and worse."

Eamon groaned.

Steph glared at him. "You loathsome little spud, are you spying on us?"

"No," he said. "I swear. It's only a job. I didn't know you lot were gonna be here." In a flash, his demeanor changed. With an oily smile at Steph, he said, "If you get your fine husband to put me down, I'll make it worth your while."

Luka snorted back a laugh.

Smiling, Steph shook her head. "Oh, I don't think so."

"Owen," Terry called. "Get in here and take a look at this rat we caught."

Now John took his turn. "You threatened to break my hives," he growled. "You tried to hurt my bees. They did not like that."

"Right, the protection money shakedown," Meaghan said, now making the connection. "I knew I'd heard the name before."

Eamon glared at Meaghan. "Who's this?"

"That's Meaghan Keele," Luka said. "You know, Matthew's daughter?"

Eamon wilted like old lettuce and began to cry. "Please, not her. The other boys are innocent. Don't destroy our home, lady. Please, I'm beggin'."

"Oh, for hell's sake," Meaghan said. "It was only the one time, and I did it to save everybody else."

Owen stepped into the crowded kitchen. He stared at Eamon, still dangling from Terry's fist, and sighed. "You're an embarrassment to the species, Eamon."

Eamon began thrashing, suddenly enraged. "You're the embarrassment, boyo. You're gonna make it all start again. Bastard." He glared at Terry. "Put me down, Sparky. You don't scare me no more. Everybody knows the lightning fizzled outta you years ago."

Steph poked Eamon with her index finger. "What did you do? Did you make that happen?"

"Ow, you old cow, quit that." Eamon continued to struggle. "Make what happen?"

"Steph," Owen said. "Let me handle this. Terry, put him down."

Terry lowered Eamon, then dropped him so he fell the last foot to the kitchen floor. He pushed himself to his feet, brushed off his robe, and smoothed his hair.

Meaghan compared Eamon to Owen. The height was similar, but the comparison ended there. Even when he was fighting the Order with her in the shattered remains of city hall, Owen had looked far less disheveled than Eamon did now.

Owen stood with his arms out. "Here I am. Do your worst."

Eamon growled and hurled himself at Owen, who did a graceful side step. Owen then grasped Eamon's arm, gave what looked like a gentle push and Eamon crashed, head first, into the wall.

He sat up, holding his nose. "Whaddya do to me? That's not fair."

"Fair?" Owen snorted. "You're complaining about fighting fair? You're the dirtiest fighter I've ever met."

"Yeah, but not like that." Eamon waved a hand in the air. "That Oriental stuff. It's not right for us."

Owen shook his head. "Since when am I considered one of the boys? You little shits threw me out, remember?"

"Yeah, but only because you was gonna get us in trouble with . . ." Eamon glanced around furtively, then whispered, "the lords and ladies."

"The fair folk?" Meaghan asked.

"Don't say their name," Eamon hissed.

"I haven't," Meaghan said. "That's a euphemism, too."

"A yoofa what?"

"Fake name," Owen said. He glanced up at Meaghan. "You see what I have to deal with? Why I get so upset when I get lumped in with these idiots? Credulous, obsequious morons, the whole lot of them."

"Oh, listen to his lordship here with his fancy words," Eamon said. "Swannin' about in his silk suits like his shite don't stink. Under that fancy hairdo, you're still one of us. A great giant wanker, yeah, but still one of us." He glared at Owen. "It's time you come home, boyo, and quit makin' trouble."

"That was never my home," Owen hissed. "I may have been born with you clowns, but it was never my home."

"Um." Meaghan raised her hand. "Excuse me, but I have a question." She pinned Eamon with a stern look. "You said you were on a job. Who are you working for? And what are you doing?"

"I can't tell you who my client is. I got a duty," Eamon said.

Owen snorted. "Duty, my ass. You really want to piss her off? You think that's a good idea?"

Eamon tried to glare back at Owen, but after a glance at Meaghan, he folded. "I never seen his face."

"A wizard?" Meaghan asked.

Eamon shrugged. "I didn't ask. That's his business."

"Eamon," Owen said. "Remember Fahraya."

"All right, all right," Eamon said. "He never said and I never asked, but I could feel big power."

"And, you agreed to do a job for a man with obvious power when you couldn't even see his face?" Meaghan shook her head in disbelief.

Eamon jutted out his chin, a defiant look on his small face. "Didn't need to see his face. I could see his money. Gold. None of that dodgy paper shite you humans like so much."

"Dodgy?" Meaghan glanced at Owen.

"Don't ask," Owen said. "Gold—it's a leprechaun thing. Modern finance is lost on these dopes."

"You're not like that," Meaghan said.

"Which is why I'm rich," Owen said, shaking his head, "and why they're still scrambling for gold. Idiots."

"It weren't only for the gold," Eamon said. "I did it for the cause."

"The cause?" Meaghan glanced at Owen.

He shook his head, a baffled look on his face.

"You know, stoppin'. . ." Eamon's voice dropped to a whisper, "the fair folk."

Meaghan glanced around the room. Everyone, including the monks, looked as confused as she was. "Stop them how?"

Eamon scratched his head. "Well, I don't know exactly, but he told me it would." He glanced around. "What? I'm doing good work here."

"He is an idiot," Dustin said. "Dude, what did you do?"

"I kept the archive locked all day. There was a spell, he said, on a warrior we need, and if the archive was locked, then the spell would have to be fiddled with to get it back open and the warrior would be set free." He beamed. "See? I'm helpin'."

"And just like that, Sparky's back in business." Terry slumped to the kitchen floor. "Shit."

CHAPTER TWENTY-SEVEN

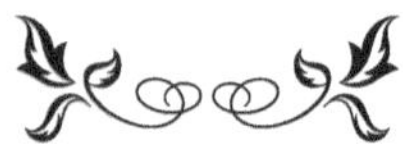

RUSS EVENTUALLY SNAPPED out of his awe of Terry and announced he was going back across the street to cook dinner and anybody hungry should follow him.

Natalie pointed at her shiny leather boots. "These are new. I'm not taking them out in this crap."

"I'm not carrying you," Russ said.

Steph pointed at Eamon. "What do we do with this?"

Todd, the monk with the glasses and shaved head, stepped up. "I'll take him back to the archive and turn him over to the brothers. Let them deal with him. Unless you guys want to talk to him some more."

"Nope," Meaghan said. She didn't need any further confirmation that Cooper was behind this. "Take him."

Dustin offered to head across the street and try to open a door to the archive in the Keeles' house. If he succeeded, they could take a shortcut.

Meaghan pulled on her coat to follow Dustin.

"Don't you want to stay out of the snow?" Natalie asked.

"You should see this place. It's like a medieval castle."

Meaghan felt a swoop in her stomach and realized the idea of venturing through a gateway into another realm felt about as appealing as going into a narrow cave.

Apparently, it showed on her face.

"You've got a magical gateway phobia now?" Natalie asked. "Need Owen to hypnotize you again?"

Part of their efforts to get into city hall during the Labor Day mess had involved a cramped underground tunnel. Owen had successfully treated Meaghan's claustrophobia, in the short term at least, with hypnosis.

But that had led to a flashback of the drug-induced psychic powers she'd gotten on her trip to Fahraya, powers she never would have had if she hadn't been attacked by a giant scorpion. She'd barely escaped with her life.

The second gateway she'd encountered led her to the stinky space squid.

Meaghan shook her head. "Every time I go near a damn gateway I get attacked by monsters." She felt her face redden. "And it's not a phobia. A phobia's an irrational fear." She stared at her feet. "Based on my experiences, my fear is totally rational."

Gee, a little more babbling and maybe you'll convince yourself.

"Is this what you need to tell me?" John moved to her side. "Is this what's been going on?"

I wish.

Her face got even redder. "No. That's . . . different."

Worse, you mean.

Shut up, Meaghan told herself. *I'll tell him tonight.*

"I'm going home." Meaghan stomped out to the front door, stepped into her boots, and pulled on her coat. She yanked open the front door, and the cold hit her like a wall. The snow was falling so fast she could barely see her house in the murky, fading twilight.

Dustin stepped to her side. "That's a lot of snow."

John was stepping into his boots. "I'll go with you. We'll flash the porch light when we get there so they know we made it."

"Me, too. This was my bright idea to begin with," Russ said as he pulled on his coat. "Let's go."

The four of them struggled across the street. The snow was knee-deep and blowing sideways. As they got closer to the Keeles' house, Meaghan saw drifts that extended almost to the second floor. The giant oak tree near the driveway was so laden with snow some of the branches touched the ground.

They clambered up the porch steps and into the house. Russ flipped the porch light on and off a few times. A corresponding flash came from the Donners' house.

"At least the power's still on," Meaghan said.

The house went dark.

"You had to say it," she heard Russ say. "You had to. Good job, sis."

"Shut up," Meaghan said.

Melanie appeared with a candle. "Welcome home. So much for a hot dinner."

Russ shrugged out of his coat on his way down the hall. "It's gas. I can still use the stovetop. We'll manage."

"Natalie's back," Meaghan said to Melanie. "Over at the Donners'. She's fine."

Melanie sighed. "That's a relief."

"We're trying to open up another gateway over here so she can cut back through the archive and not get her feet wet," Dustin said.

"Get on it," Meaghan said to Dustin. "Use the dining room."

He nodded and pulled a piece of chalk out of his jeans pocket.

"How's our prisoner?" Meaghan asked.

"Under guard, but quiet," Melanie said.

"And Sam?"

"Sleeping," Melanie said. "He's still getting his strength back from . . ." She glanced away.

"Melanie, I'm sorry I was so harsh with you earlier," Meaghan said. "Buzz told me what the stakes were back then. There were no good choices to make, only less bad ones. I get it now."

Melanie nodded. "Thank you for that, but Sam makes me wonder if we didn't pick an especially bad option." She sighed. "Let's get more candles lit. I gathered up everything I could find when the lights were still on in case this happened."

"How are we set for heat?" Meaghan asked her.

"The witches could help if they weren't using so much magic downstairs."

"It's a gas furnace?" John asked.

Meaghan nodded.

"There are ways. If I can't get it to work, maybe Terry can," John said.

"You're not going downstairs with that damn elf," Meaghan said. "No way. Let's get some light first and if Dustin can get that doorway open—"

"Done," Terry said, walking from the dining room. "Nice dry little shortcut now between our houses. You got a gas furnace?"

"Yeah," Meaghan said.

Terry nodded. "Then all you need is a way to power the fan. Let me grab some stuff from my house. I'll get you set up."

"I can help," John said.

"Not a chance," Terry said. "You need to stay away from the basement for now. But you can help me carry shit."

"Thank you," Meaghan said as Terry and John headed into the dining room.

"Now we don't have lights?" Natalie stomped out of the dining room. "This keeps getting better and better. I need to check in downstairs. I'm late for my shift."

"Where are the monks?"

"Luka's cluing them into the realities of Norse mythology."
Natalie shook her head. "Freaky stuff."

"Did you know—"

Natalie cut Meaghan off before she could finish her question. "No. Geez. I knew they'd had a checkered past, but the god thing I didn't know anything about." She shook her head. "Will you stop being so paranoid already?"

"Candles," Melanie said. "We have work to do."

"I'm not paranoid," Meaghan mumbled.

Melanie patted her arm. "You can be, dear. Occasionally."

Back in the kitchen, they sorted through the candles and flashlights Melanie had gathered. After a few minutes, a warm glow filled the kitchen. Whatever Russ was doing at the stove filled the kitchen with a delicious aroma.

Steph appeared holding a huge soup pot. "Russ, here's a pot of chili. I've got a gas stove, too, so I can help you with the cooking."

Russ peered into the pot, a suspicious frown on his face.

"The recipe you gave me a couple of weeks ago," Steph said. "I used grass-fed beef from the food co-op."

Satisfied, Russ nodded and took the pot from her hands.

Steph and Meaghan exchanged a glance and tried not to laugh. When she had the giggles under control, Meaghan asked, "Are the phones still working?"

"Let's find out," Melanie said.

Russ pulled out his phone. "No service."

"Mine's out, too," Melanie said.

"Terry broke mine with that lightning bolt," Meaghan said.

"The land line's out, too," Russ said.

They heard slow footsteps on the basement stairs and Lynette appeared.

"What are you still doing here?" Meaghan asked. "Who's down there now?"

"Gretchen and Natalie," Lynette said in a grim voice, her face haggard with fatigue. "The relief shift failed to show and nobody else is coming. We can't zap ourselves out and no new witches can get in." She pointed upwards. "Big barrier, like a dome."

"The elves?" Meaghan asked.

Lynette nodded. "Probably."

"We've got our own barrier?"

"Yeah," Lynette said. "For now."

"Why do they have to zap?" Russ asked. "Why not drive? The roads can't be that bad."

"Yeah, they can. Last we heard, it's so bad the governor's declared a snow emergency with a mandatory curfew. We called everyone we could before the phones went out. Those we could track down were too snowed in to move. Then the barrier appeared a little while ago and now we can't even make calls."

"Lynette, go up to my room and lie down, okay?" Russ said. "I'll bring up some supper in a little while.

Lynette nodded and headed upstairs.

"They're isolating us," Meaghan said. "No lights, no phone, and now no heat."

"Terry will get the furnace working," Russ said, a worshipful glow on his face.

"Not gonna happen." Terry loomed in the doorway, John right behind him, both with snow in their hair. As Terry stepped closer, Meaghan could see his face set in grim lines. "Somebody smashed up the generator in my garage."

"Magically?" Meaghan asked, feeling her anxiety grow.

No help is coming. It's all on me again.

"No, with a crowbar," Terry said. "Which means it wasn't an elf."

"Wizard?"

"Wouldn't have to be," Terry said. "Can't use magic on a crowbar. And whoever did it covered it back up neatly with the tarp. I haven't used that generator in a couple of months. It could have happened any time." He gave a small bitter laugh.

"Maybe they want me to use . . . you know." Slumping into a chair, he buried his head in his hands. "I want a drink."

"Good thing I'm here then," John said. "You have been sober this time for how long?"

"Sixty-two years, three months, and five days," Terry said.

He doesn't even have to think about it. She glanced at John, wondering if he could answer with the same unthinking ease. *I've been too afraid to ask.*

John smiled. "Oh. Then I can't help you. They don't make sobriety chips that big. I guess you have no choice then. What can I get you? Wasn't mead your drink?"

"Screw you, your majesty." Terry brushed his hair out of his eyes, a hint of smile on his face. "I'm getting schooled on this shit by the deposed king of the fairies who's got less than a year in the program?"

"So it seems," John said. "Can you use the lightning to start the furnace?"

"I'm . . . I can't . . ."

"So you say." John nodded.

"And if the wizards did this—"

"They have a reason, which we'll find out soon enough," Meaghan said. "Forget about the bigger picture for a second. Is there anything you can do to get the furnace on?'

"Not with that." He pointed his finger at Meaghan. "If I *zzzzt,* all it will do is destroy the furnace. It's huge heat and huge power, but in one concentrated place. Makes it useless for anything but frying people."

"And lighting your forge the last time you were sober for any length of time," Steph said. "Don't think I didn't know about that."

Terry glared at her.

Steph stared back, unimpressed, until Terry looked away.

"Can we go to the archive?" Russ asked. "If it gets too cold here?"

"Not anymore we can't." Dustin stood in the kitchen doorway. "The fair folk are crawling all over it. They've locked everybody in the wine cellar. They're threatening to burn the archive unless we give them Sam and . . ." He pointed at Terry. "You. They really want you."

CHAPTER TWENTY-EIGHT

"**B**URN IT DOWN?" Melanie asked, in a calm voice. "How do they propose to do that? The archive is heavily protected from fire. They can't merely light a match."

Dustin stepped closer to the table. In the dim light, Meaghan saw the panic on his face. He glanced around the room, breathing rapidly.

She rose from her seat and steered Dustin to her vacated chair. "Breathe through your nose before you start hyperventilating. Calm down, okay? We can deal with this."

Unless we can't. Meaghan shoved down her fear. Some comfort she'd be if she started hyperventilating, too. "Breathe."

Dustin took a few measured breaths, his eyes shut.

When he seemed calmer, Meaghan asked, "How are they going to burn the archive?"

"Dragon," Dustin squeaked. "They have a dragon."

Terry sighed and slumped even further in his chair. "Yeah, that would do it."

They have a dragon. Meaghan felt the denial rise up. A part of her mind shrieked that there was no such thing as dragons, but her legs knew better. She felt the room spin and would have fallen if John hadn't grabbed her.

"Now I gotta slay a dragon." Terry shook his head. "I'll have that mead now, Johnny."

Steph sat down next to him and took his hand. He pulled her close, their momentary animosity forgotten.

"No, you won't," John said. "How long do we have until this happens?"

"Dawn," Dustin said. "And he's not the one who has to slay the dragon." He glanced up at Meaghan. "You are."

Meaghan burst out laughing. She couldn't help herself. It was either that or start screaming. "Whose bright idea was that?"

"The prophecy," Dustin said. "There's a sword."

Terry raised an eyebrow. "A magic sword?"

"Well, yeah," Dustin said.

Terry shook his head. "Oh, yeah. This is gonna be great." He glanced at Meaghan. "You believe in prophecies?"

"No," Meaghan said in a squeaky voice, shaking her head. "And even if I did, any prophecy that says that I'm gonna kill a fire-breathing, goddamn flying dinosaur with a sword is flat-out wrong."

Dustin looked shocked. "But you've read it."

"No," Meaghan said. *Here's the anger.* "I haven't. What's the point? If it really is prophetic—which it isn't, because there's no such thing—then it's gonna happen anyway, right? Why do I need to know what it says?"

"Because your enemies do," Melanie said. "They'll act accordingly."

"Which means it's not a prophecy, it's a to-do list, and they'll read it to justify any damn thing they want to do, which means its predictive value is zero." Meaghan shook her head. "And there's like half a dozen versions of the damn thing, right? Which one should I worry about?"

"But it mentions you specifically," Dustin said, his voice rising. "It says you're gonna die."

"Yeah, well, news flash, everybody in this room will die, eventually, even Mr. and Mrs. Sparky here." Meaghan pointed at them. "Right?"

"We're getting older," Steph said. "So, yeah, eventually, I guess."

"So, I'll die. Wow. Big prediction. And it doesn't even mention me specifically, not by name." Meaghan folded her arms and glared at Dustin. "Plus it doesn't actually say anything about dying."

"It says they'll quench your vital spark." The panicked look returned to Dustin's face.

"That doesn't sound like fire." Meaghan rolled her eyes. "Quench sounds like water. The dragon's gonna pee on me?"

Terry started laughing, a low rumble that grew louder. Within moments, he was stamping his foot and doubled over in his chair as he roared with laughter.

"It wasn't that funny," Meaghan said.

"No, no." Terry wiped his eyes with his hand. "I wasn't laughing at that. There's a way to read that phrase that has nothing to do with death. When you make something out of iron or steel, like a blade, you heat it to make it soft enough to work with, but then once the basic shape is formed you quench it—you dunk it—in something like water or oil to cool it down fast. To harden the steel and make it strong."

"Is that the same as tempering?" Russ asked from over at the stove. "Like tempered steel knives?"

Meaghan watched her brother work. John was right. Food was Russ's magic and in his kitchen, nothing—not even talk of dragons and his sister's predicted death—flustered him.

"Tempering's the next stage in the process," Terry said. "Quenching makes the blade hard, but brittle. You temper it by heating it back up, at lower temperatures, to soften it a bit. The goal is to find the perfect balance between strength and flexibility. You want to make it flexible enough not to snap but strong enough not to bend."

"Then they've already quenched you, Meg," Russ said. "When you went to Fahraya. We're in the tempering phase, I think."

Terry smiled. "Sounds a little less scary now, doesn't it?"

Meaghan smiled back, trying to hide her panic. *Dragon. They have a dragon.*

No, they say they have a dragon, Meaghan told herself. *Not the same thing.*

"How do we know they aren't bluffing about the dragon?" she asked.

"I saw it," Dustin said in a shaky voice. "It's big."

"How big?" Meaghan asked.

"Real big," Dustin said. "You know, like in the movies."

"How do you know it wasn't an elf pretending to be a dragon? To screw with your head?"

"The fire was real," Dustin said. "The dragon torched the abbot's office. One breath in and then kaboom. You really think if elves could breathe fire, they wouldn't want to take the credit for it instead of pretending a dragon did it?"

Meaghan nodded. *Shit. Elves I can deal with. Dragons, no.* "Good point."

"What do we do about it?" Melanie looked at Meaghan. "Any ideas?"

Oh, loads, Mel, because I have so much experience in this area. "Kill it?"

"How?" Melanie asked.

How the fuck should I know?

Meaghan looked at Terry. "Would a lightning strike do it?"

Terry sighed. "Yeah, probably. Assuming I can aim it, which is not exactly a sure bet."

Steph rubbed her hand along his arm in a comforting gesture.

"You were pretty precise with it when you were using it to make steel."

"Yeah," Terry said, "but that was different."

"You were sober," Steph said. "Kind of like you are now."

Terry shook his head. "Not even close. That was the bare-knuckled version of sobriety."

"Which means you should be better now," John said.

Terry gave him a sideways look. "You honestly listen to all my bullshit, don't you?"

"I do. It's wise bullshit."

Terry shook his head.

Focus. The thought of having to fight a dragon kept pushing everything else out of her head. *What are they really up to? Why all the show? Beyond their usual love of drama?*

"Dustin, do the fair folk want us to release their guy in the basement?" Meaghan asked.

He stared at her, a puzzled look on his face. "They didn't ask about him."

"Which means either they don't give a shit about him or they want him here for some reason." Meaghan looked at Terry. "Which one do you think?"

"If he's as much a big shot as I suspect, he's right where they want him to be."

"Reconnaissance?"

Terry chewed on his lip a moment and stared into space. "That, yeah, but more to cause trouble. Unbalance us."

"It also keeps the witches busy," Russ said as he stirred something on the stove.

"Good point." Meaghan looked back at Terry and was about to say more, but thought better of it. She held up her index finger and grabbed Russ's grocery list notebook and a pen. *Time for that con,* she wrote and handed it to Terry.

He grinned and nodded. "Honey," he said in a slightly louder voice than usual. "Let's go back across the street. I need to get my head clear if I have to fight a dragon." He took the pen from Meaghan and wrote, *You and John come, too.* "You got your boots on, hon? No magical short cut this time."

"Yeah," Steph said. "Can I borrow a coat?"

"Take mine," Russ said. "See you later." He stepped over to the table, read Meaghan's note to Terry, then hugged her. "Be careful," he whispered in her ear. "I'll keep everyone calm over here."

Meaghan nodded, and she and John followed Terry and Steph back out into the storm.

The wind had picked up and the snow stung as it hit her exposed face. Twilight had given way to darkness. With the power out, the night was a snowy blur, visibility reduced to no more than a couple of feet in front of them.

"Let me try something." Terry pulled off his glove and held up his hand. Eyes shut, concentrating, he rubbed his fingers together.

The sky flashed with lightning, but all it did was light up the snowy haze and it was gone too quickly to let them get their bearings. "Hang on." He pulled off his other glove and took several deep breaths, his face smoothing into a blank.

A spark flashed between the fingers of Terry's upraised hand. It outlined him for a moment in blue light and then streaked across the street to a snowy mound. The snow exploded into steam and, for another moment, blue light outlined every leaf of the now-exposed holly shrub.

"Sweet." Terry smiled, obviously pleased with himself. "I've never had that kind of control before."

"Your hands are gonna freeze," Steph said. "Come on. Before we get lost."

The lightning left the edges of the leaves still smoldering. It wasn't much light, but enough to guide them to the front porch.

Terry pushed open the door. Meaghan heard him stumble and crash to the floor, then she felt something sharp at her throat.

"Not one more step," a voice hissed in her ear.

"Luka, that's Meaghan." Owen flipped on a flash light. "She's the only one who could walk through your spell." He shined the light in her face. "See?"

The blade was pulled from her throat. Luka stood next to her, a serrated bread knife in his hand. "Sorry. When the archive door slammed shut, we went into defensive mode."

"Ankle snare?" Terry was still on the floor along with Steph and John.

"I'm no wizard," Luka said, holding his hand out to Steph. "It's the best I could do on short notice."

"What happened?" Owen asked.

"Elves in the archive," Terry said.

"With a dragon," Steph added.

"That can't be good." Luka helped John to his feet. "What do they want?"

"Me," Terry said. "And the elf that escaped. The one without the magic."

"But not their friend in the basement." Meaghan pulled off her coat and then put it back on. It was already getting cold in the dark house. "We have until dawn to give them up, or they say they'll burn the archive."

Owen sucked in a breath through his teeth. "They wouldn't."

"Yeah, they would," Terry says. "Out of spite. They don't give a shit about knowledge."

"We need a plan," Meaghan said. "Does the archive have any defenses?"

Luka shook his head. "Not from them now they're inside. But they could pick us off one by one if we tried to attack."

I can't believe I'm about to suggest this. "Then we need to get the dragon over here, where we've got a shot at killing it, and it can't burn the archive. Make them think they'll have the advantage if they attack us directly instead of waiting for us to come to them."

"And we can lure them with the elf in the basement." Luka nodded. "Feed him a narrative that will make them change their plan."

"Exactly. We con them," Meaghan said.

Luka smiled. "Looks like we're all back in business."

CHAPTER TWENTY-NINE

THEY HEARD THE rumbling before they saw the lights. Through the window, they watched the flashing red and white lights materialize into one of the city's giant orange snowplows. Behind it, traveling in the tunnel left by the giant plow blade, was Luka's brand new pickup truck.

"Elves can't drive, can they?" Meaghan asked as the trucks stopped in front of her house.

"Nope," Terry said.

"Then Buzz is back and he's brought reinforcements," Meaghan said.

The passenger door of the snowplow cab opened and a figure stepped down. Meaghan couldn't tell who it was under the heavy parka. Another figure climbed out, then the driver emerged. The three of them helped a fourth person climb awkwardly from the cab.

The huge belly was obvious even through heavy winter clothing.

"Oh, shit," Meaghan said. "Kady. I'd better get over there. You guys stay here and start working on the con, okay?"

"I'm going with you," John said. "Don't argue."

"Didn't you say Buzz is part troll?" Owen asked.

"Buzz is part troll?" Luka grinned. "I thought he might be. Send him over, will you? He can help us."

Meaghan and John struggled back across the street, the lights on the plow guiding them.

Kady stood in the swirling snow, smiling. "I'm arriving earlier than expected. I need to talk with you before I get here." Kady's smile turned into a scowl. "Will you let me tell her first before you start yammering at her?"

"Kady, what the hell—"

Jeff, Kady's boyfriend, standing behind her, began shaking his head and waving his hands.

"Let's get inside and I'll tell you all about it," Kady said. "Brian, help Jeff haul us to the door."

Brian Cressley, Kady's older brother, stepped to her side. "Her water broke about three hours ago," he said to Meaghan. "We tried to take her to the clinic, but she insisted we had to come here."

"The clinic?"

The fourth occupant of the snowplow stepped forward. "Patrice is running an emergency shelter there. The doc lives in Williamsport and the other nurse lives out in the boonies."

Marnie. Meaghan felt her face grow hot with shame. Marnie, who had survived so much more than Meaghan.

"Emergency shelter?" Meaghan asked.

"It's bad out there," Marnie said. "The roads are a mess. No power. People are scared." She pointed at the sky. "This isn't normal. Even for Eldrich."

"Magic?" Meaghan hadn't let herself consider that prospect before this moment.

Marnie nodded. "I think."

"Where did you guys get the snowplow?" Meaghan asked. "Aren't they all in use right now?"

"This one was in my shop," Jeff said. "I did some quick-and-dirty repairs to get it running and here we are."

"They pulled all the plows off the road to escort emergency vehicles, but even those aren't moving now," Brian said.

"You're not on duty?"

Brian was an Eldrich cop and one of Meaghan's more useful companions on Labor Day. It was Brian's skill with a sniper rifle that had saved Meaghan from the balding wizard of her nightmares. "Got an emergency right here," Brian said. "My cruiser is useless in this shit and my radio is fried along with the phone. No calls coming in or going out."

Meaghan had been so focused on Kady, she'd forgotten about the occupants of Luka's trucks. She turned and saw three enormous figures trudging toward the Donners' house.

"Is that Buzz and the Millers?"

"Yeah." Brian turned to Marnie. "You okay if I go with Buzz? I don't want to be around . . . you know."

Marnie smiled at him. "Go. I'll see you in a bit."

John nodded. "I'll go with them. I think I can help more over there."

Meaghan nodded, relieved to have John away from the elf in the basement. She kissed him and then turned her attention back to Marnie. "What's going on with Kady?"

Marnie smiled. "She better tell you. It's not bad, but it's kind of weird."

I'm plotting to scam malevolent elves with the help of a couple of would-be Norse gods so I can get the chance to fight a dragon. How much weirder can it get?

Meaghan shook her head and followed Marnie. "Great. Because we don't have enough weird to go around already."

Gretchen was waiting in the doorway. "Little bastard is showing up early, isn't he?"

"Hey," Jeff said with a relieved smile. "That's my kid you're talking about."

"So, marry the girl and I'll stop calling him that."

"Gretchen," Kady said with a smile. "Good to see you again."

"Is that you or him?" Gretchen said.

"Him," Kady said. "And I wish he'd shut up until I can break the news to Meaghan."

"Sorry," Kady said. "But I won't be this version of me for much longer, and I've been away for a while."

"Are you gonna mouth off like this once you're born?" Kady asked.

"Probably," Kady said. "Once I learn how to talk again."

It can get weirder. Huh. "Would somebody please tell me what's going on?"

"Meg, sweetheart," Kady said, "let Kady and me get settled upstairs, and then we can answer your questions."

I heard Dad's voice when I grabbed her arm. The last time Meaghan had seen him, in the final moments before Fahraya had been destroyed, Matthew had told her that he'd had to call in some big favors and wouldn't be able to see her for a while.

They're naming the baby Matthew . . .

The denial tried to rise in her mind, but she ignored it. What she now suspected wasn't any more improbable than the dragon. "Dad?" she said in shaky voice. "Is that you?"

"I told you she'd figure it out," Kady said, a look of pride on her face.

"Shut up," Kady said as the pride morphed into a scowl. "I can't wait until you're just my baby again." She glanced over at Meaghan. "He started talking to me in my head a month or so back. I thought I was going nuts, so I didn't tell anybody but Gretchen. Then my water breaks and now he's talking out loud. With my voice."

Meaghan glanced around the crowded hallway. Her knees felt wobbly again. She leaned against the wall to steady herself. *I can't believe I'm about to say this.*

"Reincarnation? That's a thing?"

Gretchen shrugged. "Reincarnation, yeah. You run into kids all the time who know stuff they shouldn't, and who talk about when they were big. But I've never run into one who started talking about it while the bun was still in the oven."

"Think of me as a precocious child," Kady said.

"Are you gonna remember all this shit after you're born?" Kady asked.

"Probably not," Kady said. "At least I won't be able to talk about it."

"Thank God. Guys, I need to lie down before I fall down. Find me a bed."

"Is my room still available?"

They led her up to Matthew's old bedroom. Meaghan and Russ hadn't really done anything with it since Matthew's death. Meaghan grabbed some clean sheets from the hall closet and made up the bed.

"Sorry it's so cold in here," Meaghan said as she helped Kady onto the bed.

"I'm sweating like a pig," Kady said. "It feels good." She yelped. "Oh, shit. Jeff, honey, another contraction. Start timing, okay?"

Jeff, his face chalky in the dim candlelight, nodded, and pulled out his phone. "At least the timer still works."

Meaghan took him by the arm and led him out into the hall-way. His brown hair was sticking up in multiple directions from the ski cap he'd been wearing, and Meaghan was struck by how young he looked. They were both young, she reminded herself.

"How are you doing with this?" she asked him.

He looked at her, fear all over his face. "Which part? My girl having our baby a month early in your house or my son being your father?"

As the words came out his mouth, Meaghan began to laugh, the same nearly hysterical laughter that had been popping out of her since morning.

He smiled and began to laugh himself, quickly losing control. "Your dad is my kid," he choked through the laughter. "Doesn't that make me your grandpa?"

"Oh, shit. I don't know." She squeezed his arm. "Of all the people who could be Matthew's parents, I'm glad it's you guys."

His laughter evaporated. "Are we gonna be okay? There's big magic—bad magic— flying around, isn't there?"

Meaghan nodded. "Yeah."

"Then I'm glad we're here. Promise me you'll keep them safe."

Meaghan's heart sank. *I'm not your savior, kid. I'm barely keeping it together myself.*

"I promise," she said, hoping like hell it was a promise she could keep.

Gretchen stepped out of the bedroom. "The baby's early, but he's a good size, and he and Mom are healthy. Don't worry, kid. I've helped deliver a lot of babies over the years. Nature does most of the work. Would you do me a favor and ask Russ to make some coffee?"

"Kady can't drink coffee right now," Jeff said.

"It's not gonna make any difference at this point, hon," Gretchen said. "Kady and I might have a long night ahead of us. We need to stay awake."

"Hot water—do you need hot water?" Jeff stared at her, eyes wide. The fear was starting to set back in.

"Only in the movies." Gretchen patted his arm. "Go find Russ."

Jeff nodded and galloped down the stairs.

Gretchen let out a breath. "That'll keep him out of the way for a few minutes. Russ will have to make the coffee the old-fashioned way."

"Who's downstairs with the elf?"

"Lynette went back downstairs. Don't worry. Natalie being back perked her right up. I know more about babies so we agreed I should be up here right now."

"Is Kady okay?" Meaghan didn't like the look on Gretchen's face.

"She's young and as far as we know the baby is healthy, but he's getting here early and stuff can go wrong."

"But, you're a midwife, right?"

Gretchen shook her head. "No, I'm not. I said that to make Jeff feel better. I've pushed out three of my own and helped deliver a couple more. I know the basics, but if things goes sideways—"

"Then we'll use the snowplow to get her to the clinic," Meaghan said. "Don't worry."

Gretchen gave her a small forced smile. "You better get back in there. She—*they*—want to talk to you. I'll go help Russ with that coffee and distract Jeff for as long as I can."

Meaghan nodded.

It was time to talk to her father.

CHAPTER THIRTY

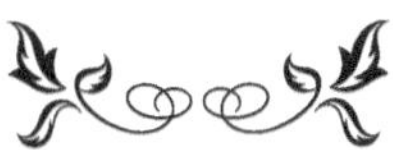

KADY SMILED AS Meaghan walked through the door. "There you are." She patted the bed. "Have a seat."

"Hey, this isn't weird. Not at all." Meaghan sat on the edge of bed. "Who am I speaking with?"

Kady laughed loudly. "I'm not exactly myself today."

"That doesn't answer the question."

Kady sighed, looking annoyed. "As if labor isn't bad enough, now I'm channeling the dead."

"I'm not dead," Kady replied. "Not anymore."

"Whatever," Kady said. "You better be a quiet baby after putting me through this. I'm checking out for a few minutes. Have a nice chat with your daughter."

She smiled at Meaghan. "Poor kid. I'm sure this isn't what she was expecting childbirth to be like. I'm arriving early, but it couldn't be helped. I need to talk to you and this is my only chance. Once I'm born, I won't be the same person. I won't be your father anymore."

Maybe I should shut my eyes. Then at least he'd only sound like Kady. "Which is a relief, I have to say." Meaghan smiled. "I offered to babysit and I'm not sure I could manage it if I knew it was still you in there."

Kady—*Matthew*, Meaghan corrected herself—leaned back against the pillow. "I guess you know about Natalie."

Meaghan nodded. "For a while now."

"I never meant for it to happen. Vivian and I were both lonely and . . . I loved your mother. I hope you know that."

Meaghan raised her hand. "It's okay. I'm not upset."

Matthew raised Kady's eyebrow.

"Fine, I was pissed off when I first found out, furious even, but . . ." Meaghan said. She shrugged. "Mom left you. It was stupid of me to think you'd spend the rest of your life alone."

"Natalie didn't replace you, you know that."

Natalie, you blabbermouth. "She told Kady?"

"I had to pry it out of her in case you were wondering."

"Was that you or Kady talking?"

"Kady." Matthew said. "Who's supposed to be napping."

"I'm not trying to eavesdrop, but you're using my vocal cords," Kady said. "How am I supposed to nap like this?"

"Sorry," Meaghan and—she supposed—Matthew said at the same time.

Meaghan added, "Kady, seriously, I need you to shut up. It's too weird listening to the both of you at the same time."

"Unbelievable. Shutting up now." Kady closed her eyes.

When they reopened, Meaghan knew Matthew was looking back at her.

"You know about the Donners?" Matthew asked. "And Luka Volkhov?"

Meaghan nodded. "I do now. Terry's lightning is back."

Matthew stared at Meaghan in shock. "Can he control it?"

"Too soon to tell, but Steph and Luka think he could now that he's sober."

"When did this happen?"

"This afternoon. We think Cooper, the wizard who leads the Order, made it happen."

Matthew's eyes narrowed. "The Order's involved? What makes you think that?"

"Eamon O'Malley. The leprechaun. He was masquerading as a monk. Said he was working for a wizard who told him a great warrior was under a spell and Eamon could help release him by locking up the archive for a few hours."

"When Dustin couldn't get in this afternoon." Matthew nodded.

"Luka tweaked the dampening magic around Terry to make it stop interfering with Dustin's hex bag and down came the lightning."

"How much?"

"Big bolt," Meaghan said. "If Terry and Luka hadn't realized what was happening, we could have been fried."

"He couldn't control it?"

"No, but he had enough time to shove us out of the way. And he did some nifty stuff right before you got here tonight, with a holly bush in his front yard. Minimal damage and what appeared to be precise control. He seemed pretty excited about it."

Matthew frowned. "How's his sobriety holding up?"

"John's with him and it seems to be helping."

"Good. Let's hope they keep reinforcing good behavior in each other." Matthew nodded. "Last thing we need right now is either of them drinking."

"The elf in the basement took a run at John this morning," Meaghan said. "Made him feel his wings and spun a lie about the missing Fahrayans still being alive."

"*What?* How did—" Kady threw back her head and howled.

"Kady?"

"Who the hell else would it be?" she shouted. "I'm the one having this goddamn baby, who's grounded for the rest of his life if he doesn't give me my body back."

Jeff ran into the room, a panicked look on his face.

"Another contraction," Kady said. "Time it."

Jeff punched the new time into his phone, then rushed to the bed. He pushed the hair from Kady's face. "What do you need? What can I do?"

"I need to get this goddamn baby out of me." She glared at him. "What do you think I need?"

Jeff gave Meaghan another panicked look. "We need Gretchen."

So much for talking to Dad. Meaghan nodded and headed for the door.

Gretchen got there first. "Here's your coffee, kiddo. Another contraction?"

Kady took a deep breath and visibly calmed at the sound of Gretchen's voice. "Yeah. A really big one."

"Hah." Gretchen handed her a mug. "Not even close, sweetie." She took Jeff by the hand. "She being mean? That's gonna get worse, too. When she starts threatening to cut your pecker off, that's when you know the baby's close."

"Give me something," Kady said, bursting into tears. "Magic, drugs, I don't care."

"No," Matthew said. "You agreed to let me talk to my daughter."

Kady flashed Meaghan a venomous look.

"I'm scared, too," Matthew said, "but I'm on my way and I need you to let me talk to Meg. I'll be your baby again soon, I promise. You can do this."

"Jeff, honey," Kady said. "I'm sorry. I don't want to cut your pecker off."

"Yet," Gretchen said.

"Your bedside manner sucks," Meaghan said with a scowl. "Stop it. Dad, we need to give them a minute." She gave Gretchen a stern look. "Gretchen and I are going to the kitchen for more coffee. Now."

Gretchen rolled her eyes and followed Meaghan out of the room.

But Meaghan never made it the kitchen. Marnie was sitting in the living room.

"You girls need to talk," Gretchen said as she gave Meaghan a gentle shove toward the sofa. "I'll be in the kitchen."

Meaghan felt the dread pool in her gut.

The bitch needs to learn her place.

Marnie gave Meaghan an appraising look. "They hurt you, too. Tell me what happened."

"What?" Meaghan stared at Marnie in shock. *How does she know?"*

"I can read it on your face and in my bones," Marnie said, her voice calm and measured. "When they took my magic, something else woke up. You know what I'm talking about. It happened to you in Fahraya." She patted the sofa. "Sit with me."

On legs that felt like wood, Meaghan tottered to the sofa. She looked at Marnie, really looked, for the first time in months. Marnie's hair had grown back, almost to the length it had been when the Order had brutally scraped it from her scalp with a knife. No longer coal black, it was a warm brown, the sharp bob replaced by softer layers.

"Where's Brian?" Meaghan asked.

"Across the street with John. Don't change the subject."

"You don't look fragile anymore," Meaghan said in a small voice.

Marnie smiled. "Because I'm not."

Meaghan sat next to her, unsure what to say.

"But you do," Marnie said. "Look fragile, I mean. If you hold it in, it festers and gets bigger. You having bad dreams?"

Meaghan, trying to hold back her tears, nodded. In a whisper, she asked, "Can you help me?"

"You mean like what Jhoro did for me?"

Immediately following Marnie's escape from the Order, Jhoro had used his psychic abilities, his shamanic thing, to make what she'd suffered less immediate. According to Marnie, it had given her the mental clarity to move on and not remain mired in trauma.

Meaghan nodded, the tears now escaping and running down her cheeks.

Marnie took her hand. "Not that way, and he didn't fix me, he just gave me enough distance to keep breathing. There's a therapist here in town who helps me. You should call her."

"They didn't . . . it didn't." Meaghan pulled her hand away and got to her feet. "Nothing happened. I'm being an idiot over something that didn't happen."

"They took my power," Marnie said. "The physical pain from what they did was bad, but the worst part was being so helpless, feeling so weak. They took my power, all of it, not only the magic. I'd never felt that helpless before. Never. I always thought I could defend myself, but I couldn't. There was—"

"Nothing I could do," Meaghan said. "Nothing."

Marnie nodded. "And that's what haunts you, isn't it? That was the real assault. So, yeah, something did happen." Marnie slipped a business card into Meaghan's shaking hand. "Call her."

Meaghan nodded, but slipped the card into her pocket without looking at it. "I have to figure out how to kill a dragon first."

Marnie smiled. "As excuses go, that's not a bad one. But I'm not going to drop this. Stop letting them hurt you. Take your power back."

Meaghan nodded again, and then fled to the kitchen.

Look on the bright side. If the dragon kills you, she told herself, *you won't have to call the therapist.*

CHAPTER THIRTY-ONE

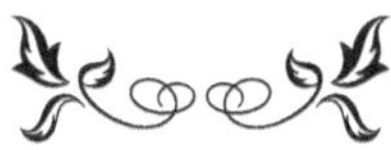

MEAGHAN POURED HERSELF a cup of coffee and stared at Russ. "You need to come upstairs with me and talk to Dad."

Russ frowned. "That's Kady upstairs."

"Yeah, and she's channeling Dad."

"Did he ask for me?" Russ refused to meet Meaghan's eye. In a stiff voice, he said, "Seems like you're the favorite kid these days."

Wow. Is that what I sound like?

"Don't be like that." She took a deep breath. "Don't be me. He's already got one peevish ungrateful child. You're the good one, remember?" *Here I go again, talking crazy shit.* "And he's about to be born. Which has to suck, when you think about it. Cut him some slack, please?"

Russ sighed. "You asking me that may be even more surreal than him talking from Kady's womb." He threw down the dishtowel he was holding. "Fine. Let's get this over with."

"You're seriously weirded out by this, aren't you?"

"Well, yeah," Russ said, following her upstairs. "I watched him die. I picked out the suit he was buried in. You're the one who's had all the post-life contact."

"Technically, it's now pre-life contact," Meaghan said, as they stood outside the closed bedroom door.

Russ gave her a sour look. "Now you're an expert on reincarnation?"

Meaghan glared back. "Will you stopping acting like—"

"You?"

Meaghan rolled her eyes. "Yeah." She knocked on the door. "Kady?" she called. "Jeff? It's Meaghan and Russ. Can we come in?"

Jeff opened the door. His eyes were red and shiny, but he was smiling. "It's good. We're good. Come talk to your dad."

"Before he's your son?" Russ asked.

Jeff nodded. "We got a little time, I think. The contractions are still far apart and she still likes me so . . . is that chili still on the stove?"

Russ nodded. "Chicken noodle, too."

"You mind me poking around and making her some supper?"

"I thought women in labor aren't supposed to eat," Russ said.

Jeff shook his head. "In childbirth class they said it was fine."

"You're the expert, I guess. Have at it," Russ said. "There's bread in the pantry and ham in the fridge if you want to make a sandwich."

Jeff headed downstairs, and Meaghan and Russ entered the bedroom.

Kady was curled on her side. When she saw Russ, she smiled. "Hey, kiddo. I'm sorry I didn't check in with you when I got here. There was a lot going on."

Russ stared at Kady, his mouth open. In a choked voice, he said, "Dad, is that really you in there?"

Kady nodded. "Sure is. Not for long though."

Russ burst into tears.

Kady patted the edge of the bed. "Russ, don't. It's okay. Get over here."

"That's Kady," Meaghan said. "She speaks a little faster."

"Sorry I got so bitchy," Kady said.

Meaghan shook her head. "No apology needed. You're doing great."

"I'm not going to be able to help you move into the new office," Kady said.

"We'll figure it out," Meaghan said. "Let us talk to Dad, okay?"

Kady nodded. "Shutting up now."

Meaghan prodded Russ in the back. "Sit down."

Kady, now Matthew, sighed. "She's a real trouper. Give her a raise when this is all over, okay?"

"I'll do what I can." Meaghan sat on the other side of the bed. "What do you need to tell us?"

"The fair folk . . . they have a—"

"Dragon," Meaghan said. "Yeah, we already know about that."

Kady—*Matthew*, Meaghan corrected herself again—looked surprised. "You know about the prophecy?"

Meaghan snorted.

"She doesn't believe in it," Russ said.

"Good." Matthew nodded. "Have you read it?"

Meaghan scowled. "Hell, no."

"Even better. All it would do is make you second-guess yourself."

"They're telling me it says I'm supposed to kill the dragon." She felt her anxiety begin to climb.

"With a magic sword," Russ added.

Matthew shook Kady's head. "Has Terry filled you in on those?"

"Yeah," Meaghan said. "Total bullshit, he says."

"The prophecy talks about a special blade that will slay the beast," Matthew said. "Which may or may not be this dragon."

Meaghan rolled her eyes. "Typical."

"That's my girl. Skeptical even in the face of magic."

Meaghan smiled. "You can sprinkle bullshit with fairy dust, but it's still bullshit."

Russ, who was holding Kady's hand, let out a watery laugh. The tears had slowed, but he still looked overwhelmed.

Matthew laughed with him a moment, then grew serious. "The prophecy may be nonsense, but the dragon is very real. And magic won't kill it. You have to take its head off and you need iron or steel to get through its hide."

"Like a sword?" Meaghan felt her anxiety crank up another notch.

"What about Terry's lightning?" Russ asked. "Won't that work?"

Matthew shrugged. "Maybe, provided he can control it and call it at will. But he'd need a precise strike to sever the head. A blade up close would work better although that has its own set of challenges."

"Like getting barbecued," Meaghan said. "I'm not impervious to fire, am I?"

"No. But you are immune to being stunned."

"Stunned?"

"A dragon exudes a powerful magical field, sort of like magical pheromones, that makes prey docile. But, provided you can avoid the flame, you can get up close to it."

"Whoa, wait a minute." Meaghan raised her hand. "Back up to the stunning thing." The anxiety kicked up yet another notch. "You're saying I'm the only one who get can near the damn thing and still put up a fight? If Terry can't take it out from a distance, it has to be me?"

"I'm afraid so," Matthew said. "The trolls can help you up to a certain point, the Millers more than Buzz. They have more troll blood. But even they won't be able to resist the spell."

"What about the witches?" Her voice sounded thin and breathy in her ears. "What about Natalie?"

Matthew sighed. "They can't help you at all. They'll be out cold. Something about their magical skill makes them even more susceptible. Dragon sleep, they call it, and it only affects human witches and wizards."

"Hang on a sec." Meaghan hopped off the bed. She grabbed the trashcan Gretchen had set next to the bed and vomited.

They really expect me to kill a fucking dragon. Me. Killing a dragon.

She wiped her mouth with the back of her hand. "Russ, would you take this to the bathroom and dump it out for me? I need to talk to Dad alone for a bit."

Russ rolled his eyes, grabbed the can without a word, and stomped from the room.

Meaghan shut the door behind him and sat at the foot of the bed. "I don't think I can do this."

"I don't see that you have any choice," Matthew said in a grim voice.

For a moment, Meaghan saw a flash of horrified concern she knew was Kady, then Matthew reasserted himself. "That's why I had to talk to you now," he said. "Why Kady's in labor early. This was the only window I had."

"Do the others know about this? They're all assuming Terry will do it."

Matthew shook his head. "Nobody knows about it. If you go under the stunning effect and somehow survive, all you remember is being frozen with fear. But very few people have ever survived a dragon attack."

"How come the fair folk aren't stunned?"

"They're less affected by it for some reason. Enough that they can feel it happen to themselves and take countermeasures."

"Couldn't we do that? Amulets or something?"

"Nobody knows the magic required. The fair folk guard it carefully, as you can imagine."

"I could tell people if I see it happening to them."

Matthew shook his head. "Humans can't feel it happen, and by the time you noticed someone acting oddly it would be late. The best you can do is keep them out of the way."

Meaghan slumped back on the bed, and ran her shaking hands through her hair. "Terry can't even help me then."

"That's where we've gotten some luck. If the lightning really is back and he can control it, then he can attack from far enough away not to be affected."

"Cooper—if he made this happen, made the lightning come back—he's helping us?"

"It appears so."

"Eamon O'Malley said the wizard told him he was helping free a powerful warrior who could help defeat the elves." Meaghan shook her head. "But I can't believe Cooper's doing this to be benevolent, to help us. If he wants Terry back in the game, it has to be for his benefit."

"The enemy of my enemy is my friend . . ." Matthew stared at the ceiling lost in thought.

"I've always thought that's a profoundly stupid concept," Meaghan said. "That's not a friend. That's a temporary ally ready to bite you in the ass as soon as their needs are met."

"I agree with you, but at the moment—"

Meaghan sighed. "We need all the help we can get. But if he's helping anybody, it's those things he's tried to free back in September."

The door opened and Russ returned with the clean trashcan and a mug. "Here's some herb tea. Settle your stomach a little. I hope you aren't getting sick. That's all we need."

"No, that was a case of gut-twisting terror. From the dragon."

"We're all here to help. I'm sure Natalie has a spell—"

"No, Russ, she doesn't." Meaghan's voice raised an octave. "Remember? What Dad said about the witches? Right before I puked?" She glanced at Matthew for confirmation.

Russ looked at the both of them, confusion on his face. "What are you talking about?"

Matthew shook his head. "Russ, son, would you be so kind as to get me a cup of that tea as well? It smells great and Kady could use it right about now."

Russ smiled. "Sure, Dad. Whatever you want." He gave Meaghan a sour look on his way out the door. "I'll rustle up some Valium for you."

Matthew looked grim. "So it's true. I'd hoped that part was merely myth."

"What part?"

"The ultimate camouflage," Matthew said. "Not only are most humans unaware of being stunned when it happens, they can't retain any knowledge the power even exists. Even Kady won't remember it and I'm using her voice to tell you."

Meaghan stared at her father in disbelief. "How the hell does that work? What if we call it something besides a dragon?"

"The idea of the dragon is enough," Matthew said. "Nobody knows why. It's why they're so dangerous."

"Only humans are affected?"

"No, every species, to a certain degree, depending on how susceptible they are to magic," Matthew said. "Which means the fair folk must be truly desperate, because they won't win any friends with this maneuver."

"Shit. So I can't even explain to everybody why I'm the only one who can do this." Meaghan took a few deep breaths, willing herself not to vomit again. "I hate magic. I really hate it."

Chapter Thirty-Two

B Y THE TIME Russ got back with Kady's tea, Meaghan had calmed down a bit. As terrifying as it was to contemplate a dragon, at least now she didn't have to worry about how she would be involved. It was now a matter of strategy, tactics, and tools. And keeping everybody else safe.

And she was kind of glad Russ couldn't remember what Matthew had said about the witches not being able to help. At least then he couldn't give her the same horrified look of pity she'd gotten from Kady.

That's all I need—people feeling sorry for me.

Now that she really understood what she was facing, Meaghan could fall back into her lifelong habit of being practical in the face of danger. Yes, it was a dragon. Yes, it could breathe fire and fly. But, its magic didn't work on her and she could kill it by chopping its head off.

The question was how.

"Killing a dragon with a sword is about as likely as killing a grizzly bear with a Swiss army knife," Matthew was saying. "A so-called magic sword is even worse—"

"Because it's made of crappy steel," Meaghan finished. "Yeah. Terry and Luka gave me the crash course on mystical metallurgy."

"Since you don't believe in prophecy," Matthew continued, "and you understand the uselessness of magic swords in general, you're free to think creatively. Anything can be a weapon if you're sufficiently motivated."

"Like a saucepan," Russ said.

Matthew smiled. "Like a saucepan."

"Or the Mangler," Meaghan said.

At Matthew's blank look, she added, "You know, that big stapler in the office, the one for court filings and huge stuff? That always jammed?"

"Must have been after my time," Matthew said.

"That was the stapler I chucked at the stinky space squid."

"I did hear about the stapler. As for the . . ." He hesitated.

He's scared. "The stinky space squid," Meaghan prompted. "I'm not glorifying them with names like 'the terror that sleeps' or 'the ancient evil.' What are they?"

"One monster at a time, honey," Matthew said, avoiding her gaze. "You have a dragon to worry about."

"A dragon Cooper wants to help us fight, not because he's suddenly developed a conscience, but because it suits his ends, whatever those may be. Provided we all get through this, those things are gonna be back and I don't want to be surprised next time. What are they?"

Matthew stared at nothing for a long moment. "They're ancient. And dangerous. But what we know about them is mostly myth. You ever read any Lovecraft?"

"Owen asked me that, too. I tried once in college, but I hated it. Not my thing."

Matthew smiled. "Which doesn't surprise me a bit. Russ, what about you?"

Russ shrugged. "Yeah, I know about his stuff. Dread Cthulhu and all that. Kind of sounds like these things."

Matthew nodded. "There are certain similarities between what Lovecraft wrote and what little information exists about them. Meg, did Owen tell you about Alastair Eldrich?"

"The guy responsible for the stupid prophecy, who went nuts and torched himself. Yeah," Meaghan. "I've heard the story."

"Lovecraft was sort of like Alastair. These things were able to reach out and speak to him."

"He didn't flambé himself, too, did he?"

Russ raised an eyebrow. "Listen to Miss Burnt Toast throw around the cooking terms. No, he died of cancer, I think. Kind of an odd duck, but nothing along the lines of Alastair."

"It's strange how different people respond to them," Matthew said. They drove Alastair mad—"

"They did a number on Jamie, too," Meaghan said. "He was a suicidal mess before we got those sigils off him."

"Is he okay now?" Matthew asked with a worried frown.

Meaghan shrugged. "He's better, but he still has a long way to go."

"Is he letting John in?"

"Some," Russ said. "More than he was, that's for sure."

Matthew nodded. "Good."

"What about Lovecraft?" Meaghan asked. "How did he react to them?"

"He wrote about them. Story after story. He bled all that poison onto the page and appeared to be unaffected."

"You sure about that? He was totally racist," Meaghan said. "Even if I liked horror, which I don't, I couldn't get past that."

"Maybe he would have been like that anyway," Matthew said. "People don't need any supernatural tampering to be bigots. But you have to wonder how much of human history may have been affected by these things planting horrible ideas in suggestible minds."

"Like John's brother," Meaghan said. "That thing fed off his resentment until it was strong enough to start wearing his skin."

Russ paled. "Can they all do that?"

"No, not the trapped ones," Matthew said. "And the Power, whatever it is, only seems to be able to do it in the presence of strong magic. Like Fahraya."

"And city hall, when all the crap was going on over Labor Day," Meaghan said. "It seems to have a chummy relationship with Cooper. How much do you know about him?"

"Not much," Matthew said. "But it fits the pattern. Whatever the source of his power, Cooper is capable of strong magic, which would keep the Power close to him."

"Owen and I were thinking it might be the other way around. That Cooper is getting his magic from the Power."

Matthew nodded. "Interesting thought. Something symbiotic, maybe? They fuel each other? But the rest of them—the trapped ones—it looks like they can only influence and corrupt from a distance."

"Like they did with Lovecraft," Meaghan.

"Actually," Matthew said, "he was one of their greatest failures, because all they managed to do through him was advertise their existence, and familiarity breeds contempt, not fear."

"Yeah," Russ said. "Cthulhu is all over the place these days, but jokey, not scary. I've seen Cthulhu cakes and pie crusts, and Cthulhu-inspired kids' clothes. Hell, there's even a Dr. Seuss-inspired parody of Lovecraft."

"I saw this sweet little Cthulhu snowsuit on Etsy," Kady said. "It would be perfect for Matty's first Halloween." She stretched and patted her belly. "Sorry. I'll shut up. But it was super cute. Fleece, with lots of little tentacles."

"Gasp," Meaghan said in a deadpan voice. "The horror." She snorted. "I've seen them—or at least part of them—and I wouldn't call them cute, but they weren't scary either. Just stinky and squirmy. Like I've been telling everybody, there's much worse stuff on TV. Without the magic and the psychic mojo, they're not very intimidating."

"It's not psychic," Matthew said. "It's all magic-based. Which means they can't affect you at all, Meg. At least not mentally."

"If those wussy-ass tentacles are any indication, they probably can't affect me physically either. The worst part was the smell."

"With some Febreeze and a chain saw, you could save the world," Russ said. "Ooh, there's an idea. What about using a chain saw on the dragon? It's not exactly a blade, but it can still slice and dice." He grinned. "Into big chunks at least."

Meaghan rolled her eyes. "Maybe on a grizzly bear, but it still looks like a pocketknife compared to a dragon. We need to think bigger."

I need to think bigger, because the rest of you are gonna be turnips if the dragon gets too close.

Matthew grabbed her hand. "You'll know your weapon when you see it."

"Because anything's a weapon when you're sufficiently motivated," Meaghan said. "Yeah, I know."

"Maybe you could throw a bucket of water down its throat," Russ said. "Put the fire out first. Ooh, or a fire extinguisher."

"It's not a grease fire, Russ." Meaghan shook her head.

"Shows what you know," Russ said. "You never put water on a grease fire. Makes it bigger."

"Actually, it is sort of a grease fire," Matthew said. "The fire is fueled by lipids produced by a gland in the back of the throat."

"What ignites it?" Meaghan asked. Could it be that simple?

"Magic," Matthew said.

"Of course." Meaghan groaned. "So you can only ignite this lipid stuff with magic?"

"No, it's very flammable. Any flame would do, if you could get close enough to try," Matthew said. "It's very corrosive and the fumes are toxic. Don't let it slobber on you."

"Dragon slobber." Russ grimaced. "Bleh."

"Then with a lucky hit, Terry could ignite its spit and blow its head off?" Meaghan felt a tiny flare of hope.

"Maybe," Matthew said, "but it would need to be a solid strike at the right moment and it's not like he could take it out with a single spark. Dragons burn off fuel as soon as they produce it, so they aren't sickened by their own fumes."

Meaghan's flare of hope sputtered and went out.

"Dad, how do you know so much about dragons?" Russ asked.

"The war. I had to do my research." Matthew scowled. "And then I had to redact it all. But they couldn't make me forget it. Only my brain turned to mush before I could tell Meg."

"And in Fahraya, we had other things to worry about," Meaghan said.

"And I've been in utero ever since," Matthew said.

"Speaking of which." Kady stretched and pushed the covers back. "You got your big bowling ball head resting on my bladder. I gotta pee, then I need to walk around a little."

CHAPTER THIRTY-THREE

AFTER A TRIP to the bathroom and few trips up and down the hallway, Kady returned to bed, Jeff at her side. After giving them a few minutes alone, Russ and Meaghan headed back in.

Jeff was massaging Kady's shoulders and neck. "Sorry, guys. I know you want to talk to your dad, but I need to look after my woman."

Kady snorted. "I'm fine for now. I've been listening. Trust me. We need as much help from Matthew as we can get."

Jeff sighed. "They have a dragon? That's fucked up."

"You can't talk like that when the baby gets here," Kady said.

"Indeed," Matthew said. Meaghan could tell now by the tone of voice which one was speaking. "What's the plan?"

Meaghan shook her head and pointed in the direction of the Donners' house. "I don't have a plan, Dad. Not yet."

"No plan?" Jeff's voice squeaked with fear.

Kady reached behind her, gave him an awkward punch on the leg, then pointed toward the floor and rolled her eyes.

"Oh," he said, with a grin.

"I'm going across the street," Meaghan said.

"Not alone you aren't," Russ said.

"You want to leave Dad?"

"No. But you can't go out there by yourself."

The wind howled, as if trying to argue his point. Russ pointed toward the window. "You can't even see their house from here. If you wander off in the wrong direction or slip or—"

"Jeff can go with her," Kady said. When he objected, she said, "Honey, I love you, but you're kind of driving me nuts at the moment. You heard Gretchen. We've got hours until go time. Help Meaghan. I'll be fine."

"Okay," Jeff said. "There's about forty feet of tow chain in the plow truck. We can hook one end to it and take the other with us. If we get lost, we can follow the chain back to the truck. It's parked right in front of your house."

Meaghan looked at Russ. "How's that for bread crumbs, Hansel?"

"Don't joke," Russ said. "You don't know anything about winter. A storm like this can kill you." He looked at Jeff. "The tow chain is a good idea. Do it, no matter what she says."

Meaghan nodded. "You're right. I'm sorry. We'll be back soon and I'm bringing everybody back here. We can't risk them splitting us up."

Let's hope the elves haven't already thought of that and the witches' barrier holds. So far, the elves seemed more focused on keeping Holly Lane isolated from the wider world but, other than the morning shenanigans in the basement, had not directly interfered. Meaghan felt certain Terry's smashed generator had been the work of the Order, not the elves.

Marnie met them at the front door. "I'm going with you. Me being here is upsetting Natalie. I can feel it from up here. We need her strong and focused."

Meaghan opened her mouth to object, then nodded. She knew from her own experience in Fahraya that Marnie wasn't merely imagining it.

They wrestled into their coats and boots, and stepped into the howling night.

The accumulated snow was now well over their knees. They tried to find the path created by earlier trips to and from the house, but the wind had drifted it closed. Even the tire tracks were gone. Holly Lane looked like the Arctic wilderness.

Bracing herself against the gusts, Meaghan shined the flashlight in the direction of the plow. It was caked with snow, but the orange paint was still visible in spots. She pointed at it and grabbed Jeff's hand. He grabbed Marnie's hand, and together the three of them fought their way through the deep snow.

Jeff pulled himself into the back of the truck bed and retrieved two large plastic buckets. He pulled a large hook from one bucket, attached it to a ring on the side of the truck. They made their way across the street, lugging the heavy chain buckets.

The tow chain had seemed silly when Jeff first mentioned it, but Meaghan was grateful for it before they were halfway across the street. The flashlight was useless. The driving snow had obliterated all landmarks.

Even Marnie, with her heightened senses, struggled to find her way. They got to the end of the first twenty-foot chain and realized they'd veered off on a diagonal toward the empty field abutting the Keele and Donner properties at the dead end of Holly Lane.

In warmer weather, it was a pleasant rolling meadow, about two acres, full of rabbits and birds and swaying grass. The end of the road was marked by a few short sections of guardrail with enough space between them to easily pass through without realizing it.

If they wandered out there now, they'd be dead long before anyone found them.

They corrected their course, attached the second chain to the first and, this time, found themselves in the front of the Donners' house.

Meaghan banged on the door.

"It's me and Marnie and Jeff," she shouted over the roar of the wind. "Let us in."

The door creaked open. In the dim light glowing from the fireplace, Meaghan made out a large figure holding a sledge-hammer.

"Oh, for hell's sake, Terry, open the goddam door and let us in," Meaghan shouted. "We're freezing our asses off out here."

"Meg, what are you doing here?" Terry pulled her into the house, with Jeff and Marnie trailing behind her.

"Sucks out there," Jeff said. "Hey, man, I hear you're like this badass thunder god."

"Huh," Terry grunted. "Not even close. What's going on? How's the baby doing?"

"He's her dad," Jeff said pointing at Meaghan. "Super weird shit."

Brian walked up, smiling at Marnie. She slipped her arm around him and gave him a quick kiss.

That's why Natalie's upset.

Brian looked at Meaghan. "Is Kady's baby really your father?"

"For the moment, yeah," Meaghan said.

"She's not in big labor, yet," Jeff said. "Gretchen says we've got a few hours to go."

"How are we doing on the plan?" Meaghan asked. "Also, I think we need to get everyone over to my house so they can't split us up. We almost got lost coming over here."

"Yeah," Brian said. "We were thinking the same thing. The plan is coming along."

Meaghan pulled off her coat. With all the people and the fire, it was reasonably warm. She followed everyone into the crowded living room. Jeff was immediately monopolized by Steph, who wanted to hear all about the baby. Marnie stayed close to Brian. Despite Marnie's earlier calm talking about her ordeal, Meaghan could see how much more relaxed she looked with Brian nearby.

Luka, Terry, and Owen sat in a knot by the fire, whispering back and forth.

But Meaghan's eye was quickly drawn to the three people sitting near the front windows.

Up until now, Buzz had been one of the largest men Meaghan had ever seen. But the man and woman who sat next to him made Buzz look small.

The Millers. Now Meaghan understood why they were so reclusive. Their size exceeded human scale. The man had to be eight feet tall and the woman wasn't much smaller. Like Buzz, the man was bald, but the woman had white hair pulled back into a braid.

She gave Meaghan a shy smile.

Buzz noticed Meaghan and grinned. "Hey, Meg, come over and say hi to my cousins." He patted the woman's arm. "This is Aggie." He pointed at the mountain sitting on his other side. "This little guy is Hank."

Those better be strong chairs. Hank had to weigh at least five hundred pounds and none of it appeared to be fat.

In a voice like the rumble of an avalanche, Hank said, "I knew your pa. Good feller, Matthew. Sorry to hear he passed."

"Thank you," Meaghan said. She decided not to mention the pending reincarnation going on across the street.

"We brought you some 'shine," Hank said.

"Rocket fuel, he means," Buzz said. "Strong stuff."

Meaghan laughed. "No kidding. I've sampled it before."

Buzz laughed, too. "Yeah, don't drink it near an open flame."

During the Labor Day struggle, the Power had used a jar of the Miller's moonshine as accelerant in their effort to burn

Marnie. At the memory, Meaghan's laughter abruptly ceased. She'd been there with a fire extinguisher to smother the flames before Marnie was burned, but in the back of her mind, Meaghan could still hear Marnie's anguished screams.

Aggie, seeing the look on Meaghan's face, swatted Buzz on the back of the head hard enough to make him gasp. "It mixes nice with ginger ale," she said in soft voice. "Don't need more than a splash, so a jar lasts you a good long time."

"What the hell, Aggie?" Buzz spluttered.

Aggie swatted Buzz again. "Hush, boy." She gave Meaghan another shy smile. "Ignore him, child."

"Ow." Buzz rubbed the back of his head. "She puts on this sweet old lady routine, but she's got a punch like a Mack truck. If that dragon shows up, Aggie can take care of it all by herself."

"Shut your mouth, boy," Aggie said. "You don't jest about dragons. They're fearsome wild beasts."

"But tasty," rumbled Hank, "if you dress the meat proper."

"You need to talk to my brother," Meaghan said. "He'd love to learn how to cook dragon."

"Tastes just like chicken," Buzz said, winking at Meaghan.

"No," Hank said, a serious look on his huge face. "It don't. It tastes more like duck, but spicy like."

"Hank, you don't know what dragon tastes like neither," Aggie said, sharing an amused look with Meaghan. "There isn't nobody around here knows what dragon tastes like because nobody's eaten dragon in over a thousand years."

She gestured to Meaghan to come closer. "Your feller is hiding across the room. He's nervous being this close to us because we make liquor and he don't want to be tempted. You should go steady him up a bit."

Meaghan glanced across the room. John was huddled in an armchair in a dark corner on the other side of the room.

She nodded to Aggie. "I'll do that."

Aggie lifted her giant hand and gave Meaghan a soft pat on the arm. "He's a good man and he's trying hard."

"I know," Meaghan said, smiling back at Aggie. Despite her size and alleged punching skills, Aggie exuded gentleness. "Nice meeting you both."

She made her way across the room to John. His eyes were closed, a look of concentration on his face. She stared at him for a long moment and felt her eyes fill with tears.

I love him and now I'll die before I can get my head straight enough to show him how much.

She shoved the tears back down. If she thought about the dragon right now, she'd lose it. "It's me. Open your eyes."

He sighed. "Are they still here?"

"Yes," Meaghan said, "with a jar of moonshine and a funnel so they can pour it down your throat."

John chuckled and looked up at her. "Don't joke. I . . . they are so large and they bring so many jars with them."

"How are you guys doing with that?"

"I'm hiding in this chair trying to meditate, and Terry is drinking even more coffee than usual."

Meaghan grimaced. "Is he bouncing off the walls yet?"

John laughed. "Soon." He pulled her onto his lap and kissed her. "How are things at your house?"

"As weird as they are over here," Meaghan said, hugging him. "As weird as they always are."

CHAPTER THIRTY-FOUR

L UKA, TERRY, AND Owen rose to their feet and headed over to Meaghan and John.

"Let's go back to the kitchen," Terry said a manic gleam in his eye. "Have a chat."

It was much colder in the back of the house. A single candle burned in the center of the kitchen table.

Meaghan pulled out a chair and sat down. "So, guys, you got a plan yet?"

Luka grinned. "Yeah, I think we do."

"Well?"

Owen yawned. "I could use some coffee, but Terry drank it all."

"Don't lie, there's more, you know there's more, plenty for all," Terry said in a rush.

Meaghan glanced at John. "You said he wasn't bouncing off the walls yet."

John watched Terry through narrowed eyes. "I was wrong. Are you okay?"

Terry snorted and waved his hand. "I'm fine. Just a little amped up." He grinned. "Amped up, get it?"

Owen sighed. "Unfortunately."

Luka stared at Terry for a long moment. "You sure you can pull this off?"

Terry stared back. "Sure I'm sure." He squirmed in his chair. "I think."

"Pull what off?" Meaghan asked.

"The fair folk have to think I'm drinking again," Terry said, avoiding John's eyes. "That I'm too drunk to be a threat."

"We are back to this again? This is a bad idea." John glared at Luka and Owen. "I thought you agreed with me. Do you think this is a game we play? That we don't fight for every day we stay sober?"

"They know the stakes," Terry said. "They were there when I was at my worst. They're as invested as I am in keeping me on the wagon."

"More," Luka said. "We had to clean up the messes."

"And there were a lot of messes," Owen added. "So many messes."

"But—"

"Johnny, if there was another way, I'd do it. But they need to believe I'm not a threat."

"But if they know about the lightning—"

"They know when I'm drunk I have very little control over it. If they know the lightning is back, then better they think the drinking came with it."

Luka leaned forward. "John, trust me. I'm not any happier about this idea than you are. But Terry's right. They want us to hand him over so they can break him and show everyone the smith is a fraud. If they think he's already broken, they'll let their guard down."

John stood up and shook his head. "I still can't agree with this. You don't need me. We already agree I need to stay away. I'm going back to the fire where it's warm." He leaned over and kissed Meaghan. "You stay. They need you."

Meaghan stroked his cheek, then he stalked from the room.

"I'll talk to him," Terry said.

"No, you won't," Meaghan said. "This is good. I don't want him anywhere near the basement. Not after this morning."

Terry nodded. "Fair enough."

"What about the rest of us?" Meaghan asked, wanting to change the subject from John. "Why would they think we'd roll over and give up Terry without a fight?"

"Partly because loyalty is a difficult concept for them to grasp," Luka said, "but mostly because they already think I can do more magic than I can, and by the time I'm done, they'll think me and my exaggerated power are on their side."

"And they'll think you, me, and Natalie are dead," Owen added. "And that Luka's going to hand them the keys to the candy store in exchange for them leaving him alone."

"And leaving me in charge," Luka said.

"You're going to play to your mythology," Meaghan said.

Luka grinned. "And they're going to buy it, because they're stupid, and because they don't understand the difference between myth and reality."

"And he has a terrible reputation, Meg. Even worse than yours," Terry said with a grin. "Hang on. I gotta pee."

"Again?" Owen shook his head. "No more coffee for you, buddy."

Terry laughed as he trotted out of the kitchen.

"Let's get back to the 'us being dead' part," Meaghan said. "How are you pulling that off?"

"With this." Owen slipped off his chair and took something from the kitchen counter behind him. He clambered back into his chair and pulled a striped dishcloth off the object.

A dagger, intricately wrought and highly polished, lay in his hands.

Luka picked it up and said, "Check this out."

He plunged the dagger into his thigh.

Meaghan gasped.

Luka pulled the knife away and showed her his uninjured leg. "Prop knife. See?" He pushed the blade onto the table a few times. "Retractable blunted blade. Looks like the real thing, but the actors don't get skewered."

Terry walked back into the room. "I sell those to high-end prop houses. I make theatrical swords, axes, all kinds of stuff." He examined the dagger. "One of my better pieces. Looks real, don't you think?"

"I'll say," Meaghan said. She looked over at Luka. "You gonna stab me with that?"

Luka shook his head. "No. Brian will stab you, if everything goes to plan. So I can prove he's held in my evil thrall." He grinned. "Bwa-ha-ha."

"You're enjoying this villain thing way too much," Owen said.

Luka shook his head. "No, I'm enjoying this conning thing way too much. I forgot how much fun it is, particularly when the mark is so loathsome."

"And all this is going to play out in my basement?" Meaghan asked. "What about the witches?"

Marnie walked into the kitchen. "I can help you there. Sorry to butt in, but Brian told me what you're planning."

Luka pulled out a chair. "Brian told us you have a new set of skills."

Marnie nodded. "But I don't have magic anymore. Did he tell you that?"

"I'm sorry," Luka said.

"Don't be." Marnie smiled. "You need a stage manager, I think. I can do that for you."

"A stage manager?" Meaghan asked.

"To tell you all when to head downstairs and play your parts." Marnie looked at Luka. "Let's figure out the cues."

The first step involved informing the witches. Marnie would tell Gretchen, who would notify Natalie and Lynette.

"They're like my backup singers," Luka said.

Owen rolled his eyes. "The Lokettes."

Luka ignored him. "Their job is to make me look like I'm more powerful than they are. It needs to look to our elf friend like they've been overcome by my magic, and I'm the one pulling all the strings."

"They'll drop the spell wall?" Meaghan asked. "Is that wise?"

Luka shook his head. "Not until I know he's taken the bait. But he needs to believe I've knocked out the witches' spells and replaced them with my own. Same spell, with a different flavor."

"The witches can do that?"

"Nat can," Owen said. "It's where I got the idea. She was talking about the nuances of magic, how it has fingerprints of a sort, and how to mask them." He glanced at Meaghan. "She was talking about your new pal, Emily. She really doesn't trust that woman."

"No kidding," Meaghan said.

"Emily's change is sincere," Marnie said. "I can feel it."

"Tell Natalie that," Owen said.

Marnie grimaced. "I really can't tell Natalie anything right now."

"Why?" Owen scowled. "Because of Brian?"

Marnie shook her head. "Oh, God, forget I said anything."

"No," Owen said. "She's still boohooing over Brian?"

Marnie sighed. "She really likes you, more than I think even she knows. But she's used to having Brian in the wings. When she could have him, she didn't want him, and when she finally wanted him, he didn't want her anymore, and she blames me. And, please, don't anybody tell her I told you that."

For a moment, Meaghan saw Marnie's fragility return. "Natalie said some awful things to Brian on Labor Day. She may not be able to admit it, but she knows whose fault it is he's moved on."

"Yeah, but she's not quite ready to accept it." Marnie stared at Owen. "It's about pride, not about her liking Brian more than you." She took a shaky breath. "Could we not talk about this anymore?"

"But—ow!" Owen glared at Luka. "You kicked me."

"Moving on," Luka said. "The next step is convincing them that I've turned on you guys."

Marnie gave Luka a grateful smile.

"By killing me," Owen said, glaring at him. "Breaking my shin wasn't part of the plan."

"I thought Brian was going to do that," Meaghan said. "Kill him, I mean."

Marnie stood up, trying to keep her face blank, but Meaghan knew the look. She'd been wearing it herself quite a lot lately. Marnie was on the verge of panic.

In a stiff voice, Marnie said, "It's freezing in here. Let me know when you've got it all figured out. I'm going back to the living room." She turned and walked from the kitchen without a backward glance.

"Nice job," Terry said, swatting Owen. "Chase her from the room, why don't you?"

Owen gave Terry a sour look.

Luka shook his head and said to Meaghan, "I need to give them a show of good faith. Then I reel them in."

"How are you gonna do that?"

Luka grinned. "By giving them the thing they most desire."

"Which is?" Meaghan asked.

"The fair folk are hurting," Luka said. "Their favorite food supply is drying up. There's still enough superstition and fanaticism out there for the elves at the top to be eating well, but nobody else is."

"Like Sam," Meaghan said.

Luka shook his head. "No, not like Sam, and that's what has them so frightened. Sam can't consume magic. He has to eat actual food."

"Which is why his skin is better," Owen said. "The fair folk can all survive on regular food if they have to. They don't need to eat emotional energy, but they're addicted to it. It's like meth. It rots their teeth and ruins their skin and makes them physically weak."

"Then why do it?"

"Because it makes them magically strong," Luka said. "Why build physical strength toiling for food when you can snap your fingers and get whatever you want?"

Meaghan nodded. "Lou mentioned that. My dad's predecessor, not you."

Luka nodded. "Dream?"

"Yeah, the night before the Order took Jamie, back in June. He said worlds that rely on magic become stagnant. They don't innovate because they don't have to."

Luka nodded. "It used to be only those like Sam—the impervious ones—who ate regular food and questioned the established order. But the people at the top, the ruling families, are hoarding their sources of emotional food, so those in the middle are losing their power and standing in society. A rebellion is brewing."

Meaghan raised an eyebrow. "The fair folk have one-percenters and a disintegrating middle class?"

"Yeah," Luka said. "Surprisingly similar dynamic."

"Said the one-percenter."

"We give shitloads of money to charity," Owen said. "Shitloads."

"We do give a lot away," Luka said, "but point taken."

Meaghan shook her head, but smiled. "You're a lousy villain, you know that?"

Luka smiled back. "Yeah, but I'm an established brand. What I lack in evil I make up for in name recognition."

Terry snorted. "I'll say."

"Okay, I get the problem, but how are you going to fix it for them?" Meaghan asked. "What are you offering?"

"Less magical food means less magical power, which means less ability to generate magical food," Luka said. "That means even less power. It's a feedback loop. A death spiral for their preferred way of life."

"And it's only going to get worse as humans grow more immune to magic," Meaghan said.

"What they need," Luka said, "is a way to turn back the clock on human evolution."

"And you're going to tell them you can give them that." Meaghan nodded.

"Their holy grail," Luka said, "which I will convince them is hidden deep inside the archive, and I'm the only one who knows where it is."

"What do you get in return?" Meaghan asked.

"A dragon," Luka said, with a grin. "I get a dragon. And the spells to control it."

CHAPTER THIRTY-FIVE

"THERE'S MAGIC THAT controls dragons?" Meaghan looked around the room, her heart pounding.

"No," Terry said. "Which is kind of the weak link in our little plan."

Of course not. That would be too easy. Stupid magic. Totally useless when you actually need it.

Luka waved his hand dismissively. "Only if we really believe that the fair folk would give me that kind of power."

"They'll double-cross you?" Meaghan asked, already knowing the answer.

Luka nodded. "Oh, yeah, absolutely."

"Then what makes you think they'll even bother bringing the dragon over?"

Luka grinned. "Because they won't be able to resist showing it off."

Meaghan scowled back. "By burning you to cinders?"

Luka shook his head. "They won't hurt me. Not until they have what I've promised them."

"So there is something in the archive?" Meaghan asked.

Luka shrugged. "Who knows? There are mountains of stuff over there."

"What if they demand you go over there and produce it?"

"Then I'll tell them I need them to free the monks to help me, and I'll wander around for a while, do some fake magic, and buy you some time. Best case, we can kill the dragon right away and I don't go anywhere. Worst case, you get an inside man. Win-win."

Meaghan raised a skeptical eyebrow. "You sure about that? I can think of a few scenarios where you lose big time. What will keep them from just grabbing you out of the basement?"

"Because we have our own barrier and the elf isn't getting out under any terms but mine," Luka said. "Trust me. I've been dealing with the fair folk for centuries. I know how they think. This will work."

Meaghan glanced at Owen and Terry. They appeared to be all-in with Luka's plan.

They're the experts, I guess, but . . . "For the record, I think it's a terrible plan. Terry told me, 'oh, don't worry, the elf can't hurt you if you keep some iron on it,' and look how that worked out." Meaghan shook her head. "We don't know what we're dealing with here. If this thing let itself get captured, then it has an end game, but we don't know what it is."

Luka gave her an appraising look.

Meaghan stared back.

Luka smiled. "Meg, I appreciate your concern, but, you've been doing this how long? Nine months? I've been doing it for three thousand years. I know what I'm doing."

The unspoken words hung in the air. *And you don't.*

She looked to Terry and Owen for support. Owen stared back at her, his arms folded across his chest.

Terry wouldn't meet her eye.

"Terry, you get why I'm concerned, don't you?" Meaghan asked. "This elf is something new, which means the old rules may no longer apply."

Terry fidgeted in his chair but didn't respond.

"What if I told you I'm the only one who can kill the dragon, because if you get too close it will stun you?" Meaghan watched as the same dreamy look she'd seen on Russ settled onto their faces.

The moment passed. "Look, Meg," Luka said, "if I'm wrong you can tell me you told me so." He grinned at her, but there was no warmth in it.

For the first time, Meaghan saw behind Luka's charming exterior. She could see the grifter.

"But I'm not wrong," Luka added.

Again, Meaghan heard the unspoken words. *And you are.*

Meaghan held up her hands in a conciliatory gesture. Grave misgivings aside, she needed their help. *He has been doing this longer than I have. Maybe he's right.*

Even as the thought crossed her mind, she knew she didn't believe it, but she also knew Luka wouldn't listen. Either way, the dragon was still on the menu.

"Fine, you win," Meaghan said. "Do the elves know how to control dragons?"

"Not well," Owen said, "but better than anybody else. Nobody knows why."

Luka smiled at her indulgently, and Meaghan resisted the urge to kick him like he'd kicked Owen.

She took a deep breath. *It's his risk to take. You can't win this.* "The fair folk can control the dragon enough to make it burn down the archive?"

"The burning part is easy," Owen said. "Jab it somewhere sensitive and it'll flame."

Meaghan started to feel the panic rise. "But how are they keeping it calm until then?"

"You can contain it with powerful enough magic, but you can't really control it," Owen said. "We know that much."

"Then why can't we contain it?" Meaghan looked around. "Easier than killing it, right?"

"Because that kind of magic takes weeks to set up," Luka said. "And we only have a few hours."

"Well, shit," Meaghan said. *I still have to kill this dragon. Me. And a saucepan and a stapler won't get it done, no matter how motivated I am.*

"You wanted the dragon out of the archive, right?" Luka gave her a patronizing smile. "They'll bring it right to us. I'll have already manipulated their greed by offering them more power. Acting like I assume they have the magic to control dragons will manipulate their egos. Greed and vanity. Sprinkle with stupidity and you have the perfect mark."

"A fat goose ready to be plucked," Owen said.

Yeah, but who's plucking whom?

Terry snorted. "And then all we gotta do is kill a dragon. Easy-peasy."

"It won't be as powerful here," Luka said. "Less background magic. And you'll have plenty of help."

No, no, he won't. Only me.

"Besides ..." Luka grinned at Meaghan. "Meg's the one who's supposed to kill the dragon, remember? With a magic sword."

"Yeah, ha ha," Meaghan said in a tight voice. "About that. Not gonna happen."

Luka sighed and the smug look left his face. "I'm sorry. I shouldn't joke about that." He held out his hand to her. "Still friends?"

He's trying to mend fences. Let him. Meaghan took his hand and squeezed it briefly. "Still friends."

Luka smiled at her, then looked at Terry. "You're our biggest gun."

"Which is apt to misfire," Terry said.

"That thing you did with the holly bush a little while ago . . . I've never seen you have that level of control." Luka paused. "Except for when you were making the crucible steel. After—"

"Luka," Terry growled. "Drop it."

"No," Luka said. "We've been dropping it for a thousand years. You had control once. For almost two centuries."

"When you were sober," Owen added.

"I wasn't sober," Terry said through gritted teeth. "I just wasn't drinking. Big difference. And I was an utter bastard if you care to recall. So much so that none of you wanted anything to do with me, thank you very much. You only came back when I started boozing again."

Luka shifted in his chair, looking uncomfortable. "Not something I'm proud of."

"You let them have me," Terry said in a low voice. "You let the fair folk have me. Best work I've ever done and I did it all in hell with those fuckers grinding away at me every day. By the end I thought I was back in . . ." He took a deep breath. "Back there. All the same feelings: the pain, the rage, the fear. A great big banquet of misery they—"

Something stirred in Meaghan's memory. In Fahraya, the Power, speaking with the voice of John's brother. "A bloody banquet."

Terry stared at her in confusion. "What?"

"The Power. In Fahraya. Bragging about how it had taken V'hren. Think about it. The fair folk don't eat pain and rage, at least not as the main course. They wouldn't want you alone and miserable with the lightning under control. They'd want you out in the world, boozing it up and dodging lightning bolts so people would believe in Thor."

Luka nodded. "Terry was the Judas goat who led all the lambs to slaughter. The elves didn't feed on him, but on the faith and fear and awe of the people who believed in him."

"As well as the dogmatism of those who came later who wanted to burn his believers as heretics," Owen added. "But he wasn't doing the god thing then. He was flying totally under the radar."

Terry shook his head. "Then they must have decided to do something new, because something was chewing on me. It was like a hole I couldn't climb out of. Every bad thing I'd ever done playing on a loop in my mind. I wanted to kill myself, but the voices in my head said I didn't deserve to be at peace."

Meaghan nodded. "Jamie said something very similar when the sigils were controlling him. That he'd tried to kill himself and whatever was controlling him wouldn't let him."

Owen exchanged a long look with Meaghan. "That thing again?"

Meaghan nodded. "Sounds like the Power, doesn't it? Which means Cooper and the squid."

"But this was like two centuries before Cooper," Terry said. "If he was still a regular human when we dealt with him, then he hadn't even been born yet."

"What ended the misery?" Meaghan asked.

Terry's face softened and he smiled. It was like watching the sun come out after a storm. "Steph came back to me."

"And you started drinking again?"

"Not right away." His smile turned sad. "There were about fifty years there when it was good. Better than good. Great. As good as it ever was until the last sixty years."

"What happened?"

Terry sighed. "I got complacent. Decided I could have a drink without it being a problem, but I was wrong."

"And then I came along and dragged him back into the magic sword business," Luka said. "He'd gone straight. Made more legitimate money as Ulfberht than he ever did as a grifter."

"Ulfberht?" Meaghan asked.

"The name I was using back then. I was a high-end sword maker," Terry said. "Ulfberht swords were the Ferraris of medieval weaponry. Much higher quality than anything being made in Europe at the time. Still baffles the experts." He smiled for a moment. "It was the steel I learned how to make in India that made them so good."

"You went to India?" Meaghan looked around the table. "You guys got that far?"

"Only me," Terry said. "I'll tell you the whole story if we survive."

"Is India where you got into the Buddhist thing?" Owen asked. "I always wondered about that."

"You're a Buddhist?" Meaghan stared at Terry. "You?"

"Yeah, but not a very good one," Terry said. "It helped me quit drinking—in a good way at first—but then I trotted back to Europe and used my newfound serenity to make weapons, so I probably should have stayed in India a little longer."

Thor's a Buddhist. Meaghan's mind filled with a picture of Terry, in full Viking regalia, sitting cross-legged and saying *Om* in his deep voice. She began to giggle and then she began to laugh.

And then she began to cry and laugh at the same time.

"John," she heard Terry shout. "Get in here."

Meaghan was distantly aware of the sound of running feet.

Thor's a Buddhist and I have to kill a dragon.

Meaghan began to sob.

Her heart raced, banging in her chest so hard she could almost hear it. She broke into violent shivering even as she felt the sweat dripping down her back under her thermal underwear.

I have to kill a dragon.

John put his arms around her and held her close. "What did you say to her?"

"Terry's a Buddhist," Meaghan managed to gasp out between

sobs. The tears and laughter had merged into something closer to choking. "But not a very good one."

"She's hyperventilating." Luka grabbed her hand and put something into it. "Here, breathe into this."

Meaghan realized she was holding a brown paper bag. Luka guided her hand to her mouth and nose. She took several frantic breaths.

"Is she all right?" John stroked her hair, a frantic edge to his voice.

Luka gently tugged the bag from her mouth. "Okay, now try to take a couple of normal breaths. She'll be fine. Panic attack, I think."

"After the last couple of days, who can blame her." Owen said.

"Now breathe into the bag some more," Luka said, gently nudging her hand toward her face.

Meaghan's felt her heart slow. She pulled the bag away from her mouth and took a couple of almost-normal breaths. "Better. Sorry."

Luka smiled at her. "No apology necessary. If you're up to it, let's go out to the living room and brief the troops."

What she wanted to do was run outside, fire up the snow-plow, and drive as far away as she could by dawn, but instead Meaghan nodded.

Out in the living room, Luka outlined the plan. He and Owen would be the first ones down the stairs. Luka would do his magical switcheroo with the witches, who would all collapse and pretend to be stunned. As Owen reacted in surprise, Luka would stab Owen with the fake dagger.

"We'll need blood," Owen pointed out.

"Can't the witches magic that up?" Meaghan asked.

Luka shrugged. "They could, but a good, old-fashioned bag of fake blood under your shirt works better. Less to go wrong."

"Russ can make that," Meaghan said.

Luka nodded. "We'll need about a pint."

After Luka had stabbed Owen, he'd begin his pitch to the elf. Brian would come downstairs when summoned by Luka and pretend to be under his control.

"Marnie, this is where you come in. Will you able to know when it's time?"

She nodded.

"Don't oversell it," Luka said to Brian. "Just do what I tell you."

"I was a soldier. I know how to take orders," Brian said.

Owen glowered at Brian, jealousy clouding his features.

Meaghan, standing next to him, swatted his arm and leaned toward his ear. "She's with you," Meaghan whispered to him. "And he's with Marnie. Behave."

Owen glared up at her, then gave a jerky nod.

"Marnie, when I signal you, send Meaghan down." Luka smiled at her. "I hear you're good at goading information out of egotistical assholes."

"Cooper, you mean," Meaghan said. "Not sure I'll get another bite out of that apple. Even he's got to have me figured out by now."

"Yeah, but the elf won't," Luka said. "I need you to put on the grand performance. Let's see what we can pry out of it. But first, before Meg comes downstairs, Brian will stab Natalie."

Brian's eyes widened as he gripped Marnie's hand tighter. "Do I have to?"

"Afraid so," Luka said. Meaghan saw him give Owen a warning look.

Brian nodded.

"Then Meg, after you react to seeing Natalie and Owen, Brian will rough you up a little, and you can cry and wail, and see what our little friend tells us."

"And then I come downstairs," Terry said.

Luka shook his head. "You need to stay out of this. John is right. I can't do that to you. Not this time. If I'd stayed away back then, maybe you wouldn't have started drinking again."

Terry snorted. "I started drinking again because I'm a drunk. Nobody did that to me. I did it to myself. Exclude me if I don't add anything to the con, but not because you think I'm too fragile to do it. If they know about the lightning, then they need to think the boozing came back with it."

Luka sighed. "I'll tell Marnie to send you down if I think we need you."

"Which you will," Terry said, "because by then, the elf will definitely know about the lightning. We need to get everyone over to Meg's house while we still can and I need to go practice if you expect me to fry Puff the Magic Dragon."

CHAPTER THIRTY-SIX

"ARE THEY GONNA burn down our house?" Russ poured another ingredient into the bowl of red gloop he was trying to turn into realistic blood.

"You got any corn syrup?" Gretchen asked, looking over his shoulder. "Or red food coloring?"

Russ gave her a horrified look. "Corn syrup?"

"Oh, right, look who I'm asking," Gretchen said. "You got a key to Edna's house? I bet she has corn syrup and food coloring. You ever taste her red velvet cake?"

Russ shuddered. "Meg, are they gonna burn down our house?"

Meaghan stared back at him. "How the hell should I know?"

She felt the panic begin to bubble again, and placed her hand on the paper bag that Luka had given her. The rough paper was soothing under her fingers, like a security blanket.

Too bad it's not big enough for me to crawl inside and hide.

"You know more about dragons than I do," Russ said.

"No," Meaghan said in a shrill voice. "No, I don't."

"They're big fuckers, I know that much," Gretchen said. "What about maraschino cherries? They got plenty of red dye in them."

"Why would I have maraschino cherries?" Russ snapped at her. "I don't have garbage like that in my kitchen."

"Right," Gretchen said, rolling her eyes. "Only healthy fake blood will do."

"Are you sure our little guest can't hear us?" Meaghan pointed at the floor.

Gretchen nodded. "Elfy's locked down tight. Natalie added a sound-dampening spell on top of the rest of it and Luka's running some noise interference, too. He's not a wizard, but he knows a few nifty things. We got it handled."

Meaghan gave her a skeptical look. "That's what everybody said before it went after John."

"It caught us with our panties down, right enough, but we fixed the problem. You can bamboozle a complacent witch, but when she starts paying attention, watch out."

"So maybe it didn't hear the first big lightning strike over at the Donners'?"

Gretchen shrugged. "Hard to say. Luka's been blocking the elf's signal as much as he can since he got here. But Natalie wasn't in the mix yet. So it would have heard and felt a boom, but might not realize what it was."

Russ stared into the bowl, frowning. "I've got some beet puree in the big freezer. Let's try that."

Gretchen poked her head into the chest freezer in the tiny mudroom. In a muffled voice, she called, "Where is it?"

"On the right side, next to the meat bin. And hurry up. You're letting the cold out. If the power doesn't come on soon, we'll have to haul everything out to the garage."

"What the hell . . ." Gretchen slammed the freezer door shut. She held up a large Tupperware container. "How about we use this instead?"

"Are you nuts? That's organic, pastured pig's blood for blood sausage," Russ said.

"You mean you have the actual stuff in the freezer and we're screwing around with honey and tomato paste?" Meaghan shook her head.

"That blood was expensive," Russ said. "What? Why are both looking at me like that?"

"Look at it this way," Meaghan said, trying not to laugh, but grateful for the moment of levity. "If the dragon burns the house down, you'll have bigger problems. If it doesn't, we'll all chip in and buy you new blood."

"Better blood," Gretchen said.

"There is no better blood," Russ said in a mournful voice. "This stuff is top of the line. I have a great recipe. I was going to surprise you."

"With blood sausage?" Gretchen grimaced. "Yeah, that'd be a surprise."

A blinding flash of light knifed through the kitchen windows, followed by a deafening crack of thunder.

Meaghan raced to the back door and pulled it open.

Terry stood in the snowy backyard next to a small smoking crater, shaking his hand with a grimace. "Sorry." He stared down into the hole. "I think you'll need a new patio slab."

"I think Elfy knows about the lightning now," Gretchen said. "Go, Sparky, go."

"I'd better head over to the meadow," Terry said.

"Oh, no," Meaghan said. "Not a chance. We almost got lost in there trying to get to your house the last time."

"Buzz and the Millers have been clearing a path bringing over supplies. I'll be fine."

"With how fast this snow is falling?" Meaghan shook her head. "And the wind? The path fills up as soon as you make it."

"Not if you make it with troll feet," Terry said.

"Which you don't have, Sparky." Meaghan glared at him. *You don't get out of this by freezing to death. You're the only chance I have to live through this mess.* "Are you trying to make this easy for the elves? How do you know they aren't hunkered down over there waiting for a chance to grab you?"

Terry sighed. "Fine, I'll go blow up your front yard instead." He stomped through the snow to the back door and held up an insulated travel mug. "Russ, can I get a top off? I don't how you're making this stuff without electricity, but it's great."

"A Chemex flask and a hand grinder," Russ said, beaming with pride, "and a goose-necked kettle to get precision control for the pour."

"You got any idea what he's talking about?" Gretchen asked Meaghan.

"You put a filter in this cone thingy, add ground coffee, dump boiling water over it, and leave it alone until it's all dripped through. Even I can do it. Easiest way to make coffee ever." She snorted. "Unless you're my brother."

"My sister is not only impervious to magic," Russ said. "She's impervious to flavor."

"However you make it, it's good." Terry held up the mug. "More, please."

Meaghan watched Terry through the windows as he trudged—coffee in hand—around the house. Kneeling on the sofa, she watched him smite another holly bush across the street.

"Weird shit happening," a male voice said.

Meaghan whirled around. Dustin slouched into the room, followed by Sam.

"Where have you guys been all this time?"

"Upstairs," Dustin said, a worried frown on his round face. "Talking."

"I will go to them," Sam said, climbing onto the sofa next to Meaghan. "You must not risk yourself for me."

"It's not only for you, hon," Meaghan said, taking his small hand in hers. "They want Terry—the smith—as well. And you're both worth the risk, believe me."

He stared up at her, his small face grave. "I will fight for you then."

Dustin groaned. "Sam, you can't. We talked about this."

"Dustin fears that I cannot help. That I am too small and I have no power."

He's impervious... maybe he can help. She abandoned the thought the moment it came to her. Sam would be as useful as the half-starved child he resembled. And she couldn't ask him to risk himself. Not after what he'd already been through.

But...

Meaghan flashed on the moment of despair she'd felt in the attic of city hall, clutching the stapler, helpless while her friends suffered. Patrice had told her she'd have a part to play before the end, but at that moment, she had excoriated herself for having no better plan than throwing a stapler at somebody.

"But that stapler saved the world," Meaghan said.

"What?" Sam and Dustin asked in unison.

Meaghan shook her head to clear it. "Sorry. Thinking out loud. Last summer, when city hall was destroyed... do you know this story?"

Sam nodded. "Oh, yes. Everyone knows this story. How you vanquished the old ones with an impervious weapon."

"That weapon was a stapler," Meaghan said. "A small tool"— she indicated the size with her hands—"used for binding sheets of paper together. A mundane piece of office equipment made of steel."

"It was not designed as a weapon?"

"Not even close. It was the most ordinary of human objects. We used it, we scorned it when it malfunctioned, we took it for granted. It had no power, and neither did I, and I felt small and useless and afraid. I felt like a fool to even consider it as a weapon. But when the time came, it saved us all. You may have a part in this, Sam, that none of us can foresee."

Geez, I sound like I'm in the Lord of the Rings. With Sam's earnest little face looking up at her, Meaghan found herself falling into his formal syntax.

Sam nodded and smiled. "I understand. Even the smallest blade can win the battle."

Meaghan smiled back. "Yes. Something like that. But wait for your moment."

"Like you did," Sam said.

The pants-wetting terror will tell you when . . .

"Exactly," Meaghan said. *Once again, I'm relying on bullshit to rally the troops.* It sounded good, but Meaghan didn't like Sam's odds against a dragon. *But I don't like my odds either.*

"So," Dustin said. "None of this giving-yourself-up talk, okay?"

"This is what the king tells me as well," Sam said.

Meaghan smiled. Nobody called John a king these days. Even the Fahrayans didn't really think of him as their king anymore, much to John's relief. He was ready for a new leader to step forward, at least for those Fahrayans who clung to the old ways. A surprising number were adapting to modern life at an alarming speed and didn't want any king at all.

In that moment, she realized she wanted him more than she ever had.

That wizard can go to hell. If I'm going to die I want to spend my last hours with John, ready or not.

"Where is the king, by the way?" she asked, trying to sound casual.

"In your chambers," Sam said.

Meaghan looked blank a moment, then said, "My bedroom, you mean?"

"Yeah. He told us to ask you to come upstairs if you have a minute," Dustin said. "So you guys can have your talk? He didn't tell me about what though."

Meaghan sighed. "I know what. On my way."

CHAPTER THIRTY-SEVEN

MELANIE AND JOHN were waiting in her bedroom. "How's Kady?" Meaghan asked.

"Mild labor," Melanie said on her way out the door. "She and your father both want you to stay here and talk to John."

Russ, you little shit. "I suppose Russ told everybody," Meaghan said in a stiff voice. "Guess there's no need for me re-hash it."

"Russ didn't tell us anything," John said. He was sitting on her bed, wrapped in a quilt. "He only tells me he is concerned for you, and you'll tell me when you are ready." He held out his hand. "You were ready to tell me this morning. I can see this weigh on you. Will you tell me now, please?"

Her moment of lust evaporated. *Which part? The near rape or the fact that if Terry chokes, I'm the only one who can kill the dragon because the rest of you will be like deer in the headlights?*

"Before we all die?" Meaghan pushed the bedroom door shut behind her. Even in long underwear and several sweaters, she could feel the cold.

"We're not going to die." John opened the quilt. "Here. We'll be warmer together."

Meaghan curled up next to him. "I hope you're right about the 'nobody dying' part. You know the plan?"

John pulled her closer. "I do. When will it happen?"

"Luka wants time to practice and then we'll get everyone prepared. We're all supposed to meet in the living room at three." She glanced at her watch. "That gives us about three and half hours."

"Why is he waiting so long?"

"He wants to head down there around three thirty. If everything goes as planned, then the elf should leave before four, and Luka says that gives the elves enough time to think they can double-cross him by showing up early, but not enough time to start asking each other hard questions about why Luka would betray us in the first place."

John nodded. "He is a clever man, Luka. Too clever, maybe."

"You don't trust him?"

"I believe he means well. He's not the monster from his father's stories. But I think he trusts himself too much. He reminds me of me before I lost my wings. I was so ... what is the word? I was so sure of myself. So sure I knew what I was doing that I never noticed my brother filling the people's heads with lies. I didn't know I was in trouble until it was too late."

"Luka's so sharp he could cut himself," Meaghan said.

"What?"

"It's a saying to describe really clever people. I've usually seen it used as a compliment, but I'm not sure it is."

"It's like the two-edged sword." He adjusted the quilt. "Warm enough?"

Meaghan nodded. *Warm and safe, but not for long.*

"Terry explained to me what it means," John continued. "It's why he made swords but never used them himself. If you're careless, the way drunks can be, it's too easy to hurt yourself as well as your enemy."

"Yeah, but in Luka's case I'm not sure it's careless so much as arrogant."

"There is the word I was trying to remember. I was arrogant in Fahraya. Luka is arrogant now."

"Yeah," Meaghan said. "He can be, but he's been doing this a long time."

"No. He did it for a long time, this is true, but he hasn't for many years now. Terry tells us these elves, these fair folk, are the most dangerous creatures he has ever encountered, but now he and Luka and Owen act like the elves are stupid enough to fall for a lie? For fake knives and fake blood?"

"We have real blood," Meaghan said. "It's pig's blood Russ had stashed in the freezer to make blood sausage, but I see your point. I tried to make the same point, and Luka didn't want to hear it."

"Which is why we need to talk," John said in a soft voice. "Tell me what is troubling you. We may not get another chance."

Meaghan sighed and tried to remember how she'd felt in the morning when she'd been ready to tell him, but now it felt like another lifetime.

A lifetime that didn't involve dragons.

"I have to kill the dragon," Meaghan said.

"We have to kill the dragon," John said. "You don't believe in prophecy, remember?"

Meaghan shook her head. "This isn't prophecy. This is a setup. The fair folk are either trying to force the prophecy forward or make people think it doesn't apply to me. I'm the only one who can do it, because I'm the only one who won't get stunned."

John shook his head. "Terry and the witches will help. I'll help."

"You can't, honey. Like I told you, the dragon has the power to make you not fight back."

John hugged her. "The witches will help you."

She pulled back from his embrace and looked at his face. He was smiling at her in an odd way.

"The dragon can stun you," Meaghan said, watching for John's reaction. "Make you calm and docile."

The effect was immediate. John's face went slack and his eyes lost focus. He wore a vague smile. "The witches will help you. And me. I'll help you."

Her heart pounding with fear, Meaghan drew him back into her arms so she didn't have to see the dazed look on his face. *I have to keep them as far away from it as I can. They won't be able to fight back or even run away.*

How the hell was she supposed to fight the dragon and keep everybody at a distance at the same time?

John ran his fingers through her hair. "Shh. It will all work out. We will be fine."

"Liar," she said, before finding his mouth and kissing him.

The bitch needs to—

No!

She shoved the balding wizard out of her mind. If these were her last hours alive, she wasn't going to give that piece of shit any more mental energy. *Brian killed you. You're dead and I'm done with you.*

Meaghan wriggled closer, straddling John's thigh. She grabbed his hand and placed it on her breast.

"Are you sure?" he breathed in her ear.

"Yes."

"Now?"

"Yes," she hissed at him. "Now. Here. No more talking."

"Are you sure?"

"Lock the door," she said. "Then get back here. I'm sure."

Meaghan stood up when he came back to the bed. She pulled up his shirt and kissed his chest as she fumbled to unzip his jeans.

"Wait," John said in a squeaky voice. "I don't know how."

"You have a son," Meaghan said between kisses. "What do you mean, you don't know how? You've figured it out at least once before."

"Stop. Please. Talk to me." He pushed her away gently. "I mean, I don't know how with a human body. Without wings. I never did it lying down before."

That got her attention. "You mean you did it in the air?"

"Yes," John said. "In flight."

"Why did you do it that way?"

John shrugged. "We had wings. Why would we not do it that way?"

"Huh." Meaghan stared at him. "Good point. I never thought about it. How do you make it work?"

"Together," John said. "The taboos about forcing sex aren't the only reason there is no rape in Fahraya."

The wizard returned to her mind, leering as he pinned her to the ground.

The tears came with him, big sobby tears, fueled by curdled lust and shame and . . .

And that goddamned dragon.

John scooped her up and took her back to the bed, this time climbing under the covers with her and pulling the quilt on top. He held her and murmured comforting sounds in her ear, but didn't ask any questions. He let her cry until she was done.

When the sobs tapered to hiccups, he handed her a wad of tissues from the box on the nightstand. "Now are you ready to tell me what troubles you?"

The story came out in a torrent of words. John didn't comment or interrupt. He stroked her hair and let her tell the story.

"The worst part was how helpless I felt," Meaghan said. "I couldn't stop him and now when you . . ." The tears threatened to return but she pushed them down. "When you touch me, down there, I can't get his face out of my mind."

"But you did for a moment, make him leave, I think, before I stopped you." He brushed her cheek gently with his calloused fingertips. "What were you thinking?"

"That I'd had enough of him and he didn't deserve any more of my time. Then you said about why there's no rape in Fahraya and he came back." This time the tears won.

"Shhh." He pulled her close. "I will never do that to you. I will never hurt you or force you. Sex is something I want to do *with* you, not to you. Do you understand?"

"I wish every man thought that way." Meaghan blew her nose.

"To think otherwise would make me less than a man," John said. "This is what I was taught as a boy. What shows you to be a man is the smile on your woman's face, not the number of women you have been with."

"Smile on your partner's face," Meaghan said, thinking of Jhoro.

"Yes." John smiled at her. "Partner. It's no different if you are like Jhoro. It's still about making your lover happy instead of making yourself happy."

"I love you," Meaghan blurted out.

"I love you, too," John said.

"I think I'm ready," Meaghan said. "Really ready this time."

She hadn't been sure how John would react, but she now realized she'd expected anger, disgust, disdain, distance. She'd expected him to tell her she was being foolish, or worse, treat her like a fragile, broken thing. She'd expected him to swear revenge and turn her pain into a slight on his manhood.

I thought he'd act like he was the one who'd been hurt.

What Meaghan hadn't anticipated was him merely listening and accepting and not trying to fix her. *Instead, I fixed myself.*

No, honey, you didn't. Nothing's fixed and you still need to call Marnie's shrink. It took you almost six months to get here. You can do better. You have to do better.

Provided she survived, of course. Provided any of them survived.

CHAPTER THIRTY-EIGHT

MEAGHAN STARED AT the ceiling, trying to control the giddy laughter. After a moment, she gave up.

John, lying next to her, grimaced. "That bad? It's been a long time, remember? I need to practice."

Meaghan rolled over and climbed on top of him. "Bad? Are you insane? That was amazing." She kissed him between giggles. "Seriously."

Amazing was an understatement.

Meaghan had been with enough men to feel she had a fairly good idea of what sex was supposed to be.

She'd been wrong.

They'd had all the usual problems associated with sex in the real world. In the movies, nobody had back problems or creaky knees or struggled to figure out where to put their limbs or accidentally pulled the other's hair. The sheets never got tangled. Nobody nearly fell off the bed. The music swelled and, depending on the film, the camera either cut away or closed in, but there was no actual conversation. No *ow, ow, no, that won't work.*

But this wasn't a movie. Along with the typical awkwardness, she and John were no longer young, and their bodies couldn't necessarily do what their libidos desired. They'd had to stop numerous times to reconsider and strategize.

Still, it had been a revelation.

I really like sex. Who knew? Certainly not Meaghan. She could see now that her celibacy had been triggered not only by disappointment with romance, but disappointment with years of lackluster lovemaking.

Meaghan kissed him again, reveling in the feel of his naked skin against hers. It had been so long. Too long. But John had been worth the wait.

"Amazing," she said.

"That's a relief," John said, stroking her hair. "Lying down . . . it's like I have an extra arm I don't know what to do with."

Her inner critic smacked the giddy joy aside. *What if you weren't any good? Did you think about that?*

"What?" he said, a concerned look on his face. "You stopped smiling."

"Was I okay? I'm not . . . it's been a long time for me, too, and I'm not sure I was ever very good to begin with and—"

He rolled her onto her back and kissed her, taking his time, then said, "Give me a few minutes and I'll show you how good it was for me."

The joy returned. He sure didn't seem disappointed.

"It's not only human men who have to wait until the battery recharges?" Meaghan smiled up at him.

"I'm a human man now, remember?"

"What about when you were Fahrayan?"

He chuckled. "Fahrayans do not have to wait."

"How much sex did you guys have?"

"A lot." He yawned. "You saw Fahraya. There wasn't much else to do. How is your knee?"

"Better," Meaghan said. "It sometimes tries to bend in directions knees aren't supposed to go. How's your back?"

John laughed. "Okay now, but for a moment I thought I broke something."

"Low back spasms are the worst." Meaghan knew she had to get up soon and go back to the madness, but right now, right here, she was warm and safe. "There's some stretches I can show you to help with that. Are you sure you're okay?"

He grinned. "I'm fine. Better than fine. It will be better next time, I promise." His grin faded. "There will be a next time, I promise you."

"You're thinking I'm thinking we're all gonna die," Meaghan said. "Honey, trust me, that's the only way we're not doing this again." She snuggled against him. The giggles returned. "You've given me a reason to live. Actually about five reasons, I think." She giggled some more. "Which has never happened before. Usually it's one and done."

John stroked her arm. "This isn't how it always is with humans?"

"Not the humans I've been with," Meaghan said. "Sid was right. You do have fancy moves."

"Sid?"

"Something he said on Labor Day about Fahrayan men having exceptional skills." Meaghan gave a contented sigh. "When you were here with your . . . problem."

The love spell's effect on John had been something akin to an overdose of Viagra. Natalie had given him a potion that had prevented an embarrassing trip to the emergency room, but Sid had seen it as a wasted opportunity for Meaghan.

John chuckled, then yawned again.

"He also said I'd be calmer dealing with the love spell mess if I got laid first." She lifted up on one elbow and stared at John's profile in the dim light from the spluttering candle. "God, you're gorgeous."

"You're gorgeous," John said, through another yawn.

"Yeah, but you're more gorgeous. Shut up and let me give you a compliment." Meaghan kissed him again. "Sid was right. I'm a lot calmer than when I walked in here."

But the dragon . . . Meaghan shut down the anxious voice in her mind before it got any further. *It's a big problem, yeah, so break it down into smaller problems.*

With her head on John's chest, she could hear his heart beat. His breathing grew shallower and she could tell he was falling asleep.

Meaghan wished she could join him, but her mind wouldn't stop running. The lawyer part of her brain didn't care about her afterglow and started to outline.

The dragon presented two main challenges. The first challenge was keeping everybody safe. She needed somebody to keep everyone else away.

The second challenge was killing the damn thing.

The panic began to rise and she shoved it back down, focusing on John's heartbeat until the calm returned.

She needed crowd control and she needed to find her weapon.

In city hall, Meaghan had used a stapler, but she'd never have had the chance if Patrice hadn't been there to clear the road.

It hit her like one of Terry's stray lightning bolts.

Marnie.

Marnie suddenly had powers nobody understood that seemed to transcend magic.

Who does that sound like? Patrice appeared in her mind, standing in the attic of city hall, bathed in golden light. *What if she's like Patrice? What if she's our secret weapon?*

"Patrice could have taken a dragon down with a stern look," Meaghan said.

"What?" John jerked back awake. "I missed something, I think." He yawned again. "Why am I so sleepy?"

"Fahrayan men don't get sleepy after sex?"

"Nuh." John's eyes fluttered as he fought sleep.

"Of course they don't, the little sex machines. Well, now you're a human man," Meaghan said. "Sex dumps a bunch of sleepy chemicals into your brain." Meaghan sat up. "As much as I'd like to snuggle here with you, I need to get up. I think I might have found my weapon."

"Patrice is not here," John said. "Whatever her powers were, they are gone now. Why aren't you sleepy?"

"I'm a woman. My physiology is different. I'm not talking about Patrice. I'm talking about Marnie," Meaghan said. "Let's see if she can do more than read minds."

She watched him fight sleep for another moment and fail. She pulled on her clothes as fast as she could in the frigid room.

On her way to the bathroom, Meaghan stepped over to the snow-crusted window and peered out. The snow fell steadily, but the wind seemed to have let up. She could see only an indentation in the snow from the path trod earlier by the Millers.

I've got the Millers, too, for a while at least. Until the stunning magic has time to work.

She glanced at her watch. Not quite two. Plenty of time to put a plan together. She knew she should be as tired as John, but instead she felt exhilarated—giddy even—with relief that she had that damn wizard out of her head.

For now. He's gone for now.

The candle in the bathroom had burnt out and she couldn't see what her hair looked like. She patted it and winced. She wet her fingers and tried to smooth down the worst of it at the back. She thought about grabbing the bedroom candle, then gave up. Everyone else had hat head. Maybe they wouldn't notice.

John snored gently. Meaghan stared at him for a long moment, memorizing every line on his face. Despite her giddy words about the future, she couldn't think past the dragon. She wanted a future with John and would fight for it, but she couldn't let herself count on it. Not yet. She leaned over, gave him a final kiss, and slipped out of the room.

Russ stood outside of Matthew's old bedroom, holding a stack of towels. He smirked at her in a knowing way. "Nice hair, sis. Gee, I wonder what you've been doing."

Her face flushed, but she smiled. "Shut up." She patted her head. "How bad is it?"

"Haystack," Russ said. "There's a candle in the hall bath."

"Does everyone know what we were doing?"

Russ nodded.

"We were that loud?"

Russ smirked. "Oh, yeah. Feeling better? You must be because you're standing here with a loopy grin on your face instead of snarling at me."

Meaghan shook her head and walked into the bathroom. Russ had been right about her hair.

And I don't care. She giggled again, then went to work with wet hands trying to pat the worst of it down. But if Russ hadn't merely been messing with her, everybody knew what she'd been doing and there was no point hiding it. She gave up and went to look for Marnie.

But first let's talk to Dad.

CHAPTER THIRTY-NINE

AT FIRST, MEAGHAN thought she'd gotten there too late. Kady squatted on a pile of pillows stacked on the bed, while Jeff kneeled behind her. No one else was in the room.

Kady looked up when Meaghan walked in and gave her a beaming smile. "Hey, boss! Did you deal with your shit?"

Meaghan smiled back. "I did. What's going on? You having the baby now?"

Kady shook her head. "Not yet, but it feels better to move around. I want to figure out the best position before crunch time."

"Can I still talk to my dad?"

"Yes, honey," Kady said in the slower, deeper voice Meaghan recognized as Matthew's.

"Jeff, would you get me some of that tummy tea from Russ?" Kady asked over her shoulder.

"Sure, babe," Jeff said. He helped her into a reclining position and then grinned at Meaghan. "Your dad is cool. I think we'll have fun once he's here."

Meaghan laughed. She couldn't help herself. "That's a pretty weird sentence if you think about it."

Jeff grinned on his way out the door. "It's Eldrich. The whole place is pretty weird."

Meaghan sat on the bed next to Kady. "Where is everybody?"

"No idea. But Steph popped in for a visit and I feel a lot better. She knows way more than Gretchen. Where did Jeff get the idea Gretchen is a midwife?"

"From Gretchen. Steph has kids?"

Kady shook her head. "Nah. Something to do with the accident that made them immortal. She can't get pregnant, but when you're three thousand years old, you pick up stuff along the way. She says my body will do most of the work if I chill out and if anything goes wrong, she's helped deliver a lot of kids over the years so we should be fine."

"Where's Marnie, do you know?"

Kady smiled. "With Brian. I think they're napping in the guest room. Brian's so cute. He thinks he's going to deliver the baby because he took an emergency medicine class a few years ago."

"He's got a cool head in a crisis," Meaghan said. "Don't count him out."

"Yeah, if somebody shot me, Brian would be great. But looking at his baby sister's hoo hoo with a little bald head sticking out of it? He'd have a stroke. He can't even buy tampons without getting woozy. And the whole your-father-is-his-nephew thing has him completely freaked out."

Meaghan laughed again. "He's not the only one. And on that note, I have to—"

"So was John as good as Sid said he'd be?" Kady asked her with a sly smile.

Meaghan buried her face in her hands to hide her scarlet face. "I can't talk about this with my dad listening in. Have the baby and then I'll tell you all about it."

"Thank you," Matthew said, "although I am happy to see you without the panicked look on your face. What do you want to talk about?"

"There's my cue," Kady said. "Mommy out."

"Marnie," Meaghan said. "Patrice, too. You know about them?"

"Patrice, yes. What about Marnie?"

"She says the Order took her magical powers but something else showed up in their place. Heavy psychic stuff. Kind of like I had in Fahraya when Jhoro gave me the funny mushrooms."

"Marnie has powers?" Kady asked, indignant. "She never told me that."

"Mother, hush, please," Matthew said. "Are they the same powers as Patrice had?"

"That's what I need to find out. What do you know about Patrice? What is she?"

Matthew shook his head. "I'm not sure, and I haven't been in a position to find out. But . . ."

"But what?" Meaghan asked. "Tell me, even if it's only conjecture."

Matthew sighed. "There's certain themes you see through folklore. Recurring motifs across cultures. One of those is the notion of the tripartite goddess."

"Tripartite?"

"Three," Matthew said. "Three manifestations of the same idea."

"Like the Father, Son, and the Holy Ghost?"

Matthew nodded. "The concept is not uniquely Christian, but the three participants are usually female. Greek mythology in particular features the tripartite motif. The Furies, the Fates, the Graces, the Harpies, for instance. And there are more. Threes or multiples of three. All female."

"But we only have two."

Matthew nodded. "Before now, I thought we only had one. And it's not only the Greeks. The concept runs throughout all Indo-European mythology."

"The Norns," Steph said, stepping into the room. "Sorry. Didn't mean to eavesdrop. How's the baby coming?"

"Better, since we talked," Kady said. "I'm way less scared now."

Steph nodded. "That'll help."

"What do you know about the Norns?" Matthew asked.

"What's a Norn?" Meaghan asked.

"The Norns are from Norse mythology. Three mystical woman who decide people's destinies."

"Whoa," Steph said. "Matthew, is that you?"

"Yes. Have you ever encountered them?"

"You mean were they real people like us?" Steph pulled a chair up to the bed and sat. "I don't know. I never met them, but I've spoken to people over the centuries who claimed they had. They said the Norns were spirits who sought human vessels to speak through. All women, all special in some way."

Meaghan felt a chill down her spine. "Patrice called herself a vessel, and Cooper and the Power taunted her that she was weak without her sisters. But she's normal. Or at least she was. Natalie and Jamie swore she'd never done magic or been even remotely psychic until Labor Day."

Matthew nodded. "When she manifested huge magical and psychic powers of unknown origin. Her background's a mystery. She was surrendered to the state by an indigent mother who snuck out of the hospital after giving birth. The mother wouldn't give her name and she refused to identify a father."

"So, basically, we have no idea where she came from," Meaghan said.

"None," Matthew said. "The maternity ward nurse picked the name Patrice after her own grandmother and Brown because the baby had brown eyes."

Meaghan shook her head in disbelief. "I can't imagine not . . . how do you know this?"

"Patrice asked me to look into it when she was pregnant with

Liddy. Between her mystery background and Jamie's magically controlled DNA, they weren't sure what to expect." Matthew grimaced. "I wish I could say I made her feel better, but I had to do some serious digging to find out what little I told you."

"What about Marnie?" Steph asked.

"I grew up in Eldrich, with my parents, Alice and Clyde," Marnie said from the doorway. "I know I'm theirs because Dad videotaped my birth and threatened to show all my boyfriends. I heard you up here"—she tapped her temple—"and figured I'd better join the conversation."

"Yeah," Meaghan said. "We need to talk to you."

"I never knew about Patrice," Marnie said. "I knew she grew up in foster care, but not the stuff about her being abandoned at the hospital. She still has all those powers. She's hiding them because she's scared." Marnie stepped over to the bed and sat down at the foot. "Hey, girl, how's the baby coming?"

"It's okay," Kady said.

"How about you, Matthew? What's it like on your end?"

"Starting to get a little crowded," he said. "I'm kind of upside down. It's not comfortable, but it means I'm moving out head first so there's some good news."

Marnie giggled. "Sorry. This is so weird." She sighed. "But then I suppose so am I. The second weird sister. And no, Patrice didn't tell me about her powers. I can feel them, and I can see the golden light around her still, even if no one else can."

"What about you?" Meaghan asked.

"So far, I don't seem to have any of the physical powers she has, but mentally I think I'm stronger. She doesn't know I can tell she's still manifesting everything and she won't unless one of you tells her. Which may not be a good idea right now. She's got enough on her hands with Jamie at the moment."

"Jamie?" Meaghan and Matthew asked at the same time.

Marnie shook her head. "Don't worry. It's the stuff you already know about. Between the Fahrayans and those squid things, he had the shit kicked out of him for a couple of months and it's going to take some time to get past it. She's afraid having a super wife will shove him over the edge."

"Will it?" Meaghan asked.

Marnie shrugged. "I can tell you what people are feeling now, but I can't tell the future. And I ... people have the right to the contents of their own heads. I only told you about Patrice because it's relevant to whatever's happened to me. We're linked somehow. And no, Matthew, I don't have any idea if there's another one of us out there. Not a clue. What can I do to help?"

"For reasons I can't explain," Meaghan said, "I'm probably the only one who can kill the dragon and almost everyone else will be a liability." *Let's do a test.* "The dragon can stun people, but you won't remember it."

Meaghan waited for the dreamy look, but it didn't come.

Marnie nodded. "I can feel there's some idea in my head I can't retain. It's like how a dream dissolves as soon as you wake up."

"That puts you several steps ahead of everybody else," Meaghan said. "I need you to trust me and keep everyone else away. I can't fight the dragon and protect them, too."

"What are you talking about?" Steph looked confused.

"Dragons have the ability to magically stun anyone who gets close and somehow they can keep you from understanding that," Meaghan said, watching Steph's face.

Steph's eyes unfocused in the same way John's had. "Tell me what you need and I'll do it."

"Stay away from the dragon," Meaghan said. "It will stun you if you get too close."

"Anything you need, Meg." Steph wore a dreamy look on her face. "I'll be right by your side."

Meaghan sighed and glanced at Marnie. She had her eyes shut and was shaking her head. "It's right there and ..." Marnie opened her eyes. "It's gone. I'm sorry."

"Steph, I need you to stay back and help Marnie. And trust me. Can you do that?"

"I can do that," Steph said, the dreamy look gone. "Whatever you need."

We do trust you, you know. Even if you don't trust yourself.

Meaghan stared at Marnie. *Did you talk to me in my head?*

Marnie smiled and nodded.

Meaghan now saw her way around the stunning problem. "I'm afraid the elves may be listening. I can communicate with Marnie in my head." *Right?*

Marnie nodded again.

"I need the rest of you to do what she tells you, even if it looks like I'm in danger," Meaghan said. "It's part of the plan."

What plan? Marnie asked her.

The plan I haven't come up with yet. Keep them safe. Promise me you'll keep them back and keep them safe no matter what happens to me.

Marnie nodded again. *I promise.* "Sounds good, Meg." *Is Terry part of this plan?*

Meaghan nodded. *But he can't get too close either.*

How close is too close?

I wish I knew.

Marnie nodded.

"Will you stop that?" Steph said. "All the silent nodding is giving me the creeps."

"Babe, here's the—" Jeff stood in the doorway with a tray. "I'm gonna need more cups."

"No, you aren't," Meaghan said. "Marnie and I are going downstairs. I think. Where's Sam?"

Chapter Forty

"Y OU'RE FEELING BETTER," Marnie said as they headed down to the kitchen.

"I am."

"You still need to call my therapist, but you already know that," Marnie said. "Sorry. I know the mind-reading thing creeps you out. Creeps me out, too. I'm learning to filter stuff out, but it's still hit or miss, and I can't shut you out right now."

"Good thing," Meaghan said.

"Normally, you're a lot murkier. You can put up some formidable walls when you want to."

"You sound like my friend in Phoenix. Elena. She's psychic, too."

"Tía Nancy's cheese enchiladas," Marnie said. "You really like those. You're beaming them right into my head."

"Russ hates them," Meaghan said. "Velveeta cheese and canned sauce."

"Oh, yeah, he would hate that."

They stepped into the kitchen. It was warmer than it had been upstairs. Russ, as usual, was at the stove, stirring something with an intent look on his face. Buzz, Sam, and Dustin sat at the table, entranced, listening to Terry.

"So then Olaf, the crazy bastard, swings the axe, but he's so drunk he misses and spins in a full circle and lands on his ass in the snow. Leif was laughing so hard, he didn't see Olaf pick up the axe, then whack! Olaf cuts off Leif's left toes. Clean cut, boot and all."

"Did he die?" Dustin asked, eyes wide.

"Oh, hell no. Those guys barely noticed shit like that. You couldn't get into Valhalla from something as piddly as lost toes. He swore at Olaf, hobbled off to the healer, and came back to the party when the bleeding slowed down. Of course, he was drunk too, so he wasn't feeling any pain." Terry grinned and drained his coffee cup. "Olaf felt kinda bad when he sobered up, but Leif was fine. He ran a little funny after that, but no lasting harm done." He shook his head. "Good times. Hey Meg, what's up?"

"Just checking in," Meaghan said. "And Marnie and I need to have a chat with Sam. How's the lightning coming along?"

"Amazing," Terry said with manic grin. "I've never had control like this." He bounced to his feet and held out his cup. "Russ, top me off, okay?"

"I can't," Russ said. "We're out."

Terry blanched. "Out? I've got some at my house."

Russ shook his head. "We drank that already. There's like twenty people in this house. You've cleaned me out."

"What about the neighbors?" Terry asked, a panicked look in his eyes.

"Nobody's here, remember?" Meaghan said. "Edna's in Florida for the winter, the Franzettis are on a cruise, Barton is on sabbatical somewhere in Europe, and the house next to you—"

"The MacDougalls," Russ said. "It's been empty since Ed's kids moved him into the nursing home."

"Franzetti drinks espresso," Terry said. "I bet he's got coffee."

"You got a key?" Meaghan asked.

Terry rubbed his fingers together. "Don't need a key."

"Not a chance in hell," Meaghan said, no longer amused.

Terry's an addict, Marnie warned her. *We need to shut this down fast.*

Meaghan nodded. "You're my biggest weapon, Terry. You can't risk yourself. This is about them wanting us to give you up. You really think running out into the snow for more coffee is a good idea?"

Terry shook his head. "But—"

"You want me to wake up John?" Meaghan asked.

"No, but, the caffeine, it's why my control is so good," Terry said.

"Terry, you got so much caffeine in you right now you aren't gonna sleep for days," Buzz said. "You'll be fine."

"Yeah, but—"

"Mr. Terry," Sam said in his small voice, "your value to us is greater than your skill with the lightning. You are the smith."

Terry stared at Sam, as regret, fury, and fear fought for control of his face. "I'm going to Franzetti's."

Meaghan stomped down the hallway after him. "Terry, goddammit, get back here." She grabbed his arm. "Are you nuts?"

Terry turned and glared at her, and, for a moment, her affable neighbor was gone, replaced by the angry thunder god. "Let go of my arm, Meg."

Meaghan felt a chill, now understanding why people used to fear him. *But I'm not one of those people.* She squared her shoulders and glared back. "Or what?" she said in a soft voice. "Because I can't think of anything you can do to me that a dragon can't do better. Go ahead. Smite me. It has to be better than being burned alive. Because that's what will happen if you aren't there to back me up."

"Back *you* up?" Terry glared for a moment, then looked away.

Meaghan relaxed a tiny bit. She'd won the stare-down, at least. "Yeah, because this dragon has magic and I can't tell you about it because you won't remember. It can stun you if you get too close."

As she expected, the dreamy look arrived on Terry's face. "Don't worry, Meg. I'll take care of that dragon." Then the look cleared, and Terry, the Terry she knew, looked back at her. "What the hell just happened? My ears are buzzing."

"Magic," Meaghan said. "That's why you need to trust me. You need to follow my orders and trust me. And right now, you can't go charging out there for more coffee."

"No need." Russ appeared at Meaghan's elbow, holding a bag. "Found some tucked into one of the boxes the Millers brought over."

Terry gave Meaghan a haughty look and plucked the bag from Russ's hands. "Let's get this brewed up right now."

As Terry sauntered back to the kitchen, Meaghan turned back to Russ. "Were you stashing that?"

"Luka asked me to try to slow him down a little, but obviously now's not the time."

Nice save, Meg, Marnie's voice echoed in her brain. *But we need to keep an eye on this.*

Agreed, Meaghan thought back. Increased control of the lightning was a good thing, but she hadn't liked the nasty look in Terry's eye when she'd tried to take his latest addiction away from him.

"Let's be glad it's only coffee," Meaghan said to Russ. "Don't let him anywhere near the moonshine."

"Aggie told me they left it out in the back of Luka's truck. It won't freeze and it keeps it away from people who shouldn't be near it."

"Where are Aggie and Hank?"

"They went back over to Terry's house," Russ said. "They aren't used to being around this many people. They'll come over after the con is run. We don't want the elves to know about them."

"No, I guess not. Keep an eye on the over-caffeinated thunder god, okay? I've got my own planning to do. I need to talk to Sam."

But everybody else wanted to talk to her first and it was nearly three before Meaghan dragged Sam into the dining room and pulled the pocket door shut behind them.

She could see her breath from the cold. "You warm enough?"

Sam nodded. "Are you?"

"Not really," Meaghan said. "But I'll be fine. I need your help."

Sam beamed. "I will do it."

Meaghan sighed. She hadn't wanted to ask him. He looked so frail, so small, like a skinny child. But he wasn't a child, she reminded herself. He'd already escaped from a slave labor camp, survived a confrontation with a wild troll, and stared down Steph.

And he'd passed the test. Everyone else—even Buzz—got dreamy at the mention of the dragon, but Sam had stared back at her intently.

"You've seen what happens when I talk about the dragon," Meaghan said. "That's part of the stunning magic. People can't remember when you warn them."

"I am impervious," Sam said. "Like you. But the others are in danger."

"Yes," Meaghan said. "Marnie will try to protect them."

"The one who was a witch," Sam said.

"She's something else now. Something powerful and she can read thoughts. She'll need your help."

"Who will help you?" Sam small face grew even more serious. "The smith . . . I fear he may not be able to help you. I upset him. I made him remember."

"Remember what?"

"Of when he was Wayland," Sam said. "When he was a prisoner."

"What are you talking about?"

"Wayland, the god of smiths," Sam said. "Surely you know the story."

Meaghan shook her head.

There was a gentle rap on the door. "Meg?" Luka called through the closed door. "It's time."

"Who's Wayland?" Meaghan asked as she pulled open the door.

Luka stepped inside and slid the door shut. "Who told you about Wayland?"

Meaghan jerked her thumb at Sam.

Luka sighed. "I knew you'd eventually connect the dots."

"Terry's god of the smiths, too?"

"Sort of," Luka said. "It's a longish story and it's why he hates the fair folk so much and after fifteen hundred years, he's still not really over it. The limp is gone, but the emotional scars are still there."

"The limp?"

"They cut his hamstrings and chained him to his anvil to keep him from running." Luka shook his head. "I'll tell you about it when this is over." Anticipating her retort, he said, "I know you hate the secrets, but we can barely talk to him about it ourselves. He's terrified everyone will hate him if they hear the story. The details aren't relevant to what's going on now beyond the fact the fair folk set the whole thing up."

Meaghan nodded. "Is this what he means when he says he used to be a major dick?"

Luka gave her a sad smile. "Partly. Terry's a good man and he would have been happy living out his life in our little Irish village casting bronze axes and making copper jewelry. Instead, he got mistaken for a god. Several gods. It's been a big burden for him to carry."

"What about you?"

Luka smile broadened. "Oh, I'm a scoundrel. Always have been. I didn't need a magical explosion to turn into a crook. All it did was give me better tools and the time to set up really long cons."

"But you're legit now, right?"

Luka shrugged. "I operate within the confines of the law. For a financier, that's not saying much." He jerked his thumb over his shoulder toward the door. "We need to get this thing rolling before Terry goes into cardiac arrest from all the coffee."

CHAPTER FORTY-ONE

LUKA WENT THROUGH the plan again with Brian, Meaghan, Owen, and Marnie. Gretchen had briefed the witches and they were ready downstairs. Everyone else was upstairs with Kady, saying their goodbyes to Matthew. According to Steph, it was getting close.

"I'm not sure I can play drunk now," Terry said before excusing himself to go upstairs. "I'm too wired."

"That's a relief, although I'm not sure this much coffee is a good idea either," Owen said after Terry had left. "Caffeine is a drug, too."

Luka nodded. "One crisis at a time. It's better than the boozing and he does have more control of the lightning now. Let's do a quick practice run with the knife. You got a blood bag on?"

"Yeah. Hang on." Owen stripped off his sweater, revealing a white T-shirt. "It's cold in here. Hurry up."

"Where's the bag?" Luka asked.

"Under my T-shirt. Russ scrounged up some balloons so we should get a good spread, but I want to make sure it works through cloth."

"You got the pin?"

Owen held up a safety pin and nodded. "Meg, you'll need to do the same thing when Brian stabs you, so watch carefully."

"I'll say 'here's my good faith gesture' or something similar," Luka said, "and then—" He took two quick steps toward Owen, grabbed his shoulder, and pulled back the knife. "Meg, watch what Owen does. He's got the pin in his hand and when I stab . . ." Luka lunged forward. "Owen will pop the balloon."

Owen grabbed the knife hilt as Luka stabbed, and in a moment, the red stain blossomed across his shirt.

"Nice," Luka said with a grin.

"Did you see how it worked?" Owen asked. "Let me see you palm the pin."

After a few tries, Meaghan could successfully hide the pin between her fingers and pop it open with a surreptitious press of her thumb.

"Now drop your head and kind of curl around Brian's hand when he stabs," Luka said. "That gives you plenty of opportunity to get the pin open and poke the balloon. Don't overdo the death scene. Make sure the elf sees the blood, then get onto the ground without hurting yourself. I broke my nose once adding a dramatic but totally unnecessary face plant."

"What happens if I flub it or drop the pin?" Meaghan looked at Luka, then Brian. "Then what?"

"I can pop it with blunt force," Brian said. "But you might get a bruise. Along with the other ones I might give you. I'll try to pull my punches. Do it like we practiced and we should be okay. And please don't kick me in the nuts. I know you're good at that."

"I promise," Meaghan said. "Are we ready?"

Luka grinned. "Oh, yeah. This should be fun. I've missed this a lot."

Her conversation with John passed through her mind.

I think he trusts himself maybe a little too much . . .

So sharp he can cut himself . . .

You noticed it, too?

Meaghan glanced over at Marnie, who was staring at her.

Meaghan nodded. *Will this work?*

Only one way to find out.

Owen stripped off the bloody T-shirt and taped a new blood balloon into place before putting his sweater back on. Then he taped Meaghan's blood pack in place.

"What about Natalie?" she asked.

"Already did it," Owen said. "She's ready to roll." He looked up at Luka. "Let's do this."

"Follow my lead," Luka said.

"I always have."

They headed down the basement steps.

Marnie, her eyes shut, tilted her head to one side as if listening. "And the spell . . . is done. The elf thinks Luka's hexed the witches."

They heard a guttural cry.

"That's Owen," Marnie said. "Brian . . ." She grabbed his arm. "Be safe down there, okay?"

He gave her a quick kiss. "You aren't getting rid of me anytime soon."

Marnie pulled him into a tight hug. "Good. Hang on." She listened for a moment. "Now."

Brian headed down the stairs. They heard him shout, then silence. Several female screams came soon after.

"There's Natalie," Marnie said. "Meg, you're up." *Luka's way too impressed with himself at the moment. Be careful.*

Meaghan adjusted the safety pin between her fingers, gave Marnie a quick hug, and headed down the stairs. The basement was more brightly illuminated than the rest of the house and it took a moment for her eyes to adjust. A glowing ball of pale blue light hung near the ceiling.

She looked down at Natalie and—even though she knew it was fake blood—gasped.

Meaghan shrieked and dropped to her knees at Natalie's side. She kept her back to the elf, screening Natalie from his line of sight. "Natalie," Meaghan sobbed. "No!"

Natalie winked at her.

Meaghan climbed to her feet and next spotted Owen curled in a ball at Luka's feet. "Luka, what the hell . . ."

Brian stepped up, his face blank. He grabbed Meaghan's shirt and spun her around so her back was to the elf. He gave her a few punches to the gut and she reacted like they'd practiced. By anticipating the blow and moving with it, the punch turned into a firm shove.

She curled to the ground and made retching noises, the safety pin still safely hidden in her hand.

"Bring her here," Luka said.

Brian grabbed her roughly by the arms, pulled her up, and threw her at Luka's feet.

Meaghan pushed herself onto her hands and knees. She glanced at the elf. It had a smirk on its face and its eyes gleamed. It was enjoying the show.

Luka reached down and twined his hand in her hair, and pulled her to her knees. Like Brian had, he was careful to make sure that Meaghan had her back to the elf so it couldn't see her face.

But the stress of the last couple of days washed over her and Meaghan didn't have any trouble feigning tears. "You bastard," she wailed. "I knew we couldn't trust you. I knew it."

"Too bad the others didn't listen," Luka said in a friendly voice. "They ignored my past and now they'll pay for it."

"You killed them," Meaghan asked. "You killed Owen. Your best friend."

"I don't have friends," Luka hissed. "Friends are for the weak. Like you. I'm going to enjoy watching you die."

"Why are you doing this?" Meaghan wailed. "You said you'd help us fight the elves."

"Why would I want to do that?" Luka pushed her back to the ground. "They'll turn me back into the god I was meant to be. Why would I want a world without magic?"

Come on, come on, Meaghan thought. *Start talking. Let me hear the evil plan.*

In a pleasant voice, Luka said, "Would you like to tell her or should I?"

The elf began to shriek with what Meaghan recognized as laughter. "Kill her."

"No!" Meaghan sobbed. "Luka, please. Why are you helping them? Why?"

"Kill her," the elf hissed.

Cooper would be blabbing away by now. Time for a new strategy.

She pushed herself to her feet. "You lying bastard. If I die, you're going with me."

Luka shoved her back to the ground.

Meaghan yelped in pain. *Not the goddamn knee again.* She'd landed on the same one she'd bashed up in Fahraya. *Hello, knee surgery.*

"Brian, kill her. Now."

Meaghan felt Brian's arm around her waist pulling her to her feet. She struggled in a halfhearted way, her knee on fire. This time Brian positioned her so the elf could see both of them in profile.

You still have the pin? Marnie asked her.

Yes.

Brian pulled the fake dagger from his belt and jabbed it into her gut at the same time she popped the blood-filled balloon with the pin.

Meaghan felt the sticky wetness spread across her stomach. She stumbled against Brian and he slumped to the floor with her.

And kept going.

What the hell . . .

She glanced at the elf, but it was staring at Luka, a greedy smile across its sallow face.

Upstairs, Marnie screamed.

The elf shrieked something and the room began to rumble.

Luka cried out in pain and dropped to his knees.

Brian slumped further to the floor, pinning Meaghan, as the room began to glow red. She looked over Brian's shoulder and saw a circle of small hooded figures closing in on Luka.

Somebody clattered down the stairs and the light turned golden. Marnie began to shout in a language Meaghan had never heard her use before.

The elves hissed as they surrounded Luka. A few screamed and fell as the golden light touched them, but the others stayed on their feet.

Meaghan heard one final wail from Luka and then the knot of elves, with Luka firmly in their grasp, vanished into the air.

Their prisoner shrieked out another screechy laugh. "You want him back, bring us your father. When you bring us the smith and the—" He screeched something and spat on the ground.

"We will make your father stay dead this time," the elf hissed. Then he disappeared too as the chains surrounding him clanked to the ground.

CHAPTER FORTY-TWO

"BRIAN," MARNIE SCREAMED. "Brian!"

She pulled him off Meaghan and checked his breathing. Her calm demeanor had vanished. She burst into panicked weeping. "No, no, no."

Then she kissed him.

The golden light poured over them both. In a moment, Brian began coughing and Marnie pulled away. She collapsed on top of him, her arms around him, as she sobbed.

"Babe," he gasped. "Shhh. I'm here. We're okay."

Meaghan glanced over at Natalie kneeling on the basement floor, a solemn look on her face. Then Natalie nodded slightly and jumped to her feet. She helped Owen to his feet, then reached a hand out to Meaghan.

"They can't have Kady's baby," Natalie said. "I don't care how important Luka is." She glanced at Owen. "I'm sorry."

He shook his head. "Don't be. If you handed the baby over, Luka would never forgive me. This is our fault. Goddamn it." He turned to Meaghan, his eyes wide with shock. "Meg, you can say I told you so now. We should have listened to you. We got played."

"And I should have fought you harder on it." Meaghan tried to put her weight on her sore knee. "Oh, that's not good. Shit. I can't walk on this."

Terry ran down the stairs. "What happened? Where's Luka?"

Owen grimaced. "Gone. They took him. The elves have been one step ahead of us the whole time. Meg was right. They've got a whole new playbook."

Terry looked queasy. "They really want me delivered, don't they?"

"Not you," Meaghan said. "My father. The baby. They want to kill the baby to make sure Matthew can't come back."

Marnie had stopped crying. She pushed her hair out of her face, helped Brian to his feet, and crouched in front of Meaghan. "Let me see that."

Marnie placed gentle hands around Meaghan's leg. Another flare of golden light filled the room. Meaghan felt a surge, like warm water, flow through her knee, then the pain disappeared, leaving a pleasant tingling.

"What did you do?" Meaghan stared at Marnie, eyes wide. "What did you do to me?"

"Healed you, right?" Brian's voice was rough and weak, but he was standing. "She did that to me, too."

"They stopped his heart," Marnie said. "I restarted it. Terry could probably do the same thing."

"Not with a kiss," Brian said. "What do we do, Meg?"

And here we go . . . everybody's looking at me. "We don't tell Kady, but we need a spell wall around her fast." She tested her knee again, then looked at Marnie. "You fixed all of it?"

Marnie, clinging to Brian, nodded. "The cartilage was a mess. I cleaned everything up."

"How?"

"I have no idea," Marnie said. "I just did it. I didn't know I could until now."

Break it down into smaller problems . . . "We have a dragon on its way. Is the house still shielded?"

Marnie shut her eyes and concentrated. A moment later, she opened them and said, "It is now."

"What else can you do?" Meaghan felt a flutter of hope. "Can you stop the dragon?"

"I think it's only defensive," Marnie said. "I can put up barriers, but the rest is sort of . . ."

"Nurturing," Brian said. "Patrice couldn't do this stuff."

"That we know of," Natalie said. "I'll go beef up the magic protecting Kady."

"What about you?" Meaghan asked Terry. "How are you holding up? Still got control?"

Through the narrow basement windows, there was a flash of light, followed by a deafening crack. "Yeah. Those fuckers are dead. I'm done with this. I'm getting Luka back."

"No, you're staying here and frying the dragon," Meaghan said. "I'm getting Luka back."

Even as the words came out of her mouth, she felt the fear begin to grow.

What the hell did I say . . .

"Back from where?" Lynette asked. She looked exhausted, dark circles under her eyes, her normally tidy silver hair in disarray. "Do we know where they took him?"

Meaghan glanced at Owen. "Any ideas?"

"The archive?" Owen shook his head. He looked tired and lost. For the first time since Meaghan had known him, Owen looked little.

"Let's get out of here," Meaghan said. "Upstairs. We need to get everybody together and figure this out."

They trudged up the stairs. The loss of Luka had hit Owen

and Terry especially hard, but everyone was rattled. The witches' barrier spells hadn't kept the fair folk out. The iron chains hadn't stopped the elf from disappearing.

Can you talk this way to the others?

Not exactly, Marnie told her, *but I can get messages to them.*

Get everybody in the living room. Except Natalie, Buzz, and Jeff. They need to stay with Kady.

Will do.

"I wonder what other magic didn't work," Gretchen said to Meaghan when they reached the living room. "Like all of it maybe?"

The living room was crowded with people, all with grim looks on their faces.

"They took Luka?" Steph asked.

"They want the baby," Meaghan said.

There was a loud clatter from the dining room. "Ow, move."

"You move. Watch it. Why did you bring that?"

"Even a crap sword is better than none."

Meaghan heard a muffled swear, then a third voice said, "Dude, get out of the way. We gotta get this closed."

There was a loud pop, and the faint aroma of Doritos drifted into the room.

Dustin appeared in the dining room doorway, flanked by two figures in jeans and hooded sweatshirts. Meaghan recognized them as the monks she'd met earlier in the day.

"Where did you guys come from?" Meaghan asked.

"I snuck in through the server room to see if I could help," Dustin said. "The elves hate technology, so I knew they wouldn't be there. But these guys were. They were trying to get over here."

"Tell me your names again," Meaghan said.

The blond freckled one stepped forward. "I'm Clint. This is Todd."

The bald one with glasses raised his hand.

"And what do you have there?" Meaghan asked, feeling dangerously calm. A rant was close, she could feel it. "Are those swords?"

"Yeah," Todd said. With shaking hands, he held up a shiny sword with a jeweled hilt. In an awed voice, he said, "This is Treasure, the sword of Tyr."

Clint was holding another sword with much less reverence. It had a simple hilt, no jewels, and wasn't the least bit shiny. "This one doesn't have a name. It's an old piece of junk."

"Let me see that," Terry said, holding his hand out to Todd. Reverently and with care, Todd presented the sword, hilt first to Terry.

"Somebody's been polishing it, I see," Terry said in a dry voice. "Where'd you get the name from?"

"The runes on the handle," Dustin said. "See? It says only a wise man may wield the sword Treasure."

Terry laughed, shaking his head. "That's not what it says."

"How do you know?" Todd asked. His awe of Terry evaporated, replaced with annoyance.

"Because I made it," Terry said.

"That's impossible," Clint said, shaking his head. "This was made by Wayland, the smith god."

"No such person," Terry said.

"Yeah, there was," Todd said. "And you can't be Wayland, because you're Thor."

"No such person as Thor, either," Terry said. "But you have no problem believing I'm him."

"Well, the lightning," Dustin said. "That's kind of convincing."

"I've been making swords a long time," Terry said. "I'm a lot better at it than I am at throwing lightning bolts around." He gave the shiny sword an experimental swing. The monks jumped backward.

Terry lifted the sword and slashed it towards the nearest

chair. The blade hit the cushioned arm and bounced. Terry presented it back to Todd. "It's pretty, but it's a piece of crap. If I used it to hit another sword or a wooden shield, the blade would shatter."

Todd stared at the sword. "But the runes . . ."

Terry shook his head. "You translated them wrong. Don't feel bad. Runes are tricky, and I was being a smart-ass so I made them even trickier. What it really says is 'treasure will slip from the hands of the foolish man.'"

The monks stared up at Terry in confusion.

"A fool and his money soon go separate ways?" Terry asked. He waved his hand in front of their faces. "There's one born every minute? Hello?"

Todd looked like he might cry. "Treasure is a fraud?"

"Yup," Terry said. "Well, I guess if you want a magic sword, then, technically, it's the genuine article. Lots of magic in it because of all the slag in the steel. Makes it sparkle if you draw it fast, it glows in the dark, that sort of stuff. But if you want a real sword that cuts stuff and won't shatter in your hands when a berserker with an axe is coming in for the kill . . ." He held out his hand to Clint. "Let me see that one."

Clint, looking as lost as Todd, handed the tarnished sword to Terry.

Terry examined it for a long moment, then smiled. "You want a sword to fight with? This is the one you want." He made a few small swings. "Don't worry, Meg. I won't attack the chair again. This blade would actually do some damage."

He glared at the monks. "Had you boys bothered to polish this one, you'd see that along the side . . ." He tapped at a darker line running along the blade near the hilt. "It says Ulfberht. With a cross between the last two letters. Not one of the later knockoffs, but the real deal, made by yours truly." He gazed at the blade with pride. "Best work I've ever done. The Rolls Royce, the Ferrari, of medieval swords."

Todd, looking skeptical, said, "That old thing? It doesn't look like very much."

"Swords don't need to look good," Terry said, scorn dripping from his voice. "Your foe won't stop and say 'oh, look, it sparkles.' He's gonna be too busy chopping you up to notice. Unless "—the pride returned—"you have an Ulfberht. Those always got attention." Terry shook his head. "Magic swords. As if humans figuring out how to turn dirt and rocks into steel isn't magical enough. Meg, you want a sword to kill the dragon with, take the Ulfberht."

And here's the rant . . .

"Do you clowns—and that includes you, Wayland, or Thor, or whoever the hell you are—honestly think I can kill a dragon with a sword? A goddamn sword? What the hell am I supposed to do with it? Make dragon kebabs?" Her hands on her hip, wearing her most fearsome scowl, Meaghan took a step forward.

The monks and Terry—eyes wide—took a step back. Meaghan felt a vicious little stab of joy. *Scared? Good.* "What is it with men and swords? Why the fuck do you think every problem can be solved with a three-foot-long steel penis?"

Steph stepped out from behind Terry and began to clap. "Amen to that. Put those silly things away, boys. To a dragon, a guy with a sword looks like cocktail weenie on a stick. Meg, what's the plan?"

Run and hide?

I can still hear you, Marnie said in her mind. *If you need time to think, take it. Smaller problems, right?*

"Smaller problems," Meaghan said.

Everyone looked at her blankly.

"I think about killing a dragon and I panic," Meaghan said. "But I remember a guy from ADOT—"

"ADOT?" Gretchen asked.

"Arizona Department of Transportation," Meaghan said. "He said building highways was like eating an elephant. The only way to do it was one bite at a time."

"You're gonna eat the dragon?" Gretchen asked.

"Eventually," Russ said. He looked around at everyone staring at him. "What? Dragon meat is supposed to be good."

"And good for you," Gretchen added, then saw the look on Meaghan's face. "I'll shut up now."

"The point of that is that the only way to deal with a problem this big is to break it down into smaller problems," Meaghan said. "What's our first problem?"

Todd stared morosely at the shiny sword in his hand. "That we're all gonna die and the dragon's gonna eat us?"

CHAPTER FORTY-THREE

MEAGHAN SWITCHED INTO lawyer mode and got to work. "First thing we need to worry about is defense. Marnie, you're in charge of this. There's magic at work that keeps those of you who aren't impervious—"

"Unlike us," Sam said in a solemn voice.

Meaghan nodded. "Yes, unlike me and Sam. There's a particular threat involved with dragons I can't explain or even warn you about because the magic won't let you hear it or remember it." She glanced around the room. She saw confusion, but not the dreamy, unfocused look.

So far so good.

"Since I can't tell you the details, I need you to trust me and trust Marnie. If she says you need to stay back, there's a good reason for it. You can't help me with this. All you can do is put yourself in danger and distract me." She looked around again. "Will you all do that? Will you trust me?"

"What has happened?" John walked into the room, his hair a tangled mess and a sleepy look on his face. "Where is Luka?"

"Gone," Terry said. "The elves took him."

"What?" John, awake now, glanced around the room. "Where?"

"Probably the archive," Meaghan said, all business. If she stopped to think about what she was about to do, stopped to think about her and John, she'd fall apart. "You missed the part where you have to trust me and Marnie."

Marnie stared intently at John.

He nodded. "I understand."

I whammied him a little. I hope that's okay.

Meaghan nodded at her. *Thank you.*

"Secondly," Meaghan said. "We need to rescue Luka. Again, I think it has to be me. Between the archive's defenses and the elves' magic, I'm not sure who else can do it."

"I can do it," Sam said in a firm voice.

"Dude." Dustin glared at Sam. "We talked about this."

"I am sorry, my friend, but this is my task." He fixed Meaghan with his intense gaze. "I know the archive, Meaghan. You do not. I escaped from their worst prison and I have eluded them for months. You have not."

Yeah, that's what Luka said, too.

Only Sam wasn't being arrogant or over-confident. He wasn't trying to shut her up, wasn't trying to patronize her. Sam was stating plain fact.

"I am not a child," he said. "I am the size of a human child, but I am an adult. The elves you have met revile me, but to many—to those like me—I am a hero. I have given them the strength to keep fighting. Do not deny me the chance to serve them again."

The quiet ferocity in his voice brought tears to her eyes. Sam was a hero, the genuine article, and Meaghan knew she couldn't stand in his way, no matter the risk to him.

"Besides, you are needed here," he said in a softer voice. "You cannot lead if you are afraid to risk the lives of your fighters."

"And they won't be expecting Sam," Owen said. "They think he's a coward. They'll be expecting you."

Meaghan nodded. "All right. Sam, you're going after Luka."

"I can leave now," Sam said, rising to his feet.

"Wait, you'll need a weapon," Terry said. "Something made of steel."

"The real sword?" Meaghan asked. "The Ulfred one?"

"Ulfberht," Terry said with a smile. "No, that's too big for him to handle easily. We need to go to my house. To my shop. Look outside."

The snow had stopped. The moon had broken through the clearing clouds and after the dark night, the moonlight reflected on the snow seemed as bright as the sun.

Meaghan nodded. "Then get right back here. Bring Aggie and Hank."

Terry pulled on his coat and held out his arms. "Come on, Sammy. I'll give you a lift."

Meaghan watched Terry struggle through the snow, Sam clinging to his back like a child getting a piggyback ride. Her stomach clenched.

I'm going to get somebody killed.

Maybe, Marnie told her, *but I may be able to bring them back. You lead the troops and I'll put them back together, okay?*

Deal.

Despite her earlier complaints about mind reading, Meaghan found Marnie's presence in her head comforting.

You're not alone, Marnie told her. *You never have been.*

Meaghan looked around the room. She was surrounded by family, neighbors, and friends. And they trusted her. She could tell by their faces. They were scared and tired, but they trusted her.

Please, God, don't let me screw this up.

This time Marnie stayed quiet.

"Okay," Meaghan said. "The third thing we have to deal with is killing the dragon."

"They're gonna burn the archive," Dustin said, trying not to cry. "There's so much stuff in there we haven't catalogued yet. So much stuff we're gonna lose."

Owen shook his head. "Luka will convince them not to. He didn't get to that part of the con before they took him—the bit about the key to stopping magical immunity being in the archive—but he'll push it now. They can't seriously believe we'll give them the baby. Luka knows he needs to convince them he's more valuable to them alive than dead."

Steph had tears in her eyes. "That doesn't mean they won't hurt him even if they think he can help them."

Owen took her hand. "Luka's tough as hell. He'll get through this."

"Like Terry got through his time as Wayland?"

"Yeah," Owen said. "That was bad, but he's still here, right? We got Terry through that. We'll get Luka through this."

Steph gave him a grim smile. "Okay, but I'm killing every elf I see—except for Sam, of course."

Owen nodded. "And I'll be right there with you, but let's get Luka back first." He looked at Meaghan. "So how do you kill a dragon? You gotta take off the head, right?"

"Yeah," Meaghan said. "I've been thinking about that..." But she hadn't come up with anything yet. How on earth was she going to kill a giant, pissed-off lizard that could fly and breathe fire?

Smaller problems, Marnie reminded her.

Smaller problems... "Is there any way to neutralize that stuff that makes the flames?" Meaghan asked. "The goop in the back of its throat?"

"You mean make dragon spit not flammable?" Russ asked.

"Yeah."

"Dad said it was a lipid, right?"

"Yeah," Meaghan said. "That's like fat, right?"

Russ nodded. "Yeah. Or an oil or a wax. All fats are lipids but not all lipids are fats, but they're all flammable. A dragon is basically an on-demand grease fire."

"But what about dish soap? That destroys grease, right?"

Russ gave her his save-me-from-fools look. "Soap attaches to the fat molecules and makes it easier to wash them away. It doesn't eradicate them."

"But it's not like a dishpan full of suds can catch on fire," Meaghan said.

"You got a giant sink we can fill up?" Russ asked. "You think you can hold a dragon's head under water? Get it to blow bubbles?"

"We could spray the hose at it," Dustin said.

Russ moved his annoyed look to Dustin. "You never took chemistry, did you?"

"Uh, well, no," Dustin said. "But you put out fire with water, right?"

"Not grease fires," Gretchen said. "Flour. That's how you put out grease fires."

"For the love of God," Russ said, exasperated. "None of you get to cook in my kitchen. Flour dust is explosive. If a pan of oil catches fire, you smother it with a lid. Or salt or baking soda, they work, too. You add water to a grease fire, you get a fireball."

"Not what we need," Meaghan said. "Okay, forget that idea. But if it ate some baking soda or salt—"

Russ shook his head. "Not for a fire that big. You'd need to dump a truckload down its throat."

"Damn it." Meaghan paced back and forth, thinking. *If we can't put out the fire . . .* "What about fighting fire with fire?"

"That means using a smaller controlled fire to burn up the fuel," Brian said, "so the bigger fire can't advance."

Crap. "A dragon makes its own fuel, so no, then."

"You're supposed to use a magic sword," Todd said in a sullen voice. "A special blade. It's in the prophecy."

"I—"

"Don't believe in prophecies," everyone else said in unison.

"Right," Meaghan said. "No more babbling about the stupid sword. Besides, the prophecy doesn't even say sword, it says blade."

Brian began to laugh.

"What?"

"I know a blade you can use." He pointed out the window. "A big blade. We'll have to dig it out first though."

Meaghan stared at him. "What are you talking about?"

"The snowplow? The big blade on the front is made of steel."

"No." Todd stood up, a horrified look on his face. "You can't kill a dragon with a snowplow."

"Why not?" Meaghan asked. "Seems more likely than doing it with a sword."

"But ..." Todd looked around the room for support. "It's the ... the ... it's not ... mythic or heroic or—"

"Suicidal," Meaghan snapped at him. "I want to survive this. If that offends your fairytale sensibilities, tough shit." She looked back at Brian. "Can I drive it? I've never driven a big truck and it's been a while since I drove a stick shift."

"This one's automatic transmission," Brian said. "As easy to drive as a car. The blade controls look like a TV remote. Up, down, right, left. Super easy. But you don't need to worry because I'll be driving."

Meaghan sighed. "No, Brian, you won't. You can't. That's the trusting me part, okay?"

Marnie put her arm around him. "You stay back with me. I'll be doing big mind stuff and need somebody I can trust next to me to keep me safe."

Brian gave Meaghan a hard look, then nodded. "I don't like it."

"Neither do I, but that's the way it has to be," Meaghan said. "Okay, I got transportation and a great big blade. Next we need to figure out how to deal with the fire. Any ideas?"

Russ raised his hand. "Maybe we're looking at this wrong way. If we can't put out the fire—"

A wailing cry filled the air, followed by a thump and running footsteps.

Marnie jumped to her feet and stared at the ceiling. "Oh, no, you don't."

Jeff hung over the bannister, panic on his face. "We need help up here."

"With the baby?" Steph asked as she headed toward him.

"With the dragon," Jeff shouted, before running back upstairs.

CHAPTER FORTY-FOUR

MEAGHAN RAN UP the stairs behind Steph, with Marnie and Owen on her heels.

Kady and Natalie were both shouting spells at the top of their lungs, punctuated by a howl of pain from Kady as a contraction hit her.

Steph, Marnie, and Owen hit the ground behind Meaghan.

Meaghan heard someone—it sounded like Buzz—shout, "Get down, Meg!"

Her heart in her throat, Meaghan looked toward the window, expecting to see a giant eye looking back.

A single elf, clad in gray, hovered in front of the window.

Meaghan's terror morphed into towering rage. She stormed to the window—everyone screaming behind her—threw open the sash, and grabbed the elf by the front of his robe. With a snarl, she pulled the elf as hard as she could into the window frame.

There was a sickening crack as the elf's nose broke. A gush of blood flowed down his chin.

Meaghan dragged the now unconscious elf through the window and dropped him on the bedroom floor. "Here's your dragon." She kicked the small body, her heart pounding. "Asshole."

The screaming abruptly stopped.

"But . . . it was . . . I saw it," Natalie spluttered.

Kady cried out. "Oh hell, this hurts."

"Relax," Steph said, before breaking into hysterical giggles. "Listen to me. Relax. Like any of us will ever be able to do that again."

Meaghan felt Marnie's panic before she heard it. "How did that thing get near the house?" She stared at Meaghan. "I'm so sorry. I thought I had it covered . . . it . . . I'm sorry."

Shaking from the adrenaline coursing through her body, Meaghan managed to push the window sash back down. "Don't apologize. It's new power and you're still learning how to use it. Can you tell what happened?"

"No," Marnie said. "I don't know what . . ." She began to hyperventilate and hunched in a ball on the floor. "I don't . . ."

Brian shoved through the knot of people at the door and knelt beside her. "Shh. I'm here. You're safe."

He cradled Marnie's shaking body in his arms. "I was afraid of this." He looked up at Meaghan. "She wants to be better so bad sometimes she pushes too hard."

Meaghan nodded, feeling the fear rise again. Marnie was her biggest weapon besides Terry.

I'll get it together, a tiny voice said in her mind. *I need a minute.*

Relief flooded through Meaghan. *You got it. Don't worry. You can do this.*

"Going to the guest room," Brian said as he carried Marnie out of the room. "She needs a little space."

Meaghan stared down at the unconscious elf, then kicked it again. "Asshole."

The elf groaned.

"So are dragons really only elves?" Kady asked from the bed. She leaned against the pillows, her face sweaty but, for the moment, calm.

Please make it that easy. I can fight these scrawny shits all day. "Dustin said he saw it flame, but it could have been special effects." Meaghan looked over at Steph. "Are they elves?"

Steph, eyes wide, shook her head. "Don't know. I've never seen one."

Meaghan looked for Owen and found him sitting on the floor with Natalie, who leaned against him with her eyes closed.

"Well?" Meaghan asked.

Owen shook his head. "No idea."

"Dad, are you still with us?"

"Not really," Kady said in a tired voice. "Kind of busy at the moment. Everything's getting fuzzy in my head. But dragons are real. I saw a skeleton in the archive." Kady groaned again. "Oh, God, I think this is it. One last thing, Meg. Use the dragon's fire—"

Kady, really Kady this time, cried out in pain.

"Use it how?" Meaghan asked. "Dad! You can't leave me now."

Steph moved to the bed and took a closer look. "The baby's crowning. Everybody out but Jeff. Take the elf trash with you." She looked up at the people crowding the room. "Now!"

A sudden wind blew through the room.

"Okay, people, she means it." Owen jumped to his feet and herded everyone toward the door. "We're out of here."

Meaghan shuffled toward the door in shock. Dad was gone.

So was Marnie, at least for the moment.

"Where's Terry?" Meaghan asked.

"Coming across the street," somebody said.

Meaghan pushed her way through the crowd in the hall and ran downstairs. She shoved her feet into her boots, grabbed a coat off the pile—she didn't bother looking for her own coat—and charged out the front door.

Aggie and Hank led the way, clearing a wide trail for Terry. Sam walked behind him, cradling a dagger that looked like a sword in his small hands. Terry had also given Sam a small helmet and what looked like—Meaghan squinted—bolt cutters.

She ran toward them. "The baby's coming. Now."

Aggie and Hank stepped aside.

"Now remember what I said." Terry crouched next to Sam. "You're immune to magic, but Luka isn't. Don't try to fight the elves. Get him out of there as fast as you can and get back here. Meg needs you."

Sam nodded. "I won't fail you."

"Kid, you couldn't fail me if you tried," Terry said. "You're the bravest guy I've ever met and I used to hang out with Vikings."

"You were their god," Sam said.

Terry nodded. "Something like that." He looked up at Meaghan. "Where are those damn monks? We need a gateway into the archive. Somewhere the elves won't be."

Meaghan heard chuffing breath behind her. Dustin arrived at her side. "The server room's still good."

"You sure?" Meaghan asked.

"Yup," Dustin said, "but when you go into the rest of the castle, they'll know somebody's arrived, so move fast. Watch your back."

"I will," Sam said.

"The gateway's in the dining room," Dustin said. "Let's go."

"We'll clear you a path, son," Hank rumbled. He gently, very gently, patted Sam's small back with his giant hand.

They moved away, leaving Terry and Meaghan standing in the middle of Holly Lane.

"Elves and trolls being friends," Terry said, "Never thought I'd see that."

"How are you?" Meaghan asked. "Can I count on you?"

Terry sighed. "You always get right to it, don't you? I'm . . . shit, I don't know how I am. I have control like I've never had before, but I'm craving caffeine like I used to crave mead, which scares me big time, and losing Luka . . ." He shook his head. "I'm a lousy excuse for a thunder god. Always have been."

Meaghan patted his arm. "You're the only thunder god I've got at the moment, so we'll have to make do."

They looked at each other for a moment, then burst out laughing.

"Oh, God. I've had such a weird life, Meg, you have no idea."

"I'm not completely unfamiliar with the concept myself. I just beat up a dragon, except he was only an elf pretending to be a dragon, so I don't think that counts." Meaghan nodded. "Oh, and Dad's gone. He's now Kady's baby again."

"An elf was pretending to be a dragon?" A hopeful look blossomed on Terry's face. "Maybe there is no dragon. Maybe this is more elf bullshit."

"Yeah, I had the same thought, but no, Dad said they're real. There's a skeleton in the archive. Or there was before the elves did their historical scrub job."

"Crap," Terry said. "Felt some hope for a moment there. You got a plan?"

Meaghan stared at her boots. "Not really. Brian said I could use the snowplow blade. Maybe I can run the dragon over and pin it while you zap it."

Terry looked skeptical. "That's your plan?"

"You say you're a lousy excuse for a thunder god," Meaghan said, still staring at her feet. "I'm a lousy excuse for a leader."

"Not this again." Terry punched her gently on the arm. "You're a kick-ass leader. You were absolutely right about Luka's plan and I'm so sorry I didn't back you up. He can be a major dick himself sometimes."

"I wish I'd been wrong," Meaghan said. "He'd have a plan."

Terry shook his head. "No, he wouldn't. Stuff like this—big epic battles against monsters—is really hard to plan for. All you can do is gather your tools and take your best shot. I'm one of your tools. So is the snowplow, and it's way better than a sword. What else you got?"

Use the dragon's fire... Matthew's final words echoed through Meaghan's mind.

"You got any idea how a dragon actually makes fire?" Meaghan looked at him. "The mechanics of it?"

Terry chewed on his lip and stared into space for a long moment. "To get fire, you need heat, fuel, and an oxidizer—usually oxygen. Block one of those three elements and the fire goes out. You thinking about putting its flame out?"

"Maybe. Dad said the dragon's fuel comes from lipids it produces in a gland at the back of its throat."

"So, a Class B fire."

"What?"

"Oil or gas." He seesawed his hand in the air. "Unless you're in Europe or Australia, then gas is Class C. And I can see by the look on your face you don't care."

"How do you know that?"

"I'm a blacksmith," Terry said. "Been working with fire for three thousand years. I'm kind of a fire code geek to be honest."

"Russ says it's basically a grease fire, which means we can't use water to put it out. Not unless we want a huge fireball."

Terry looked thoughtful again. "You kill a dragon by taking off its head, right?"

"Yeah," Meaghan said.

"And the fuel is produced in the back of the throat. How is it ignited?"

"Dad said it was magic."

"Figures. But if the fuel source is in the throat ..." He stared into space. "You ever seen a fire breather at a carnival?"

"Once," Meaghan said. "Lawsuit waiting to happen. Why?"

"They get the fire plume by blowing fuel across a heat source into the air. A dragon must operate the same way, but instead of taking a sip of kerosene in its mouth, it creates it in the back of its throat. The magic spark must be in their mouth somewhere."

"Like a pilot light."

"Yeah." Terry nodded. "Your dad didn't say anything about fumes, did he?"

"Um . . ." Meaghan tried to remember what Matthew had told her. "Yeah, he did. He said the dragon burns off its fuel as soon as it makes it so it doesn't get sick from the fumes."

Terry grinned at her. "Or blown up by them. What happens if you turn on the gas when the pilot light is out?"

"Nothing," Meaghan said. "The gas builds up." She grinned back, feeling her hope return. "Until somebody lights a match."

"Or strikes a spark," Terry said, rubbing his fingers together. "And then—kaboom."

"If we can put out the pilot light, but keep pissing it off so it makes fuel and the fumes build up—"

"We can blow the bastard's head off." Terry pulled her into a hug that lifted her feet from the ground. "Meg, I think we got a plan."

CHAPTER FORTY-FIVE

"HOW DO YOU turn out this pilot light?"

Terry whirled, Meaghan still in his arms. "Johnny!"

John grinned. "You stealing my woman?"

"Heh," Terry said. "Nobody steals a woman like Meg. She goes where she wants."

John smiled at her. "I missed you."

She smiled back. "I missed you, too."

"Yeah, not feeling like a third wheel at all here." Terry squinted in the moonlight. "Uh, Johnny, is that what I think it is you're dragging behind you?"

John looked over his shoulder. "It is. I brought it for you. This one wanted us to think it was a dragon."

About five feet behind John, a small gray figure struggled to its feet in the snow. A length of chain was wrapped tightly around its arms and chest, and locked with a padlock. It glared at them and began to hiss something.

John raised his hand to the elf. "Quiet. The only reason you are not dead now is because Steph is busy and I convinced her you were worth more to us alive."

"Iron works on this one?" Meaghan asked John.

"It appears so," John said. "My mind is clear. No wings."

"But no barrier, either," Meaghan said. "This thing punched right through everything Marnie and the witches had up."

"So barriers don't work, but iron does. Unless it's faking us out again." Terry stalked toward the elf and stopped a few feet away from where it stood. The elf pulled back on the chain, trying to get as far from Terry as possible.

Terry took another step forward and glared down at the elf. "You know who I am and you know what I can do." He gave the elf a wolfish grin and rubbed his fingers together. Static electricity crackled in the air. "And I can control it this time. Why are you shit heads doing this?"

"You broke the truce," it hissed. "You mean to destroy us."

"Well, yeah," Terry said. "We mean to destroy you now, but only because you started it. The fair folk broke the truce."

"You sent the wizards against us," the elf hissed. "They gave you your power back." The elf spat at Terry's feet. "False god."

"Look who's talking," Terry said.

I knew it. Cooper. "What do you know about the wizards?"

The elf stared sullenly at Meaghan, then spat at her. "Impervious filth thinks it deserves to speak to me."

Terry backhanded the elf across the face. It yelped and fell to its knees.

"Watch your mouth," Terry said. "Next time, I'll hit you with a big iron hammer. Answer her question."

The elf merely glared at her.

"We didn't send the wizards," Meaghan said. "They keep trying to kill us, too. You guys need to do your homework. What wizards are you talking about? You mean the Order? Cooper and his gang?"

The elf shuddered. "They consort with the evil ones."

The squid? Meaghan raised an eyebrow. "You mean more evil

than you? Because from where I'm standing, you guys are as bad as it gets."

"You want to wage war on us."

Meaghan shook her head. "Wrong. Maybe Cooper wants that, but we don't. You got any idea why the wizards want to wage war on the fair folk?"

Terry gave her a quizzical look. "You mean besides the obvious reasons?'

"Yeah," Meaghan said. "Why does Cooper want to break the truce?"

The elf glared up at her. "Filth."

Terry raised his giant fist and shook his head. "Wrong answer. Want me to get the hammer? Make some elf paste?"

The elf shrank away from Terry. "The cooper wants to clear the world for . . . *them*. The terror that sleeps."

Meaghan rolled her eyes. "The stinky space squid you mean." *Which you appear to be more afraid of than I am. Time to take advantage of that.* "I'm letting you go."

"Meg, you can't." Terry stared at her in shock. "Why would you do that?"

"Because I want to send a message." Meaghan stared down at the elf. "I'm not scared of the fair folk, and I'm not scared of your stupid evil ones. All of you can kiss my impervious ass. Go back to whatever hole you crawled out of and tell your repulsive little buddies that if they want war, they've got it." She leaned near the elf's ear and said, in a soft voice, "Tell them I'm not my father. Remind them I'm a destroyer of worlds and if the fair folk want to survive, they'll stay out of my way."

John and Terry stared at her, mouths open.

"Uh, Meg," Terry said. "Are you sure—"

"Unlock him, John," Meaghan said. "Now."

John nodded and pulled a keyring from his pocket. He opened the padlock and pulled the chains loose.

The elf shrieked and scrambled away. "You'll burn," it hissed. "I'll see you burn, filth, you're—"

Meaghan, her face impassive, took a step forward.

The elf whimpered in fear, then vanished.

"Right," Meaghan said. "That should help Luka and buy us some time. Now they'll definitely want to find any miracle cure Luka dangles in front of them."

"You played him." A smile blossomed on Terry's face. "I'm impressed."

John put his arm around her. "You okay? You're shaking."

She snuggled up against him. "Adrenaline. This always happens when I try to be tough. And I'm kind of cold."

"You don't try to be tough," John said, rubbing her arms to warm her up. "You are tough. What do we do now?"

Pilot light.

Meaghan glanced toward the house. *Marnie, is that you?*

Yeah. Better now. You guys were trying to figure out how to put out the pilot light in the dragon's mouth.

Meaghan looked at the buried snowplow. "Terry, the igniter in the dragon's mouth is magical, right?"

"Yeah, that's what you said."

"And the snowplow blade is made out of steel, right?"

"Yeah." Terry began nodding. "Yeah, it sure is. And it's bigger than any damn sword."

"A lot bigger," Meaghan said. "If we can get the snow-plow blade wedged in the dragon's mouth, it'll interfere with the pilot light, but—"

"But the dragon will be so pissed off it'll keep producing fuel." Terry slapped her on the back. "Meg, you're a damn genius."

John stared at them both, confused.

Meaghan grinned at John. "One spark and boom, we blow the dragon's head off. We need to get the plow truck shoveled out as fast as we can."

Terry grinned. "Why shovel when you can melt?"

"Don't blow up my snowplow," Meaghan said. "Don't you dare."

"Relax. I know as much about electricity as I do about fire," Terry said. "I'll start small. Let's try this first with Luka's truck."

"No," John said. "Use mine. Luka said he'd give me his new one when this is over."

"Fine," Terry said. "Which one is yours?"

John pointed at a snowy lump in Meaghan's driveway. "There."

Terry grinned. "Check this out." He rubbed his hands together, and held them toward the truck. "If I do this right, the truck functions like a Faraday cage and the lightning flashes over it, turning some of the snow to steam. Might take a couple of passes. Lightning is more than hot enough to evaporate water into steam, but water and ice are crappy conductors, so it only heats right at the surface. It's why lakes don't boil when they get hit."

"A Faraday what?" Meaghan asked.

"Cage," Terry said. "Science thing. Cover your ears. This might get loud. And bright."

There was a flash of light and a huge bang. The indistinct pile in the driveway was now a snowy truck, steam rising off it. Another flash and another bang, and the truck was free of snow.

"Sweet." Terry admired his handiwork. "If I'd had coffee back in the day instead of mead, I'd still be a god." He blew on his fingers. "This is the most fun I've ever had with the boom boom."

"That's impressive. Do the plow," Meaghan said. "And my car."

Within two minutes, Terry had cleared the snow from the plow truck and from Meaghan's Audi.

"What the hell is going on out here?" Gretchen stomped onto the front porch holding a battery-powered lantern. "Yo, Sparky? You trying to blow up the neighborhood?"

Terry grinned at her. "Snow removal. Old school."

"Terry's been smiting stuff," Meaghan said. "How's Kady and the baby?"

Gretchen grinned. "He got here right before the light show. Big, healthy boy. Mom is doing fine, too." Her grin faded. "You gotta keep him safe. You got any ideas how to do that?"

"In fact," Meaghan said, "we do." *Except for a few minor things. Like how I'm gonna get the plow blade in the dragon's mouth before it can fry me crispy.* Her grin faded. "Still working on the details. Where's Marnie?"

On my way.

A moment later Marnie, bundled up against the cold, stepped onto the porch, next to Gretchen. "Would you take a cup of tea up to Steph? I need to get to work."

Gretchen squeezed her arm. "Sure, hon. Glad to see you back in the game."

"Me too."

When Gretchen went back inside, Marnie walked out to the street. "It's a good plan. I'll try to shield you, but after the way the elves blew through the last one, I'm not sure how much help I can be."

"The more important thing I need from you is to keep everybody else out of harm's way. Once the dragon gets here, Sam and I are the only ones who'll be able to get close to it." Meaghan glanced at John, then at Marnie and Terry. "You need to stay away."

The three of them looked back, eyes clear.

Time for another test. "Or the dragon will stun you. Promise you'll stay away."

"I promise," John said, the dreamy look back on his face. "I'll stay right by your side."

Terry shook his head like he was trying to dislodge water from his ear. "That buzzing. What is that?"

"The dragon's shielding magic," Marnie said. "I saw it this time. But I don't remember what prompted it."

Meaghan, Terry, and Marnie all looked at John.

"What?" he asked, "What did I do?"

"What we were we talking about?" Meaghan asked.

"About Marnie trying to shield you."

"Anything else?" Marnie asked.

"You didn't feel that?" Terry shook his head. "Johnny, how did you not feel that?"

"Feel what?" John looked puzzled. "What are you talking about?"

Meaghan, her heart back in her throat, took his face in her hands and kissed him. *Hell, it worked in Fahraya.*

He smiled at her. "What was that for?"

"What were we talking about?" Meaghan asked again.

"You were all asking me questions I don't understand."

"Before that."

John shook his head. "The shield. What is wrong with you all?"

Marnie nodded. "It makes sense he'd be more affected. His human DNA is from the Bronze Age. More susceptible maybe."

"My DNA is as old as John's," Terry said, "but I can still tell something happened to me."

"Yeah, but you're different," Meaghan said. "You said it yourself. You may not even be human anymore." She turned her attention back to John. "Honey, you trust me and you trust Terry, right?"

"With my life," John said. "Both of you."

"Then trust us now. You need to hang back with Marnie, no matter what," Meaghan said. "You need to help her keep everyone else away, too. Promise me. I can't tell you why, but I need you to trust me on this."

John opened his mouth, the snapped it shut. He nodded.

"Thank you," Meaghan said.

"I still don't like it," he said.

"Neither do I. But it's the way it has to be."

CHAPTER FORTY-SIX

"HOW SOON IS this going to happen?" Marnie asked. "Any idea?"

"Right after Sam gets back with Luka is my bet," Meaghan said.

"If they get back," Terry said.

"Yeah, if. Since we don't know what's going on, we need to be ready to go," Meaghan said.

"Go where?" John asked. "How are you going to do this?"

Meaghan shoved down the fear once again. *Don't panic. It won't help. It never does.* She repeated it in the back of her mind like a mantra. "What was it you said, Terry? About gathering your tools?"

"And taking your best shot." Terry nodded. "You've got three main tools right now. Me, Marnie, and the snowplow. Let's get you a few more."

Over at the Donners' house, Terry began fitting Meaghan with protective gear.

"Fire protection starts from the skin up. Natural fibers only. What are your long johns made of?"

"No idea," Meaghan said. "Check the tag in the collar."

Terry stuck his hand down the back of Meaghan's sweater and searched for the tag. "How many layers are you wearing?"

"I'm from Arizona remember? I get cold when it drops below seventy-five."

Terry squinted. "Microfiber. No good. All the synthetic stuff has to go."

"Why?"

"It burns and melts. Let me get you some of Steph's clothes."

He even wanted her to change her bra. "It's microfiber and nylon. Do you really want your girls to get burnt?"

"No, but Steph's bigger than I am," Meaghan said.

"Then go without."

Meaghan sighed. "The panties are microfiber, too."

"Then they gotta go. You really don't want to burn yourself down there. Trust me. Commando is better than melted undies." He handed Meaghan a pile of clothing. "Here."

"I have clothes at home, you know."

"This is faster. Get dressed and meet me downstairs. I need to grab more stuff from the workshop."

Meaghan changed into Steph's clothes as quickly as she could. The room was so cold she could see her breath. She sent Steph a mental apology when she stripped off her underpants and stepped into the silk long johns. *If I live through this, Steph, I'll buy you new ones.*

Meaghan found Terry waiting in the kitchen with an assortment of gear.

"Is that tin foil?" Meaghan asked, poking at silvery pile.

"Aluminized rayon," Terry said. "Kevlar is better, but this is the best I got. It'll protect against sparks and reflect back some of the heat."

Meaghan held a pair of silver chaps against Steph's wool ski pants. "You wear this stuff?"

"Yeah, when I'm working."

"In the movies and on TV the blacksmiths are always bare-chested."

Terry snorted in disgust. "You ever burn your nipple? Singe off your chest hair?"

"No."

"Don't. It sucks. Every time I see a shirtless smith, I want to throw something at the TV. Only an idiot plays around with red-hot metal with no shirt on." He helped her into the chaps. "Even the most swaggering, macho types wear leather aprons."

"Is this stuff better?"

Terry shrugged. "Both will protect you fine. I like this stuff because it's lighter and easier to move around in and it deflects heat so it keeps me a little cooler. But if I'm doing a demonstration at a renaissance fair or something, I'll wear leather. I tried the aluminum once and everybody threw a fit. It's not traditional, they said. Neither is using steel you didn't smelt yourself, I told them, and they said I didn't know what I was talking about." He stepped back. "Me. I only invented half the shit they do. How do those feel?"

"I feel like a baked potato," Meaghan said.

"No, you feel like an unbaked potato. That's the point."

Meaghan nodded. *Don't panic. It won't help. Don't panic.* "They're too long."

"The gaiters will take care of that. Hang on." He slipped the gaiters around her boots and zipped them up. "Now the apron. I grabbed the short one."

It almost reached her knees.

"Short on me, I guess," Terry said, eyeing his handiwork. "Sorry. I know all this stuff is too big on you." He held up a hunk of brown leather. "This should fit better. It's Steph's welding cape."

"Steph welds? What the hell is this thing? It's only sleeves."

"It's for arm protection," he said, helping her into it. "I have a full jacket but it would be huge on you." He stepped back to look, then nodded. "Yeah, Steph helps me sometimes." He pulled something else from the table. "When we're getting ready for a show or festival."

When Meaghan saw the gray helmet in his hands, the panic—fueled by claustrophobia—came roaring to the front and she couldn't push it down this time. She took several steps back, trying to control her breathing, her heart pounding. "No. I can't wear that."

"It'll protect you if the dragon flames," Terry said, trying to move closer to her. "And the back is mostly open. It only covers the front and top of your head."

"You put that thing on my head, and I'll punch you in the nuts," Meaghan said in a shrill voice. "No. Can't do it."

Terry set the helmet back on the kitchen table and held up his hands in surrender. "The claustrophobia. I forgot. I'm sorry."

Meaghan turned away and leaned against the sink, trying to catch her breath. "Hypnosis," she managed to say. "Hypnosis helped last time. Owen hypnotized me."

"Okay, we can go see him," Terry said. "Or not. If you feel better without the helmet, that's fine."

She took a few more deep breaths, then turned to face him. "Sorry. I'm a weenie, I know."

"No, you're not," Terry said. "We all have our phobias. You've never seen me around needles. Or snakes." He shuddered. "I really hate snakes. When John told me about the giant snakes in Fahraya, I about had a stroke. Still gives me nightmares."

"Yeah, I didn't like them either. But I'd rather face a pack of them than put my head in that thing. I can't stand having stuff cover my face."

"Like I said. Everybody's got something," Terry said. "How about goggles? Can you can handle them?"

Meaghan nodded. "As long as my nose isn't covered."

"One more thing," Terry said. "I know you aren't fond of them, but it's an easily wieldable chunk of steel."

"Not a sword," Meaghan said.

He pulled it out of the pantry. "I knew I'd have to build up to this one." He held out the Ulfberht sword the monks had brought back from the archive, hilt first. "Please. It's the best thing I've ever made."

"I can't handle a sword. I probably can't even lift the thing, let alone use it."

"Sure you can. Give it a try."

Meaghan sighed. "If it shuts everybody up."

She grasped the sword. It was surprisingly light and well balanced in her hand. She gave it an awkward swing and hit one of the chairs. The blade dug half an inch into the wood. "Oh, shit." She yanked the sword out. "Sorry."

Terry beamed with pride. "What did I tell you? Nice, right? Imagine if you'd followed through on the swing."

She stared at the sword with grudging respect. "It's really easy to handle. I thought it would be heavier."

"If you jab it in the roof of the dragon's mouth, it might be enough to mess with the igniter magic."

Meaghan glared at Terry. "Like I could get close enough to do that."

"You never know. It's one more tool. Better to have it and not use it than the other way around."

"Fine," Meaghan said. "Whatever. What are you gonna wear for protection?"

"I'm not supposed to get close to this thing, right? It'll mess with me somehow?"

Meaghan nodded.

"Not having protective gear forces me to keep my distance," Terry said. "Come on. Let's go make sure you know how to drive this snowplow. You got the keys?"

I'll get them from Brian, Marnie's voice said in Meaghan's head.

"Okay," Meaghan said out loud.

Terry gave her a worried look. "Keys?"

I'll meet you outside.

"Come on," Meaghan said. "Marnie has them."

They trudged across the street. The sky had lightened to a dark grayish blue and everything looked crisper and more detailed. "Almost dawn," Terry said.

"You think they'll wait?" Meaghan said. "Or try to surprise us?"

"Luka will try to buy as much time as he can," Terry said. He took a deep breath. "If he can. If they kill him—"

"They won't kill him if they can still use him," Meaghan said.

I hope, she thought.

Marnie was waiting by the truck with the lantern. When she saw Meaghan, she stifled a laugh. "You're so shiny."

Meaghan smiled at her. "My armor." She held up the Ulfberht. "Even got a sword. See?'

"Very nice," Marnie said, holding out a key ring in her mittened hand. "The reins of your horse, milady."

Meaghan grabbed the keys. "Remember. Keep them as far away as you can. If you need to evacuate, do it. If John doesn't have my car keys, the extra is in the candy dish on my dresser. Or head down the alley or into the field."

Terry grabbed her arm. "Not the field. Bad idea. That's where they want us to go."

Meaghan looked up at him. "How do you know?"

Marnie stared, eyes wide, over Meaghan's shoulder. She raised a trembling hand and pointed toward the other end of Holly Lane, where it intersected with Sycamore. Her voice a breathy squeak, Marnie said, "That's how."

Meaghan heard growling so low it was more a vibration than a sound.

Don't panic.
She turned to look behind her.
Something huge squatted at the mouth of Holly Lane.
The dragon had arrived.

CHAPTER FORTY-SEVEN

THE THREE OF them stared at the dragon, unable to move.

Then Meaghan saw two figures, a few feet ahead of it, struggling through the snow.

"That's Sam and Luka,"Terry said.

The dragon swished its tail and took a deep breath.

Marnie screamed and ran for the house.

"Terry, lightning, now!" Meaghan dove into the cab of the truck.

She stared at the controls, her mind trying to shut down.

"Automatic, dummy," she said out loud. She slotted the key into the ignition and the truck roared to life, followed by a blinding flash of light and a deafening crack.

She could see a panel with R, N, and D, but no lever. "Shit, shit, shit. Think."

Push button, Marnie told her.

Meaghan nodded and hit D, then remembered the truck was parked in the wrong direction.

I have to do a K-turn in a snowplow with a dragon on my ass?

Meaghan stared at the transmission buttons. "Fuck that," she said, and hit reverse.

Using the side mirrors, she backed, at the highest speed she could manage in the deep snow, toward the dragon, praying she didn't hit Sam and Luka.

There was another crack of thunder.

The dragon flamed.

The cab lit up with rosy orange light. Meaghan squealed in fear but kept going. She felt a crunch and then a wave of heat, followed by a deafening roar, which quickly faded. It was like listening to a jet plane fly into the distance.

The passenger side door opened.

The sword was on the seat where Meaghan had dropped it. She grabbed it and poked it toward the door.

"Meaghan, let us in." Sam's small gray face appeared. "Help me. He's hurt."

Meaghan reached out a hand, and she pulled while Sam pushed Luka into the cab.

Luka's cashmere sweater was gone, replaced with a blood-stained T-shirt. His feet were bare, and bright red from the cold. Raw red scrapes circled his wrists.

When Meaghan got a good look at his face, she gasped. His eyes were swollen shut, the lids blistered and raw, and blood ran down each cheek, like tears.

"What did they do to you?" she gasped. "My God, Luka—"

"It's in the myth," he said in a raspy voice. "Venom in my eyes. We need to get out of here. It'll be back."

"It is circling above," Sam said. "It stunned him and he stopped, and we would be dead if you had not come."

"Get me to Steph," Luka whispered. "Steph. I need Steph."

She glanced in the side mirror. The giant blue spruce in the Franzettis' front yard was on fire, but the house looked okay.

Luka's new truck hadn't fared so well. It hadn't been burnt.

Instead, it looked like it had been stepped on. Or possibly sat upon. The cab was crushed and the rear of the truck jutted upward at an impossible angle.

Meaghan put the plow into drive and drove back down the street to her house.

We need help, she told Marnie and then, without words, sent Marnie an image of Luka's ravaged face. *Get Steph. Dragon's in the air. Can you shield us?*

On it, Marnie answered.

The gray light brightened and glowed golden. *Is that you?*
No. Sunrise.

Meaghan felt the truck rock on its axles as snow blew across the windshield.

There was a whoosh, like a giant furnace kicking on, and the empty MacDougall house burst into flames.

I can guard your house, Marnie said, *but I think that's all I can do.*
Do it. Keep them safe.

Steph rushed from the house, Brian right behind her. Steph cried out in shock when she saw Luka, but Brian exhibited the steely calm Meaghan had seen on Labor Day. He pulled open the door, asked Luka a few questions, and gently probed his neck. Satisfied, Brian pulled Luka out of the truck and slung him over his shoulders in a fireman's carry. Steph on his heels, Brian trotted into the house.

"I will stay with you," Sam said. "You cannot do this alone."

Meaghan didn't argue. He was right. "Terry will try to hit it with lightning, while we try to get some steel in its mouth. If we can pin it with the truck, or injure it and get the plow blade in its mouth, it should block the magical ignition long enough for fumes to build up and then Terry can detonate it."

"Will a sword work?" Sam ran his fingers across the Ulfberht.

"Maybe, but only if you've got a clear shot to get in there without getting fried. You're no good to me dead."

A gentle rapping on the truck window made Meaghan scream and leap in her seat.

Terry pulled open the door. "Sorry. It's circling. What now?"

"Is it injured?" Meaghan asked. "Where I hit it?'

Terry shook his head. "No, but you pissed it off big time."

"This is a good thing," Sam said.

"How is this a good thing?" Meaghan asked in a higher voice than she intended.

"Because now you are its target," Sam said. "You challenged it and it will focus its attack on you."

"How do you know?" Meaghan gripped the steering wheel to hide how badly her hands were shaking. "And how is that good?"

"I read a great deal in the archive, when I was hiding there. If the dragon is focused on you, it will not attack the rest of the town."

"But—" *Did you honestly think it would only come after Holly Lane?* "Are you sure?"

Sam nodded.

"But is it me or the truck it's focused on?"

"Both," Sam said. "It will focus on the truck's shape and your scent. Its vision is good enough to see the truck, but not you. For that, it will rely on smell."

"Oh, shit," Terry said. "Look."

The dragon landed in the meadow with a soft thump. It settled onto its haunches, its giant tail wrapped around it and twitching at the tip, like a giant, scaly house cat.

"You need to get out of here." Meaghan gave Terry a shove. "Go. You're too close."

"No," Terry said. "My ears aren't buzzing. It makes me stupid, right?"

"You remember that?" Meaghan asked. Had her father been wrong? Could the others help after all?

"No, but it makes sense it would." He stared at the dragon. "Wow, it's beautiful."

"Are you insane?"

"Meg, I'm serious. Look at it. No human has seen an actual dragon in over a thousand years. This may be our only chance. Really look."

Meaghan looked. The dragon was huge, but well proportioned, with a long graceful neck and muscular body. It looked less like a dinosaur than she'd expected and more feline. Its huge, cat-like, amber eyes dominated its slender, angular face. The dragon's scales, touched by the first rays of dawn stretching over the meadow, sparkled green and gold.

"Wow," Meaghan said in a soft voice. "It is beautiful."

"And too dangerous to exist in the human world, so we have to kill it." Terry's voice was heavy with regret. "Because of the damn fair folk."

"Aren't dragons supposed to be evil?" Meaghan asked.

"Not evil. Wild," Terry said. "It acts out of pure instinct. Utterly wild and beautiful and dangerous, and it has to die because of those fucking elves."

"Terry, I need you with me on this."

The dragon unfurled its huge, iridescent wings—like a giant dragonfly—but didn't take flight. The wings reminded Meaghan of the Fahrayans' wings. Delicate, sparkling, and impossible. Only magic could keep a dragon aloft on those wings.

Wings fluttering gently, the dragon turned its massive face toward the morning sun. It closed its eyes and tilted its head. A rhythmic rumble, louder than the idling snowplow engine, filled the air.

"Is that ... purring?" Meaghan stared wide-eyed at Terry. "Dragons purr?"

"Sure sounds like it." Terry said. "Too bad we can't just give it some cheeseburgers and a pile of catnip. I'm with you on this,

Meg. I know we have to kill it. There's no other way. It makes me sad is all."

"It is magnificent," Sam said, "but it will not rest much longer."

The dragon coughed and a spout of flame gushed from its mouth, followed by the hiss of steam as snow evaporated. It spread out its front legs and stretched languorously, then sat bolt upright. Eyes now open, the dragon fixed its amber gaze on the snowplow.

"Oh, shit," Terry said. "Showtime."

Lightning flashed and the dragon yelped in surprise, its tail flailing back and forth.

"Missed," Terry said. "Shit."

"Can you drive it towards us, but keep it distracted?" Meaghan asked. "Nip at its heels a little?"

"Like a sheep dog?" Terry nodded.

"You push it forward, but keep its attention on you."

Terry began shaking his head. "My ears, they're buzzing."

"Go." Meaghan smacked his arm. "Get some distance."

Terry nodded and ran as best he could through the deep snow towards his house and disappeared around the back.

"Meaghan, we need to go, I think," Sam said.

Meaghan put the truck in reverse and backed up as fast as she could. "I wish I knew how to work the plow."

Sam squinted at the dash. "These buttons here? Like the television control?"

"Yeah," Meaghan said. "That's it. Can you see what the dragon is doing?"

"It's rolling on its back in the snow."

"It's what?"

"Rolling," Sam said. "On its back. Wait. Now it's on its feet." Sam squeaked with fear. "It is in the air coming this way. Drive faster!"

Meaghan skidded backwards through the snow all the way to Sycamore Street. She punched the drive button, dropped the plow blade, and drove as fast as she could toward Main.

"It is following," Sam shouted. He leaned out the window, staring at the sky.

"Sam, be careful," Meaghan shouted back.

He leaned further out, craning his head to look at the sky. "It's right above and—"

Meaghan hit a ridge of snow in the road and the truck bounced hard. She heard a high squeak, and when she glanced over, Sam was gone.

"Sam!" Meaghan jammed on the brakes and the plow slid sideways into a mound of snow on the side of the road. A metallic screech filled her ears as the plow sideswiped several cars.

That'll be a claim against the city, the lawyer part of her brain told her.

She gazed in the side mirror. Sam knelt in the middle of the road and waved at her.

The truck rocked again on its axles and the snow blew sideways as the dragon passed overhead. She stuck her head out her own window, her heart hammering in her chest, looking around to see where the dragon had gone.

Then Meaghan heard a rattling wheeze from the passenger window and her blood froze. She whipped her head around. A giant amber eye stared through the open window. There was another rattle as the dragon inhaled.

Please let it be quick. John, I love you.

With a whimper, Meaghan shut her eyes and waited for the end.

Chapter Forty-Eight

NO! TERRY, NOW! NOW!!

Marnie's voice shrieked in Meaghan's mind, followed by a blinding flash and the loudest sound Meaghan had ever heard.

Static electricity crawled over her skin like a million ants. An acrid, almost chemical smell filled her nose. She coughed, choking on it.

Meaghan looked toward the passenger window. The dragon had crumbled to the ground and lay twitching, a smoking burn along its flank.

GET OUT OF THERE!

Meaghan, her hands shaking so hard she could barely hold the wheel, stabbed at the reverse button and hit it on the third try. She became aware in a distant sort of way that she was sobbing loudly.

Move, damn it. Move, she told herself. Her foot slipped off the gas.

Meg, get it together. Hang on.

Meaghan felt a wave of calm sweep over her. *What the fu—* she stopped fighting and let it happen.

"Right," she said to the empty cab. "Time to drive." She glanced in the side mirror, lifted the plow blade—*don't want to damage that, might need it*—and carefully backed away from the dragon.

This is like when Owen hypnotized me, only much, much better. She knew with absolute certainty that Marnie had done this. *Thanks, hon,* she told her. *This is awesome.*

She checked the side mirrors. Sam was nowhere in sight.

She glanced through the windshield. The dragon was struggling to its feet.

She looked back in the side mirrors again.

Terry loomed in the middle of the now-plowed road, a sledgehammer in one hand, and the other hand, outlined in flickering blue light, raised to the sky.

"Ooh, now I get the god thing," Meaghan said out loud to the empty cab. "Cool."

Meg, a little too chill, maybe? Get out of there, Marnie told her.

"Oh, right. Let's turn around while I got the space." She dropped the plow blade—*no point wasting it*—and pulled into the nearest empty driveway.

Raise the blade, hit reverse, back to drive, drop the blade. "I'm getting the hang of this."

Meg, damn it!

Meaghan felt the calm withdraw, and some of the adrenaline washed back over her. She stomped her foot on the gas pedal, spun the wheels for a second, then the truck rolled forward.

Terry stepped aside and raised the hammer in salute.

Meaghan waved back.

Sam stood on the corner of Holly Lane. Meaghan skidded to a stop, slid over to the passenger door, and reached a hand down. "Come on. It's waking up."

"The smith—"

"Is doing his thunder god thing. Come on." She stared down Holly Lane. The MacDougall house billowed smoke and would be a total loss, but the fire hadn't spread. A beam dropped, sending a shower of sparks toward the sky, where they winked out about ten feet above the house.

"No, they bounce," Meaghan said to Sam.

"What?"

"The sparks," she said. "Check it out. Marnie's doing that, I bet."

"The dragon almost killed you." Sam stared at her, eyes wide.

Meaghan smiled at him. "Don't remind me." She pulled into Edna's driveway. "Not getting stuck the wrong way next time."

"How do we get the steel into the dragon's mouth?"

"No idea."

Sam shrieked.

Meaghan looked in the side mirror.

The big amber eye was back.

Meaghan punched the truck back into reverse and stepped on the gas. Metal screeched on concrete as the blade ripped backward across the driveway and caught on Edna's retaining wall.

The blade, forgot to raise the blade. But before she could say or even think anything else, the truck smashed into what felt like a brick wall.

The truck cab glowed golden for a moment.

Meaghan felt a cushion of air surround her, right before her forehead hit the steering wheel. Something warm and wet ran down the side of her face. *Scalp wound*, she thought, feeling very far away from her body. *They bleed like crazy.*

The lightning bolt was so close she could hear it sizzle a fraction of a moment before the thunderclap hit, followed by a high keening whistle in her ears.

That can't be good.

A giant hand reached into the cab and pulled her out of the truck.

"Come on, girl," a deep voice rumbled. "Aggie's got the boy. I'll carry you."

Before she could respond, Hank swung her over his shoulder. She glanced down and noticed the plow blade twisted at an angle.

No more plowing. Damn.

Another sizzle, another deafening boom.

"Aggie, go, go!" Hank shouted. Meaghan bounced on his shoulder as he ran. Looking back, she saw Terry, a goofy grin on his face, standing in the middle of Holly Lane, staring up at the dragon. The dragon, no more than ten feet away, stared back, tilting its head from side to side, like a cat examining a mouse and mulling how to kill it.

"*Marnie!*" Meaghan shouted out loud and in her mind. "Do something!"

A shimmer of golden light, brighter than the morning sun around it, appeared between Terry and the dragon. A moment later, Terry flew backwards about twenty feet and landed with a gentle thump in a snowbank.

He struggled to his feet, the grin now gone from his face. A bolt of light shot from his raised hand, hit the golden wall, and dissipated.

The dragon inhaled and let forth a gush of fire that broke against the golden wall. Marnie's barrier held for a moment, then collapsed, and the flames shot toward the snowbank where Terry had landed.

The snow hissed into a cloud of steam, but Terry was already running toward the meadow.

Meaghan punched Hank's massive back. "Put me down."

Hank ignored her for two more steps, then other hands pulled her from his shoulder.

John, frantic, wrapped his arms around her and kissed her.

Meaghan wrestled free from John's embrace. "We can't leave Terry alone with that thing. I need to get back to the truck."

Behind her, Meaghan heard a rattling breath, and a moment later, Edna's house was on fire.

Along with the snowplow.

"It's gonna blow," she heard a male voice yell, probably one of the monks.

"No, it won't," she yelled back. "Don't you clowns watch *Mythbusters?*"

There goes my blade. Damn it.

The dragon, its flame spent, sat down in the snow and began to groom itself like a cat.

"It's purring again," Meaghan said, as a frantic giggle escaped her. She could feel another panic attack reaching into her, and took a deep breath. *Don't panic.*

Terry was nowhere in sight.

Before she could move, before she could think, the gray figures materialized before her.

"Give us the baby," one of them screeched at her.

"Fuck you," Meaghan answered.

Beside her, John fell to his knees, sobbing.

"No," Hank rumbled. "I'm a free troll. No." The words were slushy and garbled like he couldn't move his tongue. "Ag—" was all he managed to say before he stiffened like a statue. His eyes rolled wildly in his face, but nothing else moved.

"Hank," Aggie grunted, before she too froze, Sam still in her arms.

Meaghan whirled around. The monks—Todd, Clint, and Dustin—stared in awe at the air about two feet above the fair folks' heads. "They're real," Clint squeaked. "I knew it. Real elves. So beautiful."

"Fucking hell," Meaghan said. "They're still three feet tall and ugly," she shouted over her shoulder. "Ignore what your eyes tell you. It's not real."

But it was no good. Everyone was either weeping, ecstatic with awe, or unconscious.

Except Sam. He groaned in Aggie's arms and stirred.

"Meaghan," he squeaked.

The elves stepped forward.

Time for the bullshit. Meaghan hadn't gotten her chance to put on the grand performance in the basement. *Got to stall them until Terry gets his shit together.*

Meaghan buried her face in her hands and began to make loud sobbing sounds.

Marnie, where are you?

With Kady.

Is the baby safe?

For now, but I can't shield him and help you at the same time. The witches are unconscious. It's only me. And the elves are too strong.

Can they hear us?

I don't think so.

Keep everybody else in the house if you can.

The front door slammed shut with a bang.

"Please don't take the baby," Meaghan said between sobs. "My father is gone. Anything that's left of him can't hurt you now. Please, he's only a baby."

The elves screeched with laughter.

Meaghan took a quick look around her.

Sam was awake and carefully freeing himself from Aggie's frozen grasp.

Meaghan looked back at the elves. They were so busy gloating they didn't notice Sam.

She took a deep breath and wailed out some more sobs. "Please don't hurt us. Take the smith but leave the baby." *Where the hell is Terry?*

Meadow, Marnie answered. *Trying to get his focus back.*

Hell of a time for performance anxiety. She howled some more, hoping the elves were still focused on her. "Please don't hurt me. I'll never bother you again. Don't let the dragon burn me." For a moment, the sobs were real. *Not burning. Anything but that.*

More screeching laughter rolled over her.

She turned away from the elves, as if in fear, and peeked through her fingers.

Sam swung from Aggie's frozen arm and dropped into the snow, something in his hand.

"The beast is hungry for impervious meat," one of the elves screeched. It waved its skinny arm toward the dragon.

The dragon yelped in pain and cowered away.

That's how they control it. Even though the dragon had already tried to kill her, she felt a flash of rage at the fair folk. The dragon had attacked her out of instinct, not cruelty like the elves.

Meaghan now truly understood Terry's regret at having to kill it. She knew she didn't have a choice. It was either the dragon or everybody she loved, but she'd take no joy in killing this creature.

She glanced up. The dragon's tail was extended now, rather than curled tightly around its body. Behind the fair folk, Sam ran in a low crouch toward the end of the dragon's tail, carrying the Ulfberht sword in his hands. He stopped, hands raised to strike, the sword nearly as long as he was tall, and stared at Meaghan.

It flames when you piss it off . . . Marnie! She sent Marnie a mental snapshot of the scene and a moment later, a golden shimmer appeared in the air between the fair folk and everyone else.

"Sam, now!"

Sam swung the sword.

Enraged, the dragon threw back its head with a roar and took a deep breath.

Meaghan buried her head in her arms, too scared to watch.

A moment later, the screaming began.

CHAPTER FORTY-NINE

EVEN AS MUCH as she hated the fair folk, Meaghan felt a stab of horrified pity at the twisted flaming bodies. Steph had been right. Nobody, not even the fair folk, deserved to die that way.

Marnie's barrier had turned into a wall of flame.

I can't hold this much longer.

Meaghan could feel in Marnie's thoughts the effort it took to maintain the barrier.

And not only was Meaghan on the other side of it, but everyone Meaghan loved.

The dragon will follow my scent. Sam said it will follow my scent.

Before Marnie could respond, Meaghan was on her feet and running through the heavy snow away from her house. She scrambled onto the nearest car—her Audi, parked in Terry and Steph's driveway—and stood on top of it, waving her hands.

"Over here! I'm over you, you bastard. Come and get me!"

The dragon, its flame depleted, turned its head and grinned at her—at least it looked like a grin. It shifted its massive bulk and took a deep breath. At the same moment, the golden barrier vanished.

"Oh, shit," Meaghan squeaked, as she slid off the car and ran. She dove over one of the low steel guardrails that marked the end of Holly Lane, into the unbroken snow.

The dragon flamed for a moment, then unfurled its wings and flew out over the meadow.

Meaghan peeked over the guardrail and whimpered at the sight of the burning Audi. "Not again."

She felt the lightning—she'd lost her hat somewhere and now all her hair stood on end—before the thunder crack. She jammed her fingers in her ears.

Bang.

Meaghan looked out into the meadow.

Terry stood in the snow, shooting lightning bolts into the sky as the dragon circled him. Any time the dragon got near stunning distance, Terry zapped it.

Enraged by Terry, the dragon appeared to have forgotten about Meaghan for the moment, but she knew she couldn't stay huddled by the guardrail.

The steel guardrail . . .

Sam ran toward her. "We must go. It will be back. We must go."

"My scent," Meaghan said. "What carries my scent best? What will the dragon focus on?"

"Blood and sweat," Sam said. "And urine."

Meaghan had been so focused on the dragon, she'd forgotten the bloody scalp wound from the plow crash. It had dripped down the side of her face and neck, a small discomfort in a sea of chaos.

One shoulder of Steph's short welding jacket was wet with blood, as was the wool sweater underneath it. Meaghan stripped them off and draped them across the fence.

Another flash of light and a boom. Terry dropped to one knee, then got back to his feet, but his fatigue was obvious. He couldn't do this much longer.

"Hurry," Meaghan said, handing Sam the jacket and sweater. "Wrap them around the railing."

With shaking hands, he took the clothing. He pulled a rag from his gray tunic and handed it to Meaghan. "Here, wipe off the blood on your skin. More scent."

"Got a better idea." Meaghan shoved the rag in the pocket of the aluminized apron, unbuckled the aluminized chaps, and then unbuttoned her jeans. She squatted above the railing and peed on it, the urine steaming where it dripped on the snow.

The dragon circled Terry, like a sheepdog wearing down a wayward ewe. Terry stumbled again and, this time, he didn't get back to his feet.

Meaghan pulled her pants back up. She stuck her fingers in her mouth and whistled as loud as she could. "Asshole, over here!" She kicked the guardrail. "Help me make noise."

Sam banged on the railing with the sword and screeched in his native language.

The dragon turned its head in their direction.

"Go," Meaghan said, pushing Sam over the railing and then climbing after him. "Run."

"Where?"

"Away," she shouted as she ran down the middle of Holly Lane. "Away from me!"

The dragon soared away from Terry and landed near the guardrail. It sniffed once, then with a graceful dip of its head, bit down on the wad of bloody clothing.

Marnie, tell him now. Tell Terry now!

The dragon roared, but no thunder followed.

Meaghan glanced back, but couldn't spot Terry. The dragon lifted its head and sniffed the air.

With no plan, no destination, Meaghan ran for her life. The plowed road was easier to run on than the heavy snow, but slicker. She fell once and pulled herself to her feet, with no thought but to get as far away as possible. She'd made it all the way to Edna's house, when she stepped on something hard and round that rolled out from under her foot.

Meaghan fell through the air, hands out to catch herself. She felt something snap—*wrist?*—as she hit the ground and skidded another yard. Panicked breath wheezing in her chest, she tried to push herself to her feet.

The agony flared in her wrist like white-hot flame. Normally stoic about pain, Meaghan squealed and burst into tears, as her vision grew yellow around the edges. She felt consciousness starting to fade and flailed out convulsively with her other hand.

It landed on something hard and round.

A glass jar.

A jar of the Miller's moonshine.

A memory of Marnie, naked and possessed by the Power, pouring moonshine over her head as accelerant, flashed across Meaghan's terrified mind.

From behind, something nudged at her leg.

A hot foul-smelling wind blew across her.

Not wind, she thought, *breath.*

She screamed, all rational thought driven from her mind.

But the dragon didn't flame or bite. Instead, the dragon yelped in pain.

"Get away from her," she heard Sam shout.

She rolled over.

Sam stood a few feet away, the dragon's open mouth wheezing and drooling inches above his head. He was holding something . . .

The picture clicked into focus.

Sam had jammed the Ulfberht sword into the roof of the dragon's mouth.

It couldn't flame.

The dragon shook its head hard, and Sam went flying, empty-handed.

The dragon whimpered, pawing at its snout.

The sword's still in there.

Meaghan stared at the jar of moonshine in her hand.

Molotov cocktail.

She pushed herself to her feet with one hand, trying not pass out from the fire in her wrist. She wedged the jar under her left arm and used her good right hand to pull the rag Sam had given her out of her apron pocket. Wheezing with pain and exhaustion, she tried to open the lid of the jar but couldn't manage to do it with only one functional hand.

Gobs of dragon drool steamed and fizzed on the ground where Sam had stood. Meaghan swabbed it up with the rag and, with her good hand, armpit, and teeth managed to tie the sodden rag around the jar, leaving enough hanging on one end to use as a fuse.

Need a match.

Across the street, the MacDougall house burned. Behind her, Edna's house burned. "Dummy," she said out loud, as the hysterical laughter bubbled up. Edna's rosebushes were on fire, too. Meaghan hobbled toward the nearest one, and lit the rag. It sputtered for a moment and then ignited.

"Hey, Puff," Meaghan said. "Want a treat?"

The dragon wheeled its graceful head in the direction of her voice.

"I'm sorry," she said. "I truly am sorry." With her right arm, she tossed the flaming jar underhanded toward the dragon's mouth.

The dragon snapped it out of the air.

Meaghan heard the glass jar crunch between the dragon's teeth.

The explosion rocked the street. Meaghan was thrown off her feet and landed on her broken wrist. Her vision yellowed again as she howled in pain, then the endorphins kicked in and the pain receded enough to let her stay conscious.

A wet plop landed in the snow beside her and began to steam.

It's raining dragon.

The plop was followed by a solid thunk. The Ulfberht landed beside the steaming pile.

Meaghan glanced upward. The now headless dragon swayed above her.

"Oh, crap." Using the sword like a cane, Meaghan got to her feet and tried to run, but the best she could do was hobble. The dragon swayed for a moment longer, and then fell, gracefully, along the length of Holly Lane, and landed with a crash that shook the ground beneath her.

"This isn't over," a voice hissed behind her. She turned and saw the elf from the basement.

"No," Meaghan said in a soft voice. "It isn't." Still holding the sword, she pointed it at the elf. "You fuckers are next."

The elf hissed one last time and vanished into the air.

Chapter Fifty

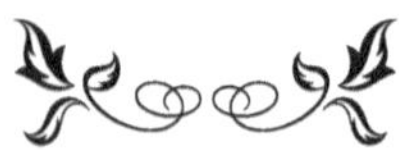

MEAGHAN SURVEYED HOLLY Lane.

We're not done yet. The archive needs to be cleaned out.

Black smoked billowed from Edna's and from the MacDougall house, but the other four homes on the street appeared unharmed. The Franzettis' blue spruce had burned itself out along with the snowplow and her Audi.

"It still had the new car smell," Meaghan said.

"I am sorry about your car," a small voice said behind her.

Startled, Meaghan yelped, and spun around. Sam, angry red burns on his face and arms, stood behind her. She yelped again, but this time with joy. "Sammy! We did it."

He threw himself at her and wrapped his small arms around her. "You did it."

Meaghan hugged him the best she could with one arm. "No, we did it. If you hadn't jammed the sword into its mouth, I'd be a lump of charcoal right now. And if you hadn't stabbed it in the tail first, everyone else would be dead along with me."

He looked up at her. "I—even with all they have taken from

me and done to me—I did not wish to see them die that way."

"Me neither."

"And the dragon. It made me sad to hurt it. Like they hurt it. Like they hurt me."

Meaghan grimaced. "You noticed that, too."

"I didn't understand why the smith felt sad to have to kill it until then."

The smith . . . "Where's Terry? Have you seen him?"

"Here," Terry said, trudging up the street. He'd exchanged the hammer for a fire extinguisher. He eyed the sword in her hand. "What did I tell you? That's a good sword. You used it well."

"I didn't use it," Meaghan said. "Sam did. He's the one who jabbed it in the dragon's mouth." She glanced at Terry's fire extinguisher. "I don't think that's gonna get it done."

Terry shrugged. "Better than nothing." He sprayed the burning rosebushes closest to Meaghan's house, then dropped the empty extinguisher on the ground. "I bet all the outside faucets are frozen solid, even if we could find a hose. And no fire department. Shit."

The street flared with golden light and all the fires winked out as if smothered.

Don't ask me how I did that, Marnie said in her mind.

Terry looked around. "Huh. Never mind. Did she do that?"

Meaghan nodded, not needing to ask who he meant.

The front door of the Keele house opened and people began pouring out, led by Natalie.

John was right behind her and ran when he saw Meaghan.

"I broke my wrist," she called, raising her arm in the air. "Gentle, please."

John skidded to a stop in front of her. "You are hurt?" He took her injured hand in gentle fingers. "Marnie will fix this."

Natalie skidded to a stop behind John. "Holy shit. You did it. Sorry I couldn't help. I was out cold."

"Dragonsleep," Meaghan said.

"Yeah, what was that? Something the elves did?"

"No, the dragon," Meaghan said. "A variation of the stunning magic. Only affects witches and wizards."

Natalie looked dazed for a moment. "Yeah, I thought it was the elves."

Meaghan rolled her eyes. "Yeah, it was the elves. Marnie picked up the slack while you guys were out."

Natalie stared at the dead dragon, avoiding Meaghan's gaze. "Brian seems really happy with her. Happier than he would have been with me."

"Owen seems pretty happy with you," Meaghan said.

"When I woke up, he was kissing me."

"Like Sleeping Beauty?"

Natalie snorted with derision. "I said 'don't be creepy' and then I punched him."

Meaghan couldn't hold back her laughter.

"I hear you guys had a big night," Natalie said, with a sly grin.

"Yeah, I killed a dragon," Meaghan said.

"Not what I was talking about."

John smiled, while Meaghan blushed. "We still have work to do," he said as he led her toward the house.

As they climbed the porch, Russ appeared at the door holding a chain saw and wearing a yellow rain slicker and safety goggles, with a blue tarp wrapped around him like an apron.

Meaghan raised her eyebrow. "You're late. The dragon's already dead."

"Yeah, and it's not gonna butcher itself," Russ said. "I've been talking to Hank."

"There's good eating on a dragon," Hank rumbled behind him. "If you dress it proper."

Russ grinned at her, kissed her on the cheek, and trotted down the steps. A moment later, Meaghan heard the burping of the chain saw.

The hallway was crowded with people.

"How are Kady and the baby?" she asked.

"Fine," Gretchen said, her voice raspier than normal. "But Terry drank all the goddamn coffee."

Everybody laughed.

"What about Luka?"

The laughter abruptly stopped.

"Upstairs with Marnie," Gretchen said. "He's in bad shape."

"His eyes?"

"Not only his eyes," Natalie said in a small voice behind her. "You better go up."

Terry pushed his way past everyone and took the stairs two at a time.

"What about the archive?" Dustin asked, in a dejected voice. "What if the elves are still there?"

"Then we will fight them," Sam said, taking the sword from Meaghan's hand and holding it out to Dustin. "You brought the weapon that saved us all. Together we will go and defend the archive."

"Hang on," Meaghan said. "Let me talk to Marnie and Luka first. And then we'll all go."

"But—"

Sam gave Dustin a gentle smile. "We will not abandon the archive. But we must make a plan. Is there food in the kitchen?"

"Yeah, but—"

"The kitchen. I must eat."

Dustin nodded and followed Sam down the hall.

With John's help, Meaghan peeled off the silvery apron and chaps, and made her way upstairs. She poked her head into Kady's room first.

"You killed a dragon," Kady said, with a beaming smile. "Bad ass. Come see what I did."

The baby lay wrapped in a cocoon of blankets in Kady's and

Jeff's arms. His tiny face was perfect, not squished like some babies, and he wore what looked like a serene smile.

"He's smiling," Meaghan said. "He's happy to be here."

"No," Kady said, brushing his tiny cheek with her finger. "That's gas. He won't start smiling for real for a couple of months. You want to hold him?"

Meaghan shook her head. "Not yet. My wrist is busted up and I'm covered in dragon snot. I need to take care of a couple of things first."

Jeff began to cry. "Thank you for keeping my family safe. You said you would, and you did."

Kady smiled. "Don't cry on the baby, you big marshmallow."

"You guys have everything you need?" Meaghan asked.

Jeff gazed at her with tear-filled eyes. "Everything. Thank you."

"Thank Sam, too. I'd be a pile of charcoal right now if it hadn't been for him."

Meaghan stopped in the hall bath. With one hand, she couldn't do much, but she scrubbed some of the blood and soot away with a washrag and washed her good hand the best she could.

Her wrist was throbbing and the pain was growing. She couldn't ignore it for much longer, but first she had to see Luka.

She let herself into the guest room. Luka lay on the bed propped up with pillows, his eyes bandaged. Steph, Owen, and Terry sat around him. He stiffened when he heard Meaghan step into the room.

"It's Meg," Steph said in a soothing voice that belied the worry on her face.

Luka relaxed. "You killed it?"

"Sam and I killed it," Meaghan said.

"The job's not done," Luka said.

"I know. That's why I'm here. Is there anything you can tell me before I go over there?"

"Don't," Luka said, an anxious edge to his voice. "Stay away from that place."

"How many elves are over there?"

Steph gave Meaghan a warning look.

Meaghan ignored her. "I need to know what I'm walking into."

"I saw about half a dozen." He shook his head. "The last things I'll ever see."

"You don't know that," Steph said.

Meaghan glanced at Marnie.

Marnie shook her head. *His eyes are gone. There's nothing for me to fix and even I can't grow new body parts.*

How do you know?

I've been trying since he got here. The other stuff I've done I only had to think about.

Meaghan felt a warm pleasant tingling in her wrist and the pain evaporated.

See? I fixed your scalp wound, too.

"Luka," Meaghan said. "Please. Any help you can give me."

"They're scared of you," he said. "I know that much. Even before you killed the dragon. And I did manage to convince them that their salvation lies in the archive."

"So they won't burn it?"

"I don't think they will. But they won't abandon it without a fight either."

"Of course not," Meaghan said. "What did they do with the other monks?"

"They had them locked up down in the cellars somewhere, but I convinced the elves to release them so they could help with the search."

Meaghan rolled her wrist around in the air, marveling at the improvement, then she remembered Luka's lost eyes and put her hand down. "Will the monks fight?"

"To save the archive?" Luka nodded. "I'm sure of it." He smiled for a moment, the first smile Meaghan had seen on his face since she'd stepped in the room. "And we've got another ally. Eamon O'Malley's wizard abandoned him over there and stiffed him on his fee."

"There's no surer way to turn a leprechaun against you," Owen said, relief on his face from Luka's smile. "Even Eamon isn't slimy or stupid enough to help the elves. Too much bad blood."

"Meg, trust Sam," Luka said. "He knows the archive as well as the monks do. He snuck me out of there, blind ..." There was a slight catch in his voice. "And in pain, and right under their noses."

"I trust him," Meaghan said. "He saved my life a few times already today. All our lives. We're going over there as soon as I get downstairs."

"Take Sparky with you," Luka said. "He's got his old firepower back." He smiled again at the shocked silence around him. "What? I may be blind, but I'm not deaf."

CHAPTER FIFTY-ONE

MEAGHAN HAD STEELED herself for another fight—literally as well as figuratively, taking the sword and her favorite saucepan—but the elves had cleared out.

The monks were sitting in the main hall of the castle with tankards of ale, toasting Eamon O'Malley.

"I'm a hero," he said, a beaming smile on his homely little face.

Terry raised an eyebrow. "Do tell."

Eamon wiped his mouth on his grubby sleeve. "Yeah, first I told them I got you back in the game, boyo, then I told them I was friends with Meaghan of Keele, the world killer, and she'd kick their arses into jelly." His voice slurred and he swayed slightly in his seat. "Then the tall skinny one, the one you had locked up in your cellar, he shows back up, and they all buggered outta here fast as they could."

"I hear your mystery wizard stiffed you," Meaghan said. "Still want to protect his identity?"

"That shifty bastard? Shite, no. T'was Cooper, that feckin' wanker what heads the Order." Eamon took another slug of ale.

"Me and the lads are going after him and his pansy wizards."
He let out a thunderous belch. "Soon as I sleep this off."

"I thought you were scared to go to other worlds," Terry said,
as he and Meaghan wandered around checking out the archive.
Monks, most of them appearing human, scurried around them,
awed looks on their faces.

"I got over it."

"After you slay a dragon, everything else is small potatoes, I
guess," Terry said. "These aren't exactly a scary bunch of guys."

"They're totally freaked out by you," Meaghan said. "Thor."

Terry snorted with laughter. "Me? A little awestruck maybe,
but it's Meaghan of Keele they're scared of. And please don't
call me that."

"What your original name anyway?"

He said something that sounded like "Taya-duh."

"How do you spell that?"

"Not a clue. I didn't learn to read or write until we headed
for Rome. Luka made me learn." The smile dropped from his
face. "His sight isn't coming back, is it?"

"What makes you say that?"

"The looks you and Marnie were giving each other. When
she fixed your wrist."

"How do you know about that?"

Terry snorted. "The beaming smile. The way you started
waving it around. Oh, and maybe how you can use your hand
again." He shook his head. "She can fix broken stuff, but she
can't make new stuff, am I right?"

Meaghan sighed. "So she says."

They roamed in silence for a few minutes longer, until Terry
announced, "What a dump. They should tear down this moldy
pile of rocks and build something new."

"But this is traditional," Meaghan said. "Mustn't interfere
with tradition."

"Why not?" Terry said. "I was a tradition until humans figured out how lightning worked. Now I'm folklore."

"And a comic book hero, don't forget that," Meaghan said. "You ever see those movies?"

"Saw part of the first one, up to the bar scene in the middle, then I had to go sit in the lobby and drink coffee and wait for Steph. You know the scene I'm talking about?"

"Never saw it," Meaghan said. "No idea."

"I had a lot of fun back in the day, but I did a lot of damage, too. Watching that big blond kid drain a beer mug brought it all back." He looked sad for a moment, then smiled. "Let's go home. This medieval crap makes my head hurt."

Much to Dustin's dismay, Sam decided to return to Eldrich with Meaghan. "My being here is too much risk to you and to the archive. Hank and Aggie, they will let me stay with them."

Terry gave Meaghan a surprised look over Sam's head.

Meaghan shrugged and mouthed, "Why not?"

The portal Dustin opened for them dropped them right next to the mangled guardrail at the end of Holly Lane.

The sun was shining brightly and the snow was already beginning to melt. A snowblower and chain saw serenaded them.

Terry headed home to check on his house, Sam in tow.

Meaghan found Russ and Hank in the middle of Holly Lane, surrounded by the partially dismembered dragon.

Russ shut off the chain saw as she walked up. "Are we definitely in the cleanup phase?"

Meaghan nodded. "Yup. For now at least. Terry says to save the skin. He wants to tan it."

"He knows how to tan dragon hide?"

"Apparently," Meaghan said. "What are you gonna do with all this?"

"Put it in cold storage. There's a couple of places down in Williamsport where I can lease freezer space. Dragon meat's considered a delicacy in the magical worlds. If I set up the food truck in the woods, Hank says folks'll stampede their gateways trying to be first in line."

"What'll they pay you with? Gold? Magic beans?"

Russ made a face at her. "Yeah, ha ha. Ever hear of diplomacy? A good meal might change some minds about you. After today, your kickass cred is solid. Time to show your softer side."

"With what? Dragon tacos?"

"Ooh," Russ said. "Now there's an idea. I could do Dragon Taco Tuesdays. Make it a weekly thing all summer."

Meaghan left them knee deep in dragon guts, Russ chattering happily at Hank about what else he could make with the dragon meat.

She found John farther up the street, clearing the Franzettis' driveway.

He shut off the snowblower. "Russ says they'll be home tomorrow and we almost burnt down their house. Their tree is gone, but at least they can reach their garage now. It seemed like the right thing to do." He pulled her into his arms. "Are you all right?"

"I'm stinky and hungry and tired," she said. "But, yeah, I'm good. How about you?"

"Better. When I remember feeling my wings, I think about last night instead." He grinned at her. "We will do that again, yes?"

"Oh, yes," Meaghan said. She kissed him, then hugged him tightly. "We will do that again. Many, many times."

The power came back on about an hour later. A quick check of the local TV news confirmed her suspicion that the snowstorm had magical origins. The rest of the northern tier of the state had gotten three to five inches of snow. Eldrich had gotten three to five feet.

The governor had declared Sylvan County a disaster area. The elevated local snow totals had the meteorologists stumped, but they were too excited by the thunder snow to care.

If you guys knew what really caused it, you'd pee your pants.

Miraculously there had been no casualties.

No reported casualties, Meaghan reminded herself as she finally climbed up the stairs to check on Luka.

The house seemed empty after the last day and night. As soon as the main roads were plowed, Brian and Marnie had taken Kady and Jeff and the baby home in Steph's SUV, and Lynette's son had dropped by and picked up her and Gretchen.

Hank and Aggie were at the Donners' house, continuing to recuperate from the elves' freezing magic. They and Buzz were stranded until the roads were clear enough to get the Millers home and Buzz back to Williamsport.

Natalie and Owen had gone over across the street, too, as soon as cell service was restored. Owen had a business empire to run and a wounded boss to cover for.

Meaghan knocked on the half-closed guest room door.

"Come on in, Meg," Steph said.

Luka lay curled on the bed, looking small and frail in the bright sunlight. Melanie sat in the armchair near the window and Steph sat next to the bed.

"You saved the archive, Luka," Meaghan said. "The elves are gone."

Luka nodded, but didn't move.

Looking at him, Meaghan realized she still didn't know anything, not really, about the animosity between the fair folk and her new neighbors. *More secrets. Still so many secrets.*

But she wasn't angry this time. She remembered what Russ had said about people keeping secrets for their own reasons and sometimes all you could do was wait until they were ready to tell you.

She could wait. For now.

Melanie gave her a meaningful look and stood up. "Meg, I need to run some things by you. Why don't we go downstairs and chat while I make lunch for everybody?" She glanced back at Steph.

Steph nodded.

"How bad is it?" Meaghan asked when they got to the kitchen.

Melanie slumped into a chair. "His eyes are . . . gone. Burnt right out of his head."

"He said something about it being in the myth?"

Melanie nodded. "Loki is an ambivalent figure in much of Norse mythology. He does good and bad things for the other gods. Some of his acts benefit them, some harm them, often at the same time, and he's usually unraveling the consequences of some mischievous act."

"And for that they burn his eyes out?"

"Not for that. He finally goes too far. He kills Odin's son, Baldur, who's young and beautiful and beloved by the gods. And as punishment, they chain Loki to a rock and a giant serpent drips venom into his eyes."

Meaghan drew in a sharp breath. "And the fair folk thought it would be fun to do the same thing to Luka. As soon as I think I can't hate them more, they prove me wrong. Can Marnie help him?"

Melanie shook her head. "Not at the moment. She's going to keep working on it." Melanie paused. "Which raises another issue."

"Marnie and Patrice," Meaghan said "It's not a coincidence they both have these big scary new powers. Dad thinks there might be a third one on the way."

"Another element of the prophecy." Before Meaghan could protest, Melanie continued. "I know you don't believe in prophecy, but you might want to start. Keep in mind, you did in fact kill a dragon with a sword like the prophecy said."

"No," Meaghan said. "I killed a dragon with a jar of moonshine and a burning rag."

"But the sword—"

"The sword was only there because Dustin tried to tick items off a cosmic to-do list. If the sword hadn't been handy, we'd have used something else. It wasn't the sword that mattered; it was the steel it was made from." Meaghan stood up and opened the fridge. "The fair folk set this whole thing up. They were the ones running the scam, not Luka. They wanted to force me to face down that dragon and lose so they could discredit me. That's conspiracy, not prophecy."

"But, Meg—"

"I won't live my life according to somebody's magical bucket list." She pulled the bag of ham out of the fridge. "Will you grab the bread from the pantry? Russ is up to his armpits in dragon guts and I'm hungry, so let's make those sandwiches."

The fatigue hit Meaghan as soon as she put her plate together. She couldn't face Luka again. Not yet. She sent Melanie upstairs with a tray and ate alone in the kitchen.

After a quiet cup of tea, Meaghan snuck upstairs, took a long hot shower, and put on her softest sweats. She dropped onto her bed and slept without waking until the following morning. She had no dreams, at least none she remembered.

CHAPTER FIFTY-TWO

THE SNOW MELTED rapidly, replaced by local flooding, but nothing serious. Spring, real spring was still at least a few weeks away, but the melting snow and sunshine improved everyone's mood. As typically occurred in Eldrich, those who were clued in lied about what had happened and those in denial gratefully accepted those lies.

The snow was a freak meteorological event caused by colliding storm fronts and the mountainous terrain. The fires on Holly Lane were caused by extinguished pilot lights, built-up natural gas fumes, and sparks from electrical shorts.

They're half right, Meaghan thought.

The dragon's stunning power turned out to be a blessing. The residents of Sycamore Street vaguely remembered a snowplow and something on fire but nothing else.

Still, Meaghan marveled at the human mind's ability to deny what it didn't want to know. It was the not-wanting-to-know part that made it work, she realized. It was a lot easier to flim-flam somebody who didn't want to know something than it was to deceive somebody who was simply uninformed.

And what denial and magic couldn't accomplish, money smoothed over. Within days, Owen had made cash offers on the burned-out properties and lined up a design team to build a new house for Luka next door to Terry and Steph. They'd deal with Edna's property later.

Edna called Meaghan to share the good news. "I'm staying in Florida. I bought a condo."

"You aren't upset about your house?"

"Hell, no," Edna said in a cheerful voice. "When I got the news, my first thought was 'oh good, now I don't have to clear all that shit out of my basement.' Between Owen's cash and the insurance settlement, I'm loaded."

Laughing, Meaghan hung up the phone. She'd miss Edna.

With everything under control at home, Meaghan headed into the office.

Emily had taken care of the carpet problem. The sigil-covered carpet was gone. "I did a thing out in the woods. Purification spell and a bonfire. It seemed more prudent than the landfill."

"Good thinking." Meaghan surveyed the new carpeting. It was a muted gray heather in a flat industrial weave. It was the most non-magical carpeting Meaghan could imagine. "It's perfect. Thank you for taking care of this for me."

"I did some checking on Bottaio Design, but I hit a dead end. They cashed the city's checks and then vanished without a trace."

"It was the Order," Meaghan said. "Cooper."

Emily visibly flinched. "He's an evil, evil man. How do you know it was him?"

"Connected some dots," Meaghan said. "Plus, he didn't pay a leprechaun subcontractor, who was only too happy to rat him out as the architect of this whole mess."

"Why did he do it?"

"Still trying to figure it out. Right after I figure out what the elves are up to."

Meaghan and her staff moved into the new city solicitor's office two days later. Her new office was bigger than her prior turret office, but with much less charm.

"This is swanky," Jamie said, a big grin on his face, as he looked around.

"It's all right. What about you? You like your new space?" Meaghan asked.

"No mystical vortices, plus a new Herman Miller office chair—what's not to like?"

At the end of the day, on her way home, Meaghan stopped to look at the little exhibit the historical society had set up in the first-floor lobby documenting the original construction of city hall in the nineteenth century.

There wasn't much to it. The building's architect and engineer, a foreigner named Böttcher, had taken the building plans and all related documents back to Europe with him when construction was complete. Welland Eldrich, the city's namesake and the project's patron, had gone insane during construction.

The historical society had done what it could with limited materials. There were only two photos. Meaghan stared first into Welland Eldrich's sad dark eyes. He still haunted the building, Meaghan knew, and he wasn't the first Eldrich who'd lost his mind.

The other photo was a group shot, about a dozen men in dark frock coats and full beards, shovels in hand to commemorate breaking ground. Welland stood in the middle and next to him stood a tall man the caption identified at "Herr Böttcher."

Meaghan squinted and looked closer.

Her stomach flipped over. Even with the full beard and nineteenth century clothing, she recognized him.

Cooper.

Cooper, using the name Böttcher, had directed the construction of city hall. Cooper had used Welland Eldrich to build a great big mystical ray gun.

Behind her, Meaghan heard a man clear his throat. She whirled around.

Cooper stood behind her. "I know we've gotten off on the wrong foot, but there's no reason we can't be friends."

"Wrong foot?" Meaghan took a step forward. "You call kidnapping and torture and trying to kill me and everyone I love getting off on the *wrong foot*?"

Cooper took a step backward. "Well, yes, I realize you might have some hard feelings about that, but we're allies now."

"Allies?" Meaghan's voice went up an octave. She could feel a tiny vein in her temple start to pulse.

"Of course," Cooper said. "I gave you access to the archive and your father's lost records. I gave the smith his powers back to help you fight the fair folk."

"A fight I wouldn't have had if you hadn't given the fair folk access, too," Meaghan said through gritted teeth. "The archive could have been burnt to the ground along with me and half the town."

Cooper waved a dismissive hand. "Collateral damage. You can't fight a war without casualties."

Meaghan thought of Luka's ravaged eyes, remembering how the blood had run down his blistered face like tears. "Collateral damage? You call what you did collateral damage?" The pulse in her temple began to thrum as her heart beat faster. "Get the fuck out of my town."

Cooper sneered and leaned over her. "Make me."

For a moment, Meaghan saw the balding wizard in her mind. Then white-hot rage swept through her like a flash flood, even as time seemed to slow.

"I should have known you were too small-minded to realize

what I'm trying to do for you," Cooper said, his hand snaking out to grab her arm. "You need to learn your place."

At 'you need to,' she clenched her hand into a fist.

At 'learn your place,' she swung her arm upward.

Meaghan hit him square in the nose. She felt something crack. *My hand?*

Cooper stumbled backward with a cry, crimson blood pouring from his smashed nose.

That's what cracked.

Meaghan felt the anger drain from her, replaced by satisfaction. There'd be hell to pay for this, she was certain, but for this one moment, life was golden.

"You bitch," Cooper said in a thin nasal whine. "I'll kill you for that."

"You'll try, asshole. You'll try. But a thousand pounds of dragon meat in my freezer says you'll fail." She turned, and without a backward glance, sailed out the front door, down the steps, and into her new car, a well-worn, ten-year-old Subaru Outback. She was done with luxury cars for the foreseeable future.

Her adrenaline rush carried her about a half mile down Main Street, then she had to stop before she wrecked the car. Hands shaking, she started to laugh and cry a little.

"That was either a breakthrough or a breakdown," she said to the empty air.

Time to call Marnie's shrink.

She pulled her new phone out of her bag and dug out the business card Marnie had given her. But before she could punch in the number, the phone rang. She yelped, but managed not to drop it.

Elena's smiling face showed on the caller ID.

"Hey," Meaghan said. "Good timing."

"Where are you?"

"In my car. I just punched a wizard."

"Where?"

"In city hall. He started it."

Elena started laughing. "Like when you punched Eddie down the street when we were kids?"

"Actually, yeah," Meaghan said, laughing along with her. "I think I broke the wizard's nose, too." Meaghan took a deep breath to steady herself. "It felt really good. What's up?"

"You tell me. Freak snowstorms, dragon slaying, thunder gods—I'm hearing all kinds of crazy shit out here."

"Yeah. Um. A lot of stuff has happened since I saw you. The thunder god lives across the street, and Russ is making dragon meat loaf for dinner tonight." She smiled at the phone. "And I slept with John."

Elena squealed. "Yes! Finally. So how was it?'

"Astonishing," Meaghan said, "and it keeps getting better."

"So, are you better? Are you over the . . . you know?"

"The attempted rape? Seems like, but I'm still going see a shrink. So much shit has happened in the past year. At some point, it's all gonna catch up with me again."

"It hasn't even been a year," Elena said. "This time last year, you were still in Phoenix, right? Blissfully clueless?"

It wasn't blissful. It was miserable. I was all alone. "Yeah, something like that. When are you coming to visit?"

"When the snow melts," Elena said, "and Russ has run out of ways to cook dragon."

"It was a big dragon. There's almost a thousand pounds of meat. Even with Taco Tuesdays, it's still gonna take a while to get through."

"Taco Tuesdays?"

"Russ's food truck. Some hare-brained scheme to make the magic types like me instead of fear me."

"Like is okay, but fear is good too," Elena said.

Meaghan didn't have a built-in, hands-free phone system anymore, so she promised to call Elena in a few days with more details and hung up. But before she started the car, she made one more call.

She got the therapist's voice mail. She almost hung up out of fear, but instead took a deep breath and left a message with her name and phone number.

If I can kill a dragon and punch Cooper, I can handle therapy.

When she got home, Russ was cooking and John was sitting at the table waiting for her.

"Where's Annie?" she asked.

"She claims a last-minute thing came up at work," Russ said, "but I think she's scared of the dragon meat loaf."

"Smart girl." Meaghan dropped her bag and gave John a big kiss. "Hi, honey, I'm home."

He smiled up at her. "How was your day?"

She decided not to mention Cooper. Maybe after dinner. "Same old, same old."

It's not exactly a lie. Fighting monsters is part of the job description after all.

When dinner was served, Meaghan eyed the meat loaf with trepidation. "Are you sure we can eat this?"

"I've been eating dragon burgers all week," Russ said. "You'll like it."

"That was dragon you gave me yesterday?" John asked. "That was a good burger."

"See, Susie Skeptical? Your boyfriend's not too scared to try it."

"Shut up," Meaghan said. "Is there ketchup?"

"Philistine." Russ sat down with his plate. "Try it first."

Meaghan took a bite. The meat was smoky and sweet with a hint of heat. "This is really good," she said. "Is there bacon in it? Chipotle peppers?"

"Nope," Russ said with a proud smile. "That's the flavor of the meat. You like it?"

She felt John's foot snake around her ankle and she smiled at him. "I like it."

They ate in companionable silence, Meaghan liking the dragon meat more with every bite. As much as she'd regretted killing the dragon at the time, she felt a curious sense of satisfaction eating it. This was what Russ was always going on about, how helping harvest your food made you appreciate it more.

She'd tell them about Cooper tomorrow. No need to spoil a pleasant evening.

Meaghan thought about her conversation with Elena. A year ago, she'd been in Phoenix, working a job she'd hated. She'd alienated her family and most of her friends, and she'd been so lonely she could barely breathe.

This was better. So much better. If the price was intermittent mortal danger, so be it. "That was great," she said, putting down her fork and leaning back in her chair. "I like it," she said, rubbing her foot against John's leg. "In fact, I love it."

ACKNOWLEDGEMENTS

Big thanks go out to my beta readers: JoAnn Bradley, Susan Emans, and Sarah Miranda. Thanks again to my editor, Susan Lindsey, Savvy Communication LLC (savvy-comm.com). And thank you to James T. Egan of Bookfly Design (bookflydesign.com) for the cover.

A Note to Readers

Gods and Swindlers is the third of seven books in the City of Eldrich series. More information about the series is available at laurakirwan.com.

www.ingramcontent.com/pod-product-compliance
Lightning Source LLC
Chambersburg PA
CBHW030653120726
47905CB00001B/188